HANGI

L M BUSH

Ozzie
Hope you enjoy
love lisa *L Bush*

First published in 2015 by:

Britain's Next Bestseller
An imprint of Live It Publishing
27 Old Gloucester Road
London, United Kingdom.
WC1N 3AX

www.britainsnextbestseller.co.uk

Printed in Poland.

ISBN 978-1-910565-57-5 (pbk)

Dedication

Supporter List

Adam Fennessy, Jo Shipp, Michelle Castle, Teri Collins, Michael Bush, Robbie Linsell, Martin Everett, Justin Edgar, Win Edgar, Tina Nash, Duncan Wallis, Andrew Males, Ana Kluman, Carol Burrows, Frank Bush, Natalie Selby, Jeff Temperley, Carla Cornell, Liz Stevens, Clair Binks, Keith Isgar, Patricia Isgar, Maureen Burr, Sarah Dupuy, Jemma Youdale, Patricia Bush, Lisa Harris, Tony Adams, Chris Vernon, Michelle Easter, Paula Tatchell, Ian Catchpole, Naomi Douglas, Yonj Djafer, Emma Lane, Angela Crane, Vix Simpson, Sarah Carter, Neeraj Shah, Aiesha Shah, Steve Collins, Leanne Gell, Maggie Collins, Endy Powar, Manjit Powar, Darren Stock, Tony & Terri Collins, Samantha Boreham, Richard Box, Suki Samra, Barbara Aitchison, Joe Hobbs, Mat Branston, Shannon Harvey, Cousha Wilson, Sophie Box, Tom Paget, Shar Bunce, Petra Sands, Michelle Brown, Kerry Osborn, Teresa Buglass, Al Hooper, Matthew Luscombe, David McCaffrey, Andrew Willis, Christine Lovell, A Heath, Lisa Burt, William Masters, Hilary Crane, Sharon McKellar, Kiri Thompson, Craig Reynolds, Ray Wilson, Victoria Freeman, Donna Richardson, Matthew Simpson, John Bull, Leah Thompson, Mary Morris, Dawn Rivers, David Masters, Dominic Bush, Bradley Osborn, Tim Graveling, Yvonne Scott, Heather Greenway, Emma Shorten, Steven Hoy, Sue Donovan, Karen Payne, Gary Walker, Sarah Newcombe, Tony Dark, Jane Beanland, Kristie Rulten, Sylvia Eldred, Doreen Halpin, Luke Weikert, Sam Catchpole, Rob Sippitt, Bailey Henderson, Olivia Harris, Victoria Knight, Paul Hardy, Gaynor Gordon, Nicole Gallagher, Matt Bartholomew, Nick Brady, Tim Hasani, Lesley Bush, Ashleigh Collins, Joe Hobbs, Judge Judgles, Andria Williams, Tamara Randall, Steve Caswell, Barbara Aitchison, Diana Maddison, Laura Atkinson, Christine Manning, Steve Evers.

Prologue

2014

A BUSY hum of chatting and laughing drowned out the live band that played in the bar that night. Most people seemed oblivious to the girl standing there singing. In the far corner opposite, a group of younger local boys were playing pool. They seemed to be getting louder and louder.

"Keep it down, lads," Pam the landlady called over. Tony eyed the group. He knew all of them from the village. He was supposed to be meeting an old friend in the pub, but as the time ticked on he came to the conclusion that this might not be the case.

"I had best drink up and get off soon," he said to the barmaid. Tony's wife Michelle would be expecting him home soon anyway. Having just uttered the words, the door of the pub swung open.

"GET THE PINTS IN, TONE!" Tony heard a shouting over his shoulder. He turned around to see his old mate Al walking through the door.

"Bloody traffic! Sorry I'm late!" Al said as he embraced Tony in a man hug. A broad grin appeared across Tony's face. *Michelle would have to wait*, he thought picking up his phone to text her. He was going to be late.

An hour or so later the pub was getting busier and the pool table was gathering quite a crowd. The regulars had moved to the other side of the bar away from the rowdiness. A loud, aggressive group of men had walked in and put their money on the table to play, but something about the way they seemed to have bullied their way onto the table had rubbed Tony's back up the wrong way. There was something shifty about this bunch, not regular faces. Being such a small village, everyone knew everyone and strange faces stood out. Tony and Al

1

walked outside to the smoking area and as they walked past, one of the strangers shoulder barged Tony and he stumbled slightly.

"Oh sorry, pal," said the stranger – emphasising the word 'pal'.

Tony could tell it was deliberate. The stranger was extremely drunk and a few of them laughed and turned back to the pool table. Tony hated being called pal; he thought it was patronising. He stared a cool grey glare at the man but said nothing and carried on following Al out of the pub.

"Who's that prick?" Al asked as he lit his cigarette.

"No idea," Tony said coldly. "Not seen his face round here before."

The weather was mild for the time of year but it was still chilly standing outside. Tony pulled the collar of his leather jacket tighter around his neck to prevent the draft blowing down his back. A small congregation of smokers were always outside the pub since the smoking ban had been enforced. Tony was always trying to pack up smoking; he'd said this week that he would stop again. However, the whole packing-up never quite went a week before he caved in again. Most of the time he wasn't a quitter in anything he did; he was an all-or-nothing man. He did things one hundred percent or not at all and he couldn't stand weak-minded people. He liked winners.

"So what's this all about then, mate?" Tony said when they were alone outside.

"I need you to take something in for me at your yard, mate," Al said shiftily.

"What kind of something?" Tony asked.

"Just one little load that will come in on the back of a lorry from Europe. It's worth fifty K to ya," Al said grinning.

"Al, mate. I don't want to get involved again with all that," Tony went to interrupt but Al held his hand up and carried on.

"It's perfect, Tone. No one around. You have plenty of deliveries coming in anyway so it wouldn't be suspicious."

"But what if it goes wrong? I'll get nicked and I've got too much to lose, Al . . . business, my family."

"Nothing can go wrong! Don't be a prick, plus you'll be helping Karl out!" Al said confidently.

"Oh yeah? How?" Tony said back sarcastically.

Al looked at him. "Since the shooting he can't do this shit himself. Come on – he needs his reliable mates and that's us. Tone . . . come on, You and me . . . like the old days. Think about it?"

Tony didn't need to think about it for long. He looked into Al's face and dropped his shoulders in defeat. "Just a one off you say?"

"Of course!" Al said throwing his arm around Tony's shoulders and laughing. Tony stubbed out his finished cigarette and headed towards the door of the pub.

"One more pint then I'm off, gotta get back home to Michelle," he said to Al.

But just as they stepped foot in the pub, an almighty punch up was breaking out around the pool table. There was shouting and scrambling on the floor, Pam was yelling for backup from some of the local men and juggling a phone under her chin trying to call the police at the same time. One of the guys had stumbled back against Tony and started thrashing about with windmill arms. Tony shoved him away. The whole crowd seemed to surge forward and then suddenly there was the sound of a pint glass being smashed.

Over the rest of the commotion Tony saw one of the strangers – the same one that had barged him earlier – grab the broken glass and thrust it into the face of one of the local boys that he had pinned on the floor. As he slashed the boy's face with the jagged glass, the boy screamed as his face turned crimson from the blood that was pumping down his cheek. Tony leapt over and grabbed the stranger by the throat. The local boy was now down on the floor and had put his hands up to his face to try and stem the blood flow. Pam was yelling for towels and another local had rushed over to help him cover his face. The entire pub was utter chaos. That was just the excuse Tony needed; he knew the boy very well that had been glassed and he wasn't having any of it.

"This is what you fucking get, *pal*" Tony said through gritted teeth as he buried his fist into the strangers face over and over again. Tony and Al had been drawn fists-first into the fight before they knew it. This wasn't how Al or Tony had pictured this evening panning out.

Another of the strangers had taken a swing at Al. In one smooth sweep, Al had taken him out and floored him. Another of the strangers had now jumped on Tony's back trying to strangle him from behind. Tony dragged him over his shoulder and slammed him onto the pool table. Before they knew it, there was a full blown pub fight going on. It had been a while since Tony had been involved in one of these – pub punch-ups were his specialty.

The sirens outside blared away as two police cars arrived on scene. PC Maguill was a short, balding sixty-year-old sergeant nearing retirement. He had worked the Serious Crime Squad in London for the last thirty years and on doctor's orders he had taken a new position of the local bobby in a quiet village for some peaceful work. He'd had a few near heart attacks back in the day and his doctor had advised him to relocate to somewhere nice and peaceful for his last few years on the force before he retired, so he was winding down gently. However, this wasn't his usual quiet Friday night that he had become accustomed to.

He stepped out of his car and walked up the steps into the pub. The scene that met him took him back to his old days on the force. Bar stools had been broken, pint glasses smashed on the floor and the pool table was wrecked. Surprisingly enough there were still quite a few people hanging around. An ambulance had arrived shortly after to take the kid who had been glassed to hospital – he was going to need several stitches in his face.

Some of the strangers had scarpered. The ones that could walk did anyway but Tony and Al had done a pretty good job in knocking most of them out.

"Just like the old days, Tone. Eh?" Al laughed after it had all calmed down. Tony decided that this was definitely the wrong week to try and quit smoking as the two of them headed outside to the smoking area.

"Names and addresses," a young policeman was asking everyone. "Everyone stay where you are. We will be needing statements and names and addresses of everyone that was here." The young officer busied himself going round getting statements.

Everybody had a story to tell. The older sergeant surveyed the scene that had occurred. Nobody could name the remaining strangers that were outside on the steps to the pub. One was holding a blood-soaked bar towel to his head, another had a badly bloodied nose and mouth, one was barely conscious, and kept throwing up as he slumped up against a wall.

As for the local boys, apart from the one that had been glassed, the others seemed not too badly scathed. A few nose bleeds and black eyes and they proceeded to fill the police in on their side of the story and what had happened. It looked like Tony and Al had done most of the damage.

"Excuse me, where do you think you're going? Names and addresses please, gentlemen!" A policeman was standing in front of Tony and Al, preventing them from leaving the bar. He put his hand out and grabbed Tony by the arm to stop him from leaving and repeated slowly "I said names and addresses . . . please."

Tony spun round and turned to face the young police officer who was still holding onto him.

"Who, me?" he said, shaking the policeman's grip off his arm.

"Yes, sir. You."

Tony took a deep breath and sighed. "My name is Tony . . . Tony Hayes."

"I'll deal with this one," PC Maguill exclaimed, cutting in sharply and staring in astonishment. "Jesus Christ! Tony Hayes, I should have guessed! What the fuck are you doing here?"

Introduction

1969

"STAND back, stand back. Come on, move it!"

The doors to the maternity unit flew open and a heavily pregnant Dottie was being rushed in for an emergency caesarean section. Although Dottie's baby wasn't due for another four weeks, the baby had decided it was time to make an appearance. Gowned-up nurses and midwives were being called over the hospital tannoy to come to the maternity unit and they came crashing through the corridors of the London hospital. The doors swung shut behind them leaving a young man and his daughter standing alone and afraid in the corridor.

The hours ticked by so slowly and Ernie kept walking backwards and forwards, up and down, trying to get a glimpse of what was happening. He couldn't see a thing. *What was happening? Why wasn't anyone coming out to see him and tell him what was going on? Where were they?* His daughter Jacquelyn was sitting next to him curled up asleep in the plastic chairs in the corridor. She was a good girl – she was only fifteen months old. They hadn't planned another pregnancy so soon after Jacki was born, but it was the summer of love back then in the '60s!

If someone didn't come out in a minute Ernie was going in there to give them a piece of his mind. He had waited and waited and after almost another hour had gone by he was still waiting. If someone didn't come out right now and tell him what was happening, he was going to storm in and give them a piece of his mind. *Who the hell did they think they were, keeping him sitting here?*

"Mr. Hayes!" a gowned-up midwife came out and interrupted his angry train of thought.

"Mr. Hayes," she said again.

"Err ... yes ... that's me," he stuttered, suddenly afraid of what had taken so long and of what she might say.

"Congratulations," she smiled at him. "IT'S A BOY!"

On the 16th of May 1969, Anthony Michael Hayes was born. A mere four pounds and two ounces – and not without major complications either. In his eagerness to arrive he came four weeks early and had to be put straight into the baby incubator for premature babies as he'd had major breathing problems. His lungs hadn't fully formed and he was so tiny it really was touch and go. Dot also had severe complications during the birth; she had haemorrhaged very badly and had caught an infection so she also had to stay in hospital under observation. This gave her the chance to keep a close eye on her son and she stayed by his bedside for many weeks, holding his fingers through the plastic unit which encased him and protected him from the world outside. Back in those days when the babies were so premature they wrapped them in foil. Dot used to laugh and say that Tony was like an oven-ready chicken when he was in there.

This meant Ernie not only still had to go to work to earn money to put food on the table, but it also left him home alone to look after Jacki whilst Dot was still in hospital. He had to make daily and nightly visits back and forth to the hospital. Family and friends rallied round and eventually the family were reunited at home together again. Life had started out tough for Tony. Although he was so tiny he quickly pulled through and grew up into a lovely little boy and proved himself to be a real little fighter.

Chapter 1

IT was the summer of 1976 and flares were the height of fashion. The Hayes family lived on a council estate in East London. Ernie was a towering and confident six feet two inches tall with broad shoulders and a fine head of dark hair. He was a strikingly handsome man with his piercing blue eyes and cheeky grin. It was often remarked that he bore a strong resemblance to the actor John Wayne. Dottie was a few years younger than Ernie and had fallen hopelessly in love with him from day one of ever laying eyes on him. Dot was a very pretty and slim young girl with long dark hair and big round blue eyes. Soon the couple were madly in love and married with a family and a nice first-floor, three-bedroom flat on the estate.

Dot loved Ernie's strong demeanour; he was a real man's man. He liked his food and loved his drink; his vices were smoking and gambling. Dot had an entirely different upbringing; she drank very little and only smoked socially. They were a very popular couple and well liked in the community, and a very happy family unit.

Ernie worked as a machine operator and a lorry driver to make ends meet. Dot worked in a supermarket during the day while Tony and Jacki were at school. That summer of '76 was one of the hottest summers recorded. It was so hot, even the tarmac was melting on the roads – kids were getting it stuck to the soles of their shoes. Tony was seven years old by now, and the kids used to all hang out together in the park opposite the flats. One day they were all playing at the park and a gang of punks aged about thirteen came in and started bullying Tony and his mates. They were drinking cheap cider out of cans and smoking cigarettes – most had pierced noses and spiked hair.

"You better get outta here if you know what's good for you, you bunch of little pricks," they all laughed and jeered.

Tony and his best mate, Rob Sullivan, were sitting on the swings. Rob was holding an ice-lolly and the oldest of the gang walked up to him and slapped the lolly straight out of his hand to the floor. "Hey!" Rob cried out.

"You wanna make a big deal out of it?" The punk grabbed Rob and threw him onto the floor.

"Lick it up!" the punk challenged Rob, laughing at him.

"Hey, leave him alone," Tony said. With that one of the other punks pushed Tony so violently that he flew backwards and landed on his back. Rob was crying and Tony didn't know what to do. The punk set about kicking Tony; this made him so angry. Another one was pulling Rob about and slapping him around the head. Tony leapt up and tried to grab Rob; he could feel humiliation burning up inside him. He and Rob managed to get away from the park and, shamefaced, Tony ran home crying to his dad.

Ernie, who wasn't often cross at his kids, was furious with Tony for allowing these boys to bully him like that and push him around. "You have got to stand up for yourself, do you hear me?"

Ernie bellowed. "How many of them were there?"

Tony explained about the punks and said they were as big as Patrick next door. Patrick next door was a tall Afro-Jamaican boy about the age of thirteen. A very tall and lean lad, very tough and popular and not to be messed with.

"Oh really?" said Ernie. "Ok." He turned and walked out of the kitchen. Tony could hear him get something from the cupboard under the stairs. Ernie came back into the kitchen and thrust a hammer into Tony's small hand. He looked at him and said, "now you look at me and you listen." Tony knew this was serious.

"You go back to that park, you hear me? You take that hammer with you; walk up to the biggest punk there and you smash him right in the middle of his head." Ernie dug his finger into Tony's forehead, motioning where to hit. "I mean it, and if you don't you'll have me to answer to. Do you understand?" Ernie bellowed, shoving Tony back out of the front door, watching him as he went off down the stairs and headed off unsurely back towards the park.

Tony kept turning round to see if his dad was still there watching and he saw him staring at him from the balcony that overlooked the park. *FUCK!* He knew he had to do this. He started to feel sick, and he could feel his legs trembling. He gripped the cold hammer tightly in his small hand, rolled his shoulders back, held his head up, swallowed hard and marched towards the park. As he approached the park he held the hammer up behind his back, his grip now becoming sweaty. He could feel the adrenaline building from his feet upwards. His hands started to shake and his heart was pounding in his chest as he got nearer and nearer the punks – they were still laughing and sitting on the swings.

As Tony got closer, the big bully that had pushed and slapped him turned around and stared at him. "What do you want now, you little prick? Go and tell your mummy did we?" he sneered, as he burped and threw an empty cider can across the floor. The rest of his gang all laughed with him. Tony didn't say a word as he stared the punk in the eye, not a single word. He never moved his gaze either; he had fixated his eyes on him. The punk stayed sitting on the swing, grinning and laughing. Tony felt a rage burning through him that he had never felt before. It had started from his feet and was surging through his veins like fire. Suddenly, Tony had lifted his arm wielding the hammer and was bringing it down through the air . . .

Chapter 2

AN almighty *THWACK* was what Tony heard as he smashed the kid right in the middle of his forehead with the hammer. The kid fell forwards onto the floor, clutching his head and screaming. Tony could see there was blood, a lot of blood. The other punks all started shouting and jumping about.

"He's a fucking nutter!" one of them was yelling.

"Get some fucking help!" another one was shouting. They were trying to grab their mate off the floor and started dragging him away from Tony. He was still screaming and holding his head. All this commotion was causing quite a scene and people were beginning to wonder what the noise and screaming was all about. Tony was still standing holding the hammer in his hand.

"TONY!" Tony could just faintly make out someone calling his name. The punk was being dragged away screaming on the floor.

"TONY!" It registered that it was his dad screaming his name. Tony thrust the hammer up under his t-shirt and ran back to the balcony where his dad was standing yelling at him. "Get up here! Quickly son, now!" Tony ran quickly up the two flights of steps and along the balcony to his front door. Ernie ushered him inside and slammed the door fast behind him.

"Give me that hammer! " he said and he threw it straight into the kitchen sink and blasted the hot tap on it. "What have you done?" Ernie said. "What have you done?" Tony looked at his dad like he was mad.

"What you told me to do, Dad!" was Tony's scared response.

"Yeah, I can see that, but I thought you were just gonna scare them with it. I didn't expect you to actually smash him in the head!" Words failed Ernie right at that moment.

"But Dad . . . " Tony stammered. "You told me to!"

13

Ernie looked at his son standing there, all young and wide-eyed. He could be in a whole heap of trouble now. Ernie had to think fast and for the first time in his life he was speechless.

"Dad, what shall we do now?" Tony looked longingly at his dad for the answer. Ernie stood and scratched his head, but all he could reply was "Jesus Christ, don't tell ya mother!"

There was no mention in the local newspaper that week about a punk who had been hit with a hammer. Luckily, the kid had escaped with minor injuries to his skull, several stitches, severe headaches and a very badly bruised ego. That group of punks was never seen in the area again.

By the time Tony was ten, he had grown into a tall skinny boy with long arms and legs. He had inherited his dad's rugged good looks and piercing blue eyes, and had dark blonde scruffy hair.

Punks were fading out and skin heads and two-tone were taking over.

Tony had made his mark at school after the hammer incident. Most of the kids had heard about it but most were too scared to say anything about it to Tony, so gossip spread like a virus on the playground. There were plenty of have-a-go-kids who started trouble to gain a reputation, but were quickly put in their place. Tony had gained a reputation as the hardest kid around school.

Despite this, Tony was a lovely boy and was very popular with the teachers. He wasn't a bully and because of the so-called hammer incident, he had developed a real hatred of bullies and quite often could be found breaking up fights and standing up for the younger ones.

Ernie decided that he wanted Tony to start boxing. However, Dot was adamant that this was too dangerous, thus causing no end of arguments. Maybe this was one of the issues that started the irreparable rift that stayed in the Hayes' household. In the end, Ernie decided his way was right and enrolled him into boxing – partly because a) Tony had the potential to be a very good boxer and b) the boxing club was next to the pub where Ernie would often be found waiting for Tony to finish. Dot never went to watch her son train.

Ernie's other love aside from boxing was the betting shop. He was very partial to a bet or two . . . or three. Most Saturday afternoons in fact he would be found standing in the betting shop clutching his betting slip yelling at the horses to "GEE UP! GET UP THERE! COME ON MY COCKER!" There most likely would be a fair amount of cash riding on these bets too and, depending on if his horse won or not, would determine whether Ernie spent the remainder of the Saturday afternoon in the pub celebrating his winnings. The boxing was a huge hit with Tony. He had won ten out of ten fights consecutively. Some of the best kids in the country had fought him and lost and Tony's reputation grew and grew.

Chapter 3

"EVERY time I see you, I'm gonna smash you up again. Do you hear me?" Tony leant over and whispered these words very clearly and very slowly. He made sure that Simon could hear them and understood them. Tony stood up, straightened himself and walked off leaving the Jamaican kid lying in the path with a bloodied nose.

At the age of eleven Tony had now started senior school and with a pretty hard reputation – most of the kids had heard that he was hard. He'd had many fights and most kids had seen with their own eyes that he was hard. He left primary school being the toughest boy in school.

When you started senior school, there were a multitude of rumours flying around. How the new kids got their heads shoved down the toilets and flushed, had their dinner money stolen off them and how they all gave you a good kicking. Tony wasn't bothered. He heard all the kids talking about this one lunchtime just before they all left primary school, saying about how they were going to hide round corners and such like.

"I'm not scared," Tony said. "What are all you lot worrying about? I'm gonna stand in the middle of the playground and if they wanna try and mess with me, I'm gonna smash each and every one of them up. They won't fuck with me. You stand next to me, you'll be fine!"

Tony wasn't at all bothered about these stories, *bring it on!* he thought. So the kids all started their new schools and very quickly they realised it was all rumours and scare tactics.

Halfway through his first year, a new kid joined the school called Simon Pharrell. He was a tall, half-Jamaican kid who could fight and came with a huge ego. His mission was to fight every hard kid in school – he won all of his fights too. He knew of Tony well as he also boxed for a rival club but he had not yet had a fight with him. He gained a huge following and all the kids hung on his every word, Tony being the exception.

One day, Tony was walking through school to another lesson and Simon barged past him in the corridor. Tony didn't even bother to react and carried on walking, so Simon and his followers caught up with him on the way home from school that evening. They all laid into him, punching and kicking him down to the floor. There must have been a good eight or nine of them. This had literally happened only a few steps from Dot's work at the supermarket. Tony knew he'd be safe in there, so he had managed to crawl into the supermarket. He looked out of the window and he could see they were all still standing there waiting for him, laughing. *What a bunch of pricks. I'll get them. I'll get each and every one of them on their own. How dare they do this to me?*

The very next day before school started, he hid in the bushes at the front and he waited. He knew Simon walked this way to school and nine times out of ten he was alone. Today was no exception. Simon came ambling down the road, hands in pockets. Tony waited till he was alongside Simon then he leapt out of the bushes and grabbed him down to the ground. He repeatedly kicked and him in the face until he was doubled over holding his head in his hands to protect himself. But Tony didn't stop. He carried on until he knew Simon could take no more. Tony bent down and grabbed a fist full of Simon's hair and wrenched his head to face him. Simon was bleeding badly from his nose and his lips. Tony had kicked a fair size cut down his cheek too. Simon was whimpering and crying and Tony leant over and whispered in his face.

"Every time I see you, I'm gonna smash you up." He threw Simon back to the ground, picked up his school bag and walked into school. One down, eight to go.

The next one to get it was a kid from the estate called Russell. Tony saw him going into the toilets at break time and shot in after him. He put up a feeble effort to fight back, crouching on the floor under the basins looking pretty pathetic. He was so much tougher when he had his posse with him.

"You had better tell the rest of your fucking mates I'm gonna smash them up too, useless prick," Tony spat at him and left the toilets.

That afternoon, just before the end of school, the remaining crowd came up to Tony. *Here we go,* he thought, *six against one again.* Tony turned and prepared himself to fight but they were all apologising and blubbering,

"Please don't get us Tony!" they said. "Please don't! Simon made us do it!" Tony laughed at their pathetic faces. At a young age, he quickly learnt that bullies hate to be bullied and that they are weak – but you have to learn to fight back.

Most kids Tony's age were too wary of him and so he made friends with a lot of the other kids that were a good four or five years older than him. Tony was almost nearly thirteen by now. He thought he knew a fair amount of what life was all about, but he had a lot to learn. And fast.

Chapter 4

1982

"HAS Dad said anything to you?" Jacki asked, walking into the kitchen one Saturday morning whilst Tony was eating his toast.

"Oi! Fuck off and make your own!" Tony spat back slapping the back of her hand as she reached down and nicked the last piece of toast off his plate. She flicked the back of his hair and carried on talking.

"Seriously, has Dad said anything to you?"

"Like what? Dad says loads of things to me."

Jacki rolled her eyes "Has he told you about the strange bloke that's moved onto the back of the estate? Apparently he's meant to be a kiddie fiddler."

Jacki loved to be the bearer of any kind of news and often would elaborate it for entertainment value.

"What? No!" Tony was shocked.

"Yes," she said smugly. "Ask him yourself if you don't believe me."

"I will!" Tony replied as he threw his plate into the sink and headed out of the kitchen.

On Saturday afternoons there was only one place Tony would find Ernie – The bookies. Tony made his way across the estate to the shops. Skinheads were large on the estate and Tony had been very much accepted by them; they liked Tony for his ballsy attitude. He would hang out with them, although they were all far older than him; Tony was almost thirteen years old by now. He found them to be quite racist though and often didn't like the comments they made regarding some of the black kids in the area.

This morning the skinheads were out in the shopping parade

outside the `Pie and Mash shop`, Tony's favourite shop. The bookie was only a few doors down so Tony stopped to have a chat with them. As he looked up across the street he saw Patrick, the Jamaican kid from next door, walking towards them. Some of the skinheads had caused trouble for Patrick before – nothing to do with Tony.

Patrick shot Tony a cold stare that held his gaze for a few seconds longer than it should have. "What's his problem?" Tony said, and laughed it off. He didn't want the gang kicking off at Patrick on his behalf. Just then, Tony saw Ernie leaving the bookies. "Oh, gotta go. Catch ya later," he said and hurried off after Ernie.

Ernie's horse hadn't come in and he wasn't in a happy mood. "What's up, mate?" Ernie said to Tony. Tony could tell that this wasn't a great time to ask his Dad about anything.

"Nothing, Dad. I just wanted to see what you was up to."

"Oh right, well I'm down at Glen's so I'm off to the Rose for a pint. Don't tell ya mother!" "Ok, Dad."

Ernie rubbed his son's head and disappeared into the pub. That was that then!

Patrick next door had turned from a nice kid into an arrogant teenager with a chip on his shoulder – not that Tony had ever done anything to him. He was just growing up that way. Tony and Patrick were never the best of friends.

Later that afternoon, as Tony was walking back to the flats, Patrick jumped out and ambushed him. He punched Tony so hard in the face that he literally stopped Tony in his tracks and momentarily stunned him. Tony reeled backwards and crouched to the floor to regain his composure.

By the time he looked up again Patrick had gone. Leaving Tony with a bloodied nose. Patrick was also a racist but against the skinheads. As he had seen Tony spending time with them he assumed Tony was in with them. He took a chance and seized his moment; with Tony having to suffer the consequences. *Patrick was going to pay for this!* Tony was left licking his wounds and he went back home and decided to bide his time. He was still quite young and Patrick was a force to be reckoned with. *I'll get him . . . the bastard, I'll get him.*

The following day Tony never mentioned to anyone what had

happened with Patrick. Luckily there were no telltale signs on his face, although Patrick had caught him full on square in the face. He had learnt from past experience not to go telling his dad about outside arguments. However, Tony did get round to asking his dad about what his sister had said.

So she had been right then. Ernie told him about Number 32. Apparently he was a convicted paedophile that had been released from prison and re-homed on the estate. Ernie hadn't given Tony too many details, but enough to warn him from going anywhere near him and to report it to an adult or a policeman if they saw him stalking about. Motor mouth Jacki would be sure to spread the news – didn't need to put posters up. Just tell Jacki and she'd spread the word quicker than any news bulletin.

Everyone hates paedophiles but everyone hates the thought of paedophiles living near them even more. Their probation officers have to release them back into a normal community environment but on an estate full of families with young kids – the local families all felt this was wrong. As bad news does, the news of Number 32 travelled through the estate like wildfire.

Families would tend to keep their kids in now and no longer did you see the kids playing freely in the park. Families were in fear of the potential danger that he posed. He took away the fun and freedom of being a child and playing out. Instead, kids were looking over their shoulders to make sure Number 32 wasn't around. Of course everyone knew who he was. A couple of kids had reported seeing him hanging around the park late one afternoon. They had rushed home and got their parents whom then walked around the parks and the streets like vigilante groups – the man was most likely was just walking to or from the shops. Some others say they saw him staring down at them from his window.

Some of the older kids, Tony included, used to throw eggs at his door and post dog mess through his letterbox. They would spray paint abusive language *PAEDO SCUM* on his front door and windows in red graffiti. The following day he would be seen scrubbing it off.

Of course the police were always about. They had to keep things from getting too out of order – but they pretty much turned a blind eye as far as Number 32 was concerned. One day, Tony, Rob and the skinheads went a step further. One of them had picked up dog mess in a paper bag, then lit the top of the bag and very quickly stuffed it through the letterbox of Number 32 and legged it. "Fucking take that, you paedo SCUM!" Tony yelled as he posted the burning bag through his door.

The silhouette that could be made out through the window in the front door was him stamping on the bag to put the fire out. They all set about laughing, knowing he would have faeces splattered up his legs and the walls – terrorism was the way forward here. They thought they could all terrify him into leaving the estate.

It was six months later, a typical Sunday afternoon in the Hayes' household. Ernie was in the pub till 2 p.m. and Dot had a roast dinner cooking. After dinner, the chores of washing up; clearing the kitchen table; drying up and taking the rubbish down to the bins fell into Tony and Jacki's laps. Tony would wind up always taking the rubbish down to the bins. This afternoon as usual he had gathered up the rubbish bag to go down.

Tony was glad they lived on the first floor. He couldn't stand the stairwells – they always stank of urine. He entered the stairwell and made his way down the two flights to the bins. He whistled as he walked down, swinging the rubbish bag around his head. Just as he turned into the bins he saw Patrick throwing his rubbish bags into the bins.

Tony quickly seized his chance. The anger of what Patrick had done to him six months earlier suddenly welled up from nowhere. Quick as a flash, Tony dropped his rubbish bag. Before Patrick had realised what was happening, Tony had pounced on him and wrestled him to the floor. Tony had Patrick pressed up against the bins holding his head ready to slam it into the bins. The bins were huge metal refuse containers with large metal rims, pushed tightly together in a line.

Tony had grabbed Patrick by the back of the hair in a tight fist . . . *this will teach him a lesson.*

Chapter 5

OVER and over again he smashed the bin lid down onto Patrick's head as he held him down with the other hand. He kept slamming and slamming. Patrick was screaming and swinging his arms about trying to grab Tony but he couldn't reach him. Relentlessly, Tony was smashing the lid again and again. With every word said he slammed the lid "YOU (slam) FUCKING (slam) START (slam) ON (slam) ME (slam) I'LL (slam) FUCKING (slam) KILL (slam) YOU (slam) YOU (slam) EVER (slam) FUCK (slam) WITH ME (slam) AGAIN (slam). THINK YOU'RE (slam) FUCKING (slam) HARD (slam) YOU PRICK (slam). I'll show you who's fucking hard!"

Tony gave a final kick to Patrick and as he let go of him he watched as he slumped to the floor like bag of rags. Tony turned and picked up his rubbish bags, popped the lid back open and swung his rubbish bag into the bin. He slammed the lid shut a final time and, wiping his hands down his legs, turned and walked back up the stinking stairwell. He was breathing hard through flared nostrils, feeling victorious over his revenge attack. He walked into his flat slamming the front door behind him.

"Don't slam the bloody door!" Jacki said as she looked up from the magazine she had been reading, "Where you been anyway?" she asked. Ernie was snoring in his chair, Dot was watching the TV.

"Mind your own flippin' business," Tony retaliated

"Mind your language!" Dot snapped, raising her head up. "I can hear you y'know!"

"Sorrry," said Tony sarcastically and sauntered upstairs to his room, mumbling that *flippin'* wasn't even a swear word.

Maybe half an hour had passed. Tony could hear his dad making a cuppa in the kitchen. He was just leaving his room and making his way downstairs when there was an almighty smashing on the front door. Someone was hammering so hard that they were practically smashing if off its hinges.

"What the bleedin' hell?" Ernie leapt up in shock to answer the door. As he opened it, he thundered backwards followed closely by a knife being thrust against his throat. It took him so suddenly that he barely had time to react. Patrick Senior was foaming at the mouth and holding a small carving knife to Ernie's throat. He was yelling about his son and that Tony had practically beaten the life out of him down at the bins. Without a moment to think, Ernie lunged back into Patrick Senior with all his might, knocking the knife out of his hand and onto the ground. He shoved the Rasta out of the door and the pair of them fell onto the balcony outside, wrestling on the floor. Ernie slammed his fist into Patrick's face as they showered menacing blows onto each other.

Dot grabbed the phone and called the police. Ernie was a big man, a good solid eighteen to nineteen stones of muscle. He was a massive figure of a man and anybody of a fighting stance would struggle against him in a fight. So what chance really did a five feet eight, mid-sized Rastafarian have against Ernie? Ernie smashed him to pieces and, with a last almighty uppercut punch, sent him flying over the balcony of the first floor and down to the ground floor below. It may possibly have been the bonnet of Patrick's Cortina that broke his fall but, needless to say, good job it was only the first floor. Patrick Junior, Patrick's wife, Rita, and Patrick's younger brother, Dwight, all ran downstairs to their dad.

A large crowd had gathered and had witnessed the attack on Ernie and the fight outside. Everyone had seen Ernie fight back and throw Patrick over the balcony. "Show's over!" Ernie barked at everyone. "Get back inside!" Everyone went back to their business, and didn't say a word to anyone. Ernie grabbed Dot and shoved her inside and slammed the front door behind them. "TONY!" Ernie was practically hyperventilating with rage. He demanded to know exactly what had happened – Patrick Senior hadn't really given the full explanation before he had launched his attack on him. Ernie knew the police would be knocking at the door anytime now.

He was sat in the kitchen at the dining room table. The chairs in the kitchen had wooden slats, with large spindles across the back. Dot slid a small shot of brandy across to him to steady his nerves.

"Are you fucking insane woman?" he stared at her in disbelief. "Do you want the ol' bill to think I'm drunk? That won't bloody go down well! Just a very sugary cuppa, that'll do."

Dot quickly withdrew the brandy and replaced it a few minutes later with a mug of tea. Ernie lit a cigarette and listened intently as Tony gave his side of the story. He explained about Patrick attacking him six months earlier, and how he had bided his time and had caught the opportune moment at the bins. Although Tony knew he had done some damage, he couldn't help feeling chuffed at his revenge on Patrick. Even though he feared the trouble he may have caused his Dad – Ernie was known around the estate and to the police for his fighting – he was certainly no mug and no one ever took him for one.

Shortly afterwards, the police arrived. They had been speaking to Patrick Senior first; he had given his version of the event. An ambulance had arrived to take him to hospital along with Patrick Junior. Pat Junior had some really bad cuts to his head, and his eyes were bruised and swollen.

The police entered the flat and surveyed Ernie. They listened to what he had to say and the whole time they were there Ernie never stood up, but remained seated at the kitchen table. He seemed to be leaning back in his chair, listening as the police carried on taking down his statement. Of course Ernie slightly elaborated his side, but being totally honest it was a brutal attack. He had said how he feared for his life and the knife was held right up to his throat and he could feel his pulse against it as it dug into his neck. There was a slight red mark on his throat which the policemen eyed and noted down.

"As I fell to the floor he kept smashing me across the back." Ernie stood up and made a big play of removing his shirt over his head to expose three very large red marks across his back. The two policemen, Dot, Jacki and Tony all gasped at the offending red marks. It looked like he had been beaten half to death with a large stick.

"I dunno what it was he was using or how many times he hit me," Ernie carried on. "But what was I spose to do? He came belting in here all guns blazing. Purely self-defence, officer. Purely self-defence."

Ernie turned to Dot, "Oh love, don't spose you could find me a small brandy or something to steady me nerves – I think I've got delayed shock coming out." Giving her a small wink he held his hands out to her, moving them to motion the shakes.

One of the officers leant in and appeared to sniff the air to see if he could smell any traces of alcohol coming off Ernie's breath. He seemed satisfied that there wasn't and closed his notepad and clicked the end of his pen off and tucked it into his top pocket

"Well, Mr Hayes. That will be all I think," said the other officer. They obviously didn't want to get involved in this. "We've got all the evidence we need. This clearly was an act of self-defence. We'll be dealing with this. We've got your statement now and I think possibly a good brandy should steady you. Good day, Sir, Ma'am." He lifted the tip of his helmet to signify that the visit was over. He turned and took one last look at Tony who stood looking like butter wouldn't melt. "Afternooooon officerrrr," Tony saluted the policeman. Dot gave Tony a short sharp kick to the ankle.

"Sarcastic little sod," she said, as Jacki showed the policemen back to the front door.

`Phew`; everyone breathed a sigh of relief.

"Dad, show me your back again," Tony beckoned to his dad to remove his shirt.

"But he never touched your back!" Dot snapped back slyly.

"I know," said Ernie matter-of-factly.

"But Dad, how did you get those awful marks across your back?"

As Ernie lifted his shirt again to show the marks, they struck an amazing resemblance to the spindles on the kitchen chairs. All the while the policeman had been talking to Ernie he had been pushing and pushing his back into the spindles of the chair, knowing for sure that they would leave a mark. He also knew that without some kind of self-defence story he would have been hauled off to the local nick for this without a doubt!

Patrick Senior wasn't charged for the attack against Ernie. Even though his injuries were also quite severe. He suffered major spinal bruising, a few cracked ribs, a broken leg – and a smashed reputation. By the time Patrick was well enough to leave the hospital, they had moved away from next door.

* * *

A week or so later, a fire engine was heard racing through the estate. Sirens wailing, alerting everyone that there was trouble. People were running from their flats to see what the commotion was. There were two engine trucks which swung to a sudden halt at the foot of the stairwell. All the firemen jumped out, throwing open the side doors to the engine, dragging hoses out and unwinding the ladders. Thick grey smoke was billowing out of a small open window from the first floor flat of Number 32.

"Stand back!" yelled one of the firemen as he kicked the front door though. They all had breathing apparatus on and charged in. The neighbours all stood around, watching and waiting with baited breath to see what had happened.

Chapter 6

AFTER the fire engines arrived, an ambulance arrived on the scene. The paedophile was brought downstairs on a stretcher with breathing apparatus on. He was unconscious from smoke inhalation. Everyone stood gawping but no one made any attempt to see if he was ok. The hum of gossip filled the air as they all just stood and stared. *Was he dead? If he was dead then it was a job well done*, some people thought – but this prank had gone too far.

Tony and his skinhead mates had graduated to throwing homemade petrol bombs through his window. That particular afternoon, the explosion was so extreme it was like a gas explosion. It had set fire to his hallway and kitchen and he had been asleep in the front room unable to get away. He had no chance of getting out. It was only because the little old lady next door had phoned 999 when she smelt smoke and could see some smoke coming from his kitchen window. In actual fact, she had saved his life and the paedo didn't die that day. However, after this, his probation officer requested to have him relocated from the estate, worried that next time . . . well . . . there may not be a next time.

Tony was starting to become a bit of a handful now, maybe a little too cock sure of himself. He was good at certain lessons in school, although school was becoming a bit of a bore to him now. Tony would spend six days a week training for his boxing; he enjoyed his sports very much. He had started swimming for his school and took place in annual swimming galas. He held records for the fastest swimmer and had broken the county record at eleven years old. He also played rugby and basketball for the school teams; he was very good at basketball. Tony and his team stormed through the semi-finals, the winning basket scored with just seconds to go. They went on to win the National Championships against another London team.

One summer during the school holidays, Dot had been taken into hospital for a hysterectomy. Jacki and Tony were sent away to stay with their aunt in Sussex for the holidays so their mother could recover. Ernie was always working away now and they didn't really want to be sent away from home for so long. They had both protested about the trip but in the end Ernie had insisted and that was that. He had taken over part ownership for the lorry firm he worked for so he spent most weeks working away long distance driving. Dot was struggling to cope on her own with the kids at the best of times, especially with Ernie being away so much. When he did come home, all they seemed to do was argue and fight.

During the month-long stay in Sussex things didn't go as planned. One of Tony's cousins, Jimmy, had been bullied quite badly for a while. He was a similar age to Tony, but a weedy ginger kid with bad skin. He got bullied on a weekly basis. After hearing that Tony would be coming to stay with them for a month he knew that Tony was really tough so he proceeded to brag and tell the bully kids that his tough London cousin was coming up and he was going to beat them all up!

Their aunt's house was set in the countryside deep in Sussex. It was a beautiful house surrounded by fields and backed onto some old train tracks where all the kids would often play about.

The old freight trains usually came past hourly at a rate of knots with their horns blowing. Tony and Jacki had been there just over a week when boredom was starting to set in. One afternoon the two boys went off and decided to mess about around the tracks. They were lying in between the sleepers when, in the distance, Jimmy heard the train coming and could hear the horn blowing. The boys had decided to see how long they could stay there

"I'm not gonna move till the last minute," Jimmy had said as he lay down further into the sleepers on the ground. Tony nervously looked over his shoulder; he didn't like this one bit. The train was fast approaching and Tony was up on his knees now. The train driver had pulled the train's horn to alert the boys to get off the track as it drew closer and closer.

"Jimmy, come on! This is stupid. Let's get off. Quick! It's coming!" Tony said.

"Ha! Chicken!" Jimmy shouted back at him.

Tony started to clamber off the tracks and as he turned round he could see that Jimmy was also getting up. As he looked back again Jimmy had fallen back down.

"SHIT! COME ON, JIMMY! STOP MUCKING ABOUT, COME ON!"

"ARGH, TONY! HELP ME!" Jimmy was writhing about on his side and Tony realised that he had his trainer wedged under the railway sleeper. Tony looked back at the train which was fast approaching

"JIMMY, MOVE! NOW! COME ON! FUCKING HELL!" shouted Tony, thinking he was still mucking about.

"I'M STUCK! I'M REALLY STUCK, TONY, HELP ME!" Jimmy squealed. The train was getting nearer.

"FOR FUCK'S SAKE JIMMY!" screamed Tony. "MOVE IT!" The train was fast upon them now.

"I CAN'T!" Jimmy had tears streaming down his face. Tony quickly threw himself over to where Jimmy was laying and, with an almighty yank, he pulled Jimmy's foot free from the trainer and dragged his sobbing cousin to the edge of the tracks and to safety. Literally a few seconds later, the train went past with its horn blowing and the driver shaking his fist at the boys.

"STUPID BOYS!" yelled the driver.

"FUCKING HELL, JIMMY!" screamed Tony. Jimmy was a blubbering mess. The train disappeared off into the distance and they both lay there for a minute, breathing in raspy lungs of air – the realisation of what had just happened dawning on them.

"We could have been killed, you moron!" Tony punched his cousin hard on the arm.

"My trainer!" Jimmy cried. "My trainer! Mum's gonna go mad as she's just bought them." Tony let go of Jimmy and stood up to go and get the trainer. His legs were still shaking as he stepped over the track and went back to where he had been trapped. There was nothing there . . . they never found the trainer, only a piece of rubber that it might have once been. On top of that, Jimmy had also wet himself.

The following day the boys decided to play away from the tracks at the local park. They hadn't even been there an hour when a group of three boys walked in. "Oi! Ginger Jimbow!" they taunted him. "Pissed your pants again have you?" they all laughed. This pissing of pants appeared to be a regular thing for Jimmy, hence why he was bullied. All that aside, Tony wasn't standing for it.

"Are these the fucking muppets, Jim?" Tony asked as he turned round and faced the boys head on.

"Oh yeah, who are you then?" The tallest of the boys stepped forward. He must have been maybe a year or so older than Tony.

"I'm Jim's cousin from London and I hear you've been picking on him."

"Oh yeah? We've heard a lot about you; think you're well hard don't ya? And what are you gonna do about it then?" they all laughed.

"A fucking lot!" Tony gave back. "Try picking on me and see what you get!" he said.

"Oh come on then!" the boy retorted. With that, Tony had punched him so hard in the face that he had broken his nose and splattered it across half of his face. Screaming, the kid held his hands up to his face and they immediately filled with blood.

"You both want some an' all?" Tony yelled at the other two who stood looking on, horrified.

"Ever start on him again and I'll be back to do ya, you wankers!" With that, they turned and ran off.

Jimmy was so thankful and proud of his cousin. He had saved his neck twice in two days.

That night, the family were sitting in the kitchen having dinner. The doorbell suddenly sounded, followed by a thunderous banging on the door.

"Oh my goodness!" Tony's aunt said, leaping out of her chair. She opened the door to find a very angry man standing there with a beaten-up kid beside him.

"Where's your Jimmy? I want to know who's responsible for this," he yelled shoving the boy forward into the light of the hallway. The kid was clearly in a bad state; his face was quite badly swollen and his eyes blackened.

"I am," Tony said immediately, standing up for himself. "And I'll do it again if he starts on Jimmy anymore."

The beaten-up kid stood with his shoulders down and his head hung in shame.

"What are you talking about – My son's no bully! Look at his face! This is disgraceful I've a good mind to hit you and see how you like it."

"Oh yeah?" Tony said. "Go on then, and see what my dad does to you. He'll come and find you and smash you up!"

"That's ENOUGH!" Tony's aunt stepped in, holding her hands up.

"I've a good mind to report him to the police – he's an animal!" the man carried on.

"I'll deal with this, I'm sorry."

"You better – that kid needs a good hiding!" the man spat back, turned and slammed out of the house, dragging his son with him.

Tony's aunt stood there glaring at him. "I think you've got some explaining to do, young man. And now!" she said with her hands on her hips.

Tony refused to apologise to his aunt – as far as he was concerned he wasn't in the wrong. Tony's aunt refused to believe his story and couldn't possibly believe her Jimmy had been bullied, as he had never said anything. Jimmy sat there and said nothing – he let Tony take all the flack.

Later that night when the boys were tucked up in bed, Tony decided to have it out with him. "How could you just sit there and say nothing? I got a right bollocking and you said nothing. No wonder you get fucking picked on. You're on your own now, Jim. You can sort your own shit out . . . I ain't sticking up for you no more."

Jimmy rolled over and still said nothing. Because of the fighting incident and the train incident, which Tony's aunt also found out about when she was looking for his trainers, she decided that Tony was just too bad an influence on her family and it just wasn't going to work with them staying there. Ernie was called back from work urgently, and arrangements were made for him to drive to pick his children up and bring them home again. This wasn't how it was supposed to have panned out. Ernie was furious and didn't know what he was going to do.

* * *

Things at home were going from bad to worse for Dot and Ernie. By now Dot had left her job in the supermarket and had taken a reception job locally in town. Tony was becoming very uncontrollable and Dot didn't know how to handle him. She would snap at him and take out her unhappiness and frustrations on him at home. Tony would back chat and get lippy – he was really quite tall now and was a good eye-to-eye level with Dot. She would stand up to him and often Tony would get a smack round the back of the head if he back chatted. Dot would push him and shove him.

She had a huge rubber plant in the hallway with a bamboo stick in the pot to hold the plant upright. One afternoon when he came in from school she had really lost her patience with him. The row started as soon as Tony came through the door.

"You've not made your bed! You've not tidied up!" She lashed out at Tony and smacked him around the head with the bamboo stick. She had tried to rule with an iron fist and Tony had started lashing out verbally at his mother. He had a foul mouth on him, as well as a foul temper. Dot was standing there shouting at him, threatening him again with the stick.

As she raised it above her head to swipe him, Tony warned her; "If you hit me with that stick one more time, I swear to God, Mum, I'll hit you back – and I won't stop either . . . I'm not taking this anymore!"

Dot didn't listen and raised her hand to hit him. Jacki was screaming from the doorway. As Dot brought her hand down, Tony grabbed her wrist and wrenched the bamboo stick from her grasp. He snatched it and turned the stick back on her. *Whack!* He smacked her across the shoulder and she fell onto the floor and rolled up into a ball. Twice more Tony brought the stick down hard across Dot's back. He had seen red and lost his temper.

Suddenly it had dawned on him what he had done. *Oh shit!* Jacki was crawling across the floor to her mum. Tony dropped the stick, but Dot had jumped up and was back on her feet . Tony turned and ran up the stairs. Dot was screaming at him. "I'm your mother! You don't do that to your mother! I'm gonna kill you, you little bastard!"

She was frothing at the mouth. She had totally lost it. Tony ran into his bedroom; he needed to think. He couldn't believe what had happened. *What on earth was he going to do?* He just couldn't take this anymore, this abuse he had to suffer. He just couldn't stand it.

The bedroom door flew open and a hysterical Dot was flying at him from the doorway, eyes blazing. She looked like she was going to kill him. She was screaming "I'm gonna get you!"

She leapt at Tony to attack him – she was so riled with rage. She landed on the bed but Tony had sidestepped her and, with one almighty pull, Tony had grabbed his wardrobe and dragged the entire thing down with its contents onto the bed on top of her. He leapt on top of the wardrobe and started jumping up and down. Dot was screaming at him, buried under the wardrobe and its contents.

Tony swept out of the room leaving his mother screaming on the bed, past a sobbing Jacki on the stairs. Jacki lunged for Tony's foot as he dashed past but he kicked out at her too. "Fuck off, Jacki!"

He grabbed his coat and stormed out of the flat. *What was he going to do now? He couldn't go back, not ever. How dare she? Oh wait till his dad heard about this one! He would go mad for sure.* Tony had never really bothered his dad with the fights that happened at home. His dad didn't get home most nights till 11 p.m. and by then arguments were over, or Ernie was just too tired to listen and went to bed. The last thing Tony wanted to do was cause grief. But not now, his dad had to hear about this.

Tony was pretty sure that Dot would have great delight in making him out to be the bad one here if she got to Ernie before he did. But Tony had to let the dust settle so he hung about the streets until he saw Ernie's car pull up – it was not far off 11 p.m. Tony was the last of the kids to be out at that time of night. He looked a sad and lowly figure sitting on the step under where the bins were. Tony left it five to ten minutes, then he mustered up the courage to go home.

Ernie certainly never knew about any of the rows that had gone on. He certainly never knew about Dot hitting Tony. Tony knew he was going to be in trouble. As he slowly stepped through the front door, he knew instantly that Dot's story had already been told and probably elaborated in detail to make him look worse.

"TONY!" his dad barked. "GET IN HERE NOW! YOU HIT YOUR MOTHER!" he screamed – he seemed so disappointed. Tony jumped in quickly. It was now or never, he thought.

Tony started blurting out to his dad; "She smacks me all the time, she belts me in front of my mates, she clumps me with frying pans, she's always hitting me, Dad, she beats me with this stick." Tony grabbed the offending bamboo stick from the plant pot that had been carefully put back in its place. Tony was almost crying by now and spitting the words out; he thrust the bamboo stick at his Dad.

Dot had made a big mistake here. Instead of standing up for herself and denying it, she blurted out; "Yeah well he fucking deserves it! Little bastard causes me nothing but grief. He deserves it!"

That was enough, Ernie spun round to face his wife. Veins looked like they were going to pop in his neck. He stared Dot in the face. *"You do what to him?"* he said in disbelief. "You hit him with sticks and pans? Tony, go to bed! Jacki, go to bed. NOW!"

Tony and Jacki backed out of the kitchen. Ernie slammed the door shut behind them. It would be surprising if the whole estate hadn't heard the argument that followed.

Two days later and the household was just starting to calm down. After another long shift Ernie had come home from work, earlier though this time. It was almost 8 p.m. and he was tired and hungry. He had been away so much; he missed being at home with his kids. He really was putting the hours in. When he came in from work that evening, he asked Dot "What's for dinner?"

Dot hadn't expected him to come home today, thinking he would be back after the weekend. She looked forlorn and said "Nothing, I've got nothing in as I didn't think you'd be back this evening."

Ernie was disappointed.

"I'll knock up ham, egg and chips." Dot said reluctantly walking off to the kitchen as all she could hear was Ernie huffing and moaning. "I've been working all bloody week. It wouldn't have hurt you to have some decent meals ready for when I'm back, would it?"

Ernie settled down to watch TV, disappointed that all he could look forward to was ham, egg and chips..... Tony and Jacki sat there looking at each other and then carried on watching the TV – Ernie's favorite programme was on. It was a snooker one called Pot Black. However, watching this proved slightly problematic for the Hayes' household as they only had a black and white TV.

"How can you watch Pot Black on a black and white TV?" Tony would ask his dad. Tony knew they were the only family left on the estate to have a black and white TV. This was his angle to try and persuade his dad to get a new TV from Radio Rentals.

"Imagine how great it would be, Dad, if we could watch Pot Black on a colour TV – you can't even see what balls are what on here!"

Jacki laughed at him.

"I know what balls are what!" Ernie joked with his kids.

About half an hour later Dot had emerged from the kitchen.

"Here's your fucking ham, egg and chips!! ." She was so angry at Ernie that she launched the entire plate of food straight at him from the kitchen doorway.

It flew through the air and it landed... *splat!* straight on his face. A shocked Tony slipped under his dad's arm to escape the dripping food that was sliding down his dad's cheek and he crawled to the other end of the sofa next to Jacki. They both sat there, mouths open, waiting for the fireworks to explode. The plate lay smashed on the floor just in front of him but Ernie didn't move; he just sat there, maybe too tired to retaliate or too shocked that she had actually just wasted his dinner. With ham, egg and chips dripping off his face and all over his chest, he proceeded to eat his dinner.

"Pass the brown sauce, Tone," he said. Tony stared, open-mouthed and quickly passed his dad the sauce bottle that was sitting on their front room table. Ernie shook it up and down then covered his chest in sauce and continued with his `Pot black`. Jacki burst out laughing and Tony sat in awe of his father.

"Want a chip, Son?" Ernie grinned.

"Nah thanks, Dad. I've had mine," Tony replied, still unable to take his eyes off him.

"Nice," said Ernie. "Hope yours came on a plate. Now turn the TV up!"

Dot was so angry and upset that she packed her bags and left that night. She just couldn't stand anymore. Dot and Ernie had quite a volatile relationship towards the end. Many nights would end in terrible arguments. One evening Dot even pulled a knife on Ernie and held it up to him

"Go on then!" he bellowed. "GO ON THEN!"

She just threw the knife down on the floor and stormed out of the kitchen.

Tony and Jacki would stay in their rooms out of the way and wait for the storm to settle – usually with one of them storming out. But the ham, egg and chips was the final straw. Dot moved out of the Hayes household for good leaving the kids with Ernie and went back to her parents' house.

Decisions had to be made, however, regarding the family. Ernie stayed at the flat on the estate and for a while he had Jacki and Tony living with him. Like many siblings, Tony and Jacki didn't get on at all and they fought and fought endlessly.

Within a year or so Dot moved out of her parents' house and got herself a small two-bedroom flat in the centre of town. She carried on working as a receptionist. In end Jacki moved back in with Dot, leaving just Tony and Ernie at the flat.

Life carried on, Tony spent less time at school and would often bunk off and stay at the flat alone when Ernie was at work. Tony was gradually losing interest in his boxing too; he had won lots of fights and had built himself an impressive trophy collection. Things took a really bad turn for the worse one day. During a fight Tony got hit in the side of the head, rupturing the veins in the back of his eyes. His vision clouded over and he couldn't see anything as his eyes filled up with blood. The fight had to be stopped and Tony was taken to hospital. Tony was ok luckily and he didn't lose any vision at all but he could no longer box. He still did the fitness training though but sadly he couldn't take his boxing career any further.

That was the day that something changed inside Tony. The young carefree boy had suddenly gone for good and in its place was left an angry young man who was more dangerous than he could ever have imagined.

Chapter 7

1983

"HAYES!" Tony felt the spit landing on his face. That's how close to him the sergeant was standing; too close for Tony's liking. Sergeant Ofarma was screaming so loudly at Tony that he was gathering white spittle in each corner of his mouth. This amused Tony; he felt the burning urge to interrupt his shouting rampage to tell him that he needed to wipe his mouth.

"WE DON'T LIKE GIRLS IN OUR REGIMENT! ARE YOU A GIRL? DO YOU NEED A SKIRT?"

The lined-up parade of Tony's regiment all sniggered, then stopped as Sergeant Ofarma sent them all a look to dare them to do it again.

"DO YOU THINK I AM FUNNY?" Tony could see the veins in his forehead rising and pulsating. His eyes were bulging as he bellowed in Tony's face.

"No," Tony replied.

"NO, WHAT?" the sergeant was really losing his temper now. "NO, WHAT?" he screamed again at Tony.

"No, I don't think you are funny," said Tony matter-of-factly.

"NO, SIR IS THE ANSWER YOU ARE LOOKING FOR! NO! SIR!"

The sergeant flicked Tony's hair with the end of his baton stick. Sergeant Ofarma was a tallish, Ghanaian kid. At age of sixteen, he had graduated through his cadets and had just earned his sergeant stripes at the cadet regiment.

Tony, who was just fourteen years old, was sporting a rather trendy blonde permed mullet of a hairdo at the time. The cadet uniform consisted of a green beret, camouflaged trousers, zip-up camouflaged jacket and shirt, green jumper and black laced boots. Tony thought he looked very smart all done up. He used to position the beret on top of his head showing off his permed mullet. It was this mullet that was the problem.

"LONG HAIR IS FOR GIRLS! GET A HAIRCUT!" the sergeant screamed. But Tony had point blank refused to have his hair cut. He didn't even want to join the cadets. "What do I wanna be in the cadets for?" he had screamed at his dad.

Tony's best mate Rob was born to be in the army and was in the cadets with him. Rob was much shorter than Tony and of a much stockier build. He had very short spiky dark blonde – hair and freckles.

"It makes them a man, gives them discipline and respect," Rob's mum had said. Ernie was struggling to have any kind of control over Tony now and he was becoming so unruly that this seemed the only option left for him.

"I... AIN`T.... CUTTING... MY...HAIR!" Tony yelled back at the sergeant. "And by the way, GET OUT OF MY FACE . . . YOUR BREATH STINKS!"

 Sergeant Ofarma was trying very hard to control his temper which was rapidly diminishing before his eyes. He suddenly reached out and shoved Tony in the chest and Tony instinctively shoved him back.

"Oh fuck!" said Rob, who was standing next to Tony in line-up. "Tony! Don't!" But it was too late – Tony had taken off his jacket and thrown his beret onto the floor.

"YOU NEED TO BE TAUGHT A LESSON HAYES!" the sergeant screeched at Tony. Everyone was shouting to Tony to *back down* and *don't do it*.

Watching on with interest from the other side of the courtyard were two colonels. "Ballsy little fucker isn't he!" commented one of them.

Tony and Sergeant Ofarma began fighting, not wrestling, on the floor. Real fighting, like a boxing match. Everyone had gathered round out of their parade line. Tony was throwing punches at the sergeant, left-right-left. He punched like he was in a fight at boxing, staying calm and focused. The sergeant was wildly swinging his arms about trying to land punches on Tony, but Tony was too nimble for him. The sergeant just couldn't get him. Tony landed another set of three punches straight into the sergeant's face and stood back as he hit the floor and was down. The boys were going wild shouting and cheering for Tony. He just stood there waiting for the sergeant to get up,

"WHO'S A FUCKING GIRL NOW?" he spat at the sergeant, who could only glare at Tony, humiliated from the floor. "STUFF YA FUCKING CADETS UP YA FUCKING ARSE, YOU WANKERS!"

As the two colonels looked on in amusement, Tony turned and walked out of the cadets. He had done well; he lasted a whole week! Tony had won that fight; however, it opened up a whole lot of trouble for him.

That evening Sergeant Peter Ofarma had arrived home. He was sitting in the kitchen talking with his sister and his younger cousin, Benny. He was telling them all about his ordeal with the cadet boy and how humiliated he had been.

"I know dat boy!" Benny exclaimed. "He's in my year at school; he lives on the other side of our estate. We had a fight years ago at da Queen's Jubilee – I hate him! I'll stab him! You leave him to me!"

Peter looked worriedly at his sister – he was slightly concerned about his cousin. The kids these days just didn't care. What with their gangs and fighting, they had no other way these days but to fight.

The following evening after school, Benny and his gang were standing around waiting for Tony as he came walking down the road with Rob; Tony knew that Benny was involved with the older gangs of boys who stole cars and dealt drugs – this was a nasty gang. As they approached, Benny motioned for him to come over. Dubiously, Tony went over. Benny's tall, slender frame was about the same height as Tony. Without saying a word, Benny threw a punch which landed straight on Tony's lip. Tony didn't see this coming and fell backwards into Rob, who instinctively shoved him back forwards towards Benny

"You bin bad mouthing on my cousin and making him look bad?" Benny yelled. His dark eyes were raging, his face stony and grimacing. With that, Tony started lashing punches out, smashing Benny in the head. Benny stumbled back and, as he did, he reached into the back pocket of his jeans and pulled a small lock knife out on Tony. Everyone froze in panic. Tony had never had anyone pull a knife on him before.

"Can't fucking fight with your hands?" Tony spat at him, feeling a mixture of rage and fear.

"Nah, man. I'm gonna fucking stab you up," Benny snarled at him.

"Is that right?" Tony challenged him back.

"Let's run, Tone!" Rob was hissing at him from behind.

"I ain't running nowhere," Tony said, not taking his eyes off Benny. The air was tense. The two boys locked gazes for what felt like an eternity.

"Tony, come on!" Rob was trying to drag Tony back by his coat but Tony slipped his arms out of it, sending Rob flying backwards. Rob scrambled back to his feet and everyone had stood around to see if Benny would sink the blade into Tony. Benny had paused like an animal stalking its prey; hands out in front of him, holding the knife perfectly still in his grip. He seemed hesitant to attack any further. Tony started backing away very slowly. As tough as he was, he wasn't going to win to a knife – he knew he was beaten this time.

"You're lucky, boy!" Benny taunted him. "You run now . . . but I'll get you another time." Tony continued his stare-out with Benny until they were a fair distance away. Rob was almost in tears.

"He pulled a fucking blade on you man – a fucking blade! Oh Jesus! I thought you were fucking done for!"

Tony said nothing as the two boys hurried up the road and approached Rob's house. Tony kept looking behind him all the way in case Benny decided to come back after him to attack him again. As soon as they were inside with the door shut, Rob bleated the whole saga out to his mum.

Half an hour later PC Maguill and PC Chambers all sat round listening to two very different versions of a story. "Tony! Tell them what happened. Tell them about the knife," Rob was going on and on.

"What knife?" Tony lied. "I didn't actually see a knife – I don't know where Rob's got that from. You must have imagined it, Rob." Rob was distraught. Tony was staring at the floor he couldn't believe that Rob's mum had called the police in.

"Tony, you must say what happened," Rob's mum was trying to

coax him into telling the whole story.

"I don't remember no knife – sorry, seems we have wasted your time." With that, Tony was ushering the two officers to their feet and was trying to rush PC Maguill out of the front door.

"Listen to me, Tony," PC Maguill said quietly at the door. "I know this gang and they don't mess about. They will pull knives out . . . and guns . . . and they aren't afraid to use them. We got loads on them. All I need is for you to tell me exactly what happened with you and Benny and I can help you. We can do something about them . . . come on, son . . . tell me."

"Nope, sorry, don't recall a thing. Sorry PC Maguill!" And with that Tony shoved them outside and closed the front door behind them.

Rob was standing there looking at him, embarrassed. "You're a mug, Tone," he said after a few seconds had passed.

"Yeah, maybe, and you're a fucking grass!" Tony threw back at him. Rob's mum was standing in the doorway of the kitchen looking sadly at Tony. Tony turned back to the front door.

"Tony dont leave........" But it was too late- Rob's voice trailed out of the front door after Tony as he slammed out of the flat towards home – checking over his shoulder all the way.

Chapter 8

LATER that evening, PC Maguill was hammering on the front door of the Ofarma's flat. There was no answer. The next day at school, the news was round the playground before Tony had even got there. All his mates were crowding around him to see if the rumours about Tony and Benny had been true. *Had Tony nearly been stabbed to death? Had Tony and Benny had a terrible fight? Was Benny's gang after Tony to stab him?*

One of Tony's mates said that Benny had been taken into the head's office first thing and no one had seen him since. Tony had to see what was happening for himself.

Without a moment to lose, he charged into the school reception and headed straight down to the head's office – a route he was rather familiar with. He needed to know what was going on and what Benny was saying. Tony slammed through the door without knocking, like a charging bull, to see Benny and the head leaping out of their seats in fright at the hurricane that had almost ripped the door from its hinges.

A terrified school receptionist shot in after him – *like she was going to stop him!* Tony lunged himself at Benny, raining blow after blow down to his head. Benny was screaming on the floor as each blow knocked more wind out of him.

"Think you're fucking hard now, do ya?" Tony spat at him through gritted teeth. "Pull a fucking knife on me, you fucker!"

Tony was like an enraged animal. The headmaster, Mr Thompson, and another teacher in the room, Mr Murray, desperately tried to peel the boys apart but they were too strong. Miss Armstrong, the receptionist, had rushed back to the staff room to get Mr Smith, the boys' rugby teacher, to help. Mr Murray was flapping about trying to pull Tony away by the back of his blazer, proceeding only to rip the coat in half up the back. Mr Thompson was trying to shove himself in between the boys.

Blow after blow kept coming to Benny; he was curled up in a ball on the floor shouting. Suddenly a large firm hand bent down over Tony and grabbed him in a death head lock. Mr Smith wrenched the boys apart and frog marched Tony by the neck out of the office and down the corridor to cool off.

Shortly after that the police arrived at school, followed by Ernie and a hysterical Dot. The police officer and PC Maguill had searched Benny and indeed found a knife. He admitted he had brought the knife into school and was going to threaten to stab Tony.

PC Maguill sat in the head's room for quite a considerable amount of time that afternoon talking with the Hayes family. Ernie felt his son was really going off the rails and proceeded to explain to PC Maguill the reasons he thought were behind this.

Six weeks ago a terrible tragedy struck the Hayes family. Phillip, a close cousin of Tony's, had been on his way home from work one evening. He had just got himself an apprenticeship as a mechanic at a garage in Dagenham in Essex. He was an only child and a good kid and was working to help support his mum Viv, who had struggled ever since he was a baby to raise him singlehandedly. He was doing well in his job. This one particular evening, Phil was waiting at the platform of the local train station to get home. As the train approached the station, Phil stepped forward close to the edge of the platform, but the slabs were all uneven and raised and, as he stepped forward, he stubbed his toe and fell forward over the edge – straight in front of the oncoming train.

This was the most horrific thing that had ever happened to the family. Ernie had been called up along with Viv and another of his brothers to help identify the few remains of the body. Something which would surely haunt him for the rest of his life. Tony had been very close to his cousin and Ernie suspected that his rage and anger was his way of dealing with his grief. He would punch walls and doors; Tony couldn't understand why life was so unfair. PC Maguill noted all this down for his records. He suggested that maybe Tony should see a grief counsellor to help him deal with his emotions and feelings. Ernie secretly thought that he had more chance of getting to see the Pope than getting Tony to see a counsellor!

That evening, as PC Maguill was knocking off his shift, he decided to take a drive home through the estate and he saw Tony walking back from the chip shop. Something about this kid had been bothering him all afternoon. He quickly parked his car up and jumped out and started walking over to where Tony was. "Oi! Where you off to, Tony?" PC Maguill called over.

"Been chippy ain't I, for me Dad," Tony said, motioning down towards the open bag of chips he was eating.

"Gis a chip!" Maguill said, reaching over and helping himself to one of Tony's chips.

Tony frowned – he hated that!   "Get your own!" Tony said, still frowning at him.

"Other people's always taste better," the copper grinned.   "How are you feeling now, son?" he questioned Tony. But he didn't wait for an answer. "Listen, I'm not buying that story for one minute your old man told me today back in school." Tony shrugged his shoulders nonchalantly. "I mean, I'm not saying I don't believe what happened, I know that's what did happen. What I'm saying is, I don't think that's the reason you're being this way."

Tony looked at him suspiciously. "What you talking about?" he asked. "I ain't doing nothing wrong, I'm not the one carrying knives am I?"

"No, but listen, Tony," Maguill carried on, ignoring Tony's flippancy. "I'm not gonna beat around the bush here . . . these gangs are serious. And the reason I'm not buying your dad's story is that, over last year or so, your name constantly keeps cropping up. Whenever there's trouble, your name is in the frame. Now, I'm not saying you start trouble, but you are getting yourself into a whole heap of proverbial here. You will end up in the nick if you carry on this way. You'll be spending your days inside when you get older if you carry on down this route. Mark my words!" he carried on, nicking another chip.

As he went in for a third one, Tony swooped the bag out and away from under his reach.

"Now get yer own!" Tony laughed and Maguill looked embarrassed.

"I'm off home for my tea now anyway, but remember what I said – and enjoy your dinner."

"I fucking will if I've got any left, you greedy fat fucker!" Tony called after him as Maguill headed back to his car. The nights were drawing in now and it was cold that evening. Tony hurried home with his food for Ernie; if he hurried he would catch the end of Pot Black!

Chapter 9

ALL that following week, the rumours were flying around thick and fast. Tony had heard that Benny's gang were after him and they were going to do him 'proper good'. These gangs were hardcore. They spent most of their days dealing drugs and beating people up who owed them money for drugs – most of them doing drugs too and smoking weed. Then there was stealing cars. They carried all sorts of weapons on them, but mainly knives and guns. Tony felt scared for the first time in a long while and he was fearful for his life.

As he approached the entrance of Leytonstone train station he checked his watch. He was running early; Lee wouldn't be here yet. "Meet me at 1 p.m.," Lee had said. Lee was Tony's older cousin. He had just come out of prison a few months back for nicking cars. Tony was so worried about Benny's gang coming after him that he had contacted Lee for some help.

Not more than five minutes had passed and Tony saw a familiar face making its way through the crowds. "Tone!" Lee called out, putting his arm up and waving.

Tony smiled and felt relief wash over him. His cousin held his arm out and hugged Tony tight. "How are you, son?" he said, roughing up the blonde curly mullet. "What's this?" he said, pulling on the long hair at the back.

Tony grinned. The two cousins made their way to a small cafe at the top of the high street.

It wasn't long before they were tucking into a hearty full English and so Tony proceeded to tell his cousin about everything that had happened. Lee seemed genuinely upset for his younger cousin.

"Oh, Tony. Mate, I wish I could help you out, but if I get into any more shit I'll end up back inside. I can't get involved with this lot mate – but you can't take them on alone. I know this gang you're talking about and they are fucking savage! They won't mess about either mate. A few lads I knew inside had had dealings with them. They'll fuck over a school kid like you in no time."

"I just don't know what to do, Lee. I ain't scared of Benny. I'll do him one on one but he's pulling out knives, and what chance 'ave I got?"

Lee thought for a minute. "Listen," he said. "I know a couple of geezers. Karl is based in Stratford, runs a cabbie at the top of the high street. I've known him a long while. He has a little side kick called Al who's maybe about five or six years older than you, if that. Couple of good geezers. I'll shout Karl and give him a head's up you're coming. Can you get to Stratford this evening?"

"Yeah should be ok, I'm spose to be training but I can swerve that – dad won't know."

"Ok," Lee said. "Take some money for bus fare." Lee stuffed some notes across the table towards Tony. "Go to KB STREET CABS, when you get there ask for Karl – tell him Lee sent you. I'll nip by later beforehand and see him too. Don't worry, son, it'll be ok," Lee said confidently. He mopped up the last dregs of his breakfast with his toast, glugged back his mug of tea and leant back, lighting a cigarette.

"You smoke?" He offered a cigarette to Tony

"Er, yeah, of course," Tony said, taking a cigarette from the packet. Lee tossed a lighter across the table and smiled.

* * *

The number 42 bus pulled into its stop at the top of Stratford Centre. Tony stepped down off the bus. He saw the high street, and he could make out a yellow `TAXI` sign poking out from the wall. He crossed the street and nervously made his way over to the cab office. He didn't know what to expect. He was beginning to feel like a small nervous kid. *Come on*, he thought. *Get a grip here, Tony.*

The last thought whizzing about in his mind as he left the flat that evening was Ernie`s words...... "*HAVE A GOOD TRAINING SESSION, SON.*" Tony hated lying to his Dad but he knew he had to about this. He took two deep breaths and stepped forward and pushed open the door to the cab office.

A thick heavy cloud of smoke filled the air.

"KB KABS," a young lady's voice from behind the counter rang through the smokey fog. "Where you going to, love? Ok and from where? Lovely, can I take a name? No problem . . . 'bout ten minutes. Ok, thanks, goodbye."

She hung up and peered at Tony across the counter, all long eyelashes and red lipstick. "Cab, love?" she asked curiously.

"Nah, I'm here to see Karl," Tony stammered nervously, staring at the gorgeous young woman.

Chapter 10

"I'VE been expecting you.!"

At the back of the office was a door with plastic fly strips hanging from the frame. A tall, slim, smartly dressed man with dark slicked hair, glasses and stubble was making his way through them, smiling; a cigarette hanging from one side of his mouth. He looked in his early thirties but the stubble may have aged him.

"Wasn't sure if you wanted salad on the kebab this time, fucking Turks! Always try and 'ave me over in there."

The door to the cabbies burst open and in came a younger boy, nearly twenty years old, if that. He was a tall, slender, mixed-race boy. Handsome, with short, dark spiked hair and a black leather bomber jacket on, holding what appeared to be a doner kebab.

"Oh well done, well done. Cheers, Al," said Karl, taking the kebab. He motioned over to Tony to follow him through to the back office. Al followed them too and closed the door behind him, leaving the gorgeous young woman in the front office.

"Don't mind me stuffing me moosh, I'm fucking starving!" Karl said as he sat down behind a desk. "Now you must be little Tony, Lee's cousin, if I`m correct? I hear you're in a bit of bother. This is my mate, Al . . . why don't you tell us all about it."

Tony immediately felt at ease. He had instantly liked Karl and Al. They had a `safe` feel here. Tony explained all about Benny and the feuds, the knife attack. He had told them what PC Maguill had said, and then about the rumours flying around about the gang threatening to get him.

"We'll sort him for you," Al said. "We'll sort it all for you."

"But I wanna do him myself," said Tony. "I'm not afraid of him but I can't handle the gang after me as well," Tony went on. "How the hell am I meant to defend myself against a gang and knife attacks when he won't fight with his fists?"

"Ok," said Karl. "Well that's very honourable of you, Tone. I like you kid . . . you got balls! You remind me a lot of your cousin Lee. How about we take care of the gang and you take care of Benny?"

"Yeah, but how? He's carrying a knife all the time," Tony said.

Al went over to a filing cabinet in the corner and opened the drawer and pulled out a long chain. "With this fucker," he said, smiling. He wrapped one end around his knuckles and the other end swung freely back and forth. "You find 'im, and then you 'ave 'im! If he pulls a fucking knife, you whip this outta your back pocket. Wrap one end round ya knuckles and, with the other end, you smash it . . . fucking hard, right down across his hand with the knife in it. He'll quickly drop it. Then you kick the shit out of him." Al was pleased with himself. "He won't pull a knife on you again, and if you put some keys on the end as well, it'll look like a keychain and not a weapon."

"Al's right," Karl cut in. "The gang won't touch a hair on your head either after we've had a word with them . . . talking of hair . . ." Karl pointed at Tony's hair. "What the fuck is going on there with the mullet?"

Tony ran his hand through his hair. "Oh yeah," he said. "I've been thinking of getting it cut, it's coming off." He said unsurely. Suddenly, Tony noticed the time. He still had to get a bus back home and it was getting late.

"Don't worry," said Al. "I'll drop you back in a cab. Come on, this way."

Tony jumped up and as he turned to leave he tucked the chain into his back pocket and turned to Karl. "How can I owe you for this, Karl? I can't pay you . . . I don't have any money. How can I return the favour?"

Karl stood up, put his hands on Tony's shoulders and looked him in the eye. "Call it all sorted, son. Your cousin Lee did me a real favour with some heavies inside . . . I owed him one. Call it quits."

He patted Tony's shoulders and Tony held his hand up and shook his hand. I'll see you soon, kid. Don't worry, and you know where I am if you need anything. You call in anytime."

As Tony left the cabbies he walked past the gorgeous woman on the phone. He gave a cocky wink at her and she smiled.

"See ya, sweetheart" she called after him.

"Not if I see you first," he retorted.

Al was sitting outside in the car ready to go. Tony jumped in.

"Cor, she's well fit ain't she!" he said as he slammed the car door behind him.

"That's Collette," Al said. "She's Karl's bit on the side." "Phoar, she's fucking gorgeous!" Tony said.

Al laughed. "She's alright. All tits and tight trousers!" he said as he sped off.

The lads chatted easily on the drive home; Tony felt like he had known Al for ages. "Smoke?" Al asked, tossing Tony a cigarette.

"Cheers," Tony said, as Al passed him the car lighter and wound down the windows.

"You got a lot of balls, mate, coming here at your age, not knowing who you're meeting.

How old are you again?"

"Almost fifteen," Tony said proudly.

Al nodded at him and raised an eyebrow and carried on. "Lee told me you're a tough one. He also told me you're an incredible fighter."

"I am," Tony said.

"That's why you gotta do this, Tone. You can't let them arseholes get away with this shit.

They wanna fight street and carry guns and knives, they gotta earn the reps in the drug business. They won't be interested in fighting your way. You gotta fight fire with fire man. You gotta smash him up and you gotta not stop . . . teach him a fucking lesson. The only way you will ever get this kid off your back is to beat him half to death and show him who you are. When he goes down, you make sure he stays down . . . you know what I mean."

Al looked at Tony, who was listening intently now, soaking up every word of Al's like a sponge. "They will run you down in the street if they want to, mate," Al carried on. "So you gotta beat him good.

Half to death. . . or to death. Then you gotta dump the chain, then burn your clothes in case you got any blood on ya. Know what I'm sayin'?"

Tony looked at Al, unable to believe his ears. "What if I kill him?" Tony asked quietly.

"Then it's a job well done!" Al laughed out loud as he pulled into the estate next the bottom of Tony's stairwell. Tony wasn't sure if Al was joking or not.

"Listen to me, Tone. After tonight, the gang won't bother you. Rest assured you are safe from them. I promise. Me and Karl will sort it. But as for Benny . . . well . . . that's your fight. You get 'im, kid. I'll keep an eye out for you an' all!"

Tony gave a half-smile. "Thanks for the lift, Al. Cheers."

Just as Tony was half out of the car – "Tone, one more thing," Al said, holding onto the back of his trousers to pull him back in the car. "Get a proper haircut!" and he tossed him a tenner.

"Will do!" Tony smiled and shut the car door.

He watched Al drive off through the dimly lit estate. Grabbing his training bag from where he had stashed it under the bins, he headed up the stairs to home.

"Is that you, Son?" Ernie called from the front room.

"S'only me. I'm back," Tony called in and popped his head round the door. His dad was watching an old film.

"How was training? " he asked.

"Yeah good, Dad, but I'm knackered so I'm off to bed."

"Cor! You been smokin'?" Ernie asked, screwing up his nose. "You stink of fags!"

"Nah . . . not me, Dad," Tony thought fast. "Andy's dad dropped me off and he smokes." *Good one*, Tony thought.

"Oh, alright. Night then, Son."

Tony dashed up to his room and threw his bag onto the bed and pulled the long chain out. He practiced holding it and wrapping it around his knuckles. Bam! Have that! He role played a fight in his mind, slamming the chain over Benny's hand . . . or his head even. You fucking wait, he thought. He tucked the chain under his pillow, snuggled down into bed and drifted off to sleep thinking about the night's events.

Chapter 11

THE tall handsome blonde lad that strode boldly through the shopping parade that following Saturday morning held a striking resemblance to Tony Hayes. All bar the hair, which was being swept away from the barber's floor and into the bin.

Tony had listened to Al, and that morning he got up, combed his mullet for the last time and headed over to the barber's shop for his hair cut. Short back and sides and spiked on top.

School was finished for the summer and it was a lovely warm sunny morning. Ernie was walking out of the bookies and he almost fell over in shock as he saw his son heading towards him with his new hair.

"About bleedin' time too! Proper boy's haircut!"

Tony was desperate for some new clothes too, but Ernie just couldn't afford the kind of clothes Tony wanted to buy. By this time all the trends were changing; Sergio tracksuits and Diadora gear was all the rage. Ernie said to Tony that if you want to have money to spend on stuff like that then you've got to go and get a job, as he simply couldn't afford it. "Fine!" Tony had said. He was getting bored kicking about now anyhow. For some time now Tony had had an interest in motors and mechanics, so he went into every car mechanic's he could between Walthamstow and Leytonstone. He asked in every single garage if there were any jobs going – anything at all he could do to earn a bit of cash. He must have been into nearly fifty garages. *This is it*, Tony thought, as he walked into a small garage at the bottom of Leytonstone High Road. *This is the last one I can try*. A pair of legs jutting out from under the car was all Tony could see at first.

"HELLO?" Tony yelled out.

"Won't keep you a minute," a gruff smoker's voice came from under the car. A few seconds later a man wheeled himself out on a low trolley. "Yes, son?" he looked at Tony. "Make it quick as I'm snowed under here. If you're collecting for the scouts, I've already sent my donation in." He stared at Tony, "Bit big to be a scout ain't ya?"

"I'm not a scout," Tony sneered. "Snowed under ya say?"

"Yes," the man said impatiently, looking back at the cars still waiting to be done in his garage.

"Well as it happens . . . I'm after a job," Tony said cheerfully.

"A job?" the man retorted.

"Yeah," Tony replied.

"What do you know about cars?" the man asked.

"I can help with anything," Tony said. "I can do cleaning, oil changes, brakes, help out on MOTs. I've tinkered about with me ol' man's cars a bit . . . I know what I'm doing . . . I'm doing motor mechanics at school an' all," Tony said.

The man looked interested. "As it happens, I could do with an extra pair of hands here, son, to help out . . . and you're sure you know how to do that stuff?"

"Try me!" Tony said. "My name's Tony," he said, stepping forward and holding out his hand.

"Reg Baldwin, and you're hired," the man replied, taking an instant liking to Tony and his attitude. "Grab an overall from the office and click the kettle on as you pass. Mine's tea, two sugars."

Reg had just turned sixty, and it was a welcome change to have some young company around him. Reg paid Tony twenty-five pounds a day for Saturday work, and one hundred pounds if Tony worked all week during the school holidays. Tony and Reg built up quite a bond. Tony was a very conscientious hard worker and really had impressed Reg with his mechanical knowledge, and what Tony didn't know, he learnt very quickly. Reg only had to tell him something once and Tony was on it.

In no time at all Reg and Tony had cleared their way through the cars building up and had more coming in. Because the work was carried out quickly, Reg had twice as much work in as normal. Business was booming; the garage had never done so well. During this time Tony also learnt to drive. Reg needed him to move cars about, in and out of the garage and up on ramps. Tony had the most basic of driving lessons. Ernie was so pleased with him for getting this job. Things were really going well at the moment.

There was still, however, the small matter of Benny Ofarma. This still hadn't been sorted out. Tony had been keeping a good eye out for Benny but he seemed to have disappeared. He had been suspended for the last two weeks of school after the fight with Tony and seemed to be keeping a low profile on the estate too.

Three weeks went by, and nothing. Then one afternoon Tony had just got home after working at the garage, when he looked up out of the window to see Benny walking across the car park. He flew out of the front door and leant over the balcony. "Oi, you wanker! Stay there, I'm gonna fuckin' smash you up!"

Tony flew upstairs, grabbed the chain from under his pillow, stashed it down the back of his jeans and raced out of the flat. Benny was heading towards the common; he wasn't alone either – he had two mates around him. As Benny saw Tony charging at him across the car park, he turned and stood facing him. As he got nearer he saw Benny reach down to his shoe as if he was about to bring out a knife. "Got another fuckin' knife 'ave ya? I'll fucking kill ya!"

As Tony got within about ten feet away from Benny he reached round and grabbed the chain from his jeans. As he came almost face to face he raised his arm and smashed the chain clear down over Benny's head. Benny screeched and slumped down to the floor. Again and again Tony was bringing the chain down on top of Benny. It must have been like smashing him with an iron bar. Benny's mates were screaming at Tony to stop. One of them tried to drag him away but he was zoned out, smashing Benny over his back and his arms – anywhere – he kept on and on. Finally, Tony gave in and stopped. Benny wasn't moving; he was so badly bloodied and smashed up. At first, it didn't dawn on Tony just how badly he had beaten him.

One of Benny's mates ran off to get help. The other was screaming on the floor next to him. Tony stopped, looked at Benny passed out on the floor, stuffed the chain back down the seat of his jeans and turned round with nostrils flared. He started walking home, stopping only to sling the chain into the bins as he passed.

Twenty minutes or so later, an ambulance was heard rushing to the scene of a horrific gang attack on a young lad on the estate. Tony could see the reflection of blue flashing lights on his bedroom wall. He drew his bedroom curtains shut and walked downstairs to the kitchen. He threw the clothes he had worn into the washing machine along with some other laundry, and went into the front room and switched on the TV. He sat there for a while and waited for his dad to come home from work.

Chapter 12

"OI . . . there's been a terrible attack on some kid on the estate tonight, Tone," Ernie said as he walked through the front door, huffing and puffing from work about twenty minutes later. "So many ol' bill, I could hardly get me bleedin' car through. Someone's done a proper job an' all. Not sure who the kid is that's been attacked though . . . think he might be some black kid from the next block . . . couldn't really tell." Ernie went on, "Gettin' a bloody joke round 'ere for them gangs, I tell ya . . . one of these days someone's gonna get really hurt. It's not bleedin' safe to be on the streets. Here you go, Son. I bought sausage and chips in. You hungry?"

"Erm . . . yeah . . . I'm starved," Tony was hardly listening to a word his dad had said. All he could think of was Benny and his bloodied face "Cheers, Dad. I didn't hear anything going on out there," he lied as he helped his dad serve up their dinner and settle down for the night.

Early the following morning Tony was woken by the sound of the dustbin men banging and clanging the bins down as they emptied them. Suddenly he remembered about last night and throwing the chain away in the bin. *Thank God the bin men had come today.* His hand hurt, he looked at the back of it to see that the chain had left a deep ridged graze across his knuckles. He leapt out of bed. Ernie was just getting ready to leave for work.

"Morning, mate. What time you startin' work today?" Ernie asked, pushing a cup of tea across the worktop to him.

"Ain't gotta be in till nine today, Dad," Tony replied.

"Oh ok, I was gonna drop you off . . . it's on me way like."

"Nah, it's ok, Dad. I'll get myself in . . . no rush, it's only just seven now." Tony rubbed the sleep out of his eyes and Ernie spotted the grazing on the back of his hand.

"What you done there then?" Ernie asked, holding Tony's hand up so he could see it. Tony hesitated for a second.

"Oh . . . that? It's nothin', Dad . . . I trapped it at the garage, that's all."

"Looks sore," Ernie said.

"Nah, it's alright. Best get myself in the bath then, Dad. Catch ya later."

"Yeah alright, see you tonight."

Tony knew he needed to see Al and Karl and tell them what had happened. Chances are they already knew. He got himself ready for work, shoved some toast down his throat, glugged the last of his tea back and set off for work. He only had a week or so before school started again; he was in his final year.

He hated school and was wondering what would happen when he went back, as Benny would be there. He was really enjoying his job at the garage and would much rather spend his days working there than sitting at boring school. As he made his way down the stairwell and out into the estate he suddenly came face to face with PC Maguill. "Going somewhere, Tony?"

"Jesus Christ! Maguill! You give me a heart attack!" Tony jumped back holding his hand up to his chest. He obviously wasn't expecting to see him standing there. "I'm off to the garage where I work," he explained.

"Nice haircut, Tony. Suits you," the PC complimented him.

"Thank you. Time for a change," Tony said.

"Been up to anything lately have we?" the officer enquired.

"Nah, not much . . . just working during the holidays, earning a bit of dosh. I'm off there now actually . . . gonna get the bus."

"Oh ok . . . I'll walk with you." The policeman proceeded to join Tony in the short walk round the corner to the bus stop. "That was bad last night, wasn't it?" PC Maguill conversed.

"What was?" Tony asked.

"Didn't you hear about the commotion that occurred here last night?"

Tony tried to paint a confused look on his face. "Nope . . . I didn't finish work till late . . . then I stayed in with me ol' man."

PC Maguill admired his alibi and carried on. "They say it was a gang of them to do such damage." PC Maguill was looking at him now.

"Really?" Tony said matter-of-factly.

"You know he's in hospital, don't you? It's serious . . . he's in a bad, bad way. Might not make it they've told me." Maguill lied trying to provoke a response which failed.

Tony slowed his pace and carried on staring at the floor.

"Listen, Tony. I can't prove anything. There were no witnesses and Benny's mates aren't saying a word. Benny's gang don't wanna know either. I've got nothing to go on . . . and between you and me . . . off the record, the little fucker deserved it. As long as he recovers, we ain't got any problem . . . have we?"

Tony said nothing and carried on looking down at the floor. "Like I said, PC Maguill, I was at home with me ol' man. Sorry to hear such bad news."

"Ok, son. Have it your way. We'll say no more on that matter . . . I know you beat him up. But please, listen to me . . . I'm trying to help you here. You are going down a bad path . . . you're going a bit over the top here, mate. There's nothing wrong with standing up for yourself, but these gangs are serious. You are a nice kid and I like your dad but I'm worried about you. Just reign it in a bit, Tony . . . please, son?"

Tony's bus was just pulling in. Maguill finished up "Listen, I'll let you get off now. You look after yourself . . . *hopefully* I won't hear or see from you for a bit!"

PC Maguill patted Tony`s arm as Tony climbed up onto the bus, PC Maguill gave him a reassuring wink, turned and walked off.

Phew, Tony couldn't believe his luck!

Later that week, Tony met up with Rob. They were sitting in the Pie and Mash Shop in the precinct. Benny was still in hospital, but luckily he was going to be ok. He was severely beaten and, apart from broken bones and bruising, he was on the mend – although he would be in hospital for a few weeks.

"So tell me what happened then," Rob was asking. "Did you really smash him up? Everyone's talking about it."

"Dunno if I should tell you. You're a fuckin' grass," Tony said, eyeing Rob.

"Oh come on, Tone. I won't say a word," Rob pleaded,

"If you wanna keep hangin' about with me you gotta keep yer trap shut," Tony demanded.

"As if I'm gonna say anything," Rob said.

"You were too quick to open your gob about the knife last time."

Rob rolled his eyes, "I apologised about that. God sake, Tone, I was in shock . . . I was scared. I'm alright now ain't I?"

"Yeah, well think before you speak from now on." Tony snapped at him.

Rob seemed genuinely sorry and Tony knew he could trust him. He thought for a minute, he then had a quick look around him to see who was about – no one. He then went on to tell Rob all the details, even bragging a bit about how Al and Karl would have had a word with the gang and were protecting him because of his cousin Lee. Rob knew all about Lee. Tony pulled a packet of fags from his pocket and lit one. Rob looked at him. "Leave it out, you don't smoke!" said Rob.

"Fuckin' do now," he retorted. "Want one?"

"Yeah, go on then. Why not!"

Chapter 13

"WHAT'S that? Fuckin' Scotch Mist?" Ernie's voice could be heard echoing through the corridors and into Tony's classroom.

"Oi, Tone. Is that your dad?" one of Tony's mates asked. Tony looked up to see his dad standing outside the classroom with his form teacher, the headmaster, Mr Thompson, and his maths teacher.

"See! I told you he'd be here . . . wasting my fuckin' time. I'll have your job!" he said, thrusting his fingers into the headmaster's chest. "And I'll 'ave your job . . . and your job! This is bleedin' harassment! You're picking on him. That's as plain as the nose on your face!" Ernie said, pointing to the other two teachers. With that, he turned back to the classroom. "Come on, Tony. We're goin' home," Ernie yelled, demanding his son leave the classroom. He turned on his heels and marched out of the school with Tony running after him.

"Dad! What's happening? Please tell me!" Tony pleaded with Ernie.

Ernie turned to his son. "For the last few weeks, I've had the school on the phone non-stop at me. Telling me you're bunkin' off 'ere, bunkin' off there . . . never at maths . . . never in geography. Never at hardly any lessons, and if I didn't believe them they said to come down the school and see for myself. Well I knew damn well you weren't at school."

Tony held his head down in shame and looked at the floor.

"I wasn't gonna embarrass myself or you by turnin' up and you not bein' there," Ernie continued. "So every time they called me I'd always say I'm busy and can't make it. Happens it was earlier today when they called and said you'd been bunkin' off motor mechanics . . . now I knew that would be the one class that you wouldn't have bunked off. So I turned up at school . . . fingers crossed you'd be 'ere of course . . . cos if you weren't, then I was gonna kill ya myself!" Ernie joked. "And there you were! I was bloomin' 'appy to see you standing there I can tell you that much." Tony grinned at his Dad. "Come on, Son, let's get home. Bloody schools!" Ernie laughed.

The following day a letter was sent home to Ernie from the school. It explained how Tony had managed to clock up eight hours' worth of detentions due to misbehavior when he was actually there – which wasn't often. It was imperative that Tony attended this detention, which was to be held on Friday after school in the hall.

Ernie contacted the school, demanding to know how this time had been accumulated and that under no circumstances would his son be staying behind for hours. Ernie was in a powerful position to negotiate now after the bunking-off scenario, and any way, Tony had to get to work after school. Reg had him in there most evenings after school till 6 or 7 p.m. The school and Ernie agreed between them that two hours would be sufficient and that Tony would carry out this detention time as agreed.

The clock struck 3:30pm. This was the time all detentions were held. Every kid that had detention had to stand in a line in the school hall and look at the clock. Everyone had their detention time and Mr Thompson, the head, would walk up and down the line shouting out who had what time left. Always the same faces every week.

"PETERS, half an hour. WALLIS, two hours. DURRANT, half an hour. RODGERS, two hours. ATKINS, two hours. COLE, one hour. HAYES . . . four hours."

Four hours? Was he having a fuckin' laugh? "No way!" Tony shouted out. "I'm not doin' fuckin' four hours! My dad agreed to two hours. That was all."

Mr Thompson spun round and turned on Tony. He was a particularly short, stubby, balding man, with red cheeks from high blood pressure and glasses perched on the end of his nose. He used to comb his hair over to one side of his head to try and cover his baldness.

"Yes well, your dad isn't here now is he? And you are not leaving this school for four hours. Do you understand me?"

At this point, Thompson was standing in front of Tony spraying a wild torrent of spit at him whilst jamming a fat stubby finger into his chest.

"Yeah well you can fuck off with your two hours. I ain't doing them now, either!" Tony retorted, pushing Thompson's arm away from him. He turned to walk out.

"YOU GET BACK HERE NOW!" Thompson grabbed him and swung him back into line, forcing him to fall backwards to the floor. Tony leapt to his feet, throwing himself at Thompson, punching and kicking him. All the other kids were shouting; "Go on, Tony! Smash 'im up!" A circle of shouting and cheering boys had formed around them. Each and every one of them was laughing and egging Tony on, all of them wanting him to kick the living daylights out of Thompson – which indeed he was.

What felt like ages was in fact about thirty seconds. Two teachers had heard the racket and charged in, wading through the fight circle to Thompson's aid. The fight was broken up and all the boys sent home. As expected, a delighted Tony was expelled from that day on.

Walking out past the school bins, he ripped off his school tie, took his lighter from his blazer and set fire to the tie, tossing it into the bin. "Pricks!" he yelled over his shoulder. He made his way to the high street to catch a bus to KB Kabs. He couldn't wait to tell Al and Karl about this.

Al laughed at Tony's story. Tony was as proud as punch with his little victory. Tony *one*, school *nil*. "Fuck school!" he said. "I don't need it anyway – I'm almost sixteen now," he said as he sat in Karl's office.

Convincing his dad of that though would be another matter . . .

Chapter 14

1985

"FUCKIN' DRIVE! They're gaining on us!"

The sirens were wailing louder behind them as they threw the car up a side street. "They're still behind us!" Rob yelled.

"I know!" Tony shouted back. "I'm fuckin' tryin'! Hold on!"

Tony threw the car down another road that led off the main street, but they were still coming for them.

"COME ON!" Rob was shouting from the back seat. Panic was starting to set in.

"Shut the fuck up and let him drive will ya!" Andy yelled over his shoulder at Rob then turned back to Tony. "Come on, Tone! You can lose them, chuck a right here."

The traffic lights flicked from amber to red as Tony flew through them, but the blue flashing lights were still hot on their tail. Tony swung the car into a sharp right hand turn and onto the estate. The police car tried to cut them off but failed as Tony took another turning. The police car realised what had happened and temporarily lost them, Tony swung the car over to the side of a kerb and the police were back on their tail. The brakes to the stolen Cortina had screeched to a halt. Andy's door flew open and he made a run for it across the estate, ripping the bunch of keys from the ignition as he went. Tony had dragged Rob from the back seat, but they were just a few seconds too slow in their runner.

"FUCK IT!" Tony said, kicking the side of the police car as he and Rob were pushed into the back seat.

"Heads down," the officer said as he leaned on Tony's head, motioning for him to bend down and closed the door behind him.

Tony could do nothing but sit and stare out of the window as they were driven away into the darkness to the police station.

"These yours?" the police officer who was conducting the interview asked Tony, as he was emptying his personal belongings out onto the table, referring to a packet of Benson & Hedges cigarettes and a lighter.

"Yeah, they came outta my pocket didn't they?" Tony shrugged as he knew his dad would be upset that he was smoking. He had been asked to empty out the contents of his pockets into a plastic see through bag by the desk sergeant when he was booked in. Ernie, who was now sitting next to Tony, leant over and picked up the cigarettes and lighter and passed him one from the packet.

"Thanks, Dad," Tony said, surprised at him whilst lighting the offered cigarette.

After he had been arrested, the police had phoned Ernie to say that they had his son at the station. He needed to come down as he was a juvenile and a parent's presence was required in order for him to be interviewed. Tony had produced a box of matches, a ten-pound note, a bit of loose change and a packet of chewing gum.

Rob had been taken into another room and was sitting with his mum, who had also been called.

As they were juveniles they didn't get charged there and then. They were bailed and free to leave for now but had to go back in eight weeks to see if they were going to be cautioned or charged.

Tony and Ernie stepped outside the police station. Tony pulled his cigarettes out of the plastic bag that had been returned to him and went to light one. Ernie slapped the cigarette out of his mouth and onto the floor.

"Don't you ever let me see you smoking again!" He clipped Tony round the back of his head.

"But Dad!" Tony exclaimed.

"Don't you take the piss," Ernie turned on his son. "The only reason I did that was so the copper didn't have one up on you. Think you're a big hard man do ya? You're stupid! You think you know it all don't ya? I am so disappointed. I haven't even brought myself to tell ya mother. I am *so* disappointed. You're nothing but a wanker, Tony. A fucking wanker!"

All this had come about because of Rob. During the time after Tony got expelled from school, he spent his days working for the garage. Al and Karl were pleased that Tony was working full time so they gave Reg's garage the job of looking after all the cars for the taxi firm. Reg and Tony had to make sure all the vehicles were serviced. During that time Tony had become good friends with Andy Weaver, another of his pub drinking mates.

Andy was a few years older than Tony and tall and skinny as a rake. Like Tony, he could handle himself and was a good fighter. He and Tony clicked as mates instantly. Andy was heavily into stealing cars and joyriding them, nicking them to order and selling them for parts. By now, Tony was a very confident driver and often went out with him.

Andy had a massive bunch of Ford keys, which pretty much fitted any kind of Ford, so stealing them was easy and a huge adrenaline rush for Tony.

One night, Tony and Andy were on their way down to the Rose and Crown. There had been a huge commotion outside and Tony could see Rob sitting on the kerb in between two parked cars. A crowd had gathered around him and Tony pushed through; Rob had been beaten up. He told Tony and Andy that it had been Nutty Ed.

Nutty Ed was a big fat skinhead who bore a strong likeness to Buster Bloodvessel. He was twenty-two years old and a big bully. He wore skin tight bleached jeans, Doctor Martin boots with studs and had bad tattoos on each forearm. He stank of BO and grease and everyone hated him. Rob had been antagonising him and after he had left the pub, Nutty Ed and his gang had jumped him and set about kicking him with their DMs. There was no major damage, but he was sore from a good hiding.

Tony was infuriated; he wasn't going to let them get away with this. "I'm gonna fucking have them," he said to Andy.

"Come on then," Andy said. "Let's find 'em."

"I wanna come!" said Rob, crawling across the pavement on his knees.

Andy proceeded to shoo everyone back inside the pub. "There's nothing to see here. Everyone back inside." He didn't want PC Maguill coming past and getting wind of this; there was nothing to see anyway.

Tony had walked up and crossed the road. He was hovering by the side of a yellow Ford Cortina Mark III with a black roof. He stood for a bit longer and when he was sure no one was looking he jiggled the door lock. Within a few seconds he had disappeared inside the car. *VROOOOM!*

The car spurted to life and Tony pulled up alongside where Andy and Rob were waiting.

"I'm gonna have that stupid fat wanker. I'm gonna run him down and see how he fucking likes a good hiding!"

"Yeah come on!" Andy said, jumping in the front seat.

"I'm coming too!" Rob said. Tony and Andy looked at each other.

"Hadn't you better get off home, Rob? Look at the state of ya!"

"Nah . . . I wanna be there when you reverse back over the cunt!" he grinned.

The three lads sped off, driving the streets in search of Nutty Ed. Tony was so furious with what had happened. He was speeding around like a maniac, screeching around and reversing up and down. He didn't find Nutty Ed and his gang. He did, however, manage to attract the attention of two police officers who gave chase.

That same evening after Tony and Rob had been arrested and let out, Tony went up the Rose and Crown with Rob and Andy. That was their main meeting ground. It was run down and in desperate need of a makeover. The tatty dark red beer soaked carpet that had worn thin around the bar area, a multitude of cigarette burns and old, trodden in chewing gum didn't help. It boasted a large circular dark wooden bar that ran right round the centre of the pub, with large dark roses engraved on the front and bar stools lining its entire length. Ray the landlord had ran the pub for years and was part of the furniture. It was a real old traditional style public house; with heavy wooden doors that creaked when opened and large stained glass roses imprinted on the windows.

From the old dated juke box in the corner to the nicotine stained drinking glasses that hung above the bar, it had all seen better days. Big heavy glass ashtrays sat along the bar top with the tatty beer mats and bar towels that were scattered about – all desperately in need of renewal. Everything was old and shabby, including Ray, but he ran a good pub.

Tony had since forgotten how bitterly upset his dad had been. *He'll get over it*, he thought to himself earlier in the day.

A few hours later they were in the pub talking about Rob's kicking, and laughing loudly about how they had been looking for Nutty Ed and ended up getting nicked. Suddenly the doors opened and there, walking towards the bar was a less-than-impressed Karl and Al.

Chapter 15

"AVE a word with you outside, son?" Karl was shaking his head and looking quite disappointed.

Tony gulped and looked at his mates. Rob was looking terrified and Andy didn't have a clue what was going, on or who they were.

Tony followed Karl outside and Rob proceeded to follow too. Al put his arm out to stop Rob. "Who are you, his fucking child minder? He don't need a babysitter, kid!" Rob immediately shrunk back and Al turned and walked outside.

"*WHAT* the fuck was all that about?" Andy said.

"Dunno," Rob stuttered. "But I don't like it. I don't like it one little bit."

Tony stood outside in the alleyway and lit a cigarette that Karl offered him. "Now then, who's been a naughty boy?" Karl smiled at Tony. Immediately Tony felt the relief wash through him as he realised that Karl had been fooling him.

"Fucking hell, Karl! I thought you were really angry at me!" Tony grinned. Al and Karl laughed. They liked this kid; he was so easy to wind up!

"On a serious note, Tone. We have heard about you getting tugged by the ol' bill for nicking motors."

"Oh yeah," Tony replied, unsure if he was to be proud of this or not.

"If you're gonna do this shit, why don't you do it with us and get paid for it?" Karl continued.

It sounded like Karl was offering Tony a job. "Are you serious?" Tony asked. Al nodded and proceeded to tell Tony about what they could do.

* * *

It was a good six weeks later when Tony and Rob were back to the police station, and luckily for them it was good news. They were both just cautioned and let off with a warning as it was a first offense for both of them.

Tony had eagerly grabbed Karl's offer with both hands and started working immediately for him. He was offered £200 for every car he stole to order, ringed and then moved on. All Tony had to do was nick the ones they needed and drop them off. The job required someone that was ballsy – Tony was more than that. It needed someone who could drive fast and get away if needed – Tony was capable of that too. He only got caught because he helped his mate. He couldn't and wouldn't have run off and left Rob, especially after Rob had just been beaten up. Tony was as loyal as a dog when he needed to be. This was another good quality that Karl had noted in him. Tony was the man for the job alright. He could use a wingman too – Rob! Al had been impressed with Rob's attitude back in the pub.

In no time at all, Tony was delivering between 6-10 ars a week for Karl. He and Rob were earning fantastic money too. They had moved onto stealing really expensive cars now. The golden rule was 'you never nicked off your own patch', so Tony and Rob used to drive out into the country to the more affluent areas and steal cars from there.

Everyone knew what he did but no one said a word. Every now and again, friends and family would ask a `favour`. Ernie had a Ford Granada Gear and he needed new wheel caps, so one week Tony had a set stolen for him. He needed new interior and Tony had it sorted for him. Ernie knew what his boy did but he never batted an eyelid; especially as his car got practically rebuilt for free.

The years ticked by and now Tony was eighteen years old. His lifestyle was lavish compared to what it could have been. Because Tony had more than excelled himself with the cars, Karl decided to move him into a more trusted nature of their business. He started doing drops of drugs and parcels, as well as cars. Karl ran a few other businesses alongside the cab firm. One was a yuppie wine bar called 'Shooters', which was now bang on trend, and also a small lap dancing club called 'Bella's' in Stratford. Bella's was quite a high-end establishment and not one of those seedy backstreet dives. Quite often Tony would run money and do drops to the club and pick up any deliveries that needed going out.

Every evening after work when Tony had finished with Reg, he would make his way over to where Karl would be and run around with whatever needed doing. It was at this point that Reg became really ill. He had left Tony to close the garage up this particular afternoon, as his wife was taking him to the hospital. He'd had a really bad chest infection that wouldn't budge. He had a cough that had got worse and really gurgled.

The hospital had kept Reg in, diagnosing him with pneumonia. He had suddenly aged quite a lot. Reg had been in his early sixties when he first took Tony on and had it not have been for the extra business that Tony had brought in, he would most likely have closed the garage years ago. He was tired of work now and getting on for sixty-seven. His health was deteriorating daily and as Tony clicked off the lights, closed the big sliding doors and clicked the padlock shut, he had an awful gut feeling that this may be the last time that garage was going to be open for a long time.

Tony was dedicated to working for Karl seven days a week now. The garage had indeed closed its doors for the last time. Later that week, Reg passed away while still in hospital. Tony was devastated. Life was so cruel, so unfair. Reg was one of the nicest men he had ever had the pleasure of knowing. He had really loved that man like a father, and Reg had certainly thought the world of him. Enough that he left Tony the whole garage and business in his will. Tony was amazed. He didn't know what to do with himself. He felt as if the bottom had fallen out of his world.

He attended Reg's funeral, a lovely small service. Tony finally got to meet Reg's daughter and his grandchildren. They had all been living abroad in France and had made arrangements for Reg's wife to go and live there with them. It was indeed a very sad day.

That night Tony went to meet Al afterwards at the wine bar. Al helped him drown his sorrows and whilst doing so had a new business proposition for Tony. Tony decided to keep the garage as it was in the same name – Reg's. He kept the cab firm running their cars through and employed Jace, a mechanic mate of his, to run it. It was never going to be a millionaire-maker, but it was always a good base to have, and a cover for the money that Tony was earning. A way to hide things – a lot of things.

Chapter 16

1987

"WHAT do you mean we are going to Tenerife?" Rob was looking at Tony through suspicious thin eyes.

"I've got you a passport and we are off, my son!"

"What do you mean you've got my passport? How?"

"Well those silly passport pictures you had done last year . . . I borrowed them. Along with some of myself, Al has had some moody passports done and we are off to Tenerife for a bit of business!"

"When?" Rob said, getting excited now.

"Tomorrow night," Tony exclaimed. "Go pack a bag, we are off to the sunshine!"

The following evening as Al was dropping Tony and Rob to the airport, he gave them a rundown of what had to be done.

They both walked into the arrivals terminal and up to the check-in desk. As they waited in line for their turn to check in they were both very excited. Neither of them had ever been abroad on their own before. This was going to be a holiday to remember.

They checked in with their proper passports, got their boarding passes and headed off to the departures. They had a bag full of fraudulent traveller's cheques and bellies full of trouble, with Rob singing "we're all off to sunny Spain, la viva España!"

The plane touched down on the hot tarmac. They got through passport control, grabbed their suitcases and headed out into the manic stream of tourists all waiting for a taxi. As Tony and

Rob slipped on their sunglasses, they smiled and knew they were in for one heck of a week.

The taxi pulled up outside the 'Costa Del Paradise '. The hotel was set against a backdrop of beaches and bars.

"This is fucking paradise!" Rob whistled, taking in the views.

"Indeed, my friend . . . this is heaven," Tony said as two girls in bikinis walked past.

"Oi oi!" Rob yelled after them. They turned and giggled and carried on walking.

After the two had checked in and slung their luggage in their rooms, they headed out onto the main strip and surveyed the scene. Tony's job was simple; he had been given thousands of pounds of traveller's cheques which he had to change up into Pesetas every day, using the fake passports. He kept ten per cent of what he changed. He handed the cheques to a local Bureau de Change, along with his ID, then they passed him the equivalent in money. That was it. The counterfeit cheques were so good they never got busted. They had a week's worth of spending money and expenses. All they needed to do was blend in with the tourists.

Tony looked at his watch through drunken, blurry eyes. It was almost 5 a.m. He shoved the lap dancer a fist full of cash, pushed her off his lap and stood up and looked around. She gave him a wink and walked off, wiggling her assets as she went. The dimly lit lap dancing club was emptying out now. It was time to bail out, but where the hell was Rob?

Tony walked up to the bar and slugged the rest of his pint down. He wiped the back of his hand across his mouth and as he did so, saw Rob emerging from a private dance room. "Dirty dog," laughed Tony as the two friends paid up and left the club.

"I weely wuv you, Tone," Rob slurred.

"I love you too, man." Tony wrapped his arm around his friend's shoulders and the pair headed off to find their hotel before the Spanish sun came up.

The next four days passed like a whirlwind. They blended in very well with Tenerife tourism and changed all the money they needed to by hiring scooters and travelling about using different Bureau de Changes. They would spend their evenings at bars, restaurants and lap dancing clubs. Rob and Tony felt this was a lifestyle they could really become accustomed to. They were surrounded by gorgeous girls whom they seemed to have their pick of. Life was a ball and they were loving every minute of it.

This was the easiest money Tony had ever made. Tony and Rob arrived home after their five days in Tenerife. They had stashed all the cash they had changed up in the suitcase in socks and wrapped in clothes. They boarded the flight back and as they walked through arrivals looking tanned and relaxed, they could see Al standing there with a broad smile waiting to meet them.

It wasn't long before Karl had another trip abroad planned for Tony. This time Tony thought his dad deserved a holiday and decided to take Ernie with him. Karl arranged the flights and hotel and, as before, had sorted out the traveller's cheques all ready for Tony to cash in.

This time it was four days in Benidorm, mainland Spain, and Ernie was over the moon. It had ages since he'd had any kind of holiday. Ernie booked the time off work and he and Tony set off. He never suspected anything dodgy about it and never questioned Tony's frequent trips to the Bureau de Change. Ernie was quite happy to sit soaking up the sun, sipping his Pernod and lemonade. He'd have a little walk along the beach and their evenings were spent slightly differently this time around.

This particular evening was their second night. Ernie and Tony were sitting in a restaurant on the main strip and a woman walked by and kept looking over at their table. "Ooooh, someone's got their eye on you," Tony teased.

"Shut up and eat your tea and don't be stoopid," Ernie laughed, embarrassed.

"Another round?" Tony ordered another round of beer and Pernods. About ten minutes later the same woman had walked by again, casually staring over. Tony laughed and gave her a little wave.

"Oi! Don't do that!" Ernie said, really embarrassed now and slapping Tony's hand down.

"What's the matter with you?" Tony said. "Only having a laugh, Dad. Jesus . . . chill out."

"Bleedin' 'ell! She's coming over now," Ernie spluttered, brushing his hair over and flattening the back down. The woman was indeed walking over to their table, but she smiled and carried on walking past them to the bar. Ernie looked mortified; he was preparing himself to smile and say "hello" when she came up, but her walking straight past had thrown him completely.

"Ha ha ha! Totally blew you out, Dad!" Tony was laughing really loudly now.

"Probably a bleedin' brass anyhow," Ernie brushed off his embarrassment and the two carried on with their dinner. Later that evening, they went to a bar a bit further up the road. There was live music and Ernie loved sitting outside in the warm summer evening breeze watching the world go by and listening to the band.

Tony excused himself and went to the loo. Although Ernie was enjoying himself, this really wasn't Tony's idea of a fun night out. On the way back to the table he spotted a cigarette machine, so he popped up to the bar to get some change and ordered another beer while he was there. He selected his cigarettes from the machine and went back to the bar to get a light. He was actually quite taken with the little barmaid there. She was a petite blonde from London who was working there for the summer.

"Another beer?" she asked, clearly taking a shine to Tony.

"Oh go on then," Tony replied, pretending to be reluctant to stay when in fact he wanted to stand here chatting more than anything. As he glanced over outside to see if Ernie was ok, he could see that his dad was not sitting alone. The woman from earlier had joined him at the table and they seemed to be in a deep flow of conversation. Ernie was really laughing; a deep belly laugh that Tony had not seen or heard him do for years. So on that note, Tony stayed at the bar all night until the barmaid's shift had finished and he offered to walk her home. As he followed the barmaid outside, Ernie was still deep in conversation. The bar was closing around them and they hadn't noticed. Tony was sure Ernie would be fine and he would get back without a problem. With that, he flung an arm around the barmaid's shoulder and they walked off into the night, leaving Ernie chatting away long into the early hours with his mysterious lady friend.

Chapter 17

IT was nearer lunchtime than breakfast time when Tony wandered back into the hotel lobby the next day, to find his dad sitting by the pool bar sipping cocktails. Though, again, he wasn't alone.

Had his dad even noticed he didn't come home last night? By the looks of it he had been otherwise occupied himself. Tony walked up to them and gave a rather loud cough, pretending to clear his throat. "Ahem," he coughed. He startled Ernie who jumped up to his feet.

"Ah . . . hello, Son," he said all sheepishly. "You . . . alright?"

"Yes, Dad," Tony answered slowly. "You?"

"Yeah, yeah . . . fine," Ernie said nervously, flattening the back of his hair down.

"Erm . . . " Tony said as he looked at his dad, then looked at the woman, then back to his dad.

"Bah!" Ernie said, reading the signs. "Sorry, Son. Left me manners behind. This is Margaret.

Margaret, this is my boy Tony. I was telling you about him."

The woman stood up and very politely shook Tony's hand. "Alreet pet. Me name's Margaret, Margaret Reece," she said in a thick Geordie accent. "How nice ta meet youz." She smiled a very warm and kind smile – Tony instantly liked her. She had big soft brown eyes that crinkled at the corners when she smiled and dark brown hair. With her tall and slender frame she was a good looking woman for her age. She was probably in her mid-forties, same as Ernie, and definitely not a brass as Ernie had first stated. Tony pulled up a chair and they all sat chatting until quite late into the afternoon.

She really was easy company and Tony could see why his dad liked her. She told Tony all about her life; she was in Benidorm alone to get away and relax. She had split up from her husband over a year ago after a volatile and turbulent marriage. She lived in Newcastle and worked as a nurse. Generally, she wasn't that forward in approaching strange men but something had intrigued her about Ernie.

Tony invited her to join them for dinner that evening. "Howay, that'd be great. As long as youz don't mind, like," she said. "What a canny lad ye are." Tony took that as meaning 'what a nice lad'.

Soon he left them to it to go back to the room to freshen up. Margaret spent the last few days joining them for lunches and dinner, evening drinks, breakfast. In fact, she met up with them all the time, which freed Tony up to nip off to the Bureau de Change and finish his business. It also left him free to meet up with the barmaid again before they went home.

The next day their flight was due to leave just after lunch. Margaret had offered to take them to the airport as she wasn't due to go back to Newcastle for another few days. It was a sweet, romantic sight to see at the airport as Ernie and Margaret hugged goodbye. Ernie planted a soft kiss on her cheek. "Ya will call uz won't ya?" she asked.

Ernie held up her hand and kissed the back of it. "You betcha I will!" he said, winking.

Oh bloody hell! Tony thought. *Pass me the sick bucket!* There had been none of that when he said goodbye to the barmaid last night; he didn't even offer her his phone number. He knew he was never going to see her again, and anyway, he was never home to call.

As Ernie and Tony boarded the flight back to London, Ernie had a sad faraway look in his eyes and Tony could almost make out a tear sliding down his cheek.

After they arrived back safely in UK, Tony met up with Karl straight away and passed the money over to him. Karl was pleased again with Tony. Karl was now branching out into selling more hard drugs; ecstasy pills were huge now on the rave scene. However, Tony hated drugs, any sort of drugs. Cigarettes and booze were his only vice.

Al had a job one day for Tony to do. Tony had arrived at the wine bar to meet Al to go over it. "Ok, so I need you to drive. We're gonna do a meet. All you need to do, mate, is just drive and know that you can get us out if we need you to. Come on."

Tony leapt into the driver's seat. Because of all the driving that Tony was doing, Karl thought it was better that Tony did in fact get a proper driving license. He arranged it with a mate of his who was a test examiner. He took Tony out on a mini test and passed him so he was legally able to drive.

Tony drove Al out to Clacton that evening. "Pull over here a minute, mate," Al instructed.

"Oh ok, no problem, "Tony said, swinging the car into the dark lay-by. Al popped open the glove box and took out a heavy black velvet wrap. He handed it to Tony. "What's this?" Tony quizzed him.

"It ain't a bunch of fucking flowers. Open it and see . . . what does it look like?" Al said.

Tony looked down at the bundle sitting in his hands. Slowly he unwrapped the velvet cloth. With eyes as large as saucers he stared in disbelief at what Al had just presented him with. He shook off the velvet cloth and held the cold metal in his hands for a second. It was a Browning 9mm handgun. "HOLY . . . MOTHER . . . FUCKER," Tony said slowly, unable to believe his eyes. "But why?

That's a bit much ain't it?" he turned to face Al who was just looking at him.

"Well I think it's about time you had one now if you're gonna come on meets with me.

You're gonna need it, mate!"

Tony just couldn't believe it. He ran his fingers over the barrel of the gun feeling its cold, shiny smoothness. He felt a shiver run down his spine. For the first time in his life Tony felt speechless.

"Ok you soppy prick, now put it away," Al said.

"Where?" Tony looked around his car.

"Stick it back in the glove box or stash it down the side panel of your door there," Al said, pointing to the inside of Tony's door. "Listen carefully to me now," Al went on. "These meets can be heavy shit. If you ever feel the need to use it, then you use it."

"But I've never used a gun . . . I don't even know how to shoot it."

"You'll learn quick, mate, you'll learn quick. You'll have to! Ha ha ha!" Al burst out laughing and Tony sort of laughed too, a nervous laugh. But deep inside he was terrified as the pair of them pulled out and drove off into the darkness.

They had been on the road about twenty minutes heading to Clacton. "So what's happening then?" Tony asked. "How does all this work?"

"What do you mean *how does this work?*" Al said. "Quite simply, we are gonna rock up and walk into the snooker club. We've both got a cue box so it won't look too suspect."

"Ahh I get it," Tony said

Al continued, "We go up to the office and we do the deal. Ninety-nine point nine percent of the time it'll go sweet as a nut, these are regulars. You'll like 'em . . . but there are a couple of them who think they're gangsters."

"Shall I take the gun in with me?" Tony asked.

"Well it ain't gonna be much fucking use sitting in here if we are in there, is it?" Al retorted. "If, for some stupid reason, they do pull a gun on you and all you're left with is your cock in your hand, then you're in trouble! It's presence, Tony. That's all . . . you are up for this aren't ya?"

"Yeah, course," Tony tutted. "I'm not sure I'll need a gun though."

Half an hour later, they pulled up outside the snooker club. It was a dump; a shabby slumlike area. Suddenly Tony felt secure with his gun as he tucked it down the back of his jeans, glad he had it on him now.

Al walked round to the boot, popped it open and took out two snooker cue cases full of drugs. Passing one to Tony, they turned and walked up the stairs. As Al pulled open the doors he said "Oh . . . one last thing, Tone. Deano is real old school, so remember your manners. Always." He smiled and in they went, closing the door behind them.

Chapter 18

THE meet had gone well. Al was pleased, and Tony never had to use his gun that day.

As they arrived back in London, Karl was standing outside the wine bar on the pavement smoking a cigarette and talking into a new mobile phone. They had just brought out the new Motorola mobile phones with huge black rubber aerials on them. Karl had a mobile which he carried around in a case with him. They were quite large, but these new yuppie ones were smaller – only the size of a small house brick. Tony was in awe; he thought they were amazing.

Karl finished his call and flicked the end of the rubber aerial at Tony. He nipped back inside the wine bar for a second and reappeared holding a carrier bag. He handed Al the bag. Inside were two brand new mobile phones and a wad of cash for each of them. "Well done, boys. Good job. There's a brand new Motorola mobile phone for each of ya and a little drink." Tony beamed with pride – he loved his job!

After dropping Al off back to the cabbies, he stopped by the Rose & Crown to see who was about. Standing by the bar was Dean with his latest girlfriend, Tania. Dean and Tony had been friends for years. Dean Freeman stood at a hefty six feet four inches and, although tall, he was lean like a bean pole with dark hair, small round glasses and a cheeky grin. He was the quieter member of the group that all hung about together. He was often the mediator when arguments broke out and he was also the one that Tony could talk to about anything and often confided in.

He hadn't long been seeing Tania. She was a really nice girl, quite tall, herself. She had a gorgeous natural face that was never caked in makeup. She had big brown eyes and long, mousy wavy hair; Tony liked her a lot. She had a little something about her that was just so likeable. Deep down Tony was a little disappointed that she was Dean's girlfriend as he had a small crush on her himself.

It didn't, however, stop him from flirting with her.

He strode into the pub and stood his new mobile phone on the bar in between them. "Alright, everyone. Who wants a drink?" he said, pulling an enormous wad of cash out of his jean's pocket.

"Blimey, Tone! Look at you! How'd ya fucking earn that?" Tania exclaimed.

"Well . . . I get paid to make love to women," he said. "Been a bit of a slow week though.

What ya drinking?" he said, as everyone laughed.

"Nice blower," Dean said, picking up Tony's new Motorola.

"You can have my number, Tania, if ya like and you can call me," Tony winked at Tania and she giggled. "Where's Rob?" Tony asked.

Dean nodded his head towards to the toilets. "Been in and outta there a million times tonight," Dean said. "He's either got a bladder infection or one hell of a nose bag."

Tony cringed. He knew Rob was getting heavy on the drugs now.

"Talking of which," Tania said. "I'm due for a little toot!" she said as she slipped into the ladies' loos.

"I thought she was knocking all that on the head," Tony said to Dean.

"So did I. We've already had words about it. I can't stand it," Dean said.

"Me neither, mate," Tony agreed.

Rob passed Tania on the way out of the men's and slipped her a wrap of cocaine, smacking her arse as he did.

"ALRIGHT, TONY!" came Rob's voice bellowing embarrassingly across the bar.

Tony could see his mate was tanked up again. This was becoming a nightly occurrence and a slippery slope, Tony thought.

"What ya drinkin'?" Rob said.

"No thanks, and I think you've had enough." Tony advised.

"Enough of what? Who do you think you are? My fucking mother?" Rob said, half-joking.

"Enough of whatever you shoved up your fucking nose," Tony retorted.

Rob laughed. "Yeah well I've got these babies for later." Rob held up the small clear bag full

of pills.

"You're such a mug. I've told you about those things." Tony was disgusted with him.

"*You* can talk!" Rob yelled. "After what you do!"

Tony shot his friend a look that warned him not to go any further. "I don't *do* drugs for this exact reason. Look at the fucking state of you!" Tony said, looking Rob up and down.

"Do you know what you are, Tone? You're a hypocrite!" Rob said. "A fucking hypocrite!"

With that, Rob turned and walked out of the pub.

Dean looked at Tony. "Right, mate," Dean said, backing Tony up instantly.

Tania appeared from the loos just then. "Oh fuck! Where's Rob gone?" she questioned. Dean and Tony looked at her.

"WHY?" Dean asked loudly.

"Well I was spose to be going with him," Tania said all panicky, charging out of the pub after him.

Pills were massive by now. Everybody was out doing them in clubs and at raves. It was getting out of control. It had even hit the headlines on the late night news that week that a young girl had died from taking an overdose of ecstasy pills.

The very next night after the row with Rob, Tony drove round to see if he could find him. But Rob was nowhere to be seen. He tried every pub he could think of. He wasn't at home and, after hours of driving about and pulling his hair out, Tony had to admit defeat. "DAMN YOU, ROB!" Tony was furious.

Later that night, Tony and Dean were found propping up the bar in the Rose. They were having a heart to heart; Dean was going to dump Tania. She also hadn't come home the night before either. He couldn't go on like this with her and Tony had to agree with his friend. He couldn't tolerate it with the drugs either. Disappearing for days on end, no one knowing where they are, it wasn't on.

Suddenly, the door swung open and Rob and Tania fell into the pub all wide eyed and wasted. Without hesitation Dean leapt up from his bar stool, sending it flying backwards across the floor. He grabbed a spaced-out Rob by the throat, and pushed him up against the jukebox, lifting him off his feet by about two inches.

"Leave it out, Dean. Leave it out," Tania was saying, but she was so wasted too it was more like slurred gibberish that fell out of her mouth.

Tony stepped in and grabbed Dean around his chest to hold him back. "Dean, don't mate. It's not worth it . . . it's not gonna happen. He's wasted . . . look at him."

Dean released his grip off Rob and he slumped down onto the floor with a silly look and bulging eyes staring back at them. Tania looked like she had all dried sick smeared across her face and her mascara had run awfully, blackening her eyes. She was almost unrecognisable as the gorgeous girl that had left here the night before.

"What a fucking shame," Tony said.

"Nah, mate. What a fucking mess," Dean seethed. Tania had leant down and was attempting to scoop Rob up and get him outside. Tony couldn't do anything but offer to help his mate, however annoyed at him he was.

As they pulled Rob up to standing, they turned around to see that PC Maguill was standing watching the whole scene. "Oh dear. Someone's a bit worse for wear there. What's he had to drink?" Maguill eyed Rob and Tania suspiciously. "Been out somewhere nice, have we?" he asked Tania, noting the state of her hair and makeup.

Tony stepped in before Tania could say a word. "Just getting him off home now, PC Maguill. He's had a row with a bottle of sambuca and he lost," Tony tried to joke. "You off duty, sir?" Tony enquired at the policeman's attire.

He wasn't in his usual uniform. Instead he was wearing a suit with a white shirt. "No, Tony. I am most definitely still on duty. However, I got a promotion last week."

"Yeah, no kidding," Tony said.

"I'm CID now, son!" Maguill said proudly.

"Ah, nice one," Tony congratulated him.

"So does that mean we won't be seeing you round here then anymore?" Dean asked.

"I sincerely hope not, son . . . I hope not. Go careful." Maguill smiled at them and left the pub.

Tony threw Rob's arm around his shoulders and proceeded to carry him outside. "I'd better get him back home," Tony said to Dean.

Dean grabbed Tania by the arm and frog marched her outside too. "Look at the fucking state of ya. We need to talk . . . I'm done with ya," he said as he threw her into his van. "Catch ya later Tone," he called out of the window as he drove off.

Tony waved an arm in Dean's direction. "Oh, Rob," Tony said looking at his old mate slumped in the front seat of his car. "What an earth are we gonna do with you?"

The very next day, Dean called Tony. He had finally finished with Tania last night. He just couldn't have this anymore.

Chapter 19

DEAN'S mum had a caravan at a holiday camp in Caister. Dean had decided he needed some time away and was going to go there this weekend and asked Tony if he fancied going along.

"Sure, why not," Tony said.

Tony called Karl to make sure it was ok and that there were no drops to be done. The two of them headed off that Friday afternoon down to Caister.

Because Dean's mum had always been there when he was younger, Dean knew a lot of the groups there. They had all spent their summers there together, and they were all about the same age.

So when they arrived Tony was introduced to everyone. There was Rick, who was into everything and knew everything; Sad Sam, who was a fat lump and appeared to be the butt of everyone's jokes; Pauley, with really bad skin; Alan, who acted like he was gay and Jack and Tom, the ginger twins.

Then there were the girls. Tony wasn't really interested in meeting the blokes but listened intently as Dean introduced the girls. Firstly, there was Lorraine, she seemed ok. She had a big grin plastered across her heavily made-up face. She was quite short with a small build and short, curly hair, quite plain and looked like she was desperate for attention. Chantel was a really good looking mixed race girl. She was tall with a curvy figure and kept checking her nail polish and her lipstick in her compact mirror. Tina was overweight with ginger hair. She had braces and could easily have been related to the twins. He'd swerve that one, Tony thought. Then boring Claire; a bit quiet, quite pretty though, with a slightly larger rear end than Tony liked. A good looking girl though, with long blonde hair that hung down her back. Straight away Tony fancied himself as a stud with this lot – easy pickings, he thought.

Dean instantly expressed his interest in Claire –probably because she had the biggest boobs out of them all. During that first night out, Tony soon realised that all of these girls were easy as they had all practically offered themselves on a plate to him. This was going to be exactly the kind of weekend he needed, he thought to himself.

They got settled in and headed out to the bars. He still had Rob on the forefront of his mind and wondered if he should have brought him with them. He really did feel bad for Rob and he knew he had to help his mate, but he just didn't know how.

His thoughts were soon brought crashing back in the room, when an already drunken Lorraine grabbed his arm and started pulling him outside and round the corner from the bar into the alleyway. "Let's get to know each other better," she purred through her heavy lipstick, unzipping his jeans and dropping onto her knees to take him in her mouth. It would have been rude to refuse, Tony thought.

A short time later, Tony zipped up his jeans and walked back in to the bar. No one had noticed he had been gone. Especially Dean, who was in the corner snogging Claire with his hand rammed up her top.

The group were trying to round everyone up to go to the nightclub up the road. Lorraine was now hanging off Tony's arm like a cheap handbag. She was going to be a hard one to shake off, he thought. He could feel her over him like a rash. He wondered how many other blokes she had made to feel that welcome and he shuddered. She was staring all dopey eyed at him.

Tony went over and tapped Dean on the shoulder. "Mate, we're off. Come on." Dean and Claire looked up. Claire stood up from Dean's lap and straightened her top. Dean swigged his beer down and the merry crowd headed off up the road to the nightclub. It was called 'Rippers' – how apt, thought Tony as he smirked. The bouncers gave him a quick body search and when they were satisfied he had no concealed weapons he made his way through to the bar.

The music was beating out some good tunes. Not too bad for a real dive, Tony thought, as he waited at the bar to order the drinks. Everyone from his crowd was in there now. Lorraine was still hanging around him like a bad smell. He took his beer and stood back to survey the scene. It was very busy.

There were quite a few large groups of men and a few hen groups.

All tacky looking and blind drunk. As he stood watching the dance floor he noticed a blonde girl; she was gorgeous. She had long blonde hair and was dancing about, swinging it around her. She was hot, smoking hot, thought Tony. And she knew it.

The magnetic draw to her was insane; Tony couldn't peel his eyes away from her. Even though he had a clingy Lorraine on his arm. *Gotta ditch this bitch*, he thought. He didn't want the blonde to see him with her. He made an excuse to go to the toilets and Lorraine tried to go with him.

Jesus! She's a maniac, Tony thought, and peeled her vice-like grip off his arm.

"I'll be back in a minute," he mouthed over the loud music.

"WHAT?" she shouted, shoving her ear at him.

"I'LL BE BACK IN A MINUTE," he shouted in her ear. "*FUCK OFF!*" was what he wanted to shout at her.

He made his way through the crowd in the direction of the toilets so he could get a better view of Blondie. He could see her now on the dance floor. She had men in every direction in awe of her, all checking her out and she was lapping it up. Tony knew he had to get near her; he kind of shimmied his way onto the dance floor and tried to play it cool. He made out he was looking for someone. Closer, he edged in. The dance floor was heaving now, all sweaty bodies dancing about. If he got close enough maybe she would just notice him. He danced a little closer, and then a little closer. He was kind of head bopping and yes, there it was! She saw him. *Play it cool, Tone*, he thought. *Be cool.* He had caught her eye. He held her stare for just long enough and then turned around and shimmied off the dance floor. He turned every now and then to see if she was still watching him. She was.

It was 2 a.m., kicking out time. Tony was waiting by the doors of the club smoking a cigarette. As he looked over, Blondie was queuing to get her coat out of the cloakrooms. Straight away she noticed him and sauntered over.

"Alrite," she said.

"Yeah, you?" Tony said cockily and gave her a little wink.

He took her by the arm and walked over quickly to the front lobby so he could get a pen. She was gorgeous; she had great big blue eyes that peered out under her heavy fluttering eyelashes. She had makeup on, but not too much. She was exactly his type; slim, with a perfect, small bottom. He couldn't take his eyes off of her. She smiled at him, displaying perfect white teeth. He scrawled his mobile number on the back of a flyer. "Call me," he said, stuffing the flyer in her hand.

"I might do," she said, and winked at him. *So cocky!* he thought. He really liked her. Although he hadn't really spoken to her all night, the eye contact was enough to seal the deal he thought. As she wiggled out of the nightclub, he knew she'd ring. So did she, as she was tucking the flyer into her bag.

Tony pulled on the last of his cigarette and turned round to see a desperate looking Lorraine, all red faced and huffy standing staring at him. "I've been looking for you for ages," she said. "You were only going to the loo. That was bloody hours ago," she wailed.

"Oh sorry, babe. Had a dodgy gut, came outside to get some fresh air," he lied. Immediately she latched onto his arm again.

"Oh, poor baby," she said, all concerned for him.

Dean and was still snogging Claire. *Had he even come up for breath?* thought Tony. They headed off back to the caravan park. Tony's head was spinning with thoughts of Blondie. He knew she would call. She had to call; she had been zapped by his charm. He pulled the collar of his jacket closer around his neck. Reality smacked him in the face when he looked back to the besotted girl clinging to his arm, desperately seeking his approval. Tonight he would just have to make do with clingy Lorraine.

Chapter 20

"CALL me! Make sure you call me."

"Yeah will do," Tony said, waving goodbye to Lorraine as she was holding an imaginary phone to her ear.

"Call me!" she was shouting, as Tony was trying to climb inside the car to go. Dean was still

snogging. *Still!*

"When will you call me?" Lorraine was still wailing.

"Later!" Tony said, as he was prizing Claire from Dean and trying to shove him into the car. *Jesus, he'd gotten over Tania pretty quickly*, he thought to himself.

"Come on, Dean. Let's go." He and Claire were like lovers parting for the last time. "Fucking hell, Dean! Come on!"

"When will you call?" Lorraine had her face squashed up against the window of the car.

"Later, baby."

"Why can't I have your number?" she whined.

"Coz I can't fucking remember it!" Tony said, revving the engine now in frustration as Dean finally unlocked lips with Claire and got in. Before he could close the door behind him, Tony was speeding off leaving the girls in a cloud of fumes.

"Bloody hell, mate!" Dean said. "In a rush, are we?"

Two days had passed and all Tony could think about was Blondie. And it was a whole day after that when finally, his mobile rang that afternoon while he was sitting in the pub with Dean and Rob.

"Hello?" he said.

"Hey," the voice on the other end replied. "It's Suzie." It was a confident, cocky voice. Tony instantly knew it was her and raised his eyebrows and grinned to Dean.

"Suzie who?" he said.

"You know who I am," she replied.

"Remind me," he teased.

"Oh fuck it. I'm going to hang up," she said impatiently.

"I'm kidding. Of course I know who it is," Tony laughed as he went outside to talk in private, away from big ears.

After Tony went outside, Dean decided it was time to give Rob a piece of his mind and tell him how worried his mate Tony was about him.

After ten minutes or so Tony came back into the pub grinning like a Cheshire cat. "Date night sorted," he said. "I'm taking her out on Saturday night!"

That evening, as Tony got home, he walked in coughing and spluttering through the thick cloud of Brut cologne that his dad had seemingly bathed in.

"Fucking hell, Dad!" Tony said, choking back on fumes. "Jesus, when the advert says 'splash it all over', it means your face! Don't fucking bathe in it!" Tony laughed.

"Do you think I've got enough on?" Ernie was unsure and a little nervous, so he gave a final splash of the potent aftershave. "One for luck!" he grinned, and stood and twirled round in the centre of the room. "How do I look, Son?" he asked Tony. Margaret was coming down and they had a date.

"You look blinding, Dad!" Tony complimented him. "Where you off to?" Tony asked.

"Gonna nip to the Italian I think . . . nice bit of steak. I've booked a table," Ernie said proudly.

"Is she staying here?" Tony asked, noting the state of the place. It hadn't been cleaned in weeks.

"Of course . . . is that ok?" Ernie looked puzzled.

"Yeah, sure. Shall I make myself scarce?" Tony asked.

"Nah, you're alright. She'll wanna see you . . . just don't come back too early!" he joked. He seemed to be hunting for something. "I've gotta go . . . I've gotta get her from the train station." Ernie was hunting for his keys.

"Here," Tony said, pushing his car keys over to him.

"Oh . . . she got the train down?" Tony asked

"Yes, Son . . . can't hang about. I gotta rush. Catch ya later."

"Ok, Dad. Have a good one," Tony shouted, as Ernie charged out of the door.

Ernie and Margaret had kept in touch constantly since they got back from Benidorm. Tony thought his dad seemed quite smitten with her. It was good to see him happy and like his old self again.

Suzie Thomas lived over in South London, about an hour or so away from Tony. It started off working out quite well. Tony went out with his mates on a Friday and then spent Saturday nights out with Suzie. They had a pact; on the nights that they saw each other, they wouldn't go to places where they hung out on Fridays. Tony knew Suzie was a flirt and she would flirt with all the blokes at the bars she drank at, and vice versa. Tony was a terrible flirt and he couldn't resist chatting up women every week he was out. He was a very good looking man – and he knew it. More often than not he would end his Friday evenings leaving bars and clubs with a different girl each week. But Tony was no idiot; he knew Suzie was doing exactly the same as him. This would lead to them spending their Saturday nights arguing over jealous rages from the night before. Sometimes Suzie would spy on Tony with her friends. He knew this and secretly he loved it. They definitely had a real love-hate relationship.

It was the week before Christmas. Karl had loads of work for Tony around this time of year. Business was busy for them as people were out partying a lot. Rob was going dangerously off the rails; he was spending all of his time wasted on drugs. If he wasn't popping pills, then he would be snorting cocaine up his nose – or smoking it. Every bit of money he made he squandered on drugs.

His mum was beside herself.

That Friday, Tony was supposed to have been seeing Rob to have a chat to see if he could try and get through his skull the dangers of what he was doing to himself. As Rob and Tony were sitting at the bar in the Rose, Tony's mobile rang – it was Karl.

"Wait here a minute. I need to take this," Tony said to Rob, as he stood up to leave the pub. Rob looked about the pub and to his delight he saw Tania over by the juke box with some of her friends. He sauntered over and before long was laughing and joking with them. They got to talking about the night that they went out. Tania reached down into her bag and discreetly pulled out a small clear plastic bag containing ecstasy pills. Rob's eyes widened. She motioned for him to go to the men's toilets and help himself. Rob didn't need asking twice. He took the bag and headed off.

He pushed open the door and had a quick look about him. No one was in there. He walked into an empty cubicle and closed the door behind him. He sat down on the loo, opened the small plastic bag and placed one small round white pill in the palm of his hand. *Oh shit, Tony would go mad*, he thought, as he rolled the pill back and forth between his index finger and thumb. It was just calling his name out. He could hear it, pleading with him to swallow it. He couldn't resist it. He closed his eyes, tipped his head back and popped the pill into his mouth, rolling his eyes back in his head as he swallowed it. He slid a second one in his wallet for later. What an amazing feeling he would have. The best hit in the world. All he had to do now was wait . . .

Tony was finishing his phone conversation with Karl. He had an urgent job that needed doing tonight. "No problem," Tony had said. He'd take Rob with him – they could chat in the car.

He finished his call, clicked his mobile off and walked back inside the pub. Rob had gone. He was no longer sitting at the bar where Tony had left him. Tony cast an eye around the pub and saw Tania. Dread suddenly gripped Tony by the guts as he stormed over to Tania. "Where is he, babe?" he demanded to know. At first, Tania played it cool, denying that she had seen Rob. "I know you're lying, Tania." She just couldn't lie to him. Tania cast a sheepish look towards the toilets and as if on cue, Rob came walking out. He seemed ok.

"We've got a job to do," Tony glared at Rob suspiciously. "Come on."

With that, Tony bid farewell to Tania, turned and marched out of the pub. Just before Rob left, he quickly scribbled Tony's mobile number down on the back of a scrap of paper. "Get me on his mobile and we'll hook up later if you want to," Rob said, handing her Tony's mobile number. Tania took the number and, smiling, she stashed it in her purse as Rob sauntered out of the pub.

Tony was impatiently revving the car up outside. "Alright, calm down!" Rob said. "Don't get your knickers in a twist. I was only having a piss," he lied. They drove off.

Karl needed Tony to do an important meet. A kilo load of pills needed to be dropped at a rave near Hampstead Heath. Karl was at the cabbies this evening and they pulled up outside. Tony rushed in to get the drop.

Rob sat in the car. He was flicking through the radio stations and came across a pirate station. "Fucking tune!" he said, turning up the stereo full blast, almost blowing Tony's speakers. He laid the car seat back and felt the rhythm of the music going through him. Pretty soon he would start coming up; he smiled and closed his eyes. The beat was pulsing through his feet and up his legs. He lay there feeling exhilarated as the sensations started weaving through his body. His head was light; he could feel the beat in his chest, up his legs, through his blood. "Oh man, this is sooooo good."

Tony slammed back into the car. "Jesus, Rob! You're fucking gonna blow my speakers!" he said, lowering the volume.

But it didn't jolt Rob from the rush he was having. He was getting lost in ecstasy, lost in the music. "YEAH!" he was grinning.

It didn't seem like there was going to be any chatting for Tony in this car this evening. Rob looked hell bent on raving in the front seat. Tony hadn't realised Rob was coming up and as he drove off into the night with the music booming he had no idea what a night he was in for . . .

Chapter 21

ABOUT thirty minutes into the journey, they were almost there. Tony was slowing down, looking for the industrial estate where he had to drop. It was around here somewhere. He was sure he had been with Al before. Al was already out on another drop, hence the reason for Tony driving. He turned up a road that was quiet and derelict with no lighting.

Rob had calmed down somewhat but was behaving oddly. He seemed to be having palpitations and gulping deep lugs of air. He had the window wound down and was practically hanging out, breathing deeply and shivering. Tony slammed the brakes on, sending Rob surging forward in his seat. "What the fuck have you taken?" Tony grabbed Rob's face by the chin, forcing him to look at him. "What the fuck have you done?" Tony was shouting at Rob. Rob's eyes were rolling around his head and he was damp from sweat. "ROB!" Tony screamed in his face. He raised his hand and brought his palm down firmly across Rob's cheek. Rob groaned. "Rob, talk to me. Tell me what the fuck you've taken," Tony screamed at him.

It was obvious that what Rob had taken wasn't agreeing with him and he was reacting. Tony needed to make him vomit, and fast. He had pulled the car over already by the kerb. He jumped out and raced round to open Rob's side. He didn't need to stick his fingers down his friend's throat. Rob threw up instantly on the kerb and slumped back into his seat, groaning.

"Let's get this done and get you back," Tony said, as he laid Rob back down in the front seat and closed the door.

He ran around to the driver's door to get in and, as he did, he noticed the road where he was supposed to be dropping. He leapt back into the car and drove up the side road which led up to another warehouse. It was pitch dark here, apart from one sensored flood light which sprang into life. Tony noticed a car parked up in the corner. He felt uneasy about this drop; he didn't know why, but something felt iffy. He reached down and felt for the gun that was hidden in the door panel. There it was. He closed his fingers slowly around it and gently pulled it out. He stuffed it down the front of his jeans.

He looked over at Rob; his eyes were closed and he seemed to be resting. Tony felt his head; he was very clammy, but his breathing had regulated and he seemed calmer. But still something wasn't right with him. He needed to find Tania later and see exactly what it was that Rob had taken off her tonight.

He pulled the car up just out of the floodlight's path. The parked car opposite him flashed its headlights twice, quickly. It was the signal. Tony climbed out of the car and went round to the boot and pulled out a brown parcel that Karl had given him. He tucked it into the inside of his jacket and zipped it up. He saw a tall slim man get out of the car. Tony reached down and felt the cold gun tucked down his jeans again. *Come on, Tone,* he said to himself. *It's ok, get a grip. Just do the drop and get the case and off we go.* With a final check on Rob, he started walking towards the man. He could see he was a tall black man with a shaved head. There was one other guy with him. As they got closer, Tony held his hand out and Lenny shook it warmly and smiled. Tony faintly recognised him, but wasn't too sure where from.

"Fucking cold night tonight, man, ain't it," Lenny commented about the night air.

Tony eyed him and smiled. "Yeah, mate. Got your order from Karl here," Tony said, beginning slowly to unzip his jacket. Lenny motioned to his guy to pass the money over. The bloke reached inside his coat. Suddenly, shouting and screaming started coming from Tony's car. A hallucinogenic Rob had flung the car door open and the next thing he was charging towards them like a lunatic waving his arms wildly in the air.

"No, Rob! Stop!" was all that Tony could remember shouting. Everything seemed to go in slow motion.

In a split second, Tony had reacted to the click of a gun loading. It took less than two seconds for him draw his gun from the front of his jeans and thrust it into the forehead of Lenny opposite him. Rob had sprung to life hallucinating from his come down and in a blind rage of panic he had run screaming from the car.

Lenny's man had drawn a gun from his back as quick as a flash and was standing there pointing it at Rob who was lying sprawled out on the floor, shivering and vomiting again. He was screaming at Rob not to move and to stay down. Instinctively, Tony had drawn his gun and now had it shoved against Lenny's head, yelling at him to get his man to drop his gun or he was going stick one in his face.

"HE'S ON FUCKING DRUGS AND TRIPPING OUT," Tony was yelling at them, referring to Rob lying on the floor. "FUCK SAKE. TELL HIM TO DROP HIS FUCKING GUN," Tony yelled at Lenny.

"DON'T FUCKING SHOOT!" Lenny was screaming. Everyone stood frozen to the spot, too scared to move. "DROP THE FUCKING GUN!" Lenny screamed at his man.

Tony was yelling at Lenny's man now "FUCKING LOOK AT HIM! WHY DID YOU PULL A FUCKING GUN OUT, YOU STUPID CUNT. DROP YOUR FUCKING GUN OR I SWEAR TO GOD, I'LL FUCKING STICK ONE IN HIS NUT."

Slowly, Lenny's man lowered his gun, not taking his eyes from Tony and Lenny. Tony didn't move. Nobody dared move a muscle. Never in a million years had Tony ever pictured himself standing holding a gun to someone's head. Rob was lying still now, panting on the floor.

"Right . . . let's all calm the fuck down," Tony said slowly, now in a quieter voice, his eyes still fixed on Lenny and the gun man. Everyone was breathing again. "Let's do what we came here to do and let's fuck off," Tony said smoothly.

Lenny's breathing regulated and so did Tony's. Tony lowered his gun from Lenny's head and Lenny breathed a loud sigh of relief. Lenny's man tucked his gun away and pulled a parcel of money out of his coat. It all calmed down as quickly as it had gone off.

"What's he taken?" Lenny asked, as he was still watching Rob on the floor.

"I don't know, but it's not this gear," Tony said, passing his parcel over to Lenny's man. "I will fuckin' kill him meself when I find out. He's a fuckin' liability!" Tony scoffed.

"Sorry about this, man. All got way outta hand," Lenny apologised.

"You can say that again, mate. It's his fault," Tony said, nodding at Rob. "I'll deal with him later."

The two men finally parted on a handshake and, as Tony was scraping Rob up from the floor, he couldn't help thinking how this could have been a whole lot worse. He had to get back and face Karl yet. He wasn't going to be impressed. As he pulled Rob onto the front seat, Rob opened his eyes and looked at Tony. "I'm sorry, man. I'm so fucking sorry," was all he kept saying. He was trying to hold Tony to his chest and hug him. He was clammy again and gulping in air.

"Let's get you sorted out," Tony said, unwrapping Rob's arms from him and closing the door. He climbed into the driver's seat and stashed the parcel under his seat. He pulled the gun out of his jeans and sat staring at it for a second. *Thank God Al had given it to him.* But the reality of actually pulling it out and holding it to someone's head had really shaken him up. Right there at that moment he prayed he would never have to pull this gun out again.

Rob slept the entire way home. Tony did poke him a few times to see if he was just sleeping and he would groan and roll away. Tony knew that he couldn't have this anymore. Either Rob sorted it out and left the drugs well alone or they would have to sadly end their friendship. Rob would never really know just how close Tony came this evening to killing a man because of it all.

Rob wouldn't remember this night. But Tony would . . . forever.

Right now he needed to re-live it all over again. Karl and Al were standing outside the cab station smoking at the door as he pulled up. *Oh fuck,* Tony thought. *Here goes . . .*

As predicted, Karl wasn't happy. Tony felt that this was the first time he had let Karl down. This could all have gone so wrong tonight and ended so badly. All because of Rob. Karl was annoyed and said that under no circumstances was Rob allowed to go on business again. He also advised of a good rehab centre down south that Rob should maybe go to.

Tony felt sad and angry at the same time as he left the cabbies to take Rob home. He was still fast asleep in the front seat. Tony decided to go straight home to his own flat and he took Rob with him.

He didn't want Rob's mum to see him like this. He knew that he had to have a real straight talk with him in the morning, but right now the only thing he needed was a damn good night's sleep.

Chapter 22

TONY woke up the following morning to the welcome sound of someone making tea. He got out of bed and, throwing on his jeans, he made his way to the kitchen. Margaret was making tea in the kitchen. "Morning, pet. Made yuz a cuppa," She welcomed Tony with her strong geordie accent and a huge beaming smile.

"Oh lovely, ta," Tony said, taking the mug from her and noting that she had cleaned the kitchen up. He could hear his dad cheerfully chatting away with Rob in the front room. "Morning," he said, walking into the room.

"Ah, morning, Tone. You alright?" Ernie was extremely bright and breezy this morning.

"Alright," Rob said, looking sheepish and embarrassed.

"I was just saying, Tone, how nice it is to see Rob. Ain't seen him for ages," Ernie piped on, unaware of any tension between them.

"You ok?" Tony looked at Rob. It was more of a rhetorical question.

"Tone, about last night . . ."

Tony put this hand up and stopped him mid-flow. "Later mate. Later."

"What you got planned today, lads? Anything nice?" Ernie asked, not really listening to their conversation. "I was thinking of taking Margaret off to do a bit of Christmas shopping today," Ernie rambled on a bit more. Margaret had come in with toast for everyone. Rob tucked into his breakfast appreciatively.

Tony sat there for a while listening to his dad and Margaret excitedly making plans. The whole time he was thinking about last night. He kept going over and over in his mind the picture of Lenny's face with the barrel of a gun pushed against it and Rob having a seizure on the floor and almost getting shot. After a while he excused himself to go and have a shower and get ready to drop Rob home.

The two boys thanked Margaret for their breakfast and headed out of the door. "Catch ya later," Ernie said as they left.

A stony silence was building between them but, as they climbed into Tony's car, Rob couldn't hold his tongue any longer. "Tony, I don't know what to say. I'm fucking sorry!"

Tony exploded. "You fucking prick, Rob! Have you got any idea what happened last night? I almost killed a fucking bloke because of you. I had to pull a fucking gun out in someone's face and you nearly got yourself blown away. What the *fuck* did you take? And I had to deal with Karl. He's fucking fuming. He's done with you. And do you know what? So the fuck am I. *You* decide now . . . it's drugs or me, coz I am never going through this again with you. DO YOU FUCKING UNDERSTAND?"

Tony smashed his fist against the steering wheel of the car. He was spitting with rage now and Rob was sobbing. Apart from the fact that Rob felt like he had the hangover from hell, his best mate in the world was walking away from him. He knew he had messed up big time – and for the last time. He knew he had a problem, but didn't know what to do. He knew he needed help, but just couldn't quite ask for it.

"If it's help you need, then just say. Karl gave me a number of a clinic, they can help you. Or is it that you don't want help? You wanna be a fucking loser?" Tony was attacking him verbally now. He hated drugs for this very reason; they ruined and destroyed people, good people. He was scared he was losing Rob and didn't want to watch his mate go down this road.

Rob sat with his head in his hands. After a long silence, Tony said "What the fuck have you got to say for yourself?" He delved into his pocket and pulled his cigarettes out and lit one.

"Give me the number. Please give it to me," Rob said quietly and seriously.

Tony sat looking out of the steamed-up car windows, he thought for a moment. "*What?*" he snapped as he turned to look at Rob.

"I said please give me the number Karl gave you. I'm serious, Tone. I need fucking help. I'm a fucking wreck . . . just look at me. LOOK AT ME!" he screamed.

Tony looked at Rob's appearance. He was a physical wreck; his usual filled-out features and chubby cheeks had been replaced by a haunted, gaunt appearance. Under his eyes were dark and sunken bags. He held his hands up and they were shaking and quivering. His frame, which once was a healthy stocky size, had shrunk down a good few waist sizes and he did look in need of a good steak. Tony couldn't bear this; he was welling up now. He thought carefully before he answered Rob. "On one condition," he said.

Rob looked up at him "Anything," he said. His dark, bloodshot eyes pleading with Tony while he held his breath.

"You let me drive you there," Tony said. "So I know you're there."

Rob nodded his head in relief and started sobbing again. Tony pulled his wallet out of his pocket and fished out the number of the rehab centre Karl had given him. He leant over and, wrapping his arm around Rob's neck, he hugged him and kissed him on the top of his head. He was relieved he had made the right choice. "We'll call them first thing in morning," Tony promised him.

Tony dropped Rob off back home and decided to call Karl to update him on the Rob situation. Karl was pleased Rob had decided to go to the clinic. He'd had a mate who went there to clean up and he said they were very good. Karl had also spoken to Lenny who said it was all cool about last night, and that Tony had handled it very well in fact. Tony was chuffed and feeling a damn sight better this evening than when he left there last night.

* * *

It was Saturday night and he had a date with Suzie. They had agreed to go to a club in Dartford. Tony hated going to Dartford as he hadn't heard great things about it, but Suzie had pulled a face and reluctantly Tony agreed to go. Earlier that day, Tony had agreed to swap vehicles with Aaron, a mate of his from the pub. Tony's car needed valeting after Rob had thrown up in it and it needed a few servicing bits done to it. Aaron only had a van so Tony agreed to take that. He was only going out with Suzie, so didn't see any harm in that.

As he pulled up outside her house, Suzie walked out and climbed in the van. She looked gorgeous. "You look a million dollars, babe." Tony lent over to kiss her.

"And so you're picking me up in a fucking dirty van?" she sneered, disgusted.

"Sorry, babe. My car's in for servicing," he said as he drove off, with Suzie still moaning.

Tony parked the van up the road slightly from the club and the two of them made their way down to the entrance. From the minute Tony walked through the doors he knew this was going to be a bad night. The woman at the doors said hello to Suzie and the bouncers at the door smiled and said hello as if they knew her. She seemed to squirm a bit every time someone looked at her. Tony knew then that she'd been here before. The pact that they had made about going to clubs where they went with their mates seemed worthless. "Have you fucking been here on a Friday with your mates?"

"No," she said. "It's just a friendly place I guess."

As he queued up to put their coats into the cloakroom, he could already feel all eyes on Suzie checking her out. She stood there swinging her hair about, soaking up the admiring looks. Tony could feel there was a bad vibe in here.

He walked over to Suzie and, putting his arm protectively across her shoulders, they made their way to the bar to get a drink. Suzie was standing by the bar dancing about to the music. Tony turned around and handed her a drink. "Thanks," she smiled back at him and carried on dancing.

Tony was wishing they had stayed at a pub this evening instead of coming here. She did seem a bit too comfortable in here, considering it was a place she'd never been before. There were groups of blokes that were hanging about and he was again feeling uneasy about the whole place.

The club was filling up now; it was getting packed in there.

Suzie was still dancing about by the bar. "Babe, stay here, I need to go to the loo. I'll be straight back," Tony told her. She nodded and carried on dancing.

Tony made his way through the crowds and upstairs to where the loos where. He walked in and up to the urinals. There were some lads in a cubicle sniffing cocaine, and a few standing about outside. He looked straight ahead taking no notice and then walked over to the basin to wash his hands.

As he was walking back to the bar where he left Suzie, he noticed a tall bloke standing there chatting to her. She was laughing and flicking her hair over her shoulder. She obviously seemed to know him. He had his arm around her waist as she was talking to him. As Tony got nearer he could make out her saying to him "My boyfriend's coming back, you'd better go." She was laughing. The bloke bent down closer to her and again she said "No, he's coming. Quick you better go," and laughed again.

Tony could feel the rage burning up from his feet as he stood up close behind the man. He leant in again to say something to her. This time, Tony tapped him on the shoulder. "Didn't you hear her the first time? She said her boyfriend will be back any minute."

Chapter 23

THE bloke spun around and stood face to face with Tony. He was a similar height and build to Tony with flashing angry eyes. He stared at him for a second and turned around, brushing him off, and carried on talking to her. Tony grabbed him by the shoulder and spun him back around. "Did you not fucking hear her? Now fuck OFF!"

The bloke squared up to him, "what did you fucking say?" he challenged Tony. As the pair faced each other now, their faces contorted with rage.

Tony repeated very slowly "I said *did you not fucking hear her? She said her boyfriend's behind you, you had better go. NOW . . . FUCK . . . OFF.*" Something in Tony's eyes made the bloke step back. He turned, looked at Suzie and walked off.

"So who's that then? Some bloke you sucked off last night?"

Suzie reared up to Tony. "NO! ACTUALLY, IT'S SOME BLOKE I USED TO GO TO SCHOOL WITH," she snapped.

"WHY DIDN'T YOU FUCKING INTRODUCE ME THEN, INSTEAD OF TELLING HIM TO FUCK OFF WHEN YOU SAW ME COMING BACK?" Tony was yelling now. "Don't give it all that. And don't talk shit to me," he said, lowering his voice now.

"WHAT'S YOUR FUCKING PROBLEM?" Suzie threw back at him. "I CAN FUCKING TALK TO WHOEVER I WANT TO!"

"COME ON, WE'RE GOING!" Tony yelled back. He grabbed her arm and stormed towards the entrance. As he passed through the crowd, Tony could see the bloke. He was talking to about six or seven other guys and was obviously telling them what had happened. The bouncers stood to one side to let Suzie through but as Tony went through there was a tap on his shoulder. He turned around and the bloke was standing there surrounded by his mates. He pointed at Tony and said "You ever come in here giving it again, we'll fucking do ya!"

"Yeah whatever, mate. No problem," Tony laughed and carried on walking through. He and Suzie got their coats and left.

They had got no further than fifty yards up the road, when he turned around to see them all coming out of the club after him. They were shouting and, as Tony turned around, the bloke was screaming, "I ain't having this off you, you wanker. Who the fuck do you think you are?"

"Oh fuck off and don't start," Suzie piped up, yelling back to the bloke. She tried dragging

Tony away back up the road to the van.

Tony could feel the rage building and he was livid. He marched up to the van, opened the door and threw Suzie inside the passenger seat. "DON'T FUCKING DARE MOVE!" he screamed at her and slammed the door shut.

The blokes were all still standing, staring at him and yelling. "Yeah go on, fuck off! Run off with ya bird, you prick. You ever come back we'll smash you up."

Tony walked around and opened up the back of his mate's van and rummaged about. There, lying amongst the tools was a spike hammer. He grabbed it tightly in his fist and, just as he turned around, the bloke was standing by the van next to him. Suddenly, Tony had a flashback to smashing the hammer over the punk's head when he little.

"I AIN'T HAVING IT. I AINT HAVING IT," the bloke was saying over and over again in his face. He was really rearing up to Tony now.

"YOU AIN'T HAVING WHAT?" Tony was in his face now. The bloke's mates were all standing on the corner of the street watching now, waiting for their mate to start the fight.

"GET IN THE FUCKING VAN!" Suzie was shouting out to Tony from the window.

"YOU AIN'T HAVING WHAT?" Tony repeated in his face.

"YOU. TRYING TO MAKE ME LOOK LIKE AN IDIOT IN FRONT OF EVERYONE," he was really shouting at Tony now.

"THAT'S NOT FUCKING HARD!" Tony said, and with that

he rammed the bloke out of his face by his throat and up against the wall by the kerb. He raised his hand holding the hammer and smashed it down hard. Not on his head, but straight into his shoulder blade, digging the spike straight through his collar bone. The bloke screamed out in agony as the hammer dangled from his shoulder. "YOU CUNTS WANT SOME AN' ALL?" Tony screamed down to the rest of them, who were all turning and running back to the club.

Suzie was screaming from the van "COME ON, TONY YOU'RE MAD. COME ON."

Tony wrenched the spike hammer out from his shoulder and he slumped to the floor, bleeding and crying. He threw the hammer back into the van, slammed the doors, climbed in and drove off with the sound of Suzie shouting and screaming at him.

As he got to the bottom of the road, he wound the window down and shouted to the rest of the gang "I'll be fucking back for you lot. I know your faces. I'll be back to kick the shit out of the rest of you. Let's see how fucking hard you are then!" and he drove off. Tony was so angry.

He and Suzie rowed the whole way home. He pulled up outside her house and she got out and slammed the door. With that, Tony sped off into the night towards home. He needed to cool off.

He approached the traffic lights. They flicked red and, as he sat and waited, he lit a cigarette. *She was unbelievable. She really was something else. Who the hell did she think she was?* Tony made his mind up there and then that he wasn't having this rubbish anymore. She was an absolute nightmare. He didn't care how good looking she was. This had to end.

As the lights changed to green he put the van into first gear and pulled away. The car came from nowhere. It roared across the high street, jumping the lights from the other direction and came speeding towards him. Tony tried to swerve to miss it but it just caught the front of his van.

"FUCK IT!" Tony couldn't believe it. *Could this night get any worse?*

Chapter 24

TONY leapt out of the van. There was no movement yet from inside the car that had hit him. He must have been going at some speed. Tony stood back to survey the damage, then the driver's door opened and a young man, dazed and shaken climbed out of the car.

"Jesus! Mate, are you ok?" Tony said, walking over to see him.

"Oh, I am so sorry," the man said, scratching his head and looking at the damage. "It's my fault I'll sort it," he stammered.

Tony couldn't agree more. He could smell booze on the man's breath and he clearly didn't want to be hanging around. Both vehicles were still drivable – Tony's van had a crunched front wing and smashed headlight, but he could get that sorted at the garage.

He kicked the broken bits of glass headlights to the kerb out of the way while the man was writing his insurance details down. Tony wasn't sure if he'd been insured on Aaron's van so he gave Aaron's name and address. The other bloke had admitted full liability anyway. He would just have to explain to Aaron and he'd get it all fixed up for him. There had been nobody about. Thankfully, it was a quiet road. There were no witnesses at this time of night and nobody had stopped either.

Tony took all the insurance details from the man and checked one final time to make sure he was ok. No one was hurt, and they both climbed back into their vehicles. Tony lit another cigarette up and proceeded to drive the rest of the way home with one headlight, still fuming about his night with Suzie. Tony would have this sorted out in no time. He would call Aaron with the bad news in the morning now. He pulled up outside Aaron's house, scribbled a quick note explaining in brief what had happened and posted the van keys and the note through his letterbox.

The following morning the phone only rang twice before Aaron's mum answered it. Aaron wasn't home but she did say he was due back in a few hours. Tony asked her to let Aaron know he'd be in the pub and could he meet him there.

He hung up and headed off to the shower mulling over his night and Suzie. He couldn't have this trouble every time they went out. He did really like her a lot though and it broke his heart to argue with her over jealousy. He had been seeing her for over a year now; they were pretty serious by his standards. Maybe that was the answer. Maybe he needed to settle down with her and stop going out with the lads and her stop going out with her mates every Friday. Maybe they needed to commit more to each other. Then there wouldn't be these jealous rows every week. Maybe . . .

He finished up his shower and as he walked into the kitchen. His dad was sitting there all solemn-faced. "What's up, Dad?" Tony asked, towel drying his hair.

"Tone, I need to talk to you, Son," Tony feared the worst. The look on Ernie's face told him something bad had happened.

"Dad, what is it?" Ernie went on to explain, holding up some papers.

"What's all that?" Tony asked.

"Well . . . it's your mum . . . she's finally filed for divorce and it's official, like," Ernie seemed sad.

Tony didn't know what to say. "It's just a bit of paper, Dad. You've been split up for years." "Yeah . . . I know, Son. It's just a bit of an end of an era I spose," Ernie said quietly.

"Dad, she's moved on and so have you got to."

"Yeah . . . I know . . ." Ernie tailed off. "That leads me to another thing I want to discuss with ya."

"Oh yeah?" Tony seemed puzzled. "Just spit it out, Dad."

"Well . . . the moving on thing . . . that's just it, Son . . ."

"What is?" Tony seemed confused. Ernie was certainly beating about the bush, whatever it was. Why didn't he just say it? "Well, Dad?" Tony was waiting.

Ernie looked at the floor. He looked at the clock. He looked at the ceiling. He looked anywhere but at Tony.

"DAD!" Tony yelled.

"Alright, alright! I'm telling ya. Well . . . it's Margaret . . ."

"What about her?" Tony said   "She asked me to move in with her." Ernie said quietly .

"Where? Here?" Tony spat.

"No, Son. Newcastle!"

"WHAT THE FUCK? Well I ain't coming with ya!" "Why not?" Ernie seemed genuinely hurt now.

"What the *fuck* do I wanna move to Newcastle for? My life is *here*, Dad. My mates are here . . .

I'm with Suzie now. I've got business here, Dad. I ain't moving to fucking Newcastle! No way!

Sorry."

Ernie looked sad again. "How can I move and leave you here, all by yourself? How you gonna cope? You won't go and see ya mother, or your sister. You hang about with these dodgy people getting up to all sorts of dodgy doings and stuff . . . you come in at all hours of the night. I can't bleeding well just swan off and leave you here . . . no one to watch over you, can I? I can't move on coz I got *you* to think about." Ernie was bellowing now.

"Oh, pardon me for spoiling your fucking life!" Tony cut in feeling stung. But Ernie was having none of it.

"Ain't it about time *I* had some happiness too? After everything I've ever bleeding well done for you .... I wanna move on and it happens to be moving on in bloody Newcastle," Ernie stared at his son.

"I'm just fine. I can look after myself," Tony could hear himself shouting at his dad now. This was escalating into an argument. He'd had enough of them lately and could do without another one tonight. "I can take care of myself just fine, thank you," Tony said.

Ernie retaliated, "You could do with a fresh start. A new life. Get away from all this shit."

"Oh yeah . . . right . . . ok . . . and Newcastle is the place to be is it? I've got the garage to deal with. I have responsibilities here. I have a *life* here, Dad. You can fuck off to Newcastle if you want but I promise you this now; I AIN'T COMING!" With that, Tony grabbed his jacket, keys and cigarettes and slammed out of the flat. Ernie let him go; they both needed to calm down. That was pretty much the reaction Ernie had expected from him.

"FUCK Newcastle!" Tony huffed as he stormed off to the pub. "FUCK Newcastle and FUCK him!"

As he pushed the doors to the pub open and walked in, he saw Aaron sitting waiting for him at the bar. He turned and smiled at Tony. "Alright, mate? You look like you need a pint."

Chapter 25

AARON was absolutely fine about the van. He and Tony had only known each other for a couple of years due to drinking in the same pubs. Gradually, they spent more and more time together and it ended up being a regular Friday night meet. Aaron Harris was the same age as Tony. He spent most of his time working up the gym pumping weights; he was training mad. He was slightly shorter than Tony but twice as wide and had a chest and arms that were pumped up like Michelin Man. He had dark, short shaved hair and a big square jaw and wore muscle vests to emphasise his huge frame.

"Mate, it's alright," he said. "Don't worry, it's a work van, it's covered. You did the right thing with the insurance shit," Tony breathed a sigh of relief. "I'll get it all sorted out, mate," he said.

He was pleased Aaron had taken it as well as he did. He was telling Aaron about the club and his evening and Suzie and his dad. "Fucking hell, Tone. What a nightmare," Aaron sympathised.

Later that evening Tony thought he needed to go back and make things right with his dad. He'd had a think about it, and had to admit that he'd overreacted. As he walked through the front door his dad was making a cup of tea in the kitchen. Ernie turned and looked at his son. "Dad, I'm sorry," Tony said instantly. "I shouldn't have shouted at you like that." "It's ok, Son. I'm sorry too," Ernie replied.

"Dad, you go to Newcastle and be with Margaret. Honestly, I'll be ok here. I can take over the flat."

"I don't know, Son," Ernie said. He had obviously been giving this some real thought. "I don't think it's right I shouldn't go and just leave you."

"DAD!" Tony insisted. "Listen, I'm almost twenty years old. I can handle it on my own. And if I can't then . . . well . . . I can always come up later if I need to. You're only a few hours away, and I'll come and visit."

"Well I would bleedin' well hope so!" Ernie smiled and leant forward and gave his son a hug.

He was so proud of him. He just needed Tony's ok to go.

"Anyway," Tony carried on. "I was thinking about the flat and being here on me own . . . I could maybe ask Suzie to move in . . ."

* * *

Monday morning, and Tony's flat phone was ringing. It was an anxious Rob on the other end. He told Tony that he had received a call from Karl earlier that morning. Karl had rung the clinic ahead of Rob and booked him in. Karl had paid the bill upfront for a four-week stint and recovery program afterwards. All Rob had to do was pack his bag and wait for Tony for drive them there.

Tony was pleased for him and extremely grateful to Karl for his help; these clinics were not cheap. Karl had paid around ten thousand pounds for Rob to stay there. He knew that this was the right thing to do for Rob.

As promised, Tony got his stuff together and made his way round to collect Rob. They were heading down there just before lunchtime. Rob hugged his tearful mum goodbye and climbed into the car. With promises of phone calls and letters the two boys drove off, leaving Rob's mum standing on the pavement waving them off down the road.

"Promise me you'll see this through and get sorted," Tony said.

"Mate, I *promise,*" Rob said. "After the other night, I never ever wanna go through that again. I was a fucking wreck! I couldn't believe it. I keep thinking it over and over in me mind. I can't believe I could have fucked it all up for you too, mate. I really am sorry. And after Karl has paid out for me to do this . . . they ain't cheap . . . I know that much, mate! How will I ever repay him for this?"

"Just get clean," Tony said sternly as he lit a cigarette. He passed one to Rob and proceeded to tell him about the bad weekend he'd had.

Tony had booked Aaron's van in to be repaired later that week. He had also made amends on the phone with Suzie. He had planned to meet her one night this week, as there was something he wanted to talk to her about. Ernie had thought that it was a great idea for Tony to see if Suzie wanted to move in. He needed to know that someone was going to keep an eye on his son. This might be just what he needed to rein him in a bit.

Tony and Rob arrived at the rehab centre. It was a very pleasant place and not like the vision Tony first had. There were no iron railings and bars at windows, no patients running around in strait jackets being chased by men in white coats. On the contrary, it was like a country hotel with lovely gardens and very nice bright, clean rooms.

"Jesus! This is a fancy hotel," Rob laughed, looking around his new temporary home.

"It's gonna cost a fortune," Tony whistled in agreement. He hugged Rob goodbye and promised he'd call all the time to see how he was doing. As he pulled away from Rob, he could see huge tears rolling down his friend's cheek. "It's for the best, mate, come on," Tony said softly.

"I know, I know. Come on, leave me. I'll be fine," Rob said, pushing Tony away from him and towards the door. "Now git outta here!" Rob said, smacking him on the back. "Oh, and cheers for the ride!"

"Anytime," Tony winked and turned and left. He held it together as he walked back into the lift and out through the lobby towards the car park. As he turned around one last time to look, he could see Rob standing at the window watching him. He gave a final wave and Rob waved back. As Tony got into the car, he couldn't stop the tears from falling and stinging his eyes. He pulled out of the clinic and started his lonely trip home. He was going to miss that fella!

The following Friday he met up with Dean in a pub at the other end of town for a change. There was a pool table there and he needed a good beer and a game of pool – that would cheer him up.

Whilst setting the balls up on table, they casually touched on the whole Tania and Rob episode. Dean had seemed really cut up over Tania. "I did really like her, mate. But seriously, I couldn't deal with that shit."

"That's exactly why Rob is where he is. I can't lose me best mate to that shit."

"Well I ain't got that option for Tania. And she don't seem to wanna stop either. That's the problem," Dean said. Leaning over, he took his pool cue. "My break?" he called, smashing the balls up into a frenzied panic. "Ooh, reds," he smiled, as a red one disappeared down into a pocket.

The pub was filling up; it was a busy Friday night. Out of the corner of his eye, Tony noticed two girls standing by the bar. The girls were watching Tony and Dean and giggling every now and again. They were both gorgeous looking girls albeit a bit cocky. He liked that though. He didn't recognise them from the pub. The pool tables were by the toilets and the girls slowly walked past to go to the ladies' – one wearing the tightest pair of white trousers he had ever seen a girl squeezed into. "Phoar! Fucking hell!" he commented to Dean as they wiggled past.

Dean looked up just as he was taking a shot, sending the white ball off target and missing his ball completely. "Oh! Two shots to me!" Tony laughed.

"Bastard!" Dean said.

"The one in the white was a bit of alright, eh?" Tony said rather loudly to Dean.

"I'll have a look," Dean said. Tony walked round to line up the first of his two shots. "Anyway, you're spoken for," Dean said, as Tony sunk his ball into the pocket.

"Still got two shots," he smirked, walking round the table. "No harm in looking," he said, as he lowered down to take his shot. At that moment the girls sashayed past them from the loos putting Tony completely off his strike.

"Ahh! You missed!" Dean retorted.

"You talking about me?" the girl in the white trousers asked in a rather pointed, rude tone. Instantly, Tony took a dislike to this attitude that she had. She thought she was the bee's knees. He already had one girl like that; he didn't need grief with another one.

Tony stood up tall. "What makes you think we are talking about you?" Tony threw back at her. He turned back and leant over to take his final shot. The girl seemed more than annoyed that she didn't have his undivided attention, something she was clearly used to getting with men.

Dean also turned away from her and carried on with the game. Slowly and carefully Tony lined up and took his shot and smiled at Dean. "Just the black one now, my son," he smiled.

The girls stood there by the bar now, glaring over. In one smooth movement, Tony pulled back his arm and struck the ball, sending it flying straight into the pocket he was aiming for. "And that, my friend, is how it is done," he stood and took a mock bow at Dean who was laughing. "Fuck I'm good!" Tony laughed.

"Alright, smart arse," Dean laughed.

Tony could feel the eyes of the girls boring into him. "Oh, by the way, love . . ." Tony turned to the girl in the white trousers, who was still glaring at him. " . . . I think you've just come on," he said, motioning down to her trousers.

The girl looked down briefly. "Oh fuck off!" she slammed back furiously and turned and stormed off with her friend following after her.

"Prats," Tony said. He downed the last of his pint as he and Dean headed over to the bar. The bar now was at least two people deep. To get served quicker they split up; Tony stood by one end of the bar and Dean the other to see who could get served first. While Tony was standing there he noticed the girl in white trousers standing with a group of men. She appeared to be pointing over at him.

Tony managed to get served before Dean. "Two pints please, love," he called over to the barmaid. He signalled to Dean that he had been served and Dean began to make his way over to him through the crowds.

"Alright, Tony?" Tony turned to see a bloke standing there who he vaguely recognised from school. "Ain't seen you for a while, how's things?" the bloke carried on babbling.

Suddenly, Tony could see the man had been used as a decoy to distract him. From the corner of his eye, he just made out an arm coming flying towards him. The punch landed on the side of his head, momentarily stunning him – but not for long enough. Tony grabbed whoever it was that was beside him and the whole bar surged forward. Tony had brought him down to the floor and a terrible fight had broken out. The guy that had been chatting to him set about kicking him whilst he was down. Tony was raining punches on the bloke he still had on the floor. Every time they kicked Tony he punched the bloke harder and harder. There must have been four or five of them now, all piling into Tony on the floor. Relentlessly, Tony carried on like an animal hitting the man. He grabbed at another one and started raining punches down. Someone else had smashed him over the back with a pool cue. The pub's doormen had come charging over; they were friends of Tony's. They started pulling the blokes off, but Tony was zoned out now. He had leapt to his feet yelling, unaware of Dean at this point.

The bouncers had broken the fight up "FUCKING KEEP 'EM IN HERE!" Tony screamed at them. The bouncers were trying to keep the blokes inside and Tony bolted outside and up the road to his car. Wrenching the boot open, he grabbed a hammer and began storming back down to the pub. He knew their faces now. He was going to have each and every one of them. Just as he was storming back up the road, he saw Dean come staggering towards him. He looked in a really bad way and had received a severe beating by the looks of it. They had got him on the floor and just kicked him relentlessly. His face was a bloodied mess and he looked at the hammer in Tony's hand. "Let's fucking have 'em!" Dean yelled, spraying blood everywhere. Dean wasn't a fighter but he'd have a good go.

"COME ON THEN!" Tony raged. At that point they saw that the blokes had got out of the pub and were climbing into a silver Orion. They had the girls with them. The white trouser girl was crying now as she climbed into the car. Tony had clocked the number plate as the car screeched off into the night.

Chapter 26

IT had been an eighty-year-old ex-postman that had stepped in and dragged Dean out from under the barrage of kicks, otherwise they most probably would have kicked him to death. Tony spun around and looked at Dean. He was looking like he was going to faint. Tony knew it was bad so he threw his arm around him and slowly they walked back up to Tony's car. "I'm taking you hospital, mate" Tony said as he helped Dean into the passenger seat. He ran to the driver's side, jumped in and spun it around and headed off to the A&E ward.

They had kicked him so badly that they had shattered his cheekbone and the bone had splintered into his eye. He could have gone blind. They kept Dean in for nearly a week.

Tony was so angry. "All over stupid fucking birds and a stupid comment," he said. He felt absolutely terrible about this; he was going to get them big time.

Dean had made Tony promise in the hospital that he would leave it and not go after them as he didn't want any come back. "Promise me, Tone, you'll leave it. Please don't do nothing." Dean said. He'd just had all his wounds cleaned and dressed again and was so badly bruised he was almost unrecognisable.

Dean's mum was at the hospital too. "Please let it go, Tony. You've got to calm down and stop all this fighting."

"Of course," Tony had promised, crossing his fingers in his pockets. As if he'd leave it! After what they'd done to Dean. No way! He was going to get them. He knew their faces now. He knew he was really going to hurt them,

About a week later, Tony went up and saw Andy Weaver who agreed to go out with him looking for them. They stole a van and drove about for hours until they saw the Orion car parked up outside a pub on Peterborough Road. They parked a few cars behind it up the road. Tony and Andy ran down and had a quick nose through the pub window to make sure it was him. There he was, the mouthy one who had started it all. Just him and his silly girlfriend, with the same white trousers on.

Tony and Andy walked back to the van. They would have to sit and wait.

It must have been a good two hours later when Andy saw them leaving the pub. As they walked up to their car, Tony and Andy ducked down out of sight. The pair climbed in, started their car up and drove off, with Tony and Andy following them down the road in close pursuit.

It wasn't long before they came to a stop sign at the bottom of a quiet road and Tony and Andy seized their chance. As the car stopped, Tony rammed his foot down onto the accelerator of his van and smashed straight into the back of the Orion. Quick as a flash Tony and Andy pulled the balaclavas that were rolled up on their heads down over their faces, pulled on a pair of gloves and jumped out of the van.

The bloke jumped out of his car but Tony was up and alongside him now, fast. He dragged him down onto the floor, screaming. The girl was screaming too. Andy dragged her from the car and threw her down onto the kerb as she scrambled to get away. Tony was kicking and stamping on the bloke now. Andy whipped a hammer out of his jacket and passed it to Tony and, as Andy held the man down, Tony raised the hammer. Bringing it down hard, he smashed every single bone in both of his hands. The noise was sickening, as bone after bone was smashed to pieces. The man struggled and Andy was holding him down steady. He couldn't move. Tony was kneeling on each of his arms.

"Tough guy now, ain't ya?" Tony spat at him through gritted teeth. The bloke was still screaming and Andy grabbed his head and covered his mouth with his hand squeezing his jaw bone to stifle the screams. The bloke's eyes were rolling back into his head with the pain. As he now struggled to breath too all he could do was listen as Tony said; "Like to gang up on people and give them a kicking, do ya?"

As every blow came down across his hands and wrists, more bones smashed and disintegrated beneath the hammer. "Let's see how fucking tough you are now when you can't even wipe your own fucking arse." With the final blow, and every single bone broken in his hands and wrists, the bloke finally passed out on the floor in pain. The girl was still screaming. Andy ran round and, grabbing her by the hair, screamed in her face to stop it or he would give her something else to scream about. She spat in his face and Andy brought his hand down hard across her cheek and she fell to the ground, sobbing. "Fucking slag," he spat the words back at her.

Tony gave the bloke a final kick then they both ran back and jumped into the van. They reversed back out of the Orion; it was a bit smashed up and bent now, but still drivable. Leaving the bloke unconscious on the floor and his terrified screaming girlfriend, they drove the van half a mile up the road near where Tony's car was and dumped it. Ripping their balaclavas off they jumped into Tony's car drove off.

"Nice one, mate. Job well done I reckon. Fancy a pint?" Andy said, pleased with their evening.

"Fucking do I," replied Tony and the pair drove to the Rose in time for last orders.

Earlier that week, the conversation with Suzie about moving in hadn't gone quite as Tony had planned in his head. She wasn't overwhelmed with emotion at the idea. As she pointed out, her job was in South London so that meant an awkward commute for her. She also didn't seem too keen to give up her Friday nights with the girls to spend more time with Tony. She had said she would half move in, maybe just weekends to start and see how that went. Tony said it wasn't really worth it, but went along with it anyway.

Ernie had made his plans now to go to Newcastle the following week. He was very excited about his move. Tony was happy for him but sad to see him go. Ernie had specifically said he didn't want any leaving do or surprise party. Tony offered to take him to Karl's lap dancing club but Ernie politely declined. He wanted a few beers with Tony in the local and that was all. Tony thought it was going to be weird being on his own, especially if Suzie wasn't going to be about. However, on the flip side, if Suzie wasn't about . . . what she doesn't know doesn't hurt her. If she wasn't willing to commit, why should he? He would just resume his usual lifestyle and see what happened.

Suzie used to spend a lot of her time with her best friend, or sidekick, as Tony referred to her, Natasha. Tony didn't like Natasha very much. He thought she was a troublemaker and a sneak; he never quite trusted her. Suzie and Tasha always went everywhere together. She was also a very good looking girl and she knew it. She was mousey brown as opposed to Suzie's blonde, and had a fantastic figure. She had big blue eyes and wore quite heavy makeup as opposed to Suzie's more natural face. They were always out on a Friday together; they also worked together. Suzie spent more time with Natasha than she did anyone else. So when Suzie did come and stay at weekends, Tash sometimes came with her. This annoyed Tony no end.

"What the fuck does she always have to come for? You spend all fucking week with her.

Can't you bear to be apart?"

"So what!" she slammed back. "If I do decide to move in. And *if.* I am allowed to have my friends over too y'know."

"You might as well give her her own fucking door key. She'll be wanting to fucking sleep in bed with us next," Tony said stroppily, thinking he probably wouldn't argue about that one though.

However, this weekend Suzie came up alone. All that week Tony had heard rumours. He hated rumours – and the people that spread them. People had been coming up to him in the pubs saying "*Aaron's after you." "Aaron's got the right hump. You fucked him over with his van; he's gonna do ya. Have you seen Aaron? He's really fucked off about his van. He's gonna smash you up.*"

After about the fourth or fifth person had said this, Tony decided he was going to go to Aaron's himself and see what he had to say. He hadn't heard a thing from Aaron lately, so it did seem feasible. He'd had the van repaired good as new, but because he had Suzie moved in most weekends he wasn't out with his mates as much as he used to so hadn't really seen Aaron about. He walked up to Aaron's front door and knocked loudly and waited. Aaron opened the door and glared at Tony. Sure enough, he had the hump.

Chapter 27

"WHAT'S all this I hear about you having a problem with me?" Tony said straight away without making any small talk.

"Yeah, that's right," Aaron glared at him.

"Oh, so the soppy wankers up the pub aren't making it up then. Well here I am. What's the fucking problem? I'm here if you wanna smash me up."

"You fucking cost me three points on my license because of that headlight being smashed. And I got nicked," Aaron said.

Tony reared up to him, "What are you fucking talking about? I offered straight away to replace it and you said fucking leave it, the firm will get it fixed. I had the body work all sorted and you said you'd get the light done that afternoon. Ain't my fucking fault." Tony couldn't believe what he was hearing.

"No you didn't," Aaron shot back.

"You're a fucking lying prick," Tony was getting really angry now.

"Yeah well that's why I've got the fucking hump, ain't it," Aaron said.

Tony was losing his temper. He could feel the rage building inside him again. "So because you go to the gym pumping your fucking iron and you got a big chest, you think you're bad, do ya? You think you can go around telling everyone that you're gonna do me, do ya? DO YA? Well, let's fucking have it now ya cunt! If you're gonna *do me,*" Tony was rearing up now against Aaron's huge frame.

"Nah, I'm eating my fucking dinner now," Aaron backed down. "But you'll get your comeuppance, ya prick," he said.

"Whatever! Fucking look forward to it, ya fat cunt. You're a fucking idiot. Next time you start making fucking threats you better find out who you are really dealing with. Could save you a lot of fucking pain.

Oh, and when you *do me,* as you put it, make sure everyone's there . . . I'll have the last fucking laugh with you. WANKER!" Tony yelled over his shoulder and slammed out of his front garden, kicking the gate as he went.

Tony couldn't believe this; Aaron had been absolutely fine when they'd spoken in the pub about it and the van had been repaired to perfection, apart from the head light. There had to be more to this than Aaron was letting on. Aaron wasn't interested at all in settling it either, and the feud went on and on for a good month. Tony continued to hear the rumours in the pubs about Aaron wanting to *do him.*

"Yeah well, I've been round his house and he ain't done nothing yet has he?" Tony would tell them. "I've been round and fronted him and offered him out and he didn't wanna know. He's all muscles and mouth. He's a fucking tosser!"

A few weeks had passed by now and it was one Saturday that Tony had agreed to go to the cinema with Suzie. He wasn't a lover of the cinema but she wanted to watch the latest release, *Sex, Lies and Video Tapes.* So reluctantly, Tony agreed to go. By now, everybody knew about what had happened between Tony and Aaron. It was public knowledge.

It was particularly busy at the cinema as the film was a new release and everybody was queuing up to go inside; the queue was huge. Tony had to park his car up the road and he and Suzie were walking down to join the back of the queue. There were a lot of people there that Tony knew. They all stood there chatting and laughing. Just then, Tony saw Aaron and his girlfriend, Lydia, crossing over the road and walking towards them. They were walking up past them to join the back of the queue.

"This is awkward," Suzie piped up. Aaron pumped his chest out even further and walked right up to Tony and stood directly in front of him, squaring up to him with his muscly frame. Tony just stared at Aaron, smirking, as if the muscles were there to intimidate him.

"Alright?" he said, and suddenly he gave a small slap to Aaron's face to get a reaction. Everybody was watching. Aaron would have to hold his hands up and fight. He retaliated, and with his pumped-out chest and inflated arms all he could do was throw a roundhouse punch which caught Tony on the side of the temple. Tony instantly reacted and landed three blows to Aaron's face; one, two, three. There was an awful cracking noise as the last two blows hit Aaron. That was it. The fight was over and Aaron had hit the floor. The fight was finished as quickly as it had started. There hadn't even been time for a huge crowd to gather round. There was blood everywhere. Someone in the queue said they had heard his nose crack and his jaw break. Aaron was crouched down on all fours on the floor with blood streaming from his face like a tap.

Tony stood over him and tapped him on the back of the head, "I could have really hurt you, you stupid cunt. But you ain't worth it . . . you just ain't worth it." Suzie was pulling Tony away. Lydia was trying to help clean Aaron up with blood-soaked tissues. The queue was starting to move inside now. The show was over. Tony wiped his hands on the back of his jeans and he and Suzie followed the queue inside to the pictures, leaving Aaron and a hysterical Lydia on the floor outside.

About half way through the film, Tony started getting blurred vision and had a headache, obviously from Aaron's one and only punch. He nipped out of the cinema and into the men's toilets. He looked in the mirror and could see that his eye was heavily blood shot; the veins had leaked from his boxing injury. It was no good, they were going to have to leave the cinema. He popped back into the film to get Suzie and the pair left. Tony couldn't drive, so Suzie did. When they got home, he rinsed his eye out with eye wash and thought no more about it.

The following morning Suzie had to go home. She had a few bits to do and she had work the following day. She gave Tony a kiss goodbye and left him to his Sunday morning chill out. She couldn't have been gone longer than an hour when there was a loud banging on the door. It was one of Tony's neighbours from a few doors down. "Tony! Come quick! There's three blokes downstairs, they're all smashing your van up."

Tony quickly ran over to the balcony. There below, was Mark, Aaron's older brother, with two of his mates all smashing Tony's van up. Mark was another pumped up version of Aaron – all muscles and mouth. He had smashed the windscreen and the other two had set about letting tyres down and smashing the headlights. There was broken glass all over the floor.

"OI, YOU WANKERS!" Tony hollered over the balcony. He ran downstairs as quickly as he could, and as he came flying out of the stairwell to the car park, Mark turned around and fronted him. Tony was a lot quicker than Mark had given him credit for. Tony's fist came unexpectedly crashing down straight into Mark's face, flooring him instantly and knocking him down like a skittle. The second bloke had run around from the other side of the van to help Mark. As Tony turned, he'd landed another punch and this bloke had gone down too and was lying in the broken glass from the van. Tony was in a rage and he turned to see the third bloke running off. Tony gave chase. The bloke was quick but Tony was quicker. In no time at all Tony had gained on him. With his long legs he stretched out and kicked the bloke's foot, tripping him up and sending him reeling forwards, face down on the floor, splattering his features across his face. Tony grabbed him by the hair and slammed his head down into the pavement. The bloke was practically unconscious. Tony kicked him and then ran back to his van. Mark was just about getting up. As Tony ran past him, he lashed out with a kick to his head, sending him down to the floor again.

Tony stormed back to his flat without even looking back. He grabbed the phone and dialled

Aaron's number.

"Hello?" Aaron's mum answered the phone. "You've got a fucking nerve calling here. What have you done to my boy?" she shouted when she realised it was Tony on the phone.

"Don't fucking start all that. You've got another son coming home battered now," Tony bellowed. "Put fucking Aaron on the phone," Tony was livid.

"Come here and talk to him and get it sorted. I don't want all this shit all the time." Tony could hear her talking to Aaron as she held her hand over the mouth piece to stifle her voice.

"Huh? What?" Aaron said down the phone.

"What is your fucking problem? You wanna fucking send ya brother and his mates round here to vandalise my fucking van, you dirty cunt!"

Aaron didn't deny it. "You're a cunt," he mumbled into the phone.

"Is that the best you can fucking do? I suggest you send someone a bit fucking harder next time. You wanna fucking start going down that road, I'll come round there and fucking finish you off for good. You're gonna want to MOVE by the time I'm done with you! I'll put you in a fucking box or a bullet in ya fucking nut, you wanna mess with me," Tony was livid. Aaron just hung up the phone without another word.

That afternoon, Tony decided he would call Ernie in Newcastle. Ernie answered the phone after the second ring. "Hey, Dad" Tony said.

"Hello, Tone. Alright?"

"Dad . . . I think I need to come and stay with you for a bit." Tony told his Dad the whole story. His dad was quite fond of Aaron and he was so shocked when Tony finished telling him what had happened.

"That's out of order," Ernie said. "What a total misunderstanding." He didn't understand what Tony had done wrong and agreed with Tony that there must be more to it than just this.

Suddenly there was a loud knocking on the door. "Dad, hang on. I'll just get the door," Tony said. He placed the phone receiver on the side and went to answer the front door.

Tony opened the door to see two police officers standing there. "Yes?" Tony said, shocked. "Mr Anthony Hayes?"

"Err . . . might be," Tony replied cautiously.

"Anthony Hayes, you are under arrest on suspicion of an attack on a Mr Aaron Harris. You are going to have to accompany us to the station."

Tony was taken aback. *Aaron, the fucking weasel,* he thought. Ernie was still on the end of the phone. He could hear everything that was going on. "Tony? Tony?" he was yelling loud to be heard on the phone. "TONY! CAN YOU HEAR ME?"

"Sir," the police officer carried on. "You are going to have to accompany us to the station for questioning," the police officer stepped forward into the flat.

"I need to speak to my dad. Can I quickly speak to him? He's hanging on there," Tony said urgently, pointing to the phone. The police officer allowed Tony to quickly finish speaking to Ernie but stood next to him the whole time. "Dad, just get me a fucking solicitor and call Karl. You're gonna have to come back now and meet me at the station. *Quick, Dad!*"

Chapter 28

TONY was sat in the police station. The interview room was bare and cold with nothing more than a small table, four chairs, an ashtray and a large recording device for company. It had felt like ages ago since they'd arrested him. He'd been pacing about in his cell before they finally brought him down to the interview room a few minutes beforehand. He had no idea what was happening. Hopefully his dad had contacted Karl and a solicitor was on his way. Karl wouldn't let him down. He stood up and paced about this room now. The mirror on the wall was obviously one-way glass; he knew they were watching him. The door opened suddenly and an officer walked in with a suited man. He was small and ratty looking, wearing a pin striped suit and small round glasses, carrying a briefcase. The man took a seat and opened his briefcase.

"Could you give me and my client a moment please?" the suit asked the officer.

"Certainly – five minutes?" The officer turned and left the room.

"Mr Anthony Hayes. Is it ok for me to call you Tony?" Tony nodded.

"My name is Mr Vernon Jackson," the suit carried on shuffling papers in his briefcase. He looked up briefly over the rim of his glasses. "I am a solicitor representing you. Mr Karl Bateman has arranged for me on your behalf."

Tony wasn't sure what to say or do. He nodded to show he understood him. They only had a few minutes left before the police officers came back in to start the interview. Tony wasn't sure about this suit. He must be good though, Karl had sorted him out. He just needed to sit tight and do what he was told.

Vern Jackson looked at him purposefully. "This is a serious allegation, Tony. I need facts."

"It was just a fight. A stupid fight," Tony protested.

"I'd advise you to say *no comment* to all of the questions and we'll postpone questioning until such time that I can sit with you and thoroughly go through everything. Understood?"

Tony nodded obediently and, as if on cue, two officers entered the room. They offered Tony a hot drink and his cigarettes and proceeded with the interview, clicking the tape recorder to RECORD.

"For the benefit of the tape, persons present are PC Simms; Chief Inspector Maguill; defendant, Mr Anthony Hayes and Mr Vernon Jackson, acting solicitor. You are under arrest on suspicion of the attack on a Mr Aaron Harris. You do not have to say anything, but it may harm your defence if you do not mention when questioned something you later rely on in court. Anything you do say may be given in evidence. Please answer loudly and clearly when instructed to do so. Do you understand?"

Tony leant forwards and picked up a cigarette. Putting it to his lips he lit it, inhaling the smoke deeply.

"Please tell us your full name."

Tony leant in. "Anthony Michael Hayes," he stated.

PC Simms produced a series of photographs from a plastic folder. "For the benefit of the tape, defendant is being shown a series of photographs of a Mr Aaron Harris."

The photos they had taken of Aaron seemed to be quite horrific. Maguill looked at Tony with sadness in his expression. "Tony, where were you on the night of Saturday the eighteenth of July?"

"No comment," Tony looked at Vernon. He nodded at him to continue.

Maguill slid a picture of Aaron across the table for Tony to see. "Have a good look at this picture, Tony. Can you see what you have done to Mr Harris?"

"No comment," came Tony's answer, loud and clear.

"Were you at the cinema on the High Street on the night of the attack on Mr Aaron Harris?" "No comment," came Tony's answer again.

"Were you in the queue outside the cinema with your girlfriend?

We have a lot of witnesses that say they saw you there on the night."

"No comment."

Vernon kept quiet, noting everything down. Every single question that Maguill asked him he fired back thick and fast "No comment".

"Interview terminated at sixteen o five," Maguill said, standing up and clicking off the tape recorder. PC Simms stood up too and left the room. There was an uncomfortable silence in the room for a second or so. "Tony . . . come on," Maguill said very quietly. "I can't help you, son, if you don't work with me. You need to tell me what happened. You have to talk to me," he genuinely seemed to be reaching out for Tony.

"I believe you are goading my client," Vernon jumped in.

"NO COMMENT," Tony replied. "NO COMMENT."

Maguill passed another cigarette across the table to Tony. "Tony, please," Maguill pleaded with him now. "This is very serious, Tony. Come on, look at these pictures. Look at them!" he thrust them at Tony across the table. Tony took the pictures in his hand, stared at them for a second then tossed them back across the table – slightly too hard, sending them all fluttering down to the floor.

"Damn you, Tony!" Maguill shouted now.

"NO COMMENT," Tony replied.

"That's enough!" Vernon cut in and stood up to signal the end of the interview.

Tony was taken back to the cells. He was charged with GBH with intent.

As Vernon walked with him, he said "We'll get bail and deal with this, Tony. I'll be in touch, well done. Karl's waiting for you outside," he shook Tony's hand and turned and headed off.

Tony was released on bail. When he got outside, Karl was there. Ernie had also just arrived after a manic drive down from Newcastle in record time. Tony walked up to his dad and never before had he been so glad to feel his arms around him hugging him.

Karl patted his shoulder, "It's ok, Tone. We'll sort this, don't worry. Everything's gonna be ok," Karl said confidently. "It's all ok."

The three of them headed off to the nearest pub and Tony proceeded to tell them about the interview and the pictures of Aaron.

He couldn't believe he had done this much damage to him with only three punches.

Because Tony was due to appear at the local magistrates court, Ernie had decided to stay down in London for a while. Karl had arranged a meeting with Tony, Ernie, Vernon and himself to go through every detail of what happened. Vernon's confidence in his case made Tony feel a lot better about the whole deal but, having never appeared in court before, Tony was very nervous to say the least.

The day of the hearing arrived and Tony waited outside the court with Vernon to go in. He was all suited up and extremely nervous.

"It's only natural," Vernon said encouragingly with a warm smile. Karl and Ernie were waiting inside the court.

"HAYES. COURT TWO," the court usher called them in.

Everyone entered the court and took their seats. Tony stood up at the dock. There were no other witnesses or anyone there for that matter. Aaron hadn't even appeared in court that day.

The court had been informed by the CPS that Mr Hayes had apparently threatened to kill Mr Harris, as well as making other threats after the GBH event had taken place. Tony pleaded *not guilty*. Tony was charged with GBH with intent and malicious wounding. The judge gave Tony conditional bail which meant he had to sign on every day at the local police station while they waited for a Crown Court date. It was going to take months, possibly even a year, to get a court hearing.

They left the court that day with a very heavy cloud hanging overhead.

Chapter 29

1989

"GET a fucking grip, man!" Karl told him one afternoon. Tony had headed down to Karl's wine bar and was wallowing in self-pity at the bar. "You're doing yourself no favours. This court date could take months and months, maybe even a year to come through. You cannot spend the time waiting for it sitting here half-drunk all the time," Karl scolded him.

"Yeah ... well ... I gotta keep my nose clean, ain't I?" Tony whined.

"Doesn't mean you have to become a fucking nun either. I've got drops to be done, meets that need doing, stuff picking up. I appreciate you're going through a hard time, but you're not the only one that's ever had a hard fucking time. You wanna hear a hard time, spend an afternoon talking to Al about his life story. But you don't see him all down and boo hoo over shit. You need to wake up and smell the coffee. It can get a lot tougher than this, too. I thought you were tough, Tony. I thought you had it. I thought you were cut out for this shit!"

"I am," Tony threw back at Karl. He felt hurt; he thought Karl was on his side.

"Listen, Tony. It's good to be tough and be a fighter. You are an amazing hands-on fighter. But you need to be a smart fighter too, and it's not all about using your hands. You gotta use your head too. You need to learn to think right. Think smart." Tony seemed to digest this information carefully. Karl looked at him and gave him a half-grin that let Tony know that it would be ok. "You know what I'm saying." Tony nodded and smiled back

"Right! Ok then, get yourself up to the cabbies and you can go with Al. Just get up, wipe your fucking arse and get back out there. You've got an hour!" Karl made it clear that it was non-negotiable.

With that, Karl stood up signalling the conversation was over. "An hour, Tony. Right?" Karl walked out the back of the bar leaving Tony to mull over what he had just said.

Ever since the magistrates court, Tony had been feeling really bad about himself. Karl didn't want to see him on that slippery slope and decided Tony needed a buzz again. He needed that reason to get up in the mornings. He was gradually wearing himself down and Karl would be damned if he was going to sit here and let that happen to Tony. He was so fond of him; he now thought of him as one of their own.

Tony pulled up outside the cabbies. Just as he switched off the engine, his mobile rang.

"Yeah," he answered.

"Alright geez!" a familiar and friendly voice boomed down the other end.

"ROB! How are you, mate?" Tony was over the moon. It was Rob and he sounded brilliant.

He had completed his four-week rehab program.

"I'm on the mend, man. I'm all fixed! I'm coming home!" he sounded chuffed.

"Ah, mate. That's brilliant. When?"

"Day after tomorrow . . . hopefully. Can you come get me?"

"Of course I can. Let me know for definite tomorrow and I'll arrange it and I'll be there to get you."

"What's been going on then? Any news?" Rob asked.

Tony paused. "Nah, nothing new . . . this and that. I'll save it for the trip home."

"Ok, buddy. Can't wait to see ya," Rob said and hung up.

Tony clicked off the mobile. This was exactly what he needed right now; his best mate back in the saddle with him. Feeling better already, he stepped out of the car and walked into the cabbies with the good news of Rob's return.

"Afternoon, Collette," Tony called over as he passed through the front of the smoky cabbies. She was as usual busy on the phone booking cabs. She gave him a cheeky little wink and blew him an imaginary kiss. He pretended to catch it and stick it on his lips. She giggled and carried on with her phone booking. She was so bloody gorgeous – Karl was a lucky man. There were a few punters sitting waiting for cabs. Tony carried on through to the back and, knocking gently on the back door, he walked into the office. Al looked up and was pleased to see Tony looking more like his old self. Tony told him about Rob. Al jumped up and gave Tony a quick high five.

"That's great news, mate. Come on, you can tell me about it in the car. It's a drop the other side of Heathrow airport. Straight forward drop and collect. All good, no probs and we'll be back later." Al tucked two brown paper parcels into his jacket, and they made their way out through the back door.

They had a good few hours each way in the car and Tony thought he'd open up to Al about his chat with Karl in the bar earlier. He briefly touched on what Karl had said about toughening up and that life gets harder than this. He didn't mention to Al that Karl had used him as an excuse for hard lives. He didn't need to. Al must have really trusted Tony as he openly volunteered the information. "You wanna hear tough life, mate? Listen to this . . ."

Little Alfie Tyler was born in North London in 1964. As an unwanted baby he was unloved and neglected. His father was 'unknown' on the birth certificate. He may have been of Jamaican blood; that was all his mother could say on the matter. To be truthful, it could have been any number of men that would often spend the night. His mother was a Londoner, born and bred. Alcoholic, brass and junkie. Baby Alfie was often left alone in his room whilst his mother 'entertained' her guests. She would have wild parties until all hours and the neighbours would bang on walls and make complaints about her to the police and the council. By the time the parties finished the following morning she would be passed out on the bathroom floor or crashed out on the sofa. Alfie was over the age of two by the time he realised that crying himself to sleep didn't get him anywhere. He was left hungry and alone and was dangerously undernourished and so thin.

The morning after her parties, she would be so hungover that she would often crawl to her bed and stay there until the evening, leaving

Alfie to his fend for himself. When she was drunk she would often scream at him if he got in her way. She would stumble past him in her drunkenness and often kick him out of her way if he tripped her up or got under her feet. Quite often she would be sent sprawling across the floor as he scrambled around her legs to get her attention. She would throw things at him, beat and abuse him. Sometimes she would even stub cigarettes out on him to make him stop crying when she was drunk. Then, she couldn't bear to listen to him cry so she would throw him back into his room. The rashes and scabs he had on his backside were so bad they would bleed and pus.

He would rummage through the bins looking for scraps of mouldy food that had been left on tables or the floor. He would sit for days in the same soiled nappies. On the rare occasions that she was of sober mind, she might give the odd affectionate hug. But every time she looked at him, he reminded her of what a disgusting excuse of a human being she was. She remembered how and why he was here; she had used her body to pay for drugs again. Poor little Alfie was the result. She despised herself, and that was the reason she ended up smashed every single night.

He was three years old the day the door was smashed through and Social Services came in and rescued him. His mother hadn't moved for ages. She had been asleep on the bathroom floor and she was never going to wake up. Alfie was so hungry he had crawled into his mother but she lay still on the floor where he sat staring at her face. He was so filthy, emaciated and weak from malnutrition and infection. His ribs were protruding from his tiny frame.

The stench was so overwhelming that, as they hammered through the door, they had to cover their noses and mouths as they all reeled back violently from the stench of her dead body and excrement. A neighbour had complained that the smell was foul and had grown increasingly worried about the child that had been crying for days on end.

She had been dead for three days when she was found lying on her back, face up on the bathroom floor. Her features swollen and purple coloured, her face and hair smeared with dried vomit. Earlier that morning, having still been blind drunk from the night before, she had staggered to the loo and lost her balance and collapsed. She smashed her head on the toilet bowl as she went down, knocking herself out cold. In her unconsciousness, she had been sick, swallowed the vomit and had choked to death.

Thankfully, Social Services had saved poor little Alfie Tyler that day for he would surely have died if left for much longer. He was taken straight into hospital and kept there under strict observation. He was instantly put on a drip to rehydrate his poor, starved body.

Several months down the line, his sores were healed and his skin eventually recovered from the pusing wounds that bled and wept. To this day, the scars still remain and will forever. Images sometimes flooded his mind when he looked back on a childhood filled with fear and sadness. He was kept in care and was shipped out to foster homes and children's homes, but he never settled. He ran away from the children's homes that took him in and by the age of twelve he was living on the streets, homeless. He was stealing and pick-pocketing to survive. He'd eat from bins, soup kitchens and homeless centres when he could get to them. Social Services always tried to find him and brought him back, but he would run away again and again. They would re-home him somewhere new, desperate for him to find that love and secure home that he needed.

By the age of thirteen or fourteen he had fallen in with a group of youngsters, all homeless and living in squats through the city. Always on the run from the police, they would steal cars, shop lift, thieve and mug. One night, they had stolen a car and had smashed it up at the top of Stratford High Street. The other kids scarpered, but Alfie was straggling behind. It was pouring with rain and he didn't know where to go. He had lost his crowd and wandered aimlessly around as the night set in. In the end, he curled up in the doorway of a cab office. It was so cold and windy that Alfie had pulled all the rubbish bags from a nearby bin and covered himself with it to keep the cold off. He was wrapped up in a plastic bag to keep any warmth in. He pulled the hood of his sweater tight around his face and buried himself as low to the ground as possible. Eventually, with the sounds of the night surrounding him, he drifted off to sleep.

The following morning he was woken up by a kicking and a mumbling of someone clearing the rubbish back up into bags. A sudden gasp followed as the owner of the shop doorway realised that there was a body buried underneath the rubbish that had been strewn across his doorway. "Oh my goodness!" said the gentle voice of a man, and he started pulling the rubbish away from the boy cowering in the corner. "It's ok, I won't hurt you, kid," the man said to Alfie, sensing his fear.

Alfie peered in fright as the man held his hand out to help him up. "My God, child. What an earth are you doing here?" Alfie didn't answer but lowered his eyes to the floor. The man could see then that he was homeless and in need of a good bath and home cooked meal. He helped Alfie to his feet. "Won't you come inside for a hot drink and some shelter at least?" He had a kind face and twinkly eyes. Something said to Alfie to go with him; he'd finally be safe.

That kind man was Karl's dad, Ed Bateman. He owned the cabbies and he took Alfie in and gave him a roof over his head, a warm, dry bed and food and asked no questions. He treated him with kindness. Ed had finally rescued Alfie and saved his life. Alfie would be forever grateful to him and his new-found family – Ed and his wife, Kathy, and their two sons, Karl and Kane. Karl was almost ten years older than Alfie, so he treated him like his younger brother. Kane was two years older than Karl and they all got on well together but Alfie bonded more with Karl than Kane.

When Ed finally retired from the cabbies, Karl and Kane took over. Alfie worked for Karl, being his little side kick, and doing all his running around for him. Kane was completely different to Karl. Karl had the brains to run an organisation, whereas Kane soon got bored and moved onto money lending.

Alfie had settled here. He decided to shorten his name to Al instead of Alfie and was never ever tempted to cut his losses and run away again. He finally felt wanted, a feeling he had never experienced before – and he liked it. They really made him feel like part of their family.

Tony had listened to Al's story with such empathy and sadness. "Bloody hell, mate! And I thought I'd had it rough!" Tony couldn't believe it.

"Life's a bitch, mate," Al laughed. "I was lucky that Ed found me, God knows where I'd have ended up, eh?"

Tony didn't really know much about Kane, and Karl hardly ever mentioned him. The brothers were close enough that they would bail each other out of problems, but they didn't speak very often – unless there was trouble afoot.

"Anyway, that's enough of that shit," Al brushed off a flicker of a memory that shadowed across his face. Tony felt privileged that Al had shared this with him.

Tony had been so engrossed with Al's story that, as he looked up, he suddenly realised that they had arrived at their destination.

Chapter 30

THE meet had gone well, and several hours later Al and Tony were on their way back to Karl. Tony was feeling much better in himself; Karl had been right. A good drive out and a chat with Al had made him realise his life wasn't that bad at all. He looked at what he had in his life; a good money earner, good friends, a gorgeous girlfriend, his health – not bad for a twenty-year-old. On that note, he needed to call Suzie. She would be at the flat now. He had still been thinking seriously about the whole commitment issue. He felt that, seeing as they had been together for over two years now, maybe it was time to get engaged. He thought he should really grab this whole serious relationship idea by the horns and go for it. He wasn't interested in going out with the boys and pulling women anymore – he could still window shop. He was happy and he was sure Suzie was too.

The pair pulled up outside the cabbies, Karl was there and he came out. He was pleased to see Tony a lot more upbeat and positive. "Thanks for the prep talk earlier," Tony said quietly to Karl.

"Anytime, mate," Karl said patting his shoulder. "That's why I'm here! Have a good evening.

What you got planned? Anything nice?"

"Actually I have," Tony smiled as he bid goodnight to Karl and Al and headed off home.

Fishing into his pocket, he pulled out his mobile phone. He'd give Suzie a quick call and see where she was. He was replaying over and over in his mind how he would ask her to marry him.

Would he get down on one knee traditionally?

He didn't have a ring to give her yet. She was such a fussy one. He'd better take her to choose a ring. Chances are, she wouldn't like the one he chose. He dialled the flat telephone. Strange – it just rang and rang. He'd let it ring a bit more in case she was in the bath. She'd eventually answer it.

Upstairs in the bathroom Suzie could hear the phone ringing. *Oh fuck off!* she thought, as she felt the familiar gut-wrenching upheaval coming again. *Jesus*, she thought to herself. *Why was she so sick?* She'd been hanging down the loo for the past half hour. Surely it couldn't have been something she'd eaten. She frantically cast her mind back to her meals over the last twenty-four hours. As she threw up again she felt the wave of sickness pass over; she'd been feeling bad all day.

She was sweating now too. She laid down on the floor and pressed a cold damp flannel to her head. One minute she was ok, then the next a wave of sickness took her over and she just physically couldn't control it. There was no way she could go out tonight with Tony for a meal. He'd understand when he came home and saw how sick she was. All she could think of doing now was getting herself back to bed and resting before the next bought came.

Tony rang off. He'd try again in five minutes. Maybe she'd popped out to the shops. He'd be home in fifteen minutes anyway. He wondered if Suzie would see the romantic side if he bought her a jelly ring to put on her finger when he proposed. Probably not – but he'd give it a shot anyway. He saw an off-license and pulled the car over and parked up, chuckling away to himself. He could picture her face now; *"Suzie, will you marry me?"* and he pulls a jelly ring from his pocket and slips it over her finger. *Worth a laugh*, he thought, as he headed inside the shop.

It hadn't been more than five minutes when Suzie thundered through to the bathroom again, hand over her mouth to stop the sickness from projecting up the hallway and the bathroom walls. *This is insane*, she thought, as she hung over the toilet rim, retching. Suddenly, an awful sinking feeling came to mind. She hadn't had her period. She scrambled to her feet and headed back to the kitchen to grab a glass of water and her handbag. She downed the water, wiped the perspiration from her forehead and fished about in her handbag for her diary. The phone started ringing again. "Damn it!" Suzie said, snatching it off its cradle. "Yes?" she snapped into the receiver.

"Hey, it's me," Tony said. "I've been trying to call you. You ok?"

"Oh ... yeah ... sorry ... I was in the bathroom," she said. Although she could hear Tony chatting away, she had no idea what he had just said. She was trying to count back the days since her last period. If this diary was correct, she was late. A whole week late.

"So, what do you think then?" Tony went silent on the other end of the phone.

"Sorry . . . I missed that. Say it again," Suzie said, still only half-listening.

"I said, shall we go somewhere nice for dinner this evening? There's something I want to talk to you about."

Suzie wasn't really interested in what he was saying. All she could do now was get a test, and quick; she had an awful gut feeling.

"Sorry, babe. Not tonight, I feel rough and just wanna go back to bed." With that she hung up the phone as the next nausea wave took over her body and she darted back upstairs to the bathroom.

Tony's mobile flat lined. *Terrific!* he thought. He wasn't looking forward to spending the night indoors with her now. She sounded miserable and annoyed. He could feel the bag of jellied rings weighing down in his pocket. He'd been so excited and had a speech all planned out in his head. It would have to wait for another time now. She didn't sound like she was in the mood at all.

His fingers darted into the bag of sweets and he took a few rings out. "Waste not, want not," he said. He decided to swing past the Rose on the way home and grab a few pints. There was bound to be more exciting company in there rather than heading straight home if she was going to bed anyway.

About ten minutes later, a small figure wrapped up in a tracksuit and coat headed out of the stairwell and up to the shopping parade. If she hurried, she could catch the late night supermarket before they closed.

The shop bell made a dinging sound as she opened the door to alert staff that someone had entered. The checkout girl, casually chewing gum with an open mouth, glanced up at Suzie and looked annoyed at being disturbed and went back to reading her *Women's Own*. Suzie made her way round to the aisle of toiletries and pharmaceutical items. Her eyes frantically scanned the shelves until she saw what she needed. There, next to the medicated creams and ointments lay the home pregnancy testing kits. She grabbed one and hurried to the checkout; she needed to get home before Tony did and also before she starting vomiting again. The fresh air had seen her well and held off the nausea waves for now.

As she walked up to the checkout, the girl raised her eyes from her magazine. She rang up the kit in the till. "Five ninety-nine," she said slowly. The gum she was chewing could be seen rolling about in her open mouth. She cast a knowing glance at Suzie and raised an eyebrow. Suzie huffed impatiently; she wasn't in the mood for small talk now. She thrust the money across the counter, and shoved the kit deep into her coat pocket. The girl tutted at her and gave her the change. Suzie snatched it out of her hand and stormed out of the shop, slamming the door behind her. The shop assistant wasn't phased and went back to reading her magazine, smacking her lips together attempting to blow bubbles with her gum.

It was barely ten minutes later and Suzie was curled up on the bathroom floor after another sickness bought. She tore open the packet of the kit and read the instructions,

Remove cap, hold the absorbent tip pointing downward directly in your urine stream for at least 10 seconds until it is thoroughly wet. Replace cap and wait for 5 minutes. Results shown in window – a blue line for negative and a blue cross for positive.

Simple enough, she thought. She couldn't understand how this had happened. She and Tony were always careful and used protection. She sat on the toilet and waited to wee. There was no way she could go through with this if she were. Her parents would be furious for a start; she was only just nineteen and wasn't ready to be a mum. She could barely look after herself. She certainly wasn't ready to settle down yet.

After she had replaced the cap and washed her hands, she sat on the floor of the bathroom and waited. *Jesus Christ, this was the longest 5 minutes ever.* The flat was silent, the only noise she could hear was the kitchen clock downstairs, ticking away those long minutes. She never realised how loud that damn clock was, *tick tock tick tock.*

Oh come on, surely that was five minutes by now. She was just thinking that she hadn't thrown up for a while when a sudden wave of sickness took over and she was again hanging over the side of the toilet bowl vomiting. By the time she has composed herself much longer than five minutes had passed. She looked at the stick laying on the floor . . . there would definitely be a result now. She splashed cold water on her face and then, with trembling hands, she turned the stick over to see what it said . . .

Chapter 31

IT was past midnight when Tony tiptoed – or tried to tiptoe – through the front door. He'd had slightly more to drink than he should have. He was shushing himself to try and be quiet. He hadn't meant to stay out all night, but she hadn't called him to see where he was. She didn't care – that was obvious. Well if that was the case, he was going to show her who cared or not. He would sleep on the settee then. Probably for the best, as he looked at the stairs and decided he probably couldn't tackle them anyway. He didn't realise how steep they were. It seemed much easier to just sit on the sofa – he'd deal with the stairs later. He was just going to rest there for a bit. He kicked off his shoes, laid back and stretched out. *This is a very comfy sofa*, he though. So comfy that within less than a minute he was snoring away.

Upstairs in the bedroom Suzie had heard Tony come in. She opened her eyes and looked at the clock 12:14 a.m. She rolled over and tried to go back to sleep, pulling and hugging the duvet tighter around her.

It was 7:05 a.m. the following morning and Suzie had already paid the first of her visits to the bathroom to be sick. She was fine during the day. It was just mornings and evenings – classic morning sickness. She got herself together and quietly crept downstairs. Tony was still asleep on the sofa and the sunlight was just starting to stream in through the curtains. He'd feel dreadful when he woke up so she decided to leave him there to sleep it off.

Grabbing her coat from the hallway, Suzie left the flat. She had arranged to meet Tasha later that morning for a coffee to tell her the news. She just needed to stop off at the chemist on the way.

"OH MY GOD!" Tasha exclaimed, blinking at her with her heavily made-up eyes and thick black lashes. "Are you sure?"

Suzie emptied her bag out onto the table. Six pregnancy tests all tumbled out.

Tasha looked at Suzie. "What the hell!"

"I needed to be sure," Suzie shrugged. "They all said the same result . . . positive."

"What the fuck are you gonna do?" Tasha asked Suzie, eyes welled up with tears.

"I don't know," she sobbed, ramming all the tests back into her handbag.

"Have you told him?" Tasha asked.

Suzie shook her head "I don't know what to say to him. He didn't come home till well late

last night . . . and he was drunk. I said I didn't feel like going out so he stayed in the pub all night. He didn't even call to see if I was ok." Suzie looked pale, like she was going to be sick. "I feel like shit,

Tash. I don't wanna eat . . . I look appalling. Look at my face. I look fucking hideous."

Tasha smirked. "Well . . . I have seen you look better, hun. Listen, Suzie, this isn't gonna go away. You cannot ignore this. You have got to sort this out. It's not like you can hide it and forget about it. People will start to notice in a few months . . . know what I mean?" Tasha pointed to her belly, which was flat now, but soon enough would give the game away.

Suzie sat with her head in her hands. Just behind them in the corner of the café sat a woman with a baby. The baby had started crying loudly and the woman was desperately trying to shove a bottle into its mouth to settle it and stop the crying.

Tasha looked at Suzie. "Urrghh you've got all that to come."

"OHH DON'T!" Suzie wailed, fear written across her face. The baby still hadn't stopped crying and it was getting louder and louder and wasn't settling for its bottle or a dummy. The woman picked up the baby and was holding it against her shoulder rubbing its back. On and on the crying went. "I can't deal with this!" Suzie stood up and, swinging her bag over shoulder, stormed out of the café.

Tash looked at the woman who was smiling apologetically back at her. "Oh kids eh? Who'd have 'em!" Tash said as she hurried out of the café after Suzie.

"How am I spose to even think with all that fucking noise in my ear?" Suzie cried.

"Calm down, mate. That's what babies are all about. You haven't got the patience to look af-ter a goldfish . . . let alone a fucking baby!" Tash said back to her.

Suzie tutted at her friend. "What am I gonna say to him, Tash? He's not gonna wanna know is he? And to be honest, I don't wanna know either. I'm not ready for this . . . this is too big a deal for me. We have only just started living together."

Tash put her hands on Suzie's shoulders and turned to face her. "I can't tell you what's right or not . . . but if you ask my opinion . . . I'd say he would run a mile. He won't wanna know at all. You're gonna scare him off with this. He's a player, Suzie. He's not the settling down type, is he? You always say that you can't trust him as far as you can throw him! You know how I feel about him . . . he's not for you. He's a wrong'un."

Suzie looked hurt. "Bloody hell, Tash! Don't hold back, mate, will ya . . . say what you think!"

Suzie replied.

"Just saying . . . that's all. He's a loser! But it's your decision," Tash said nonchalantly. "I've got to head off," Tash continued. "Call me later. Good luck with telling him!" she called over her shoulder.

Cheers, thought Suzie, *she was gonna need it . . .*

As she put the key into the door of the flat she could hear Tony whistling in the kitchen. He didn't sound too hungover.

"Babe, I'm home," she called out.

Tony's head popped around the doorway from the kitchen. "Hiya, how are you feeling now?" he said, walking towards her to give her a cuddle. He noticed her dark eyes and tired face.

"Yeah, I'm ok. Just felt a bit sick yesterday. Must have been something I ate," she brushed it off. "What happened to you last night anyway? You got back late," Suzie questioned him, as he was busy making a cup of tea for them. She could still hear Tasha's words in her mind . . . *'he's no good . . . you can't trust him'.*

"I nipped into the Rose and Crown and got chatting, babe. You know what it's like . . . time flies and all that shit."

Tony passed over a mug of steaming tea to her. Instantly she felt her stomach turn. "Oh God, I don't want that!" she refused the tea.

Tony looked hurt. "What's up?" he questioned.

"Nothing. I've just had a cup with Tash . . . that's all," she lied. Tony made a face at the mention of Tash's name. "What's up with you now?" Suzie said snappily.

"Nothing! Calm down! Bloody hell, you spend all your time with her, that's all. I just get a bit sick of her name constantly . . . Tash this . . . Tash that," Tony said honestly. Tony thought for a second before saying, "Let's go out this evening. Just you and me. Let's have a nice meal somewhere, and a chat. There's something I wanna talk to you about."

"Yeah, that'd be nice," Suzie said quietly – thinking there was something she needed to talk to him about too . . .

Chapter 32

"TABLE'S booked for eight o'clock. Babe, we're gonna be late!" Tony hollered up the stairs. He had been waiting for her now for ten minutes. *Why the fuck was she taking so long?* Tony was on a high today as he'd had the call from Rob to say he could pick him up from rehab tomorrow.

"I'm coming!" Suzie yelled out as she flushed the remaining dregs of vomit down the toilet. She washed her mouth out, splashed cold water on her face and stood back and surveyed her appearance in the bathroom mirror. *Fuck . . . that would have to do.* She combed her long blonde hair, added a touch of lipstick and waltzed out of the bathroom, trying very hard to act normal.

"You look gorgeous," Tony said, as he patted her backside and they headed out of the flat.

As they sat at their table glancing over the menus, the waiter started pouring the wine.

"Oh, not for me," Suzie said, covering the top of her wine glass with her hand.

Tony stared at her. "What! Why?" he quizzed her.

"Still feel a bit sick from yesterday, babe," she said. "I'll just have water please," she turned and smiled at the waiter.

"Yes. Certainly, miss," the waiter smiled and topped up her water glass.

Tony looked at the waiter and said nothing. He had a bottle of champagne being chilled out the back. He reached into his pocket and felt for the jelly ring he had bought yesterday – he had even put it in a ring box. He hadn't eaten them all last night. He had saved one, the one he wanted to put on her finger when he asked her to marry him. He felt nervous. He had planned his speech and had booked a table at his favourite Italian restaurant. He would wait until the dinner had been cleared away and then he'd get down on one knee and pop the question – and hopefully she would say yes. Everyone would applaud and she would be happy and Tony scores points again!

Suzie was looking at her watch. "Keeping you from somewhere, am I?" Tony joked.

Suzie smiled back at him. "Don't be silly. I just wondered what the time was."

Dinner was a quiet affair; Suzie didn't order any starters and she picked at her main. Tony had bought her a proper steak dinner, but she seemed distant and uninterested. She certainly didn't have any appetite. A few times she had excused herself and nipped to the ladies'. Maybe she was still feeling under the weather. She looked like she had a lot on her mind. *Best get this over and done with then and put a smile back on her face*, he thought, while Suzie was in the toilets again.

As she sat down, Tony looked at her and smiled. He took her hands in his and cleared his throat. "Suzie, you know I love you, babe, don't ya?" She looked at him and nodded. "Well I've been thinking, and . . . I was wondering . . . well . . . I was gonna say . . . coz I do love you . . . and we are living together now and . . . " he was stumbling. The prepared speech had gone out of the window.

"What?" she asked.

"Well . . ." Tony grabbed the ring box out of his pocket and slipped down onto one knee in the middle of the restaurant and looked up at her. He opened the box displaying a jelly ring and, smiling, he said "Will you marry me?"

Suzie gasped, the rest of the restaurant gasped too and waited with baited breath to hear

Suzie's answer. "*Is that a jelly ring?*" was the first thing that everyone heard.

"Errr . . . yeah. I wanted to pick a ring together. It's just a funny ring till we can buy one,"

Tony said quietly and winked at her.

Everyone was still waiting. Tony was still down on one knee. Suzie looked about the restaurant; she was absolutely gobsmacked. She had no idea Tony would have wanted to get engaged.

Everyone was looking at her – she loved an audience and she certainly had one now.

"YES! YES I will!" she replied loudly. Tony slipped the jelly ring onto her finger. Everyone clapped and cheered and Tony jumped up and hugged her. The champagne cork popped and the waiters were pouring out two glasses of champagne. Suzie went to refuse and covered her glass.

"Oh, come on," Tony said. "Just have one. We're celebrating ain't we!"

It may have been the bubbles in the champagne, it may have been the excitement of the marriage proposal, or may simply have been the pregnancy that made Suzie so violently sick that night. Tony felt awful for her as he lay and listened to her retching and hurling in the toilet until the early hours of the morning.

"Spose a blow job's out of the question then?" he said, as she crawled back into bed. He was only half-joking as she took a swipe at him.

She held up her hand with the jelly ring on it, "It's quite sweet really," she smiled. "I don't know whether to keep it or eat it!"

Tony laughed. "Keep it till it's replaced with a proper one." He snuggled her into his arms and drifted happily off to sleep.

Tasha's got it all wrong about him, Suzie thought as she lay in the darkness. *She's got him all wrong. She doesn't know him at all.* She thought tonight was the sweetest thing he'd ever done. *How on earth was she ever going to tell him about the baby?* she thought, as she gently ran her hand over her tummy.

Chapter 33

"YOU'RE WHAT?" Tasha screamed down the phone in disbelief.

"Engaged! We're engaged! I'm flippin' well engaged!" Suzie said again. She kept repeating it, as if it weren't true. Suzie told Tash all about the whole restaurant and the ring. "It was soooooo romantic," she cooed.

"I'm sure it was," Tasha said disapprovingly. "And did you tell Mr Romantic about the other thing yet?" an awkward silence fell over the phone.

"No, not yet. But I will," Suzie replied.

"The longer you leave it, the worse it'll be," Tasha spoke of 'it' like it was a disease. Suzie ran her hand over her stomach again.

"I will, I will. I just need the right time."

"Where's Mr Romance today then?" Tasha sneered.

"He's picking Rob up from rehab. He is so excited to tell Rob our news. I think he's gonna ask Rob to be his best man . . . talking of which . . . you will be my chief bridesmaid, won't you?"

"Of course. I'd love to," Tasha said quietly.

* * *

"YOU'RE WHAT?" Rob yelled at Tony in disbelief.

"Engaged. I asked her to marry me. She said yes," Tony's was a much shorter version of the story than Suzie's.

"Blimey! That's great news, mate!" Rob said.

"I'm gonna need a best man, Rob. Think you're up to it?" Tony said.

Robs face lit up. "Abso-fucking-lutley!" he yelled.

Tony had arrived to collect Rob that morning from the clinic. He had been signed out and given a follow-up program of meetings to attend. The journey back to London seemed to take no time at all. Tony filled Rob in on everything that had happened whilst he had been away. Rob was shocked about the whole Aaron fiasco and being arrested, the court hearing and so on.

"So I'm waiting on a crown court date as we speak," Tony concluded his story.

Rob was gutted for his mate. "It'll be ok though won't it, Tone?" he asked.

"I hope so, mate . . . I hope so," came Tony's unsure reply.

As they pulled up outside his flat, Rob reached over and hugged his mate, "It's so good to have you back, man" Tony said to Rob, slapping him on the back.

"I'm all good now too, Tone. I promise. I can never thank you and Karl enough for what you did for me."

Tony looked at him. "Rob, just don't let *yourself* down more importantly," Tony winked at him.

Rob jumped out of the car and ran over to hug his mum who was waiting patiently at the front door to see her son. As Tony drove off, he had a good feeling inside.

Over the course of the next few days, plans had to be made; phone calls had to be made, parties needed to be organised and most importantly rings needed to be bought.

Tony pulled up outside the cabbies and walked in; it was unusually quiet today. Karl and Al were going over some paper work in the front office. There was no Colette today either. *Must be her day off,* he guessed. They both looked up as Tony walked in.

"Whoa! What are you looking so chuffed about today?" Al commented.

Tony sat down on the swing chair, swung his feet up on the desk and proceeded to tell them all about his proposal and the ring. Immediately, Karl was on his feet and shaking Tony's hand.

"Congratulations, Tony. What fucking fabulous news, well done, son."

"Well done, mate," Al congratulated him too. "When's the party then?" he asked.

Karl insisted Tony have their engagement party at the wine bar. They could have a Saturday in a few weeks' time. He said he'd pay for the lot; they could have a buffet and a band too. Tony couldn't possibly accept that generous offer from Karl, but arguing about it wasn't going to change Karl's mind. He was adamant. He wouldn't hear another word about it. Al said he'd help Tony sort out the band and the food. That was that!

That evening. Tony spoke to Suzie and told her about Karl's offer for the party. Suzie couldn't believe how generous Karl was. The following day the decision was made and Tony called Karl back to accept his offer and to thank him again.

"Better there than the lap dancing club I spose," Suzie said sarcastically. It was all booked for three weekends' time. That gave Tony plenty of time to go out and get a nice sparkler of a ring for Suzie. A real Bobby Dazzler!

He called Ernie up in Newcastle that evening and told his dad the latest news. "Oh blimey. That's nice, Son," was all Ernie had to say. He wasn't a big fan of Suzie. He thought Tony could do better and thought his son had chosen unwisely. "*She's not trustworthy*," Ernie would say. "*Can't trust her, she's got suspicious eyes and I don't trust her!*"

Tony was well aware of his dad's opinions when it came to Suzie. He let it all go over his head. Ernie wasn't a fine example to counsel on relationships. Tony didn't take it too much to heart.

"You will come back for the party, Dad, won't you?" Tony said.

"Margaret and I will be there, yes," he didn't sound too convinced though.

Tony never told his mum about the engagement. She had never even met Suzie for that matter. He hardly ever spoke to Dot these days. He still got birthday and Christmas cards, usually sent via 'Jacki post'. Jacki would pop over every now and again to drop stuff off. Tony rarely asked after his mum.

Suzie's parents also were dubious. But as long as their baby was happy, they were happy. They felt Suzie was punching well below her weight and deserved someone who was, well, 'better' quite frankly. They certainly didn't like the fact that they thought he hung about with some rather unsavoury characters. His temper also left a lot to be desired. Tony, again, didn't give a toss. Her parents had wanted their daughter to marry a suited and booted business man that worked in the city poncing about with shares and banking. Tony would show them that he could provide for their daughter; didn't need a poxy briefcase and a silver spoon up his arse to do so, he thought to himself.

Everyone else seemed genuinely pleased for the happy couple. Except maybe Tasha.

Chapter 34

THE weeks flew by and it wasn't long before Shooters Wine Bar was decorated with balloons and banners displaying *CONGRATULATIONS TO THE HAPPY COUPLE!* There was champagne at the door and the buffet was a lovely spread. A live band was playing on the stage and the place was full of friends and family all wishing the happy couple well. The place was heaving. The ring that sparkled on Suzie's finger was absolutely stunning. Everyone complimented her on the diamond that shone like a bright light – Suzie was in her element.

Ernie and Margaret had travelled down from Newcastle and Jacki had come along with her boyfriend, Stuart. Suzie's family were there; her parents and a few aunts and uncles had also arrived and were all mingling in well. Ernie was having quite a chat with Suzie's dad. This pleased Tony as they'd never really met up before. Dean was standing at the bar with Andy and calling the drinks in.

Colette had come with Karl – Suzie took an instant dislike to Colette. Colette did look stunning as always and Suzie just couldn't handle the competition. Colette had walked straight up to Tony and, throwing her arms around his neck, she had planted a whopping big red lipstick kiss straight on his lips. "Ahhh, what a shame you're off the market now, kiddo," she teased him playfully, holding onto him a little longer than Suzie had cared for. Tony blushed a crimson colour in his cheeks. Shy wasn't usually a trait of his, but Colette had this effect on him. Suzie stood there open mouthed staring at the blatant cheek of this woman!

"Who the fuck does she think she is?" Suzie said, turning to Tasha, who was also standing there unable to believe this woman.

"See, I told you. He's a snake. Can't be trusted. What do you expect!" Tasha said in a matter of-fact tone. However, Suzie wasn't standing there listening anymore. She had moved alongside Tony who had released Colette from his arms. Tony was still blushing as he turned and looked at Suzie, who was looking at him sour-faced.

"What?" he said.

Suzie ran her thumb along his lips and smeared the offending bright red lipstick across and down his chin. "Not really your colour, babe, is it? She couldn't hold the sarcasm out of her tone and, flicking her hair over her shoulder, she stormed off through the crowd to mingle.

Al was standing next to Tony. He began laughing at him. "She's a livewire that one. I thought the colour kinda suited you, mate, but I'd probably go and wash it off if I were you."

Tony smirked and shrugged his shoulders and made his way to the toilets to wash his face. *Fucking hell! This shit stains!* he thought, as he rubbed at his chin where Suzie had smeared it unnecessarily. It was very red now and sore from excess rubbing. *Jealous cow,* he thought. He had to admit though, he had liked the Colette kiss! He would store that one away in the memory bank.

As he came out of the gents', he decided to nip outside in the garden and see who was there and have a quick cigarette. It was a nice evening and the cool breeze was welcoming from the stifling heat inside. Rob was outside sitting on the bench chatting to Tania. Tony ambled over; they weren't in a deep and private conversation and immediately Rob shifted over so Tony could join them. "What's happening, people? Nice to see you, Tania," Tony said as he lit his cigarette and drew a deep breath in, before blowing the fumes out into the night air. He lent down and gave Tania a kiss on the cheek.

"Congratulations. Can't believe she snared you," Tania said dryly.

"Oh, bitchy!" Rob said, standing up.

"I'll get us some drinks. Same again, Tan, Tone?"

"Yes please," they both chorused.

"Do I detect a hint of sarcasm in your tone, Tania?" Tony said, grinning at her.

"Oh, is it that obvious? You're too good for her. She doesn't deserve you. There . . . I said it."

Tony took a long drag on his cigarette and blew little smoke rings at her. "Why do you say that? What makes *me* so special that's she's not good enough for me?" he asked.

"I just think she'll shit on you. She'll use you . . . she's gonna hurt you. I can see it a mile off." Tania really had a dislike for Suzie. The feeling was mutual; they didn't like each other. Girls could be so bitchy! Tony thought.

"Since when did you become a relationship expert? Let's look at your love life."

"It's not me or my love life we're talking about here. It's yours and I just think you could do better, that's all. It's just my opinion," Tania said honestly.

"Like who? Who do you have in mind then?"Tony said flirtatiously, giving Tania a little grin and a wink. He knew she liked him and he liked her too, but seeing as she was Dean's ex he would never go there. He stubbed his cigarette out as Rob came back with their drinks.

"Tania was telling me that she's off to a rave later tonight after your bash, Tone," Rob said innocently. Tony instantly shot them both a look of disgust. "Bloody hell, mate. Calm down! I'm not going!" Rob back pedalled quickly, realising how that must have sounded.

Tania jumped in quickly "It was my fault, Tone. I fucked up. I had forgotten where he'd been and I asked him if he wanted to come but he refused and said *no*, Tony. Don't panic! He's a good boy now, ain't ya, Rob!" Tania put her arm round Rob's shoulders and gave him a friendly hug.

"Yep. I am," Rob said proudly.

"Glad to hear it too,"Tony said forcefully.

On that note, Tania stood up. She downed the vodka and tonic Rob had got her. "Listen, I'm gonna bolt. I've wished half of the happy couple well . . . as well as they can be. I'll pass on the other half if that's ok! Good luck, Tone . . . you're gonna need it, baby!"

Tony stood up and folded Tania into his arms, giving her a huge hug. "Take care, babe," Tony whispered into her hair, kissing the top of her head. He hoped she didn't get too wasted again.

He hated the thought of these raves.

Tony could feel the burn of someone's eyes boring into him. He was still holding Tania and, as he stepped back and let her go, he saw Tasha standing there watching him – her eyes like fire with smirk on her face.

Tania leant over and hugged Rob with a big bear hug too. "Have a good one, babe," Rob said, kissing her cheek. Tania turned and left the pub through the garden without even going back inside.

Tony sat back down and lit another cigarette.

"I'm off to the gents', man. Back in a sec," Rob said, scooting off in the direction of the loos.

"Oh dear, oh dear. Suzie wouldn't have liked to see that, would she?" Tasha's patronising voice was low and seductive as she purred at Tony like she was stalking and tormenting her prey. She was standing in front of him now, holding an unlit cigarette in her mouth. He lent forward and offered to light it for her. She took a deep drag as she breathed in and then blew the smoke out very slowly, never taking her eyes off Tony.

"Suzie wouldn't have liked what? What did you see, Tash? Eh? Me saying goodbye to a dear friend of mine?" Tony challenged her.

"Looked like more than that to me," she sneered.

"Well it would do to you, wouldn't it!" he snapped back.

"So hostile, Tony, aren't we?" Tasha said as she sat down on the bench next to him. "I don't know why you don't like me," she carried on. Tony rolled his eyes; *here we go*, he thought. "I've never done anything to upset you. After all the nice things I say about you as well. I'm always backing you up. I'm hurt."

"Oh yeah, right, Tasha. I'm sure . . . like . . . what . . . coz you're my number one fan right?"

Tony was trying his hardest to be civil to her.

Tasha continued "Well I say things like *'she's mad going off with other guys still when she's got you now.'* But you know what they say . . . leopards don't change their spots do they, Tony? Once a cheat, always a cheat." Tasha took a deep long drag on her cigarette and, still keeping her eyes on Tony, she slowly exhaled, blowing the smoke into his face before she carried on. Tony slightly moved his face away and then back to her as he listened.

"Bless Suzie. It's just her way. I'm sure she doesn't mean any real harm. And I know she loves you, well, she says to me she loves you. But I do say to her that she's crazy. I mean, if I had someone like you, I'd never cheat on you." Tash sat down next to Tony and was running her hands around the back of his neck, drawing small circular rings in the back of his hair. Tony shifted uncomfortably and felt frozen to the spot. He didn't know whether to slap Tash away or listen to some more.

Curiosity had got the better of him and he stayed where he was. She must have been telling lies – Suzie wouldn't do that to him. Mind you, Suzie had been off-ish for last month or so. "She has been a bit distant lately, but she's snowed under and busy at work," Tony said, backing Suzie up.

Tasha laughed loudly, stubbing her cigarette out by Tony's foot and lingering her foot over his long enough for Tony to feel uncomfortable and move his foot. "Is that what she tells you? Don't forget I work there too, Tone. It's not busy. It's not busy at all. She'll never meet anyone like you again." Tasha was running her hands up and down through the back of Tony's hair now. He shifted on the bench to move away from her touch. Suddenly Tasha was too close to him. She pulled his face round to meet hers. "She's no good for you, Tony. She's still sleeping about with some of the guys at work . . . ask anyone . . . they all know she's using you. She doesn't love you. She won't make you happy. She loves winding you up. She loves it. That's what this is, this fiasco of an engagement party . . . one big wind up."

Tony went to back away and say something but Tasha had pulled him onto her lips and kissed him hard and deep and desperate, almost suffocating him. It took a few seconds to sink in and register what had happened. Tony pushed Tasha back off him. "What the fuck!" he spat at her.

"She's spose to be your best friend! What the fuck are you doing?"

"I'm serious, Tony. She's no good for you. She's a liar, you deserve better than that." "Oh like you, ya mean?" Tony blurted out.

Tasha nodded as she was pulling Tony towards her again. "I can make you happier than she will." Once more, she kissed him hard on the lips. He was trying to resist her, he really was. Her hand was holding him tight by the back of his neck as her tongue delved in and explored his mouth.

No! This was wrong, so very wrong.

Tony gave a final push and pulled away from Tasha's vice-like grip. "I can't do this to her. Not with you. You're bang out of order, Tasha." He shoved Tasha away from him and she stumbled back slightly.

"Don't say I didn't warn you when she shits on you from a great height," she said to him spitefully. He shook his head in disbelief and pushed past her and made his way back to the party.

"Ah, babe. I've been looking for you. I was just coming out to find you. Your dad's been chewing my ear off!" Suzie was heading towards the garden.

"Sorry, baby. I got chatting . . . I won't be a sec." Tony felt flustered and sick. Confused, he slipped into the gents' toilets to splash cold water on his face. He needed to think. Tasha was really something else. *Was it true what she said? Did Suzie still act like that? Was she sleeping with blokes at work?* He couldn't believe Tasha had just come onto him and kissed him. Who would do that to their best friend? Maybe it was true then, otherwise why would she say all that? What she said made no sense though; he felt so hurt and confused.

Rob came into the loos, "Tone, what's up? Suzie said you came charging in a bit distressed. You ok? You ain't got bad guts have ya? Coz I fucking have. Have you eaten the buffet? Maybe it's the vol-au-vents! I went back outside a minute ago and you'd gone . . . only that mate of Suzie's there, that Tasha bird. She's a funny one, ain't she? I quite fancy her though . . . is she single? Maybe we could double-date some time?"

Tony turned and looked at Rob and smiled, "Yeah maybe, mate. I'm ok . . . just a bit too much to drink, that's all. Come on, let's get back to the party." Tony needed to digest all of this. He'd deal with it later. For now, he had to put a front on and act as if everything was ok.

Tony was unfeasibly quiet for the rest of the night. He stood with Dean at the bar for a while, chatting and mingling and trying to ignore what had happened. He painted on a smile – and played the part very well. But in the back of his mind he couldn't shake off Tasha and what she had said. He was terrified it was true. He knew Tasha was a vindictive bitch, but why deep down did he believe her and keep going over and over her words? Then there was the kiss – oh my God! The kiss had stirred something inside him – it was so wrong.

It was almost twelve midnight. Everyone was merry and dancing, however Suzie wasn't behaving normally either. As the evening wore on, Tony thought there was something very wrong with this picture. He had noticed that she wasn't drinking much – she was usually knocking back vodka and cokes like they were going out of fashion. She'd normally be legless by now. Tony thought he had heard somebody ordering her just a straight coke. She would normally be found throwing herself around the dance floor with Tasha. She seemed very-low key this evening. Maybe Tasha was right, maybe this was just a front. The party was in full swing but would be winding down soon.

Tony walked back outside; he needed to get his head straight. No one was outside. He was all alone – he could think here. He sat on the bench and lit up a cigarette. Suddenly he could hear a phone ringing. It was his mobile. He fished it out of his pocket – *who could possibly be calling him at this time?* Everyone he knew was here at the party.

Chapter 35

TONY was up and on his feet and running through the bar "ROB! ROB!" he was searching frantically for Rob. Rob was standing talking to Tasha – of all people. "ROB! WE'VE GOTTA GO NOW! IT'S TANIA!" Tony ran past, grabbing Rob as he went and dragged him out of the bar and up the road to his car.

"What the fuck's happened?" Rob was scared and scrambling to keep up with him.

"I'm not too sure. Some girl called Carly rang my mobile. I couldn't really understand what she was saying – she was begging me to come and get Tania. She kept saying it over and over again." He leapt into the car and started it up and shot off into the night.

"I know her. It's Tania's mate who they go clubbing with."

"Whereabouts exactly did she say they were going to this rave, Rob?" Tony demanded to know.

Rob thought for a second. "Bethnal Green, at the back of Cambridge Heath Road, at the warehouses by the lights I think. Tony, what's happened to her?" Rob was panicking.

Tony didn't answer. He just put his foot down and drove faster, jumping a set of traffic lights that had just turned red.

"Where the fuck has he gone now?" Suzie yelled to Tasha, demanding to know as she saw the two of them running out.

"Told me he was meeting up with Tania," Tasha said.

"Fancy leaving your own engagement do to go and meet another bird!"

Suzie glared at her friend. *Maybe she was right about him after all – he had been acting really strange this evening. Firstly, having that stupid Colette bitch all over him, smothering him with her whore lipstick. Then disappearing for ages outside. Tasha said she saw him with his hands all over that Tania tramp too.* Suzie didn't like it at all. She knew Tania fancied Tony – *and now he's buggered off to meet up with her, leaving her alone at their engagement party! Surely he wouldn't have just run out on her? What the hell was she going to tell everyone? Wait till he gets home! He's going to be very, very sorry for this! In fact – fuck it*, she thought, and decided she wasn't going home. She would stay at Tasha's instead. *That would teach him to run out on her. Who the hell did he think he was? If he thought for one minute that getting engaged meant he could start treating her like this then he could think again!* She was starting to feel really sick again and rubbed her belly.

"Tash, can I stay at yours tonight? I don't wanna go home alone."

"Course, babe. Come on, let's go," Tasha said, linking her arm through and into Suzie's. The two girls left and Suzie drove back to South London to Tasha's.

Tony had called Karl on the mobile from the car and explained what had happened. Karl said he would deal with the situation and wrap the party up for him. He told Tony to call him as soon as he had any news. Karl looked for Suzie to explain but he couldn't find her anywhere – she must have left already.

As Tony and Rob pulled up into the industrial estate off Cambridge Heath Road, Rob could see the warehouses and knew by now that the rave would be in full swing. It was almost 1 a.m. Tony had been trying to call Carly back on her mobile but there was no answer. Panic was setting in now and he needed to find Tania and make sure she was ok. He wanted to see what had happened and what she had taken. He thought back to when Rob had his bad one. He didn't want to see Tania in that state. "Oh God, please let her be ok," he silently prayed.

Tony's eyes were scanning the people that were milling around outside. He couldn't see

Tania or Carly anywhere. Rob ran off to see if he could find them or anyone that knew them.

"Tony. Tony Hayes. Is dat you?"

Tony spun around to see Benny Ofarma looking at him. "Oh fucking hell! Benny Ofarma!

Long-time no see, you alright?" Tony was hesitant, as he thought back to the last time he saw Benny.

Benny stepped forward and held his hand out to Tony. Tony shook it instantly.

Benny smiled and said "Yeah, I'm good, I'm good. Just checking shit out, man. Ya know what I mean," Benny looked at Tony shiftily. "You at dis rave den?"

Tony looked shocked, "Oh . . . *no!* I don't do raves, man. I'm here to pick someone up. Is this rave anything to do with your lot, Ben?" Tony asked.

"Nah, man. As it goes, I'm here to chat with da lot dat are running it . . . turf shit . . . ya know what I mean."

Tony was looking about to see if Rob had found her yet.

Benny continued talking "Listen, Tony. About what happened . . . I'm sorry, yeah?" "A lot of water under that bridge, mate. I'm sorry too," Tony said apologetically.

"No one ever beat me like dat before . . . respect to ya!" Benny laughed.

Tony grinned "Sorry, mate." Again, the pair shook hands. "I don't mean to be rude, Benny but I've gotta go, mate. I'm looking for a mate of mine. She called and needed picking up. I gotta find her."

"What's her name? I saw a girl come out a while back. They were round the back there waiting for the ambulance. Dunno who she was doh."

"Cheers, mate," Tony said, patting Benny's shoulder and turning away to run around the back.

"Take it easy and catch up soon, bro," Benny yelled after him.

Tony ran to the back of the warehouse. He could see the reflection of the blue flashing lights as he turned the corner – the ambulance was already there. A crowd of people had gathered around and he could see Rob standing over there. Rob looked up. "Tony, Tony. Come quick! It's Tania!" he was crying.

Tony barged his way through the crowds and there was Tania, in the back of the ambulance, strapped down to a stretcher and covered with blankets with breathing apparatus over her face. The paramedics were rushing around to get her in. "What the fuck has happened?" Tony turned to Carly. She was sobbing and shaking her head.

"Ok, we are cleared to go. Stand back," they said as they locked Tania's bed in. One of the paramedics jumped in beside Tania and was holding up tubes and breathing equipment. The doors slammed shut behind them.

"Wait! Where are you taking her?" Tony asked, trembling with fear.

"The Royal. Follow us." The driver ran around to the front of the ambulance and hopped in.

With lights flashing and sirens blaring, they made their way out of the estate and into the night.

Tony ran back to his car with Rob and Carly, who was struggling to keep up. Tony grabbed his cigarettes from his pocket and shoved one into his mouth and lit it as he drove off chasing after the ambulance to the hospital.

"I didn't know what to do, Tony." Carly was really crying. Rob had jumped into the back alongside her and was cradling her in his arms. "She said she felt weird and breathless . . . she wanted to go outside . . . she just kept saying 'call Tony.' She gave me her phone and said to call you.

She said she needed you here and you'd help her . . . you'd come and pick her up. That's when I called you. I gave her loads of water and she was fine. We were outside, then she started fitting and collapsed on the ground. She was being sick."

" Who called the ambulance?" Rob said.

"There was a bloke that was sitting on the kerb next to us. He said he'd anonymously call them as she looked really bad and needed to get to hospital. He had a bottle of water and said to get as much in her as possible . . . but she was just vomiting it back up and all frothy at the mouth," Carly sobbed.

Tony was shuddering at the thought of Tania. "WHAT DID SHE TAKE?" Tony was yelling angrily now.

"A pill," Carly cried.

"WHAT PILLS? WHERE DID YOU GET THEM FROM?" he shouted.

"I don't know. Tania had them . . . said she got them a few days ago," Carly was really crying and Rob held her tighter.

"Have you taken one?" Rob said calmly.

"Yes . . ." Carly said, shuddering with uncontrollable sobbing. "I only took half, I think Tania may have took a couple . . . I'm not sure."

"FOR FUCK'S SAKE!" Tony was furious. In no time at all he pulled up outside the A&E unit.

He flicked his cigarette away as he jumped out of the car and ran into the hospital.

The ambulance had arrived and Tania was being rushed in already. A big nurse stood in the doorway and held her hands up to stop Tony from charging any further. "We can take it from here, sir," she reassured him. "Please take a seat in the waiting room and someone will be with you shortly."

"Is she ok? Will she be ok?" Tony was saying over and over, trying to look over the nurse's shoulder to see Tania.

"*Sir, please just take a seat. We are doing everything we can. Please try and remain calm and take a seat. I'll be back soon.*"

The forcefulness of the nurse made Tony step back. Rob and Carly were behind him now.

"Let's just sit here," Tony said, motioning to a row of plastic seats behind them.

"Someone had better call her mum and dad," Rob said. "They should *be* here."

Carly started crying again. Tony looked at Carly's face all teary and smeared with makeup. "Pass me your phone, I'll do it," he said as he snatched the phone from Carly's hand and stormed outside.

Within half an hour, Tania's parents were seated alongside Carly in the waiting room, anxiously awaiting news of their daughter. Tony and Rob were outside pacing up and down, waiting and smoking constantly,

The nurse had come out and asked Tania's parents and Carly to go through to a room with her so she could take down all Tania's personal details and the night's events. "Are you immediate family?" she had asked, referring to Tony and Rob. That was all that was allowed in at this time. As they weren't, she had asked them to wait outside for the time being.

Tony checked the time on his watch – it was almost 2:45 a.m. He wondered if Karl had managed to get hold of Suzie. He'd better not call her at this hour; she would go mad if he woke her.

Tony and Rob wandered back in to the waiting area. "Wanna tea?" Rob asked, fishing around in his pockets for some loose change. Tony shook his head. He didn't want tea. What he did want, however, was Tania to be ok. He wanted this night to not have happened. He wanted to be anywhere but sitting here watching time tick slowly away. He didn't want tea.

"No thanks, Rob," he said eventually.

Rob sat down with his tea, which could only be described as resembling dirty dish water. Tony gave the tea a look of disgust and pulled a face.

More than half an hour had passed. Tania's parents and Carly came back out and were sitting in the waiting area again. The nurse had explained that Tania had suffered a huge seizure due to the amount of ecstasy that was in her system and that this had led to a cardiac arrest. They had her stable at the moment, but she was in a very bad way and her heart rate was dangerously low.

Tania's mum was crying. Tania's dad was just sitting there stony-faced unable to believe what had happened. They had no idea Tania frequented these places. Carly's parents had also been called.

Suddenly, a very loud alarm sounded and chaos descended on the emergency unit. Doctors and nurses began running back up to Tania's room. "She's gone into cardiac arrest again," a nurse was overheard saying, as she ran into Tania's room and slammed the door shut behind her.

Tania's dad jumped up and began pacing up and down frantically in the waiting room. Rob leapt up, knocking the foul tea crashing to the floor. Tania's mum and Carly were crying. Tony felt so helpless. They could do nothing but continue to wait . . .

Chapter 36

IT was 4:55 a.m. The emergency room fell quiet. The on-call doctors all stood back in defeat. "Are we all agreed?" The team all nodded in silent agreement. The lead doctor placed the defibrillator paddles back. "Stop CPR," he said. He checked the stopwatch on his coat and let out a long, hard sigh. This was devastating. They had tried everything to save her. They had been working on her for almost an hour, such a shame. She was only young.

"Time of death, four fifty-six a.m." A nurse was writing this down in the notes. Another nurse was pulling the stickers and tubes from Tania's lifeless body. They pulled the sheet up and over her head. She was gone.

The door opened slowly into the waiting room. Everyone held their breath as they looked up. The solemn look on the face of the nurse said it all. "I'm so, so sorry," she said, shaking her head.

She was almost in tears herself. "We really tried everything we could to save her. I'm so sorry."

Tania's mum collapsed on the floor and began wailing uncontrollably "NOOOOOOOOOO!" she was screaming. "NOT MY BABY! NOT MY TANIA!"

Tania's dad was immediately by her side. He was holding his wife and crying too. Carly dropped her head into her hands and sobbed. The colour had drained from Rob's face and he started crying. Tony stood up; he was running his hands wildly through his hair. He was utterly speechless. He didn't know what to do. It wasn't true. Surely not. It couldn't be. Not Tania.

* * *

Tony put his key into the door of the flat. It was almost 8 a.m. when he had dropped Rob off. He kept going over and over in his mind about last night. He couldn't believe she was gone. Tania was gone. Less than ten hours ago he was holding her in his arms. He could remember what her hair smelt like, the perfume she wore, her smile as she kissed him goodbye. He was absolutely gutted.

Rob was just sobbing the whole way home. The two hardy exchanged any words at all – there wasn't anything to talk about. They both took the opportunity and made the most of the silence to think about her. The police had arrived at the hospital to take down statements. Tony had explained that he received the call from Carly on his mobile to go and get them and had arrive to pick her up, but was too late and the ambulance was there before him. There wasn't much more he or Rob could tell the police, so they were allowed to leave. Tania's parents were unable to speak to them at that time.

The flat was dark and cold. It showed no signs of anyone having been there. Tony wearily climbed upstairs to the bedroom, but it was empty. Suzie wasn't there. She hadn't slept there at all. *Where the fuck was she? Why hadn't she been home?*

Karl had closed the party down, so he knew she wouldn't still be at the wine bar. He grabbed his mobile – there were no missed calls. *What the hell was going on?* Maybe she had gone back to stay with her parents at their house. Ernie and Margaret had gone back to Jacki's flat that she had just started sharing with Stuart.

Tony dragged his tired body into the front room. He pulled the curtains closed to block out the sunlight that would be streaming through soon and collapsed onto the sofa, kicking off his shoes and slipping out of his jeans. He couldn't think about anything at the moment. He closed his eyes and slipped into a deep sleep. The next time he opened them it was 3:35 p.m. and his mobile was ringing. "Suzie?" he said into the phone as he quickly answered it before it rang off.

"Tony . . . it's Dean. . ." Dean was quiet, almost whispering into the phone. Hearing his voice, Tony suddenly recalled last night. He'd suspected he would have to be the bearer of bad news but, by the sounds of it, Rob had beaten him to it. Tony looked at his watch and realised the time – it was late afternoon. He'd completely passed out.

"Is it true . . . what Rob told me . . . is she dead?" his voice was quivering.

"Yeah . . . it's true," Tony said softly into the phone. He could feel his heart heavy in his chest as he said the words.

Dean was angry and upset. "I fucking knew something like this would happen!" he ranted.

"Why the fuck wouldn't she listen to any of us? And now look . . . look what's fucking happened. FUCKING HELL."

Tony didn't know what to say to him. He stayed quiet for a moment. "Dean?" he said after a while. The phone call had gone silent on either end. Tony heard Dean sniff as he was trying to hide the tears that were streaming down his face.

How Tony wished he could turn back time. If only he'd stopped her from ever going to that rave. If only he'd stopped her from leaving the party. All these regrets.

The two friends finished their conversation with plans to meet up later in the pub. Tony needed to call Suzie and find out where she was. Rubbing his eyes, he dialled her number. It was ringing, no answer. That was strange. He tried again. Suddenly he remembered Tasha's advances on him and he shuddered. Still Suzie's phone was just ringing and ringing. As he hung up he walked over and turned the TV on. A picture of Tania was staring back at him on the screen. There were two main news stories that filled the headlines that evening – Tania's death being one of them. The other was of a young man who had been shot dead in Bethnal Green behind a night club.

'ECSTACY PILL CLAIMS ANOTHER VICTIM' was the headline. **"A drugs alert has been issued following the death of 19-year-old Tania Davies from East London, who died from a heart attack following reports that she had taken the drug ecstasy at a private rave held in Bethnal Green, London, last night. Tania had collapsed and was rushed to hospital by ambulance after suffering a seizure, followed by a cardiac arrest, shortly after leaving the club. She died three hours later in the early hours of this morning in hospital."**

Tony couldn't watch anymore; he turned the TV off. He needed desperately to get hold of Suzie. *Why wasn't she answering her phone?* Pacing around the kitchen he was getting frustrated. Her phone was just ringing. He had texted her too and she wasn't responding. Maybe she was annoyed at him. Surely she had seen the news by now and would have at least called him about it. She would certainly have known what had happened last night.

Tony decided he would call Karl. "I'm at the cabbies with Al, mate. Come over," Karl said.

Tony hung up the phone and, grabbing his car keys, headed over.

Karl and Al had the portable TV on in the back office when Tony walked in. There was Tania's face on the evening news. Karl stood up and gave Tony a hug. "I'm sorry, mate. I really am. That's terrible. I know she meant a lot to you." Tony thanked Karl for his kind words. She *had* meant a lot to him, there was no denying that.

"What rave was she at last night?" Al said.

"Back end of Cambridge Heath Road in Bethnal Green. Why?" Tony asked.

"Some geezer had his brains blown out there too last night," Al said, pointing to the TV that was now showing a picture of a young man. The news said that he had been shot in the head at close range.

"I think I know what that's all about," Karl said, reaching over and switching off the TV.

* * *

It was nearly 6 p.m. on Sunday and a very tearful Suzie was curled up on Tasha's sofa.

"Shall we put the TV on, Suz?" Tasha asked.

"No! I don't wanna watch anything." Suzie had been in her pyjamas crying all day.

"I'll make us some more tea," Tasha said, getting up from the sofa.

"I hate him, Tash. I hate him," she sobbed.

Tasha picked Suzie's phone up. "You've got another two missed calls!" Tasha said.

"I don't care. I don't want to speak to him," Suzie sobbed as she got up and went to the toilet.

After a minute or so, Tasha noticed the answer machine in the corner was flashing with a message on it. *'You have one message'* it announced, then a long beep . . .

"Suzie." It was Tony's voice. He must have rung here last night

looking for her. *"Suzie, it's Tony. Where are you, babe? I can't get hold of you. I wondered if you'd be with Tash. I need to speak to you. Please call me back when you get this"*

It beeped and said *'end of message.'* Quickly, Tasha held her finger over the delete button and within a second the message had been deleted and was gone forever.

Suzie came back from the toilets and was still ranting. "It's our engagement party and he's supposed to be engaged to *me* and spending the night talking and dancing with *me*," Suzie carried on. "And he's in the garden flirting with that fucking Tania bitch. And then he's got that whore Colette hanging off him, smothering him in her fucking whore lipstick. Then he disappears off all fucking night and doesn't even contact me and tells you he's off to meet fucking *Tania*!"

"Suzie . . . there's something I really need to tell you about last night . . . but I'm not sure how to tell you . . . " Tasha said quietly to her friend.

"I must be the biggest fucking mug in the world to have trusted him," Suzie went on without hearing Tasha. "He's so wrapped up in fucking *Tania* . . . and he fucks off to meet up with *her* and leaves *me* on my own at *our* fucking party! Who the hell does he think he is?"

"Suzie! I really need to tell you something!" Tasha snapped.

Suzie stopped her rant and looked at her friend with concern from under her lashes. "Oh yeah . . . what?" she said tearfully.

"I didn't know how to tell you . . . I didn't want to upset you anymore, but seeing as you are gonna finish with him anyway and get rid of *y'know*," Tasha pointed to Suzie's stomach and carried on. "It's about Tony . . ."

"What is it?" Suzie asked quietly.

"Ok. I'm just gonna say it . . . ok . . ." Tasha braced herself.

"What?" Suzie looked at her friend now, waiting for her to speak.

"Well . . . basically . . . he tried it on with me last night at the party. Outside in the garden when you were inside," Tasha said.

"He did *WHAT*?" Suzie was beside herself now. "AAARRGGHH! I *really* fucking hate him now. What did he do?"

Tasha was beside her friend now, holding her in her arms and hugging her. "Ah, Suzie. Don't get upset. This is why I didn't want to say anything. I told him straight. I put him right in his place!" Tasha told Suzie how Tony had tried to kiss her and that she had pushed him off and said that she'd threatened to tell Suzie about him. "I told him you deserved better and that I was gonna tell you everything. *See!* I knew he was a snake!"

"Oh my *God!* I knew he couldn't be trusted. And with my best friend as well!" Suzie was balling by now. "I hate him. I hate him! And first thing tomorrow, I'm going to the clinic for an appointment. I don't want this fucking baby of his. I don't ever want to see him again. I'm *so* lucky to have a friend like you," Suzie wailed.

Tasha gave her friend another hug. "It'll be ok. I'll come with you tomorrow. We'll both book the day off and I'll come with you. And when you go in, I'll be with you." *That'll teach that scum bag,* Tasha thought to herself.

Suddenly, Suzie's phone started ringing again. Suzie looked down – it was Tony. She picked up the phone and threw it on the floor and smashed it. "FUCK HIM! He can go to hell for all I care."

"I'll make us that tea," Tasha said, getting up and kicking the broken phone across the room as she sauntered off into the kitchen.

* * *

"That's weird," Tony said to Karl. "Her phone was ringing and now it's just cut off like a dead line."

"Maybe she's in a bad area, mate. Try her later. You know what these phones can be like." Karl had recently bought more new mobiles. These were smaller and square, just slightly bigger than Tony's hand. Tony had got two – one for him and one for Suzie.

Tony was still at the cabbies with Al and Karl. He wanted answers to questions. He wanted to know where she got the pills from. He wanted to know who had put the rave on. He wanted someone to blame for Tania's death.

Carly didn't know the answers to the questions either, and the following morning the police arrived at her house to question her. Carly was in such a state and had told the police all she knew. She didn't know where the pills came from, who had supplied them, who was running the rave they were at. She didn't know anything. All she did know was that Tania had taken them voluntarily and so had she. Tania's death was indeed caused by a heart attack from the result of taking the ecstasy tablets. The hospital had run all the blood test and the results had come back conclusive: *Death By Cardiac Arrest – Caused by Narcotic Overdose.*

HANGING TOUGH

Chapter 37

IT had been just over a week since Tania had died. Tania's parents had finally been allowed to arrange her funeral and it was to be held a week on Thursday.

A few days later, Suzie sat quietly in the waiting room of the hospital. It was 7:30 a.m. She had been given an early morning appointment by her GP and was waiting to be admitted into the day centre for the abortion. Tasha had taken the day off to be with her.

"Sure you wanna do this?" Tasha asked her quietly.

"I'm sure," Suzie said quietly. She hadn't spoken to Tony now for nine days. After smashing her phone up, he couldn't call her anyway He had left a few messages at her work but she had refused to call him back. After what Tasha had said he'd done, she'd never forgive him ever again. First Colette, then Tania – and now her best mate. It was unforgivable. She couldn't and wouldn't be with a man like that.

"You know what you need?" Tasha said.

Suzie looked at her. "Yeah, what?" thinking it would be probably be the last thing she needed right now.

"You need a night out with the girls! Get back out there and start enjoying yourself. You've been moping about all week over that prick. It's time, obviously once today is over, that you get out there and get back on that horse . . . a new start. Forget him! Best way to get over one bloke is to get under another one . . . right?"

Suzie knew that Tasha meant well, but she wished she would just shut up and let her get today over with.

`Suzanne Thomas,' Her name being called out made her look up. It was her turn to go in and see the nurse. She needed to get gowned up and wait to go through to theatre.

"That's me," she called quietly.

"I'll be waiting for you when you wake up, babe," Tasha said, hugging her friend. Suzie stood up, Tasha held her hand and gave it a tight squeeze. Suzie let go of her hand and turned to follow the nurse through the corridor. She looked back one last time to give Tash a half-smile, as she disappeared into a large room and the doors closed behind her.

Tasha was going to be waiting here for at least two hours. She settled back in her seat and looked around the waiting room, wondering what all the other girls were in here for. She looked over and spotted a magazine table across the room. She walked over and shifted through the magazines and papers. Someone had left a local paper lying on the table. Startled, she reeled back in shock. There, staring at her from the front page of the *East London Advertiser* was Tania's picture.

Oh my God! She was dead!

Tasha couldn't believe what she was reading. She knew about the man getting shot that night which was also featured on the front page, but she hadn't heard about Tania. So that must have been where Tony and Rob went that night. For a split-second, Tasha had a wave of guilt wash over her. That must have been why Tony had left her the message on the answer phone to call him back urgently. He must surely have been going out of his mind with worry, what with losing Tania and not hearing from Suzie. Tasha felt like a bitch. She thought about her friend lying in the other room – *what would Suzie think when she found out? Would she feel guilty for not answering his calls?* It would be too late by then. There was nothing Tasha could do now. She decided to say nothing. Going back to the magazine table she stuffed the paper to the bottom of the pile so it wasn't staring up at her and took a magazine from the top instead. *Ignorance is bliss,* she told herself.

It was almost two and a half hours later. Suzie opened her eyes to find a pretty young nurse sitting at her bedside holding her hand. For a second, Suzie didn't recall what had happened.

"You're ok. You're in recovery," the nurse said, smiling at her.

Suzie's mouth felt dry and she tried to swallow but her throat hurt. Suddenly her eyes welled up with tears. "Is it over?" she asked the nurse.

The nurse stroked her hair away from her forehead. "Yes, it's over now. Your procedure was successful. Just close your eyes and rest for a while. You might feel slightly queasy from the anaesthetic, but you're ok. We'll get you up and out soon."

Suzie laid back and closed her eyes again. She could remember the anaesthetist talking to her before and asking her to count backwards. She can't remember where she got to, but suddenly she was here, awake, and it was all over. She'd had her abortion. She ran her hand over her stomach, she felt nothing. A dull ache maybe deep inside, but nothing else. She looked down at the empty space on her finger where the engagement ring had been only a week before. All that was there now was an intravenous drip into the back of her hand. She had been so happy, so in love. She didn't understand; it didn't make sense. *How could it all go so wrong so quickly? Why had all this happened?* Again, she ran her hand over her stomach and let it rest over her belly button this time. She was sorry and she felt a deep sadness in her heart – a sadness she would never forget. She had known from the first instance that the baby would have been a mistake. She was also adamant she didn't ever want to see Tony again. Ever.

That night she was curled up in her own bed at her parents' house. She never told anyone where she had been that day. *This is the first day of the rest of my life,* she thought, as she quietly cried herself to sleep. *I'll never trust anyone ever again.*

Chapter 38

1989

THE atmosphere was tense at Gatwick arrivals. Flight number BA734 had landed on time as scheduled. The serious crimes police unit, headed up by Inspector Maguill, waited patiently at passport control. "Here we go. They are coming. Easy . . . easy. Get ready to go," he motioned to his unit over the police radio.

As the five young men all approached passport control with their passports in hand, Maguill and his men swooped in. "Samuel Ichanga? I am arresting you on suspicion of the murder of Martin Perry. You have the right to remain silent, but anything you do say may and will be used against you as evidence in a court of law." Maguill had thrown Samuel face-down on the floor and was handcuffing him behind his back. Samuel cast his head round and looked back to his friends. He saw they had all been arrested, cuffed and were having their rights read to them. As Sergeant Maguill and his men led the five lads out and through to the waiting squad cars, he couldn't help feeling smug at his capture.

* * *

The persistent ringing of his phone surely signalled bad news. Benny leant over and, grabbing the phone, he answered it impatiently. His eyes widened as he listened for a minute. "Oh NO! Fuck it!" he spat as he hung up. He sat bolt upright and wiped the sleep out of his eyes. He needed to think. "Fuck fuck fuck!" Benny didn't have much time to act. He got his stuff together as quickly as he could, checked his passport and his wallet and left for the airport.

Benny Ofarma checked his bags onto the next flight from Ibiza to the UK, as planned. The phone call hadn't been good news. It was from Corinne, Samuel's girlfriend, from the UK. She had told Benny how Samuel and his mates had been arrested at the airport two days ago for Martin Perry's murder. She had been told by another gang member to alert Benny that the Old Bill knew which flight he would be on and would surely be waiting for him to arrive.

Martin Perry belonged to a gang which organised raves in run down warehouses throughout the UK. They dealt mainly in ecstasy pills and, as ecstasy was the new high, acid and raves were all the rage. Everyone was popping these tabs like they were going out of fashion. Benny and his crew worked for a rival gang and the two gangs had come to a mutual agreement that they didn't cross on each other's paths. They didn't work the same areas – bad for business too, so this had been settled after a number of fights and turf wars. They kept putting raves on in the same areas and eventually the two heads of the gangs met up and up mutually agreed that they would have their own areas. It was all settled by a handshake.

This seemed to work well until Benny got wind that the other gang had put a rave on in Bethnal Green at Cambridge Heath Road. Benny and his crew decided to drive up there and check it out. They arrived and, sure enough, the rave was on. They hung around outside for a while to assess the situation. After a while, Benny saw a young girl had been taken outside. She didn't look well and it wasn't long before she was being rushed away to hospital by ambulance. *Maybe another victim to fall foul of the ecstasy overdose*, he had thought.

Benny watched on quietly from the shadows. A while later, he saw Martin Perry from the rival gang. He was outside and seemed to be dealing out pills. Benny waited for the group to disperse and then walked up behind Martin. In a single sweep, he had slung a bag over Martin's head and dragged him by the bag around the back and down an alleyway. They were only supposed to beat him up and scare him. Benny had really laid into him, kicking him. Suddenly, Samuel whipped the bag off his head and dragged him onto his knees and pulled a small gun from his back pocket and thrust the barrel of it against Martin's temple.

"Leave it out, Sammy" Benny said, taken aback. "That's too far, man!"

Samuel was fixated and staring coldly at Martin. "Nah," he said, "you gotta fucking teach dem. Teach dem mother fuckers that we mean fucking business."

"Sam, leave it!" another of Benny's gang was yelling. "We've beat 'im up. Done with it. Leave it, man, leave it."

Martin was on his knees, eyes squeezed shut tight, trembling with fear with the gun still digging into his head. Benny was shouting. Everyone was shouting now. Samuel was shouting too. "Gotta be taught a fucking lesson," Samuel spat. "Fucking mugging us off."

Benny went to lunge for the gun in Samuel's hand.

The shot that rang out in the clear night air and was drowned out by the sounds of the rave. Martin's body slumped to the ground. The hole in the side of his temple pumped the last dregs of his life through it. Samuel fell back in shock. He hadn't meant to kill him. He just wanted to scare him. That wasn't supposed to happen.

Benny jumped over and grabbed the gun off the floor. "Fucking hell, man!" he said. "Get outta here *now!*"

Panic flooded amongst them. Samuel was in shock. Jason, another member of their gang, started dragging Samuel across the ground. "We gotta go, man. Come on!"

Samuel started crying. It was dawning on him what he had done. He was splattered in Martin's blood. A black BMW with blacked out windows and a private plate screeched to a halt alongside the kerb. Benny's mate, Vincent, flung open the doors and was shouting for them all to get in. Benny and Jason stuffed Sam into the back seat and slammed the doors. They speed off in the darkness leaving a huge pile of lifeless retribution lying in the alley.

The front pages of the newspaper the following day had described it as a *'savage attack on a poor young man whom had been shot at close range in the head'*. The portrait picture of Martin that was featured painted him as a clean-cut young family man. A husband and father who was enjoying a night out with friends and had been brutally murdered for no apparent reason.

The very next day, Samuel, Benny, Vic, Jason and two others all boarded flights to Ibiza to lay low for a few days. This was a whole heap of trouble and they needed to work out what was going to happen next.

The airport loud speaker rang out **"Flight now boarding at gate seven to EINDHOVEN."**

Benny walked up to the gate and handed over his boarding pass. The young air stewardess looked up and smiled, "have a nice flight, sir."

"Oh I will," Benny said. "I will."

"Last call for flight number BA744 leaving for Gatwick. Last call leaving for Gatwick. Could the last remaining passengers please make your way to gate number four. Gate number four. Your flight is ready to leave. Thank you."

The tannoy was still calling for the last remaining passenger to board the UK flight back to Gatwick that evening. Eventually, the cabin crew had to locate and offload the luggage that had been checked in by the missing passenger, who was now going to miss his flight. They couldn't hold the flight up any longer.

Benny had settled back into his seat for his flight to Holland. Having booked his luggage onto the UK Gatwick flight he had then bought himself a one-way ticket to the Netherlands. From there he could make his way back to Ghana. There was no way they were going to get him. He had outsmarted the Old Bill this time.

Chapter 39

TONY was furious! "Fuck her, if that's how she wants to play this. Let her fucking sulk," he had told Rob and Dean in the pub earlier that week, after not having any calls returned or any messages from her whatsoever. "It's not like she's *not got* a mobile phone, is it? I fucking *bought* her one! I've got enough shit going on at the moment without her adding to it with her stupid fucking tantrums. Bollocks to her and her fucking mate!"

Tony told Dean and Rob what Tasha had done at the night of the party. "OH MY fucking

God!" Rob said. "Gutted. I well fancied her!"

"That's not quite the point here, Rob. It's Suzie's best mate," Dean said, as usual in Tony's defence.

"Yeah well, still gutted. I'd love to have her throw herself at me . . . I wouldn't say no," Rob whistled.

"If it's got a pulse you wouldn't say no, Rob," Tony said.

"Any hole's a goal mate," Rob said smugly.

"You're so inappropriate!" Dean said, frowning at Rob.

"Get the pints in, Rob" Tony said, rolling his eyes at him.

It was the night before Tania's funeral. Tony was still angry about Tania and he was no closer to finding out who had supplied her with the drugs. He wanted to find them. He wanted to kill them. He wanted to hurt them the way he and everyone else was hurting from losing Tania.

Someone was going to pay for this.

Karl had said to Tony that the rumour on the streets was that Benny Ofarma's gang had been responsible for the shooting that same night that Tania had died. Tony was shocked – he had been talking to Benny that same evening outside the rave. He had told Karl about the conversation they had had. He knew Benny's lot weren't responsible for the rave.

Tony was like a ticking time bomb waiting to go off. He was so angry about Tania. Unfortunately, that night it was a small group of army paratroopers that had come into the pub that were going to get the full front of Tony's anger . . .

Tony had had quite a lot to drink by now. As fast as the pints were being bought, Tony was knocking them back and ordering another one. "Pint!" he said, calling the round in again. Dean and Rob couldn't match him pint for pint and after a while they gave up chasing and let him carry on downing his pints. One after another. Dean had had enough and decided to stop drinking and keep an eye on Tony – he could feel trouble brewing. Tony needed to get drunk and let some anger out, but they were fearful as to where it would be directed.

A few of the regulars in the Rose were watching Tony from across the bar. "What you fucking staring at? D'ya want a fucking photo?" Tony slurred at them.

"Jesus, Tony. You're knocking them back a bit tonight ain't ya? What's a matter with you?" one of them said, keeping a safe distance from across the bar.

"Mind yer own fucking business!" Tony slammed back at them. "Fucking nosy cunts!" Tony said loudly, pointing to his own nose. "Keep that outta my fucking business."

"Tone, mate. Come on . . . calm it. It's ok," Dean said, trying to simmer him back down again.

He was like a pressure cooker that was ready to go any minute. "It's ok, they didn't mean any harm – you've known them ages. Don't be that like that to 'em, come on," Dean said, resting his hand on Tony's arm.

"I've pushed out shits longer than I've known them cunts!" Tony laughed at his own joke and as he stood up he toppled slightly, sending his stool flying backwards across the floor. Rob was laughing now and so was Tony. "Oh fuck it." he said drunkenly. "I'm having a slash . . ." and he turned in the direction of the gents' toilets.

As Tony walked round to the toilets, he pushed past some TA paratroopers that were there having a drink at the bar. He stumbled into them, sending a pint that was sitting on the bar sprawling across the floor. "Oopsie! Sorry, mate," Tony said all bleary eyed. He stepped back to look at the men and noticed their t-shirts. They were all dressed in matching regiment t-shirts, which read *'Paratroopers TA Regiment'* and their numbers.

"You fucking will be sorry . . . spilling my pint!" said one of the troopers. He stood up to face Tony.

"Ah s'alright, mate. Calm down. I'll get you another one," Tony said, slurring, trying not to focus on the fact that he desperately needed a wee.

In a flash Dean was standing behind him. "It's alright. I'll deal with this. Another pint please," he said, calling the barmaid over to replace the pint.

Tony turned and headed into the toilets. As he stood there finishing up, he replayed the paratrooper conversation in his mind – *'you fucking will be sorry.'* He kept repeating it over and over again. *Will I now?* he thought. He felt the rage start burning up from his feet; a burning rush that was making its way up through his veins. He couldn't control it.

Zipping his jeans up he smashed his way back from the toilets and, in one sobering instance, was standing face to face with the offending paratrooper. "Fucking sorry?" he screamed in his face. "I'll be fucking sorry will I?" With that, Tony rained a continuous stream of punches straight into his face. The paratrooper fell to his knees and Tony continued his bombardment of punches.

Suddenly, a stool came crashing down across the back of Tony's head. As he turned around, he could see another paratrooper standing above him, wielding the remnants of the smashed stool. Tony leapt to his feet and grabbed the stool, sending the TA sprawling across the floor. He then set about beating him up with his fists. Rob had come charging across the pub and rugby tackled two of the other TAs down to the floor as they attempted to join in on the attack on Tony.

It had all happened so fast that Dean turned around and was still holding the replacement pint in his hand. "Oh well, he won't be needing that now then, will he?" Dean smirked and proceeded to drink the pint himself, knowing his friends could more than handle the situation.

Tony was like a wild animal. Between him and Rob they had taken out the entire group of paratroopers. Tony stood back and looked at what had happened, nostrils flaring and eyes blazing. The paratroopers were all on the floor, beaten up. "You bunch of wanker weekend warriors!" Tony spat at them all. He turned and looked at Dean. "Is that my pint?" he asked.

Dean stared at him. "Is now!" he said, passing the drink over to Tony and ordering two more pints.

Tony looked at the TAs who were starting to scramble to their feet. He sneered at them, "I suggest you bunch of pumped up pricks fuck off right now if you don't need a fucking ambulance.

And don't fucking come back!"

Tony noticed Ray, the landlord, staring over at him and shaking his head. "You smashing my pub up?" he said to Tony sternly.

"I never fucking started it!" Tony said, holding his hands up in the air.

The nosy regulars from earlier backed him up. "Nope, he definitely didn't start that one, guv" they said to Ray. "It was them paras."

Tony turned and smiled at them appreciatively, now feeling bad about his comment earlier. "Sometimes it helps being a bunch of nosy cunts," one of them said to Tony, grinning.

He turned around, apologised to Ray about the broken stool and went back to where he had been sitting with Dean and Rob. "Same again," Tony called another round in. "Get one for the nosy cunts over there an' all please!" Tony felt better after getting that out of his system. He needed a good fight!

It wasn't long before the three of them were all standing in the queue at the kebab shop.

"Large doner. Kill it with chilli sauce, Youssef," Tony said to the owner across the counter.

"Where you boys bin tonight?" Youssef asked. He was a lovely old Turkish man in his fifties and had known the boys since they were young. They often dropped by here after a session in the pub to soak up the beer and over the years had built up a real rapport with him.

"Same ol', same ol'," Rob replied, smiling at the old boy.

They all got their kebabs and stood outside under a street lamp. "What time tomorrow then?" Dean asked, sobering up at the thought of Tania's funeral the next day.

"Midday at the church," Tony replied. "The cars are leaving her parents' house at eleven thirty a.m. so we'll make our way straight there."

"Shall we all meet outside here at eleven and see if we can sink a quick one for Dutch courage?" Rob said, nodding at the pub.

The wake was back at the Rose afterwards so Tony was sure Ray would let him in for an early one beforehand. "Good idea," Tony said. On that note, the three parted ways and all headed home.

Tony had indeed had a skinful that night. He made his way across the estate, up the stairwell to his flat.

It was dark when he put the key in and opened the door. He stumbled on the post which had been lying there for a few days now. He bent down and, scooping the pile of letters up, tossed them onto the kitchen worktop. *He'll look in the morning now. He was too drunk to open anything tonight.*

He missed Suzie not being there; he was lonely. The flat was cold and unwelcoming to come home to. He couldn't be bothered to climb the stairs, so again he staggered into the front room. He flopped down onto the sofa and as he kicked off his trainers, his cigarettes fell out of his pocket and onto the floor. Bending down and grabbing them, he scrambled about for a light and found one. He lit his cigarette and lay back. Breathing deeply, he blew small smoke rings out. He stuck his finger through one of the rings in the air.

He started thinking about the last week's events – so much had happened. He was dreading tomorrow and the funeral. He wondered where Suzie was now. He wondered how long they would stay mad at each other for. *Would she turn up tomorrow for the funeral?*

HANGING TOUGH

Chapter 40

THE early morning sun streamed through the curtains in the front room, waking Tony from his sleep. The light was stinging his eyes and he rolled over to get away from it. But rolling the wrong way, he sent himself flying off the side of the sofa and onto the floor waking up with a jolt.

His head hurt, his mouth was like sawdust, his eyes burned. He was thinking he may have gone a little over the top last night with the drinking. He remembered what day it was today . . .

He looked at his watch; it was 8:55 a.m. He had plenty of time to get ready. First things first, he needed a shower to wake him up properly and a cup of tea. He walked into the kitchen and as he was filling the kettle up, he noticed the stack of mail on the worktop. There must be at least four days' worth there that he hadn't opened.

He made his tea and carried it upstairs with him. He laid all his clothes out on the bed; he had chosen a smart black suit with a new crisp white shirt and a skinny black tie. Rob had meticulously polished his smart black shoes for him a few days ago and they sat in the corner, shining like new ready to go.

He turned the shower on and as he stood under the hot water it ran over his body, blasting life back into his soul and reviving him. It was a mere thirty minutes later and Tony was standing by the sink showered, shaved and admiring himself in the mirror. With a final squirt of aftershave, he gathered his stuff up and headed back downstairs. He was unusually way ahead of time today.

He clicked the kettle back on to boil and decided to tackle the post. "Junk, junk, junk, bills, junk, more bills, Dad's stuff, more junk." Suddenly he paused. There was the letter he had been dreading. It was stamped 'ON HER MAJESTY'S SERVICE - CPS', postmarked special delivery to Mr Anthony Hayes. Hands trembling, he turned the letter over and tore the envelope open. Here it was– his court date set. He scanned the letter, speed reading down to where it said the date. *Monday, May 28th.* That was six weeks from now. It was also twelve days after his twenty-first birthday. *Oh well, there was nothing he could do about it.* He stuffed the letter into his inside suit jacket pocket – he would deal with it later and speak to Karl.

It was 10:45 a.m. and time to go and meet Rob and Dean over the road. "Let's do this," he said to his reflection as he gave a final check in the mirror. He took a deep breath in, then out, and stepped out into the morning sun closing the front door behind him.

The church was standing room only. There were easily over 500 people whom had all come to pay their respects to Tania and her family. Tony, Rob and Dean had taken their seat in the church early about three rows from the back. Soft music was playing in the background. Tony saw Tania's parents and her younger brother all walk in and sit down in the front row. Tania's dad nodded and smiled a sad, half-smile at Dean as they passed.

"I cannot believe how many people are here," Dean said as he turned and looked around the church. Suddenly the organ started playing and everyone seated stood up as Tania's coffin was walked in. Everyone had been presented with an order of service as they came into the church. As Tony turned his over, there was a picture of Tania on it looking back at him. It was a beautiful picture of her; she was smiling without a care in the world. That's how Tony would remember her. He glanced over at Dean who was running his finger across the picture of her face with a sad look in his eyes.

The service was lovely. The wake was to be held at the Rose and Crown afterwards and everyone was welcome. As the three of them made their way into the pub, Carly ran up to Rob and threw her arms around his neck hugging him. Tony smiled at her and he and Dean carried on to the bar.

Tania's mum suddenly was beside Tony. "Tony, I just wanted to say thank you . . . for trying to help Tan out that night . . . and for being a good friend to her. I know how close you two were. And Dean . . . how are you, sweetheart?" She gave Dean a hug and kissed him on the cheek.

Tony didn't know what to say. He bent down and gave her a kiss on the cheek. "I'm so sorry, Mrs Davies," was all that would come out. She gave him an understanding smile and gently squeezed his arm and turned and made her way back through the crowds of people that had arrived.

They had been standing at the bar for quite a while when Tony suddenly remembered the letter in his pocket. He dug it out and showed it to Dean, just as Rob came back up to them. "Mate, that Carly's in bits," Rob said sadly. Then he noticed the serious look on Dean's face as he was reading the letter. "What's that?" he asked Tony.

"I got my court date, ain't I," Tony said glumly "When for?" Rob asked.

"In six weeks' time, just after my twenty-first . . . so you can all get wankered at my birthday with me, celebrate my twenty-first . . . then hopefully we can be celebrating as this court bollocks will be over with."

Rob's face dropped. "What date is it, mate?"

"Twenty-eighth of May. Why? What's up?" Tony eyed him suspiciously.

"Fuck it! I'm not gonna be here, Tone," Rob said.

Dean and Tony both looked at him and waited for him to carry on. "Why?" Dean repeated.

"Well . . . I've gone and joined the Army," he said. "I'll be on my six-week training program by then. I got my enrolment date yesterday. I wasn't gonna say anything until after today was over with."

"WHAT? No shit!" Dean said disbelievingly.

"You better believe it, buddy. It's the truth!" Rob said proudly.

Tony didn't say anything to start with, he just looked at Rob. "So you're bailing out on me? The biggest thing to happen to me, and you won't be there?" Tony tested him. Dean was staring from one to the other. Rob looked mortified.

"Tone, I don't know what to say, mate . . . I'm sorry," Rob stuttered. "I had no idea when your court date was . . . you hadn't mentioned it for weeks. I could probably see if I could change my training dates . . . but it wouldn't look good and . . ." he trailed off when he saw a smile break out across Tony's face.

Tony couldn't hide it any longer. "As if I'd make you change it, you knob! Come 'ere, I'm fucking with you!" Tony hugged his mate and patted him hard across the shoulders. Dean was laughing too.

"Ah, you guys are wankers!" Rob said as the relief washed over him.

"Listen, mate. It's a good move for you," Tony said.

"Yeah, well I thought so. My rehab program has finished now and I've wanted to do this for a while . . . well, ever since fucking cadets. And it'll get me proper on the straight and narrow . . . y'know what I mean. I'll make something of meself there. I'll be someone . . . not just a recovering druggie from rehab!"

"Listen, mate. I think it's a good thing for you. I'm proud of you," Tony praised him.

"You'll let me know how it goes though, the court case and shit?" Rob said nervously.

"I'll keep you informed, mate. Don't worry," Dean reassured him. "Especially if he's behind bars and can't!" he said, nodding at Tony and grinning.

Tony punched out playfully at Dean. "Oh yeah, cheers! You're fucking funny, ain't ya!" Tony looked at his watch and realised the time. "Listen, I'd love to sit here talking bollocks with the pair of ya, but I gotta get a move on. I'm due to meet Karl to go over all this shit with him," Tony said, folding the court letter and slipping it back into this inside jacket pocket. He downed the rest of his pint and stood up.

The pub had thinned out a bit now from the funeral gathering. Most people had left. There was still a fair amount of food left over on the buffet table. He had a feeling that Rob and Dean would be there for the remainder of the evening and would help clear that up. Grabbing a sausage roll he headed out of the door, waving to Rob and Dean as he went.

Tony was disappointed that Suzie hadn't shown her face at the funeral. *Heartless bitch*, he thought. She must have known about Tania – it's been all over the news. He decided that now he had his court date through, he would go and meet her tomorrow evening. She would probably be called up as a major witness in court and he needed to know she was going to be there. He stood by the side of his car and delved into his inside jacket pocket for his cigarettes. As he pulled them out, the order of service for Tania's funeral was folded up around them. He stood and looked at her for a second and a small pang of sadness flooded him again.

He jumped into his car and, opening the glove box, he stashed Tania's service booklet in there for safe keeping. He lit his cigarette and headed off towards Shooters wine bar to see Karl. He decided that, as it was Friday tomorrow, he'd take a drive over to see if Suzie was about and if she felt like talking this through yet. He needed to clear things up with her and find out where they stood now. *Were they still engaged? Was it off now?* It had been two weeks and no contact. He was still really upset that she hadn't called him at all. He pulled up outside Shooters, flicked his finished cigarette into the kerb and strode into the bar where Karl and Vernon Jackson were waiting for him. Vernon needed to go over some details with Tony as he had already been furnished with Aaron's statement.

Tony pulled up a chair – this was going to be a long night . . .

* * *

Tony checked his watch. It was 10 p.m. on Friday night. Suzie's car wasn't outside her parents' house. He had driven past Tash's place too and there was no car there either. Maybe she was out having a drink with Tash somewhere, having a girlie heart to heart as women did. No problem, he was here now. He might as well sit and wait. She probably wouldn't be too long. He settled down into his car and waited. He wound the window down and lit a cigarette. It was a nice warm night for the middle of April. He blew smoke rings out of the window and into the night sky and watched them float up. After he'd smoked about six cigarettes he was bored. He had the radio on, but that was boring him too now. He flicked it off and a silence fell upon the car. He pushed his car seat back to extend his legs and stretch out. By now it was almost 11:30 p.m. She'd be home soon, any minute, he was sure.

The next time he looked at his watch, it was 2:48 a.m. The sudden jerking of his head as it rolled forward jolted him awake. He jumped with a start. He rubbed his eyes and focused on where he was. Her car still wasn't there. She must have gone back to Tash's place. *Damn it!* Tony sat up and rubbed his eyes again. He grabbed a cigarette and, lighting it, he noticed a car coming down the road towards him. The car's headlights were bright and they dazzled his eyes. He couldn't quite make out the registration plate. The car pulled up and parked outside Suzie's place. *Was it her?* He couldn't tell. The headlights went out. It was dark. He could make out the first half of the car's number plate. It was definitely her car but still he couldn't see who was in there. *At last, where the fuck has she been?* he thought. He sat and waited for her to get out of the car. *What was taking so long? What the fuck was she doing?* Several minutes had passed and she still hadn't got out of the car. He couldn't see if it was her in the driver's seat. He finished his cigarette and climbed out of the car. He stretched his arms up in air; he was achy and cramped from being asleep. She must have been to a club with Tash. Maybe they were sitting in the car talking. *That would be awkward*, he thought. He started walking towards the car. As he got alongside level with the passenger door, he bent down and reached for the handle and swung the door open.

Chapter 41

SUZIE screamed in fright as the car door swung open. The bloke that she had been snogging didn't have a chance to react, as Tony grabbed him by the scruff of his shirt and wrenched him up to his feet and against Suzie's car.

"What the fuck?" the bloke yelled, trying to cover his head with his hands.

"Get off him! Get off him! What the fuck are you doing here?" Suzie was screaming at him.

Tony had his fist poised, ready to bury it in the bloke's face. "What the fuck are *you* doing you mean!" Tony was furious. He had the bloke around the throat and was squeezing tighter and tighter in a vice-like grip. The bloke was choking now and had lost all the colour from his face. He looked like he was going to pass out. His hands were desperately clutching at Tony's grip around his throat and he was gurgling, his eyes bulging.

"Fucking let him GO, you fucking animal!" Suzie was jumping on Tony's back now, trying to prize his hands off the bloke. "He ain't done nothing, Tony. Fucking let him *go*!" Suzie was hitting Tony's back.

"Who the fuck is he?" Tony screamed. "Tell me before I kick the cunt to death!"

The bloke couldn't do a thing and was helpless under Tony's strong hold. Suzie was screaming. All the way up the road, bedroom lights started clicking on and curtains and windows were being opened. People were looking out to see what all the noise and commotion was about.

"Please let him go! He ain't done nothing. It's got nothing to do with him, Tony," Suzie pleaded now.

Tony looked at the bloke's face; eyes all swollen and puffed out as he struggled to breathe. In an instant, Tony released his grip from his throat, dropping the bloke to the floor. The bloke threw his hands to this neck and began making an awful rasping noise.

"Get the fuck outta here now!" Tony snarled at him and kicked him away from his feet and into the kerb. "FUCKING NOW! If you know what's good for you," Tony yelled again at him. The bloke didn't need asking twice. He was on his hands and knees crawling away from Tony, stopping only briefly to turn and look at Suzie.

"Just go, I'll be fine. It's ok. I'm ok with him. You go or he'll fucking kill you if you don't. I'll be ok . . . Mum and Dad are just up there if I need them. Just *go!*" she was panicking now. Tony looked up to see Suzie's parents staring down from their window at what was happening. The bloke scarpered off up the road, terrified for his life.

"I think we need to talk," Suzie said, trying to be calm. She turned to her parents who were still looking down on them. "It's ok. I'm fine. I'm ok," Suzie yelled up. They nodded in response, but hesitated for a moment before closing the window and drawing the curtains again. Gradually lights were being turned off and the commotion had died down.

"Get in the fucking car. NOW!" Tony said through gritted teeth, grabbing her arm and frogmarching her back to his car. Suzie went to argue but the look on his face told her to get in the car and say nothing. He didn't want to be in her car after what had just happened. Tony was so angry he could feel his blood boiling over inside and it took every ounce of self-control that he had not to blow up.

"We are spose to be fucking engaged . . . or had you forgotten? Fucking engagement party . . . diamond ring . . . two weeks ago . . . ring any fucking bells with you? Not spoke to you for two fucking weeks and I find you with your tongue buried down some geezer's fucking throat! What kind of a fucking prick do you take me for?"

"Yeah, engagement party! You've got a fucking nerve showing your face round 'ere! Oh yes, I know all about your little tricks. Tash's told me *everything*. I know all about you, you're a fucking arsehole to think you can do that to me on *our* engagement party. Who the fuck do you think you are?" Tears were now streaming down Suzie's face.

"You fucked off and left me to go off with *her* and then Tasha told me you fucking tried it on with her and got all funny when she knocked you back and and . . ."

"*You what?*" Tony butted in and interrupted her flow now. "Tasha said fucking *what?* She told you that I tried it on with *her!* Is that fucking right is it? How about the other fucking way around? *She* tried it on with *me* in the garden! And what do you mean I fucked off with *her?* Are you referring to Tania?"

Suzie glared at him. "Oh yeah . . . that's right . . . Tasha said you'd deny it! And YES I mean Tania . . . whatever her fucking name is. Spose you've been out with her for the last two fucking weeks crying on her shoulder. Oh yeah I bet . . . or fucking her!"

Tony stopped dead in his tracks. "What did you just fucking say?" he said in a calm and chilling voice.

Suzie repeated "*Tania!* Fucking *Tania!*"

Tony's eyes glazed over in disbelief that she would say such a spiteful thing. "How could you say that after what's just happened, you bitch! How can you fucking sit there and *say* that?"

"What the fuck are you talking about?" Suzie snapped back at him.

Tony turned to stare at her in shock. "You *do* know she's dead don't you?

"WHAT?" Suzie spat at him.

Tony flung open the glove box and shoved Tania's funeral book into Suzie's face. "Have a fucking look yourself if you don't believe me!" Tony sat back in his seat and ran his hands wildly through his hair shaking his head. He grabbed a cigarette, took a deep drag and tried to calm himself down. In a very low voice, he said "Tania *died* the night of our engagement party. I got a call on my mobile from a friend of hers saying that something had happened and could we go and pick her up. Rob was with me, and *if* I was *fucking her,* as you put it, would I have taken Rob with me? We left the wine bar and Karl was looking for you to tell you but couldn't find you. Tasha was there when we left. She *knew* we had gone to get Tania! Don't you watch the fucking news? Read a newspaper? It's been all over the news the last week or so . . . for fuck's sake, Suzie!"

Suzie couldn't believe her ears. "And why haven't you answered your fucking mobile I bought you? I've been ringing and ringing. I left a message on Tasha's machine. I've been driving myself mad trying to call you . . . and I've been going out of my mind trying to understand what I'd done wrong!"

Suzie sat there in stunned silence looking at Tania's face staring back at her. She couldn't believe it. Tony looked at Suzie. It was all calming down now. In a quieter voice he asked, "do you *really* think I'm like that? Is what you *really* think I'm about? You don't know me at all, do you?"

"I thought I did," she replied quietly. "Tasha said you were just gonna mess me about and . . ."

"Oh what the *fuck* does Tasha know about me, eh?" Tony was off again. "She knows nothing. Abso-fucking-lutley *nothing!*" he spat back at her. "That's your fucking problem . . . always gotta listen to Tasha! Tasha told *me* that *you* were fucking about behind *my* back. Tasha told *me* that *you* were shagging a bloke at work and that you were playing about and the whole e*ngagement* was just a fucking joke to you! If I listened to every fucking single word that *Tasha* told me, we'd all be up fucking shit creek, wouldn't we? The girl is a compulsive fucking liar and a shit stirrer! If I would have *wanted* to be with Tania, then I would have *been* with Tania. But I love *you*. So I was engaged to *you*. It's not fucking rocket science! And I see you've taken the ring off already. I can't believe you, Suzie."

Suzie was crying now. "Yeah well, what was I spose to think? You just took off and left me. And Tasha's not a liar . . . she's a good friend and was there for me after the abortion and I don't know what I would have done if she wasn't . . ."

"The WHAT? *What* did you just say?" Tony reeled back in shock, like he had just been slapped round the face. "I had an abortion," Suzie said quietly in an almost muted voice with her head down now to avoid any eye contact with Tony.

"*WHEN? WHY?*" he stuttered his words out, unable to believe what he was hearing. "Was it mine?" he was yelling again now.

She turned on him in defence, "*YES OF COURSE IT WAS FUCKING YOURS! WHO ELSE'S*

COULD IT HAVE BEEN?" Suzie screamed.

"*WELL ACCORDING TO TASHA . . . FUCK KNOWS!*" he yelled back in her face.

Suzie slapped him hard across his face, sending him back in his seat. "I'm sorry," she immediately said. She reached out to touch his face where the slap had landed, which now was bearing a large red hand mark.

He pulled away from her and lowered his head in his hands. "How could you do this to me? How could you not tell me about the baby? Then you just swan off and you're over me and snogging someone else a fortnight later." Tony felt like his whole heart had been ripped from his chest and stamped on in front of his face. "When did you know? When did you find out about the baby?" he asked very quietly, his voice muffled by his head still in his hands.

"When you proposed . . . I had just found out. That's why I was so sick."

"All that time you knew and you didn't say a word . . ." he said softly, still in shock.

"Babe, I'm so sorry," Suzie whispered, reaching up to touch Tony's head. He instinctively pulled away from her touch. "Oh, Tony. Please don't," Suzie cried. "Please don't be like this . . . it's not been easy . . . I didn't know what to do."

"You should have spoken to *me!* That's what you should have done. Spoke to *me* . . . not Tasha! It wasn't Tasha's baby. It was mine!"

"I didn't think you'd wanna know," Suzie was crying now.

"Well it would have been nice to have had the option. " Tony said bitterly. "Who went with you? Oh, second thoughts . . . don't answer that, I think I can fucking guess that one by myself," he snarled.

"Tony *please* don't," Suzie sobbed.

"DON'T WHAT? DON'T CARE? Bit late for that. I do care . . . or *did* care should I say. I think we can safely say we are done here."

"I thought we were over. I was so upset," Suzie said, really crying now.

"Yeah! So upset that you're already out pulling other geezers," Tony scoffed. "If you had answered your fucking phone and spoke to me, *SPOKE TO ME,* you would have known what was going on and none of this would be happening right now, would it?"

Suzie shook her head, tears streaming down her face. She knew she had hurt him. "Who was that bloke then? Someone from your Friday nights out with Tasha? She said you were still pulling on your girls' nights out. How long you known him for? Or is he a *new* one? Great mate she is to you, ain't she!" Tony sneered.

"Tony, don't be like that."

"Don't be like that! How do you expect me to be? My fiancée . . . the one person I loved more than anything in the world . . . the person I wanted to spend the rest of my life with . . . ignores me for two fucking weeks, goes off fucking other geezers, and then drops a bombshell like this on me! And you expect me to take all this and sit here and fucking be happy about it? I asked you a question. WHO THE FUCK IS HE? You better tell me, Suzie, or I swear to God I'll find out myself and I'll smash his fucking head in anyway. Did he fucking know about me? Did you tell him you were fucking engaged? Or did you tell him you were single?"

"Calm down, Tony. *Please,*" Suzie was pleading with him now.

"No I fucking *won't* calm down. How would you like it if you turned up and I was snogging some other bird?"

"Well according to Tasha you was!"

"So you still believe what she says? Did she tell you about the message I left on her answer machine begging you to call me? Did she tell you that? If she was such a good mate, don't you think she might have mentioned all this to you, knowing what you've been through? Think about it, Suzie!"

"Well . . . she didn't, did she? Argh! We're just going round in circles!" Suzie said in defeat.

"Who the fuck was that geezer, Suzie? Tell me now!"

"Oh, for *fuck's sake!* He was just some fella I met in the pub a few nights ago when I was out with Tasha. He seemed a nice bloke and he asked me out and so I said yeah. We met at the club and that's it. That's all!"

"SO WHY WAS YOU BRINGIN' HIM HOME THEN?" Tony shouted again.

"Oh, Tony. *Don't!*" Suzie sighed.

Tony was losing his patience now. "I think you're right, Suzie. We ain't getting anywhere. We're going round in circles. I need time to take this all in . . . I can't deal with this . . . it's too much," Tony said eventually.

Suzie laid her hand on Tony's arm. "Tony, I'm sorry. I really am. I had no idea what had happened to Tania. I'm sorry what I said about her. Tasha must have got it all wrong. I'll talk to her. Can't we work this out? We can start again."

Tony shook his head and moved his arm away from Suzie's touch. "You gave up on us too easily, Suzie. You just threw it all away . . . literally got rid of everything. You got rid of us . . ."

"I didn't realise, Tony. I'm *sorry*, we can work it out. We *can*."

Tony shook his head, a sadness shadowed across his face. "I'm a fighter, Suzie. And I'll fight for anything in this world . . . if it was right and worth fighting for . . ." he stopped talking and looked at her.

"But you won't fight for me. Fight for us . . . no?" she said, her face full of hope.

He shook his head and looked straight ahead out of the windscreen "There is no 'us', not anymore".

He knew in his heart it was over, and so did she. He could never trust her again. "Where's the ring?" he asked quietly.

"It's at Tasha's house . . . I left it there. She's got it, shall I get it for you?" Suzie said quietly

"NO! It's ok, I'll get it myself. There's a few things I'd like to say her anyway . . ." Tony had a faraway look in his eyes now.

"I'd better get in. It's getting late," Suzie said, noting that the car clock said 4:05 a.m.

Tony turned and half-smiled at her, "sure," he said. "I'd better get home."

"Tone, will I see you again?" Suzie asked hopefully.

"Yeah. I'm in court on the twenty-eighth and you're up as a witness!" Tony said sarcastically.

"You know what I mean," Suzie said sadly.

"Let's just leave it there for now, eh?" Tony looked ahead again as Suzie stepped out of the car and closed the door behind her. He watched her walk away from him and up to her house. He was sad to see her walk away and, as she went, she took an irreplaceable piece of his heart with her.

Inside he was dying. But she would never know that.

All he could think about now was Tasha. He couldn't believe what she had done. He would have his revenge on her. *He was going to fuck her good and proper now – in more ways than one,* he thought.

Tony was in a blur all the following day. After leaving Suzie's, he'd headed straight home and eventually crawled into bed just after 5 a.m. Although sleep was the last thing he could do, he lay there with the sun coming up, his mind going over and over what Suzie had said. The baby, Tasha, the bloke she was snogging, the court case. There was no way he could sleep, so after a while he gave up and decided to get up. It wasn't far off 7 a.m. He clicked the kettle on and made himself a strong coffee.

He had managed to survive the entire day on strong coffee and cigarettes, and later that night he was sitting in the local Indian restaurant confiding in Dean everything that had happened.

"I don't believe it," Dean said. "You can't be serious?" Dean was as stunned as Tony was.

"Nah, mate. I'm fucking serious alright. And Tasha's gonna pay for this I swear it! I've lost everything because of her. She's worked us all like fucking puppets!"

"Well . . . it *does* look like that . . . after you knocking her back an' all. Surely she wouldn't be *that* cold as to let Suzie go through with an abortion though and not say a word?"

Tony explained how Suzie knew nothing about Tania. "She had no fucking idea mate! She was shocked. Either that, or she's a fucking good liar!"

"So what you gonna do?" Dean asked quietly. "Or don't I wanna know?" he cringed. He knew

Tony was mad as hell.

Tony thought for a minute. "Let's just say revenge is gonna be bitter fucking sweet. I'm gonna pay a little visit to Tasha's place tomorrow evening. There's a few things I need to collect."

It was Sunday evening and Tony was sitting alone in his car outside Tasha's flat. He checked his watch, 6:25 p.m. Tasha's car was there. She was in. He could see the lights on in her flat. He prayed that she was home alone – she usually was on Sunday evenings. He walked up to her front door and, taking a deep breath, reached out and rang the doorbell . . .

Chapter 42

TASHA'S face fell when she opened the door and saw Tony standing there. He was the last person she expected to see. "FUCK OFF!" she said quickly, and went to slam the door but Tony was too quick.

He had his foot in the doorway, stopping her from closing it.

"What's the matter, Tash? I thought you'd be pleased to see me," he said patronisingly. Pushing the front door open with force, he sent Tasha flying backwards. He stepped in through the front door and slammed it shut behind him.

"Who the fuck do you think you are? You can't come in here like that!" Tasha yelled at him.

"*Really?*" Tony smirked at her now. "I thought it's what you wanted, Natasha? I thought you wanted me to come round. Wasn't that what you said the night of the party? You made it pretty fucking obvious that you wanted me that night . . . what's changed, babe? Eh?"

Tony's voice was scarily calm and smooth. He was talking very quietly at her now. He could feel the rage in him but, for now, it was controllable. Although he wanted more than anything to throw his hands around her throat and squeeze every last ounce of life out of her, he was controlled – for now.

"What do you want?" she fronted him through gritted teeth, trying to regain her composure. She was scared now but she wasn't going to let Tony know that. It was starting to turn her on – he looked gorgeous standing there. He was rugged from stubble that was a few days old, his hair was a mess and he had a wild look in his eyes. Tasha was standing against the kitchen sink. There was nowhere for her to go. Her one-bedroom flat was barely large enough to swing a cat in. Tony's forceful entry had pushed her backwards straight into the kitchen. He was up close to her now. She stood flat against the worktop and he stood with a hand either side of her waist resting on the counter top. He was so close she could feel his breath on her.

"So hostile aren't we, Tasha?" Tony said slowly, mimicking her words to him the night of the party. Tasha's eyes fell briefly to the floor, then quickly back up to meet Tony's gaze. He could smell her fear. She was doing a good job though of trying to hide it, but he could sense it. She was quivering slightly. He only wanted to scare her a little bit – he had no real intention of hurting her.

"And . . . I believe you have something that belongs to me?"

"I don't know what you're talking about," she sneered.

"Is that right? Shall I give you a little reminder?" he grabbed her hand and held it up to her face. He pointed to her ring finger. "I believe you are looking after a little sparkly thing of mine for friend of ours."

"Oh yeah, that . . . sure, I got it . . . it's in the other room," she nodded towards the bedroom. Tony looked over to where she was pointing. "If you let go of my hand, I'll get it," she tried to wriggle her hand free from his grip but he suddenly grabbed it again and tightened it around her wrist.

"Ouch!" she said, as he tightened his grasp, turning his knuckles white. She could feel the pulse throbbing in her hand. "You're hurting me," she said, wincing.

"Am I?" Tony said quietly, his stare fixed on her now. Then, in a single step, he had shifted close to her, body to body. He rammed his legs in between hers, forcing them open wider and stood in between them. His other hand flew to the back of her head, grabbing her hair into a fist and wrapping it around his fingers. He was close to her face now. He brought his mouth down to her ear and in almost a whisper, he said "someone's been a bad little bitch, haven't they, Natasha? A very bad, vindictive little bitch. And do you know what happens to naughty little bitches like you?"

She couldn't move, apart from her eyes, which were now wide in both fear and excitement.   Keeping hold of the back of her hair, he half-lifted, half-dragged her a few inches off the floor and out of the kitchen into the hall towards the bedroom.

"I'll show you what bad bitches get! You wanted me. You can fucking have me. NOW!" he was growling under his breath. Kicking the bedroom door open he threw Tasha down onto her bed.

Ripping his coat off, he threw it on the floor and slammed the door shut behind him.

Half an hour later, Tony emerged from the bedroom wearing only his jeans pulled up to his hips. He sauntered across the kitchen and opened up the fridge. There wasn't a great deal staring back at him, but he did spot several cans of *Holsten Export* lager. Grabbing them and Tasha's cigarettes from the side, he walked back into the bedroom.

Tasha was lying there grinning like a Cheshire cat. She had got her just desserts, but Tony couldn't help feeling that she enjoyed every minute of it. He wasn't sure what kind of lesson he had taught her. He did feel better for using her, however. The fact remained – vindictive little bitches did seem to get *exactly* what they wanted. She had wanted Tony and had finally got him.

He lit a cigarette and passed it over to her. She laid back on the bed in her naked glory and inhaled deeply. "So what happens now?" she purred quietly, feeling victorious.

Tony lit his own cigarette and, blowing the smoke out into her face, he smirked back. "What do you mean '*what happens now?*' Nothing fucking '*happens now*'." Holding the beer can up, he pulled the ring pull back and the cold lager frothed over the rim of the can, sending a spray over his naked stomach and making him jump. Tasha sat bolt upright and stared at him. "Wanna sip?" he offered her.

"No thanks, "she said. "I mean, what happens next? What do we say to Suzie about us?"

Tony spat his lager back out in laughter. "*US! US!* There *is* no *us!* Jesus Christ, Tasha. Get real!

It's simple babe . . . you wanna fuck with me . . . I'll fuck you back! "

Tony pulled his shoes on, stood up and pulled his t-shirt over his head. "Oh, aren't you forgetting something?" he said, holding his ring finger up.

Tasha tutted and leant over to the bedside cabinet and rummaged in the drawer. Pulling out the ring box, she threw it at Tony with more force than necessary. Tony caught it awkwardly in his arm. Just to be sure it was in there, he opened the box. A sudden pang of hurt stabbed him in the chest as he saw Suzie's ring sparkling at him. He snapped the box shut quickly and picked his coat up off the floor. Pulling it on, he buried the ring box deep in the inside pocket.

Tasha wrapped the bed sheet around her naked body and was up on her knees. "Don't go yet, babe. I'm not finished with you," she said, slowly running her hand up his chest and then down to his waist. She hovered there for a second, before slowly running her hand down around the inside of his thigh.

"You never even got started, *babe!*" he said nastily, grabbing her hand and throwing her back on the bed away from him. He turned to leave the bedroom.

"You're a fucking animal, Tony!" she spat at him, as she tried to scramble off the bed whilst

still trying to cover herself with the sheet. "You can't just walk out of here like that! I'll tell Suzie everything!"

Tony spun around to face her now, with a venom in his face. "Yeah . . . well you're good at that. You told Suzie a lot didn't you? You're a spiteful little cunt, Tasha! I know about it all, about the baby, the lies, the deceit. You're a back stabbing, lying little cunt! Tell Suzie what the fuck you want.

You usually do, and I don't give a flying fuck!"

"Bastard!" she yelled after him. Her eyes frantically searched for an object to throw. Picking up the phone from the table, she threw it at him with all her might. But it was too late. The phone smashed against the front door that had slammed shut behind him.

Chapter 43

IT was a night of celebrations a few weeks later – Tony's twenty-first birthday and Rob's last night of freedom before he went away to the Army. The two of them had decided to have a joint party at the wine bar.

Rob's mum had nipped in after work to have a quick drink with the boys. "Ah . . . my boys," she said, bursting with pride. She had known Tony since he was a nipper in socks and sandals. And she was so proud of Rob, turning his life around with the help of Tony and Karl. She wasn't overjoyed at him leaving to go away and join the Army, but Rob had always been that way inclined. Being in the cadets when he was younger, plus his father had been in the forces – maybe it was in his blood. His father had also been a two-timing rat bag and had left them for another woman when Rob was a toddler. She hoped that Rob wasn't like him in that way. She beamed as she watched him chatting to his friends. She loved him dearly.

Ernie hadn't been able to make it due to work commitments, but was coming down in a few weeks for Tony's court hearing. He was staying on for a while then, too. Jacki and Stuart had also popped by. She was laden with cards and presents.

"What's all this?" Tony asked, as she thrust a carrier bag at him.

"It's your cards and presents . . . it *is* your birthday, right?"

"Oh lovely. Cheers, Jack. All from you?"

Jacki opened the bag and started sorting the presents and cards out into piles. "These are from me," she said, passing him her pile. "And these are from mum!"

"Thanks for yours," Tony said, moving them to one side. He picked up the carrier bag and began placing the gifts from his mum back in the bag. Jacki's face dropped when she saw what he was doing. "You can give these back to her. I don't want 'em!" Tony said, as he thrust the bag back to her.

"Tony, don't be like that," Jacki started to protest.

"Jacki, please don't start – it's my birthday. Thank you for coming to see me and having a drink with me, and for my cards and present from you, seriously . . . but please leave it there. Now . . . what are you both drinking?" Tony stopped the conversation there before it escalated into an argument.

He had never really spoken to his mum since she left. Although he was much happier when she did leave as the beatings stopped, for now he despised her. He was his dad's boy through and through. Jacki turned and frowned at Dean who was standing beside Tony. Dean shrugged and turned back to the bar.

The evening was brilliant, but it didn't stop there. The night was winding up and, after most people had left, Rob requested to finish the night off at Bella's, Karl's lap dancing club.

As they walked through the door, they were greeted by a couple of gorgeous, scantily clad girls who showed them to a tall bar table. Karl walked behind the bar and pulled out a bottle of champagne and ordered the bar staff to arrange glasses for all of them. Rob was drooling over a girl who was dancing provocatively in front of him, wrapped around a pole wearing just a lace thong. The music was seductive and low but through the dimly lit, smoky club Tony could see it was a very packed out night. The tables were all full at the front of the stage where the girls danced – that was most likely where Rob would be all night.

Tony had got to know some of the girls that Karl had working there. They were all really nice, and a few of them really fancied Tony. After the whole Suzie saga though, he wasn't interested in any kind of relationship at all. He would never trust women again. He would go back to being the way he used to be where women were concerned.

Rob had now moved onto stuffing a fistful of cash into the dancer's thong. Karl was trying to get his attention to come back to the bar for a minute. "I'll get him," Dean offered.

Karl held the champagne bottle up and flicked the cork out. There was a 'pop' followed by a short, frothy spray in the air. He proceeded to fill the glasses that had been put out on the bar.

Rob came back with his tongue hanging out. "My God! These

birds are amazing, Karl! I could stay here all night with them."

"You pay them enough and they just might!" Karl laughed.

"Don't tempt him," Dean said. "He's already spunked nearly fifty quid and we've only been here ten minutes!" Everybody laughed.

"Let's make a toast to my boys!" Karl announced, holding up his champagne glass. "Does everybody have a glass?"

Rob now had a buxom blonde draped around his shoulders and Dean was passing the glasses around to everyone.

"A toast!" Karl held his glass up. "Happy birthday, Tony. Twenty-one today, son. We are all very proud of you," Karl winked at him and a chorus of cheers and whoops followed. "And to Rob, who leaves us tomorrow to fight for his Queen and country. Stay safe, son, and come back soon."   Another round of cheers broke out, followed by a clinking of glasses. Rob downed his glass and the blonde took him by the hand and led him off to a quiet corner somewhere.

"Happy birthday, Tony," a smooth voice purred at him. A young girl dressed in black lace underwear had come over and, taking Tony by the hand, she led him off to a private room courtesy of Rob.

Dean laughed – Tony didn't need asking twice. "She's a *new* one!" Tony raised his eyebrows in approval. "Get a round in, Dean. I won't be long," Tony grinned, calling over his shoulder as he followed the girl out to the back of the bar.

"Sure thing," Dean burped and ordered the same round again.

Karl was talking to a few of his bar staff. Al and Dean were the only ones left. "Not your kind of thing?" Al asked Dean, as he nodded towards the dancers on stage.

"Oh yeah . . . but I'm just more subtle than Rob!"

Al laughed and agreed. "Yeah, he's a dirty dog ain't he!"

In any case, Dean had taken a real fancy to one of Karl's barmaids. Her name was Coco and she was absolutely stunning. Karl regarded her very highly and always said she was worth her weight in gold. So much so, that she also worked in Shooters and helped out at Bella's when it was busy. She was a short bubbly girl with gorgeous dark hair that hung down her back in waves. She had huge big brown eyes that twinkled at Dean. She had a cute, hourglass figure and was wearing a short black skirt and low cut black top. Dean was quite mesmerised by her and happily sat watching her run up and down the bar serving customers. "When you're ready, babe," he called over to her. She turned and gave him a wink and huge sparkling smile. *He wouldn't bother with lap dancers this evening*, he thought, *he was well in here*.

Tony came back about twenty-five minutes later with a cigarette hanging from the corner of his mouth. "Mate, she was smoking hot," he grinned. "Did you get the beers in?"

Dean was still at the bar and had been chatting to Coco. Rob was still with his blonde in the corner. Karl and Al had joined them at the bar again. "Are you having a good night, Tone?" Karl called across to him.

Tony was just about to answer him when he spotted Vernon Jackson walking up to them. He was looking slightly harassed. It was past midnight and a little late for Vernon to be out and about.

Must be serious. "Evening all. Karl, Al, Tony," Vernon politely addressed everybody.

"Vern, have you come to celebrate with the boys tonight? Pull up a stool and have a drink with us," Karl said to him, and motioned to Coco to grab another beer for Vernon.

"That's very kind, Karl, but I really must speak to you as a matter of urgency. In private first, if that's ok. I've been all over looking for you – the cab station, wine bar, thank goodness I've finally found you."

Coco pulled Vernon a pint and passed it over the bar to Karl. Passing the drink to Vernon, he grabbed his own and excused himself from the table. "We won't be long," he said to Al, motioning to keep an eye on things while he was gone.

Nobody said a word, but everyone went quiet and carried on sipping their drinks. Suddenly, there was a loud "whoop whoop" from the stage. Everyone turned around to see a drunken Rob swinging himself around a pole on the stage. The crowds were laughing at him, and the girls on the stage were clapping him. Someone in the audience was even throwing money at him, and he was bending down trying to scoop it up and stick it in his pants. Tony could see the doormen heading over to get him down before he did himself, or someone else, some serious damage. He tried to protest that he was trained as a pole dancer, but they lifted him off the pole and back onto his chair. Everyone was cheering him. No harm done.

"I'm gonna miss that funny fucker when he's gone," Tony said, wiping the tears of laughter from his eyes. Dean agreed and went back to his conversation with Coco. He had almost persuaded her to go on a date with him. The doormen had resumed their posts at the door – just as Karl appeared at the bar. He motioned for Al and Tony to join him in the back room. He looked very serious.

The pair followed him into the office out back and Karl closed the door behind them. Vernon had taken his glasses off and was rubbing his eyes wearily. "What's happened?" Al said. Tony said nothing, but sat in silence looking from Al. to Karl, to Vernon and back again.

"I'm afraid it's not good news as far as Kane's court case is concerned," Vernon said, addressing Al.

Tony was shocked, as he knew nothing about any court case that Kane was involved in. He knew that Vernon had been about a lot lately and they were always discussing something or other. Tony learnt that night that Karl's brother had been arrested for an assault on someone that owed him quite a bit of money and was up in court for ABH.

Karl told Tony the story . . .

It was about eighteen months ago. Kane's businesses are money lending, and he runs a large loan shark company. Some guy owed him a lot of money and was dodging him on the repayments.

Kane had sent his men round to collect but they always came back with a sob story. Kane decided enough was enough and he decided to pay the bloke a subtle visit himself. He'd scare him and get the money out of him. He found the bloke running a small bar in the quieter side of town. Kane walked in and the man's face dropped. They argued and Kane had reached over, grabbing the bloke by the scruff of his shirt. He'd lifted him clean across the bar by his throat and threatened him.

Tony sat there in silence. Karl went on to say that Kane had been reported and arrested for it. However, over the course of the last year he'd been in and out of court and was facing a possible minimum of two years, maximum five years, for ABH.

But Vernon was worried now. Each time over the last year that Kane had been in court, the case had been adjourned for one reason or another. The judge had adjourned again, only this time it was adjourned until next week – the week before Tony's trial. But this time the prosecution had come up with a key witness that had positively identified Kane, saying that he had attacked the barman.

"That's it! He's fucked!" Karl said.

"But what happened then?" Tony asked.

Karl finished his story. "He was holding the geezer by the throat, or the scruff of his shirt . . . I dunno . . . I can't remember . . . but he had him with one hand and threatened to punch him. The bloke was screaming at him to stop. I don't know if Kane actually hit him or not. Two days later, the

Ol' Bill arrive at his house and arrest him. You know the rest."

"Well," Vernon moved his glasses to the end of his nose and peered at Karl over them. "We do have to consider that Kane has no record or previous convictions. That will go in his favour. However, it would seem that the prosecution have this witness who was, in fact, sitting *at* the bar when Kane allegedly made the attack. It was a gentleman, I don't have his name here a present, who owns the key cutting and locksmith shop directly opposite the bar where the incident took place. He was having a late drink in the bar and knew the man that Kane assaulted, saying he saw the whole thing and is quite happy to stand up in court and testify against Kane in court next week. He is *the* only witness that has come forward. What a silly fool!"

"Oh great! Yep, that's it! Kane's definitely fucked!" Karl said angrily. "Such a prick! I've always told him *'don't do your own dirty work'!*"

"Only if the witness turns up though," Al jumped in. Everyone looked at Al. "No *witness*, no *case*," Al said smiling.

Vernon hesitated before answering. "Yes, indeed Al is correct in that assumption. They will have to adjourn it again and, as this will be the sixth time of attending court and having to adjourn, the judge might just rule in our favour and throw the whole darn thing out. Or, more than likely, continue for the case to be heard anyway without the witness present and rule in our favour regardless as there will be no concrete evidence. But the chance of the witness being a no-show . . . I'm afraid to say . . . very slim. He has already submitted his statement and the court date is next Wednesday."

"What if he *can't* make it?" Tony said slowly, getting Al's point.

Al nodded in agreement, pleased that Tony was on his wavelength. "What if he were *otherwise detained*. Know what I'm saying?" Al said to Tony.

Karl was very quiet and smiling to himself.

"Ahem. Just a minute, gentlemen," Vernon said, as he removed his glassed and wiped his brow with his handkerchief. "May I remind you that this is not a conversation, nor a conspiracy that I would wish . . . nor want . . . to be part of. And also, Tony, may I remind *you* that you are up in court yourself in no more than a few weeks' time. So I wouldn't recommend taking any irresponsible risks at this stage."

"Vern's right, Tone. You can't take any risks," Karl said as he stood up. "I need a fucking drink. Hold on." Karl stormed out to the bar to get some more drinks.

"Don't worry about it, Vern. We'll take care of it," Al said confidently.

"Yeah we will," Tony said, nodding at Al. "I'll do whatever it takes for Karl and his family."

"May I suggest that's also another private conversation to be had when I'm not present in the room," Vernon reminded them.

Karl reappeared with some more drinks.

"Good Lord! Is that really the time? I must be heading off," Vernon said, noticing it was just short of 1 a.m. He stood and gathered his paperwork up into a pile. "I'll be in touch with you, Karl, and Kane before this week is out to go over things in finer detail. I just wanted to give you a head's up. Now, I errr . . . haven't had time to find Kane and inform him of this yet as it's only come to light this evening. I'm not sure how he'll take the news."

"Thanks, Vern. I'll deal with Kane," Karl shook his hand. Al and Tony stood up and they each shook Vernon's hand in turn.

Vern eyed them suspiciously and nodded his head. "Good evening, gentlemen," he said and turned and scurried out of the room.

Al sat down and lent back in his chair. "That's easy, Karl," Al was smiling now. "Geezer's just gonna disappear for a while!"

"There'll be no keys cut that week!" Tony laughed.

Karl looked at his two boys with pride. Sitting down in his chair he pulled a packet of cigarettes from the top drawer and, lighting one, he threw the packet on the desk and smiled a slow, wicked smile that Tony had not seen before. "You know what to do, Al. You know what to do."

* * *

Three days later.

"Ok, have you got everything? Karl was sitting in the back office of the cabbies.

"I think so. Let me check," Al said, pulling out a drawstring bag and emptying its contents on the table in front of him. Just then, Tony walked in. "Just in time, Tone," Al winked at him.

Tony was dressed in old jeans and an old zip-up bomber jacket, scruffy old trainers and a baseball cap. Al looked pretty similar. "Ok . . . couple of sacks, rope, knife, gaffa tape, blindfolds, a bat, bread, chocolate, balaclavas, gloves, toilet roll. There's a bucket and enough food and water for four days' supply in the van. There's an old mattress in there too." Al turned to Tony, "All set? Know the plan?" Tony nodded – he understood.

Karl turned to Tony. "Tony you don't have to do this. You are in enough trouble as it is. If this goes wrong, you'll go down for a fucking long time. Kidnap is fuckin' serious shit on its own . . . let alone kidnapping a key witness to a court case!"

"It won't go wrong. Me an' Al got it all worked out. We know who he is, we know what time he closes his shop up, he's always alone and we've already been up to where we're going to hide out. It's all good!" Tony said confidently.

"You know what I mean, Tone." Karl walked over and put his arm around Tony's shoulder.

"This means a great deal to me, Tony. The fact that you are prepared to do this for my family."

Tony beamed at Karl. "Like I said, Karl. Whatever it takes. You've looked after me enough . . . time to repay favours."

"Listen, Al. Don't mark his face, whatever you do. You're not gonna kill him. Don't beat him up . . . just scare him. If you mark him and he squeals to the Ol 'Bill when he gets back, then we're fucked. If he goes squealing off and he's not got a mark on him, it's gonna look like he was running, scared ain't it? I mean it, Al. NO MARKS. Is that clear?"

"Crystal!" Al said, grinning.

Two hours later, the two of them were parked up in an old white transit van which they had stolen and had ringed earlier in the week. They had been staking out the shop for the last few days. They knew every movement this bloke made, as well as he did. They knew what time he opened, what time he closed, what time he had lunch, where he lived and pretty soon they even knew what time he went the toilet! Their mission was to kidnap him and hold him hostage until Kane's trial was over.

They had a good two hours to wait until he was due to close up the shop. They decided to stake out for the whole afternoon, just in case he finished up early today. Kane's case was to continue tomorrow when the witness was due in court to testify.

"Egg and cress sandwich?" Al said, passing over a packet of sandwiches.

Tony turned his nose up and declined. "Nah thanks. Wonder how Rob's getting on with his training," Tony said.

They'd had a brilliant night last week. Rob had really enjoyed himself at the lap dancing club and it had been a bit of a sad goodbye the following day. Rob's mum was tearful and Rob had decided to take himself off on his own and didn't want a lift there. It had felt weird to Tony saying goodbye to him again. But he knew Rob would be back after his training before he went off somewhere. This was where Rob belonged.

"He's loving it, I reckon," Al said. "He's proper Army, ain't he? All that 'yes sir, no sir' shit!"

Tony told Al about his short lived time in the cadets with Rob and the time passed quite quickly as the two chatted easily. Al looked at his watch. It was 5:26 p.m. The man was due to lock up the shop any minute now . . .

Chapter 44

IT was 5:30 p.m. on the dot. The door opened and the skinny balding man in his early fifties stepped out into the warm evening. He pulled the shop door of the locksmiths closed behind him and locked it. He pushed back on the door to check it was shut. Reaching up, he pulled the long shutters down. He produced an enormous padlock out of his bag and threaded it through the shutters' hooks. Then, slamming the heavy padlock shut, he jiggled it to make sure it was secure. It was then as he was jiggling it that, out of nowhere, a white transit van pulled up alongside him. The side door flew opened and a figure in a balaclava jumped out. He ran up behind the man and pulled a straw sack over his head. In a single swoop, he had gathered the man and his bag up and bundled him into the side of the van. The doors slammed shut and the van drove off into the evening, leaving not a trace behind.

Gregory tried to open his eyes. It was dark and fuzzy. He couldn't see anything and he had an excruciating pain in the back of his head. He tried to move – he couldn't. His hands were bound behind his back, and suddenly he recalled what had happened . . .

One minute he was locking his shop up, the next, he felt something over his head – a bag maybe – and he was being dragged backwards. He didn't know what was happening. Then he hit a hard surface, maybe a hard floor. A man's voice was threatening him. He couldn't recall what it said but it was menacing. He had winced as he felt a short, sharp kick into his stomach. He could hear an engine revving and driving off. He realised he must have been kidnapped; he could remember no more.

His head hurt; it was hot and throbbing. He must have been hit over the head with something and knocked out. All he could hear was his own breathing, loud and rasping. He could taste blood in his mouth. He held his breath to see if he could hear anything – just the engine. He was being driven somewhere. Very, very faint muffled voices were talking in the front, but he heard nothing he could make out. As he lay there trying to remember, he thought about how much his stomach hurt. He seemed to be lying on his side so he tried to roll over, but the pain took him and he curled back onto his side. He was bound by his wrists and his ankles. All he could do was lay there and wait to see what would become of this nightmare he was in.

An hour or so later, the van came to a stop. Gregory must have slipped into a light sleep, but he woke with a start as he heard the engine noise turn off. He held his breath again so he could listen. The two front doors opened and then slammed shut again. He could make out someone walking. The footsteps got closer. A loud grinding noise was suddenly by his head. It sounded like the side door of a van being pulled opened. That's where he must be, in the back of a van. The whole floor seemed to move suddenly. He could hear that someone had jumped up next to him, moving things around. He didn't dare to move. He held his breath again. He was terrified. Why would anyone want anything to do with him? He was just a lowly locksmith.

He couldn't hear any voices at all, but he could still smell. He could smell grass, a damp, forest smell. Suddenly a gruff voice said "sit up." He was being dragged to a sitting up position by his head. He tried to stretch out his fingers; his arms ached from being tied tightly around his back. His wrists were sore and he had pins and needles in his fingers and his feet. He wasn't sure how many of them there were or how many voices he had heard but he couldn't hear a thing now. He still had something over his head. He didn't know what, but he could make out very small holes – like a straw effect and he could breathe easily enough. Whatever it was, it was being wrenched off his head as quickly as it had been thrown over. Gregory screwed his face up as the light hit him. Pain seared through the back of his head; he must have cut his head open. He couldn't open his eyes, for they had become too accustomed to the dark – they stung. He tried to blink but the next thing he knew he was being gagged. He put up little effort in fighting back as he realised that resistance would be futile. He had seen the movies where this happened – it was best not to resist and go along with it. He would know soon enough what lay in store for him. He was very thirsty. Again, he was being thrown back down onto the floor of the van, but this time there was a soft landing. A musty smell surrounded him and he could see that he was lying on a mattress. He felt so scared. As he lay there he blinked his eyes and his vision, which at first was blurred, was now starting to come into focus. Again he could hear the gruff voice.

"Do you need a piss?" the voice asked. The words didn't register with Gregory at first. He was trying to turn his head in the direction of the voice. His gag was tight and digging into his jaw.

"DO YOU NEED A FUCKING PISS?" louder this time, and impatient.

Gregory nodded as best as he could from his lying position. He was suddenly desperate for a wee. He felt himself being dragged up and back out of the van and into a standing position.

"Don't try anything or we'll stick a fucking bullet in your nut. Do you fucking understand?"

His ankles were still tied and his legs were weak, but he felt his wrists being released and they sprung free. His arms immediately fell down to his sides.

"You can get your own fucking cock out," the voice said. Gregory tried to look at the man whom the voice had come from. He was wearing a balaclava and Gregory could see his eyes and his mouth. That was all. He could also see that there were two of them. Fighting the pain of the pins and needles that was searing through his hands and wrists, he fumbled about and unzipped his trousers and proceeded to go for a wee. He felt something being thrust into the side of his temple. It was a gun. Gregory's legs started to quiver and tremble with fear. He finished off and zipped his trousers back up.

"HANDS BEHIND YOUR BACK. NOW!" the second man shouted at him.

Gregory clenched his fists as his arms were dragged behind his back again and tied at the wrist. He felt himself being dragged back up into the van and down on the welcoming, soft mattress again. The side door to the van slammed shut behind him and he was left alone and scared in the darkness once more.

Spots of rain had begun to fall. Gregory could hear the drops' pitter patter on the roof of the van. It was very dark. He had absolutely no idea what the time might have been.

The door of the van slid open, making his jump. He was still gagged and now he was thirsty.

One of the men hung up some camping torches in the corner of the van, lighting the whole area up. Gregory blinked in the light to adjust his focus. He tried to look at the men; they were both still wearing balaclavas. One of them pulled Gregory up into a sitting position and started to untie his wrists.

"Don't do anything stupid or we will shoot you. Do you fucking understand that?" he growled at him.

Gregory nodded in response, his eyes wide with fear. They untied the gag from around his mouth. "Thank you," Gregory said quietly as he rubbed at his sore wrists.

"Thirsty?" one of men said, thrusting a bottle of water at him.

Gregory nodded and gratefully accepted the water. He unscrewed the cap and guzzled the cold liquid down; it was a welcome feeling.

"Hungry?" the man asked, kinder this time. Gregory shook his head; he wasn't hungry. He had no idea how long he would be here for, but peering around in the light of the van now, he could see a fair supply of food and water.

"Why are you doing this to me?" Gregory asked shakily, like a child.

"Don't fucking ask us questions or we'll fucking gag you again. Understand?" the other man growled at him. "*We'll* be asking the questions. Now shut it!"

Gregory closed his eyes tight so as not to make any eye contact. He didn't want to anger the men.

"You'll have plenty of time to talk later," the other man said in a calmer voice. "But for now, it's time to get some sleep. You're gonna need your strength for tomorrow," he said in a quiet, scary voice. The other man laughed in agreement as he leant over Gregory.

"I'm gonna gag you and tie you up again, so have another swig of that water." Gregory obeyed and then passed his hands behind his back to be bound and then gagged.

The kidnappers secured him in the van for the night. Reaching up, they clicked the torches off, plunging him back into darkness

"Night night, princess. Sleep tight!" one of them laughed, as the door was slammed shut behind them and he was left alone once again.

It was early. Gregory could hear birds singing. He knew he hadn't died and gone to heaven as he could also hear somebody scrabbling about outside the van door. The kidnappers were close by; he recognised their voices.

The door slid open, allowing a burst of sun to rush in, temporarily blinding him. He could just make out a silhouette against the sunlight of one of the men.

"Wakey wakey, Sleeping Beauty. Rise and shine!" the voice said. Gregory blinked against the blinding rays. He was pulled up into a sitting position.

"I'm gonna untie your feet so you can stand and walk about a bit, okay?" the second man said to him. Gregory nodded. They untied his ankles and dragged him to the edge of the van so he could stand up. "Need another piss?" the man asked. Gregory nodded. "I'm standing right behind you, so don't even think about leggin' it, okay?" He hadn't even dreamt of it. He desperately needed a wee, and a drink too.

Gregory could see that they were deep in a forest – God only knew where. He could smell the woodlands and still hear the birds singing, he was grateful for that. He finished his wee and zipped his fly back up. He walked back towards the van with the man close behind him. He desperately wondered if anyone knew where he was. He doubted it.

There was a fresh bottle of water and a muffin cake for him. They let him sit in the van and he glugged at the water. The two men were standing in front of him now, looking at him. He was terrified.

"Eat!" one of them ordered aggressively. He bit into the muffin. He hadn't realised how hungry he was. He hadn't eaten since lunchtime the day they kidnapped him. He thought that might be yesterday, but he wasn't sure. He hadn't a clue what they could possibly want with him. He looked at the two of them. They were both wearing balaclavas; Man A was slightly taller than Man B. They both had very strong London accents and they both equally terrified the life out of him. Was it money? Did they want his money? He didn't have much, seemed a bit extravagant to kidnap him for his money. They could have just grabbed the takings – he had them in his bag. He would just offer it to them and see if that sufficed.

Man A lit a cigarette and blew the smoke at him. Gregory had scoffed the muffin down and finished the remainder of the water. After he had finished, he held his wrists out for them to tie him up again. Man B laughed and pointed to a shovel. "You'll be needing your hands to use that!"

"I ddddont understttannd," Gregory stuttered, looking at the shovel. "Is it mmmoney?

Ddddo you want mmmoney?"

"That depends on how much you got," Man A said, cocking his head to one side and rubbing his balaclava-covered chin, tormenting him.

"You ccccccan have it all. I have the takings in my bag. Jjjjjjust take it all," Gregory stammered, his eyes welling up.

"Don't start fucking crying yet!" Man B said. "We ain't even fucking started on ya!"

"What do you want with me?" Gregory pleaded. "Please tell me. What do you want? I don't have anything."

"*Ohhh* . . . but you do, Gregory Garvey. You have a big gob. That's what you have, sunshine.

And you're a dirty grass. And we don't like dirty grasses, do we?" Man B said to Man A.

Man A shook his head sadly and very slowly. "No! We don't like grasses," he said back. Man A continued, "so *you* have to be punished. We are gonna hold you here till we get a call and, depending on what that call says, depends on whether we shoot you or we let you go. But seeing as we are waiting for the call, you might as well make yourself useful for once. You can start by helping us dig your fucking grave."

Gregory's face fell and he started sobbing as he realised what the two men were referring to. "I'm supposed to be in court today," he said, the realisation of what was happening led to tears sliding down his cheeks and snot running from his nose.

"Oh we know that. That's why you're here," Man B said.

"All I was doing was helping a friend out who runs the bar. You see, it was my birthday and I was in the bar that night he was attacked. He was having a drink with me, as I don't have many friends . . ." Gregory was babbling now.

"You fucking loner," Man A said.

"Well, I don't have many friends and no family," he carried on.

"Well no one's gonna fucking miss you then, are they? So shut up and start fucking digging!"

Man A snapped at him, tired of his sob story now.

Gregory put his head in his hands and started really sobbing.

"Christ all mighty! We've got a right one 'ere, ain't we! Best just fucking do him now . . . put him out of his misery," Man B said loudly.

Man A stifled a laugh behind his balaclava and, grabbing the shovel, he walked round the back of the van. "Right! Let's start him digging here then," Man A said when he had composed himself. He had marked out a grave-sized area underneath a tree. "I reckon here will do the trick."

Man B bundled Gregory over to where Man A stood. Passing Gregory the shovel, he said, "well go on, what you fucking waitin' for? Christmas?" Gregory heard the click of a gun being loaded. He turned and saw Man A holding a gun out pointed at him. "Well go on then! Fucking dig!"

Gregory turned to the marked-out grave and began to smash the shovel into the hard ground. He swung the shovel above his head and smashed it down with every sob that burst out of his mouth. He had snot streaming down his nose and into his mouth. As tears burned his eyes he said, "I was only trying to help a friend out."

"Thought you said you didn't have any friends," Man B said, lighting a cigarette. *How the hell were they going to put up with this blubbering baby for four days?*

* * *

"Court rise," the usher said, as the judge entered the courtroom from his chambers. It was

10 a.m. on Wednesday morning – the day of Kane's trial. Karl shifted in his seat as he sat next to Vernon. Kane stood in the dock waiting for the judge to address him.

The prosecution were frantically pacing about outside. Their main witness was to appear in court first thing this morning, but he was late – very late. The judge had again asked the whereabouts of a Mr Gregory Garvey. He had granted the prosecution strictly one hour and he had returned to his chambers in a terrible mood while they searched for Gregory Garvey.

Vernon watched and counted down as the final minute of the hour struck. They waited in the court room patiently. It was eerily silent apart from the mundane ticking away of the second hand on the clock. The court room boasted a beautiful heavy wooden panelling that lined the walls of the entire room. The solid wooden judge's bench and panels were all lined with a dark green leather covering. Green leather chairs all congregated beneath the desks, giving a very grand and regal feel.

Sitting in a line towards the front of the court were the court officials and police, with ushers darting here and there. Various people were entering the room and leaving again. There was nobody seated in the public gallery today either and the courts were unusually quiet.

"Court rise," again the usher addressed everyone and they all stood as the judge entered the room. "Court be seated," the usher said loudly, turning to bow after the judge had taken his seat at his bench. The usher called the jurors through and Karl watched them all proceed into their panel and take their seats.

The judge peered around the room, looking over the top of his small half-moon spectacles. To his left stood Kane, and Kane's lawyer on their panel. To his right, the prosecution panel were still shuffling uncomfortably about with endless pieces of paper

"Permission to approach the bench, Your Honour," the prosecution immediately asked.

The judge leant down to hear what they had to say. It appeared not to be the good news he had been waiting for. "Well, this is utterly ridiculous. We cannot possibly grant any more time in waiting. We have already had to adjourn this case now for . . . let me see." The judge read his notes for a moment and let out a rather long and tired sigh, "This will be the sixth time and I am afraid that this just isn't feasible to request another adjournment at this late stage. You will simply have to proceed with your prosecution without your witness."

"But Your Honour, with all due respect, this witness *is* . . . or was . . . I beg your pardon, Your Honour, our prosecution. Without it would be one's word against another and, as I am fully aware, we wouldn't have any grounds to go ahead as we have no other evidence, photographic or likewise to present to you at this stage, as we were fully reliant on the witness."

The judge stared down at the prosecution in disbelief. "Yes, I agree. Something I feel will be quite problematic for you. I wonder . . . do you think that perhaps My Garvey didn't realise the seriousness of the case and has taken himself off on a jolly holiday?"

The courtroom sniggered at the judge's attempt at humour. "And may I add, quite simply, that for future reference, you could perhaps reiterate this with your witness and find some clarity in your cases to avoid further and unnecessary vain attempts."

Turning to address the court room, the judge dismissed the prosecution from the bench. "Ladies and gentlemen," he said, turning to face the accused and his defence bench. "Do you have anything you would like to add in these circumstances accumulating to the facts?"

"Permission to stand and approach the bench, Your Honour," Kane's lawyer said, leaping into action.

"Granted," the judge agreed.

Kane's lawyer continued, "Certainly, if my learned friend or I had failed to appear and the witness were present, I wouldn't be entitled to a last minute postponement. So I respectfully ask that the court dismiss this case for lack of prosecution and in the interest of justice, Your Honour."

The judge sat silent for a minute. Everyone held their breath in angst. Finally, the judge said, "I move to dismiss this case, based on the fact that the prosecution has completely failed and ignored all requests to provide a reliable and steadfast witness as proposed. I have here a copy of that request, made at the previous case on March the fifteenth. So therefore, I have no alternative but to dismiss this case on procedural grounds due to prosecution not following the full procedure and a dismissal with prejudice. Case dismissed. Mr Bateman, you are free to stand down and leave."

The judge then turned his attention to the members of the jury,

"Jurors, I am afraid to say that I have to relieve you all of your duties today. But I thank you all for you time in appearing here. Good day to you all." The jury all stood and, at the usher's signal, they all turned and left the court room.

"Court rise," the usher said and with that the judge turned and swept out of the room, slamming the doors to his chambers behind him.

Vern looked at Karl who gave a silent whistle and raised his eyebrows. Kane was grinning from ear to ear. He shook his lawyer's hand and Vernon scurried over to discuss details. Karl gave Kane a hug and patted his back.

"Let's celebrate!" Kane said.

"Indeed we fucking will!" Karl said. "But first, I got a phone call to make."

* * *

It was almost lunchtime and Gregory was still digging. He was smothered from head to foot with dirt. The taller of the men offered him a drink and something to eat. He was too scared to eat, but figured he should, just to keep his strength up. It was a cheese sandwich and a chocolate bar. He gratefully demolished the lunch offering and had drunk almost a bottle of water. He was parched too. He surveyed the grave he had been digging; he was only just beyond knee deep.

"How far down do I have to dig?" he asked.

"Just keep digging till I say stop," was the reply he got.

Gregory kept imagining himself being thrown in and covered over with the soil until he couldn't breathe. He imagined having to claw his way out through the soil – that's if they buried him alive. Or would they shoot him?

"Please don't kill me!" he whimpered quietly. "I'll say nothing. I won't breathe a word of this to anyone for as long as I live."

"Well that's good of you, as you've only really got about . . . I'd say . . . maybe twenty-four hours left . . . give or take a few. So if you can keep your trap shut that long, I'll be impressed," Man A said harshly.

Man B stifled his laugh to a cough and spluttered, "keep digging!"

"I promise I won't say a word. Please, please let me go! I'm sorry! I really am so sorry!" Gregory sobbed again. He lay on the floor by the grave begging for his life, almost hyperventilating with fear. "I'll tell the police I can't remember anything . . . I'll say I forgot it all and can't remember anything . . . I'll say I don't recall anything and I was drunk. Please, please don't kill me!" he was wailing now.

"Shut the fuck up! We'll just have to see what happens when the call comes through, won't we?" was all the reply he got.

Chapter 45

IT was early evening when Al's mobile rang. It was Karl with some good news. Al had walked away to take Karl's call, leaving Tony in charge of Gregory.

"All good, mate. Case thrown out. What's happening your end?"

"Jesus, he's crying and snivelling like a bitch. Tone made him dig his own grave, it's quite funny actually. The geezer's pissing his pants, he ain't gonna be saying nothing though. He's shitting himself . . . keeps begging us to save him and not kill him. We'll rough him up a bit and make out we gotta nut him, then we'll make him think we've gone soft. Shall we drop him where we said, in

Peterborough? Tomorrow evening?"

Karl laughed, "Good job, boys. Tell me about it when I see ya. I'll be waiting at the bar for ya.

See you tomorrow."

Al hung up and headed back to see Tony. He was starving now and was sure that the others must be too. "Well, well, well . . . seems your gonna be needing that grave after all," Al growled at Gregory.

"NO! NO! Please don't kill me. I'll do anything! Please!" Gregory flung himself onto the floor and was now hysterical.

"Shut the fuck up!" Al yelled, giving him a light kick in the stomach. Al looked at Tony and winked to say it was all ok.

Tony grabbed Gregory and threw him into the back of the van, down onto the mattress. Gagging him again, they threw the sack over his head so they didn't have to look at his tear-stained, sobbing face. They tied his hands behind his back and slammed the door shut, leaving him in the dark.

"He's dug quite a decent hole to be fair!" Tony laughed. "What's happened?"

The pair walked away from the van up into the woods a bit and removed their balaclavas. Tony lit up a cigarette and passed the packet to Al.

"Phew," Al said, tucking the balaclava into his pocket. "Glad to get that off for a bit. It went sweet as a nut. All went to plan. Thrown out. Karl said he'd fill us in on details tomorrow night. We gotta take silly bollocks to Peterborough where we said. We'll dump him near a train station . . . or fucking bus station . . . or something, and let him find his own way back."

Tony thought for a minute, puffing away on his cigarette. "Do you think we've scared him enough? Is he really fearful for his life? I dunno, Al . . . will he fucking blurt it all out to the Ol' Bill when he gets back? "

"Well he'll be nicked for a start for missing court. We'll threaten him that we'll be watching him. Every day we'll be there watching him and waiting for him to fuck up again . . . then this time, we *will* kill him. He'll be too shit scared I reckon," Al said.

The two of them finished their cigarettes and headed back to the van. It was quiet in there.

Tony held his ear up to the door and listened for a second. He could hear the faint sniffing sound of

Gregory. "Shut the fuck up and go to fucking sleep. NOW!" he yelled at him and banged on the door.

Tony and Al sat in the front of the van and put their feet up, glad to be heading off and back to reality. It was almost 9 p.m. and getting dark. They settled down to sleep, ready for the long drive tomorrow.

The sun seemed to be up all too soon for Tony and Al. They felt like they'd only had a few hours' sleep. Tony felt absolutely shattered. They could hear Gregory moving around in the back. "Come on, let's do this," Al said, jumping out of the front of the van and stretching up, before pulling his balaclava back down over his face.

"All set?" Tony said, pulling his down too and wrenching the side door of the van open.

The sunlight streamed in on Gregory. Tony pulled the bag off his head and ungagged him.

Poor fucker, he thought – he had been gagged all night. Tony sat him up. "Same as yesterday, okay?

I'm gonna untie you so you can take a walk and a piss."

Gregory gratefully got up and rubbed his wrists. They were sore and ached – as did the whole of his body. He stood out in the early morning sunlight and blinked up at the sky. He looked awful.

"Listen to me now," Al said. Gregory turned and looked at him. "You said you'd do anything

if we spared your life."

Gregory nodded. "*Anything*. I'll do *anything*. Please let me go. Please don't hurt me."

"How about keeping your fucking trap shut for starters?"

"Yes, I won't breathe a word to anyone," Gregory fell over the words. He couldn't get them out fast enough.

"It was opening your gob that got you into this shit, weren't it? How can I trust you not to fucking open your trap again, eh?" Al said, standing next to the grave that Gregory had dug. He turned and pointed at it. "How can I be sure that you won't be needing this after all?" Al said, tormenting the man now.

Tony was leaning up against the van, smoking and listening intently.

"Coz it's here . . . all fucking ready for you. We could just nut ya and pop you in. No one would ever know, would they?"

Gregory was shaking his head, his eyes squeezed tightly shut as if trying to shut Al out. He had dropped to his knees now. His hands were tightly squeezed together as if praying, begging Al to spare him. "*Pleeease*. I'm just a silly locksmith that *had* a big mouth. I'll not say anything to anyone ever again. I promise. I know I'm in trouble with the police for not going to court but I'll say I had amnesia and forgot . . . I'll say anything you want me to say . . . *pleaaseeeee!*" he begged.

"I reckon we might be able to do a deal. What do you reckon?" Al nodded at Tony.

Tony finished his cigarette and squashed it under his trainer into the dirt. "I reckon maybe," he agreed.

An hour later and they were all back in the van and travelling up north to Peterborough. Tony and Al managed to string the time out till it was late afternoon. They were a good two hours away from home. If they left now, they would be back at Karl's by 8 p.m.

They pulled up into a secluded parking area. They knew the train station was a good mile away by foot. They knew Gregory had money on him, but thought maybe he had been through enough so didn't bother to rob him of all of his money as well. They left him enough to get home with.

They made sure they were well out of sight and, jumping out of the van, they pulled their balaclavas down and opened the back up to let Gregory out. Tony swung the door open and Gregory sat up.

"Here's where you fucking get out," Al said. "Come on, move it!" He grabbed him by the scruff of his shirt and flung him out of the van and down on the ground. Gregory rubbed his wrists. Tony jumped back into the van and took the driver's seat. Al grabbed Gregory's bag and slung it on the floor beside him with a spare bottle of water. Slamming the van door shut, he climbed up into the front.

Just before Tony drove off, Al wound the window down. "You can make it from here, stations that's way . . . somewhere. But you better fucking remember this . . . you had better be looking over your shoulder every day for the rest of your fucking life. We'll be watching you and you never know when we'll just pop by and pay you a visit. Don't even think about moving or running anywhere as we will find you and you will be very, very sorry. You open your fucking gob and breathe a single word of this to anyone, and you'll be in that fucking grave quicker than you can say sorry. Do you fucking understand me?"

Gregory was still on his knees and nodded very quickly. "Yes I do understand, I do. And thank you for sparing me and I will be eternally . . ."

But Tony had already screeched off and out of the parking area, leaving Gregory still on his knees in a smokescreen of gravel and dust.

Gregory had absolutely no idea where he was – but he didn't care. He was alive! HE WAS ALIVE! He wanted to shout it from the roof tops that he was alive, but he thought better of it and started off down the road in search of the station.

A few weeks later, Tony was driving past the locksmiths at the top of the road. He slowed right down to watch. It was exactly 5:30 p.m. He saw Gregory step out and close the shop door of the locksmiths behind him. He locked it and pushed back on the door to check it was shut. Reaching up, he pulled the long shutters down. He produced an enormous padlock out of his bag and threaded it through the shutters' hooks. Then, slamming the heavy padlock shut, he jiggled it to make sure it was shut. It was then, as he was jiggling it, that he kept looking over each shoulder to see who was around – to see if there were any vans sitting nearby watching him. He turned and hurried off down the street, checking over his shoulder – just to make sure.

Chapter 46

TONY stood up to make a toast. He looked around the room at everyone that was there; Ernie, Karl, Colette, Al and Kane had come along too. Dean and had brought Coco from the club; the two of them had become somewhat of an item lately. Andy Weaver had popped in and Jace from the garage had also come along. Vernon had joined the evening too. The only one that was missing from their crowd was Rob.

Tony stood at the bar of the wine bar and held his glass up. "I'd like to firstly thank all of you for coming this evening to have a drink with me. This could be my last night as a free man," Tony joked. They all jeered and booed at him.

"Don't be stupid!" Al shouted back at him.

"He's alright, Vern, ain't he!" Kane jeered over at Vernon.

Vern smiled a nervous and uncomfortable smile. "We'll certainly try our best," he said awkwardly.

"Let him speak all of you, shush!" Karl quietened down the rowdy group.

Tony carried on, "Well . . . it is what it is. I am shitting myself, to be honest with you all. But I am sure I am in good hands with Vern. But my toast is to good friends and family and also to Vern and the British Justice System!"

"Here, here! May it rule in our favour," everyone chorused, followed by a clinking of glasses.

"One doesn't want to be too presumptuous, but at most I am hoping for possibly a fine and bound over to keep the peace. After all, it was a petty argument amongst friends," Vernon said stiffly.

"Let's hope you're right, Vern," Karl said. "Cheers to Tony. And good luck tomorrow."

"You having another round, Tone?" Dean asked.

"No, mate. I'm gonna call it a night tonight. I've got an early start and I don't wanna be rough when I appear in court. I'm gonna slip off after this one."

Vern smiled an approving smile at him.

"You should have got a bleeding haircut before tomorrow if you ask me!" Ernie piped up.

"Yeah, Dad. Turn up looking like a fucking skin head and a thug shall I?"

"Tony's correct, Mr Hayes," Vernon jumped in. "We did advise him to grow out the shaven and spiky style, and to perhaps adopt more of a college boy look . . . so as not to give rise to any assumptions amongst the jury."

"Oh *la de dah*," Ernie said mockingly.

"Dad! Leave it out!" Tony said, shooting him a look.

Vernon seemed offended and readjusted his jacket and tie uncomfortably. "On that note, I must also be off myself. Good evening everyone, Tony. Good evening and I'll see you outside court at 8 a.m. sharp!"

Tony shook his hand. "Thank you, Vern. Goodnight."

"Right! Drink up, mouthy. Let's get off," Tony said, glaring at his dad. Ernie finished his light ale in one and the pair stood up to say goodbye to everyone.

Collette threw her arms around Tony's neck and hugged him tightly into her chest. "Good luck, sweetheart. I'm crossing everything for you," she breathed into his ear and gave him a big kiss on the cheek, leaving her lipstick imprint on him. He could have stayed in her embrace all night. Reluctantly, he pulled away from her and fought the urge of a deep stirring below in his jeans.

Karl held his arms out. "I'll be there with you, son. See you in the morning." Karl patted his back and now Al was patting him too. Tony went round in turn saying goodbye to everyone. He had a sad feeling, but wasn't sure why. He was nervous for tomorrow, there was no denying that, but his confidence was draining by the hour.

The following morning he was awake early at 5:30 a.m. His eyes had sprung open. He couldn't sleep again, no matter how hard he tried. He thought back to last night, suddenly a vision of Colette filled his mind. He could remember her smell and her pressing up against him. He slid his hand down his stomach and felt his morning glory. Fifteen guilty minutes later, he jumped into the shower. He was sure he wasn't the first person to fantasise about Collette!

"How do I look, Dad?" Tony asked as he walked into the kitchen.

Ernie took a step back and admired his son's appearance. "You look fantastic, Son!"

Tony was dressed in a smart dark suit, a crisp white shirt and smart red tie, shiny shoes and no jewellery, apart from his watch. His face was clean shaven, his hair combed smartly and parted to one side. He had achieved the look of the clean-cut businessman that Vernon would have wanted to see meeting him at the court. It really suited him. Ernie was bursting with pride at his son.

Tony had gone through his whole statement with Vernon. He had his story straight. Aaron had attacked him and he was acting in self-defence. Aaron had sustained the damaged due to Tony being a skilled fighter. Tony had witnesses on his side, saying that Aaron had started the whole fight. Vernon had advised Tony not to admit to slapping him first and that Aaron threw the first punch.

Karl had gone over and over with Tony that Aaron had slapped him first. Karl had said, "Make sure you believe yourself. You must believe in what you are saying, coz if you don't, then no one else will." This was the best bit of advice Tony had ever received.

Tony read his statement over and over again, memorising it as best he could – word for word. Glugging down the remains of his tea, he and Ernie left for court.

Vernon Jackson was waiting for Tony outside the court in the car park. It was 7:55 a.m.

"Perfect timing, Tony," Vernon said warmly, shaking his hand and then Ernie's. "How are you feeling this morning?" he asked, as he looked Tony up and down very much in approval of his appearance.

"Yeah I'm ok. What do you think then?" Tony said, brushing down the front of his jacket with his hand and motioning to his suit

"Splendid, Tony, splendid" Vernon said. "Right, come on then, quickly. Follow me." He scurried inside the court with Tony and Ernie following him.

"We have a meeting here in this room first." Vernon held his hand out to Tony, beckoning him to the room. It was like a small chamber room, and there sitting at the desk was a barrister. He stood up and introduced himself to Tony.

"Good Morning, Mr Hayes. My name is Mr Colin Moore, I'll be representing you today," he stood up to shake Tony's hand.

Tony stood back, confused. "No ... hold on ... he's not representing me. He doesn't even know me. He doesn't know my case," Tony burst out. "Vern? Why aren't you doing this with me?"

"Tony, please calm down. It's crown court, I'm not allowed to. You have to have a barrister," Vernon tried to reason with Tony. With that, there was a knock on the door. "Enter," Vernon said loudly, and in came Karl.

"Karl, have you heard this shit! I can't have Vern!" Tony blurted out immediately. Karl put his hand on Tony's shoulder and ushered him to sit down.

He held his hand out to Mr Moore and shook it. "I'm Mr Bateman. I'm here with Tony. Morning, Vern," Karl nodded to Vernon.

"Mr Hayes," Mr Moore addressed Tony now. "May I call you Tony? I have been in touch with the CPS. The prosecution have said that if you plead guilty to ABH, they will appeal and indicate to the judge a sentence of no more than two years imprisonment."

"TWO YEARS! TWO YEARS! Are you having a fucking laugh!" Tony leapt of his chair.

"Tony, calm down." Vernon was up on his feet now too, holding his hand out to Tony.

Tony's outrage continued, "That fucker starts a fight on me and I'm supposed to be pleading fucking guilty! He starts on me and I get taken to fucking court and *I'm* the one that ends up in prison! No! I won't fucking calm down!"

"Mr Hayes, *please!*" the barrister was frantically trying to calm Tony down.

"TONY!" Karl was in his face now, urging him to calm down and think.

The barrister continued, "I must advise you, Tony, if you go along with the prosecution, you could get fourteen months . . . you'll be out in eight months."

Vernon tried to appease him, "Tony, if the jury *do* rule in his favour and find you guilty of this offence, it could be up to seven years. Or, worst case scenario, it carries a maximum of fifteen years in prison."

Tony turned on Vernon, "*seven years! Seven fucking years!* If I get any time inside, that cunt

Aaron will be in a box! Karl! Do you know what I'm saying!"

"*Tony!* Just calm it, it's not gonna happen!" Karl said, turning to look at Vernon. "This is ridiculous!"

Tony turned to the barrister now, "Seven years!" Tony felt like his life was being torn from him. He started to feel panic rising up in his throat.

The barrister continued, "Hence why I say that if you go along with what the prosecution are proposing, you may be out in fourteen months."

"No fucking way! No one talked to me about a possible prison sentence. I'm not fucking guilty and that's it. I ain't going to prison. I'm not guilty. Fuck the lot of ya!"

The barrister sat back in his chair and held his hands together. A big, broad smile crept over his face displaying a perfect pearly-white smile as his eyes lit up from the insides. Karl and Tony stopped and looked at him. Vernon had loosened his tie slightly and sat back in his chair too.

"Now *that's* what I wanted to hear! That's *exactly* what I wanted to hear," Colin said, grinning from ear to ear. "I knew it was in there! Okay, so we know where we are with this then. I've read the paper work; it's six of one, half a dozen of the other. It's a silly fight. So on that note, let's go and take that *fucker* down and win!" Colin said, jumping up to his feet.

Chapter 47

TONY sat with Colin for an hour, going over crown courtroom etiquette. "You always look the jury straight in the eye, every time you are asked a question. You always say *Your Honour* when addressing the judge. Do not look at Mr Harris at all. Do not make any eye contact with him, his family or his friends." Tony was soaking this up like a sponge, listening intently to everything Colin said to him.

Vern and Karl were waiting quietly in the hallway with Ernie. "I'm sure it will be ok," Vernon said to Ernie. "It's going to be a long few days for you. And Tony won't be heard on the stand until the last day – we have to hear the police evidence first, then the prosecution and then witnesses are cross-examined. Tony will be up last on the final day. However, I am confident it will be ok. Colin Moore is very, very good."

It was 9:55 a.m. Court was due to commence at 10 a.m. sharp. Tony had been walked through to the dock and was sworn in and seated with a custody officer next to him. Karl and Ernie were seated in the viewing gallery. Ernie was fidgeting uncomfortably in his seat.

Colin Moore was seated on the defence bench. He was dressed in his black gown and short white wig. He had spun around and was discussing something very quietly with Vernon, who was seated on the solicitor's bench directly behind him. Tony looked around the huge courtroom. His dock was a semi-partitioned platform opposite the judge at the back of the court.

Heavy oak wood panelled every wall and bench, including the judge's bench at the front. It was very tall and boasted an impressive royal coat of arms on the wall behind it. Tony looked at the front desks where court clerks and similar officials were sitting, scribbling down short hand notes.

He took a deep breath in. It smelt of polish and a musty, unfamiliar smell that he didn't recognise. Alongside where Colin sat was the jury's bench. Opposite them was the witness box. Tony wondered who would be called up, and briefly thought about Suzie. *Would she be here?*

His thoughts were brought back to the room by the door opening. A court clerk came in and sat down, facing the court in front of the judge's bench. Tony could see Aaron's family sitting in the galleries too.

"Court rise," the usher said loudly. The custody officer motioned to Tony to stand now. The entire court room stood and the judge entered.

He sat down at his large bench and looked around his court room, dressed in his long black gown with a red and purple sash. He had a long white wig on and a stern look on his face that gave him an aged and weathered appearance. Tony felt his leg start to quiver – just one leg, and it was uncontrollable. He could feel his nerves running through his body and he had a sick feeling in his stomach. There were two police officers present and, at the judge's request, the usher proceeded to call the jury in.

Tony watched as the twelve jurors all walked into their bench, took their oaths and were sworn in and seated. He looked at each and every one of them, as if searching for their souls behind their eyes – some of them looked back at him. Then they all turned and faced the judge as he spoke to them, advising them to listen to the evidence that was to be presented before them.

Aaron's barrister stood up and addressed the court and began talking. He had a weasel-like appearance, a very odd looking man indeed. Tony took an instant dislike to him. Colin had forewarned Tony that the prosecution would try and trip him up and make him flustered. This barrister in particular was known for his aggressive approach.

"Don't panic," Colin had advised. "Just stay focused and breathe each time before you speak. If I think that they are goading you, I'll object. It'll be fine."

Tony's leg was still quivering.

The prosecution were first to give evidence. Tony noticed it was the arresting officers that had come to his house. They gave their statement and Tony watched them very closely. He noted their body language, how they stood and how they composed themselves. This officer in particular was standing holding onto the rail in front of him and seemed very confident. Tony made mental notes to adapt the same kind of confidence and composure.

It wasn't long before Aaron was called up to the stand. Tony couldn't believe his eyes – he looked like a hooligan. He had shaved his hair very short and was practically bald. He was wearing a scruffy suit that needed pressing; he really did look like he had just got out of bed.

Aaron very nervously read through his witness statement. The whole time he had his eyes lowered and not once did he attempt to make any eye contact with anyone. He stammered and stuttered his way through. It was at this point that the prosecution produced the photographs of Aaron's injuries.

The court room was suddenly filled with gasps and tutting sounds, with loud intakes of breath from the jury as they looked at the pictures of Aaron's face. Tony looked across at their faces – they were glaring at him now. He felt his cheeks flush scarlet and his stomach drop as he thought that was it – he was done for. The response from the jury was exactly what the prosecution had wanted. Tony felt like he could read their minds; o*h poor Aaron* and *what an animal Tony is.* That was it, he was going to lose. Colin turned and gave Tony a brief reassuring look but he couldn't help but feel his confidence sinking to his feet. Even the judge had looked at Tony in disgust.

It was now Colin's turn to cross-examine Aaron. Colin stood up and flicked his gown behind him. Armed with Aaron's statement he approached Aaron on the stand. Aaron briefly looked at him. "Good morning, Mr Harris!" Colin addressed him and he nodded back nervously. "So, let's go all the way back to the night in question, the night of the cinema. Can you tell the court what film you were going to see?" Colin said cheerfully.

"Sex, Lies and Videotape," Aaron said quietly.

"Speak up please so the court can hear you!"

"SEX LIES AND VIDEO TAPE," Aaron said louder.

"Sex, *Lies* and Videotape indeed. And on the night in question you state that you were in the queue waiting for the film. Now, the court has yet to hear my client's statement. *He* clearly states that *he* was *already* in the queue. Now what we need firstly to ascertain here is where exactly you parked when you arrived at the cinema. You see, this is somewhat important. Now, I have a small map here of the area and the road where cars are parked. Could you please, for the benefit of everyone in court, show me and point to *where you actually* parked your car?" Colin handed a small map to Aaron.

"I parked here, on this road," Aaron said, pointing to a road on the map.

"Oh I see, you parked *there*. That's lovely. So you would have had to walk across the road here to get to the queue, thank you. Now, when you were in the queue, did you by chance see what direction Mr Hayes walked from?"

Aaron thought for a second. "Well . . . he just kinda walked up to me."

"He just walked up to you . . . what, from behind you? from in front of you? from the left? the right? Did you see him cross the road in front of you? Or did he just seem to appear magically in front of you? I need to be sure which direction he came from."

"I dunno . . . I was in the queue but he came from behind me. Yep, definitely behind me. Then he stopped and turned around," Aaron said.

Colin raised an eyebrow at Aaron, "He *did?* Okay, now, you state that you parked here," Colin again indicated on the map where Aaron had parked. "Are you absolutely, one hundred per cent certain of that fact?"

"Yep," Aaron said cockily.

"Okay. Now, you also said My Hayes walked from behind you. Now if that was the case, where would you suggest that Mr Hayes had parked? Or did he not park?" Colin asked.

"Well *I* don't know," Aaron said bluntly.

"OBJECTION!" Aaron's barrister jumped up. "How can you ⌐˅⌐ect my client to know the whereabouts of a parked car? You cannot ˅ed with this line of questioning."

ʼerruled. Please continue, Mr Moore," the judge let Colin

"Well my client states that he parked *here,*" Colin pointed to the map. "Could he have possibly parked here?" Aaron nodded. Colin continued, "And the queue was along here and quite long, is that a fact?" again, Aaron nodded. Colin went on, "So the nearest place to park by that time would have actually been where you parked? My client says in his statement that he saw you walk from up the road, which is about thirty yards, then across the crossing and then you came up from the front of the queue towards him, which suggests that you could have only come from that direction. And that direction was *exactly* where you have pointed out that you parked . . . the exact spot where you just *confirmed* you parked. So remembering that you *are* under oath, I put it to you that you arrived *after* my client, given the location of your parked car. So would it be possible to state that indeed you did arrive *afterwards* and can now perhaps confirm that Mr Hayes was in the queue first?"

Aaron started fidgeting in his seat uncomfortably. He shook his head at Colin.

"You *will* need to *answer* the questions *verbally* Mr Harris. The jury may misread a head shake. Before we go on any further, are we to assume that you may have indeed fabricated the rest of your statement too?"

The cross-examination continued with Colin battering down Aaron's statement and pulling him to bits. Aaron kept looking at the floor.

"My Hayes and yourself were good friends, were you not? And Mr Hayes and yourself would often socialise together on a Friday evening, is that correct?"

Aaron nodded and answered "Yes".

"And I believe you and Mr Hayes had fallen out over the lending of a vehicle. Is that correct?" Colin tricked Aaron into telling him about the incident with the accident and van. Colin and the entire court room listened intently as Aaron's story unfolded before them.

"So am I correct in believing that you had grounds to attack Mr Hayes then? You were so angry that he had crashed the front of the van? And you state that he *hadn't repaired it to your liking*, that you were *bad mouthing* him and threatening to *beat him up*? PLEASE REMEMBER THAT YOU ARE UNDER OATH, MR HARRIS!"

Aaron was losing his temper now and getting himself flustered as Colin went on and on.

"Mr Harris, you say that Mr Hayes threw the first punch and instigated the fight. I put it to you that Mr Hayes did *not* throw the first punch and that it is quite clear here for everyone to see that you had motivation to attack Mr Hayes. So I put it to you that the reason you *do not* know where Mr Hayes parked his car was because he was in the queue before you. You did not see him arrive, as you suggested, but the other way around. You approached him as you were angry about your van and you instigated the fight."

"NO, NO, NO!" Aaron started to shout at Colin.

Colin turned to the judge. "We do have witnesses, Your Honour, that elude to the fact that Mr Harris did indeed instigate the fight and was also seen and heard going around the area in their local drinking establishments informing all of their friends that he was going to *beat Mr Hayes up.*"

The judge raised a bushy eyebrow. "Please continue with your examination, Mr Moore, unless you and your learned friend are ready to start calling on your witnesses?"

"I am indeed finished, Your Honour. No further questions." Colin returned to his bench. Tony sat there in awe and suddenly he began to feel hopeful. He turned and saw Karl smiling and saying something quietly to Ernie. The sinking feeling that he had earlier was diminishing by the minute.

"We will break for lunch and court will commence at one p.m. sharp," announced the judge.

"COURT RISE," the usher said loudly.

Chapter 48

"WHAT'S the matter with you? You've got a face like a slapped arse!" Stuart yelled at Jacki, as she sat there in silence.

She looked at her watch. It was almost 2:30 p.m. Tony would still be in court. She hadn't heard from Ernie and she was worried. "Nothing. I was just wondering how Tony was getting on, that's all." Stuart tutted loudly and dismissed her. "He *is* my brother and I am allowed to be concerned," Jacki carried on sulkily.

"Oh who *gives* a shit! He's a fucking wrong'un," Stuart spat at her, a cigarette hanging from the corner of his mouth. "He deserves to be banged up! Serve him fucking right! He walks about giving it the big *I am* . . . fuck him!"

He stopped and looked at Jacki who was shaking now at his raised voice. "What you fucking shaking for? Ain't you got anything better you could be doing? Ironing or me dinner? Instead of just sitting there wasting your time worrying about him . . . it's not like he fucking worries about you, is it?"

"All I wanted to do was go to the court and support him," Jacki said snappily

"Shut the fuck up or I'll shut you up. You're boring me now. Your place is here with me in this flat. You ain't got time to fucking run around after him. You should be running around after me."

"But I just wanted to go. It's not like Mum's there . . . he needs all the support he can get. It wouldn't have hurt to let me pop there for a few hours. I've not got loads to do here. I'm up to date with the washing, and shopping can be done later . . . and I'm not working at the moment. I've got plenty of time to iron and clean," Jacki was wailing now.

"You're not working because I said you're not working. I know where you are when you're at home," Stuart snapped back.

"But I don't want to stay at home all day. I want to go and see my brother."

"DON'T FUCKING START! I'm warning you. Shut up!" Stuart said. His eyes had turned to cold blue slits and his nostrils were flared with anger. He stubbed his cigarette out in the ashtray.

Jacki started sobbing, her body shaking from crying.

"SHUT UP!" he screamed at her, but she only sobbed harder. In an instant, Stuart leapt up out of his seat. Raising his hand above his head, he brought it down hard across her face, sending her sprawling to the floor and into a ball. He kicked her hard in the ribs making her scream out in pain. Jacki felt sick and her head felt fuzzy. Her vision was blurring and she could feel a nauseas sensation. Her arm started jerking – she knew what that meant. Any minute now she was going to have a fit. Jacki was epileptic. She had been since she was a small girl and prone to fitting whenever she was tired or stressed. It was starting. Her body began to pulsate and jerk. She was having a fullblown fit.

About half an hour later, Jacki opened her eyes. She was lying on the floor on her side. She looked around her and for a second she had forgotten where she was. She went to roll over onto her back and her stomach burned in pain. It was her ribs. It was excruciating pain. Her head was pulsing and she knew then that she'd had a fit. She had a metallic taste in her mouth and her throat was dry.

She tried to sit up. She listened around her but there was no noise. *Was anyone in?*

"*Stuart!*" she called from the floor. "Stu. Help me, *please!*" Again, her only reply was silence. He must have gone out and left her again. She suddenly remembered an argument – she must have wound him up again. She was always doing that. He always got so cross with her but she didn't know why. Slowly, she managed to sit up. She thought she must have definitely broken a rib. With every breath in and out, the pain seared through her like a knife. Slowly, very, very slowly, she managed to get her feet. She held onto the side of the sofa as she gently and slowly took tiny baby steps towards the kitchen. She needed a glass of water. As she made her way up the hallway, she passed the mirror hanging on the wall. She glanced into it. Staring back at her was someone she vaguely recognised. Only the girl looking back at her had an enormous bruise on her cheek and her eye was black and swollen so badly she could hardly see out if it. *Damn it, I must have smashed it when I had a fit and fell,* she convinced herself, turning to look away.

Stuart Wright was a thirty-four-year-old delivery driver from London. He was a good ten years senior to Jacki. They had met three years ago when she was working at the same firm. She had just turned twenty and was working as a part-time telephonist.

He was funny, he was charming and made her laugh. He had wooed her. He had taken her out for fine meals and dazzled her with trinkets. Jacki had never been much into boys. She was quite a shy girl in comparison to her younger brother – and very naive

Jacki had suffered from epilepsy ever since she was 11 years old. This had held her back in her confidence to go out. She was quite a tall, slim girl who had inherited her mother's dark hair and Irish looks. Tony and her were like chalk and cheese in every single way. Having lived with Dot right up until she had met and moved in with Stuart, she had never experienced independence as Tony had, and was very heavily reliant on others. Dot was thrilled when Jacki had taken Stuart round to meet her, although there was something about him that Dot just could not put her finger on. Something didn't ring true about him. He was shifty and would often leave Jacki waiting around when he was supposed to meet her. He was always late and sometimes he just never showed up at all. But Jacki always forgave him and when he eventually said they should get a flat together, Jacki was over the moon.

They moved in and Dot had come round to help them. She had bought a moving in present – a rubber plant. The flat had a cold and unwelcoming feel to it that Dot had instantly picked up on. Jacki was running from room to room looking for bits and trying to unpack while Stuart sat drinking cans of larger. Dot had nipped to the shops across the road and picked them up fish and chips for their supper, as there hadn't been time to cook. Later that night, it was almost 10 p.m. when Dot bid farewell and left them to it.

Stuart seemed quite drunk and he had staggered to the kitchen to look for another ashtray. "Why did we have to have fucking fish and chips? What you letting your mum treat us to that for? We don't need fucking charity. She best not start coming round 'ere sticking her fucking nose in my business. This is *my* house!" he yelled through to Jacki as she was unpacking boxes in the bedroom.

"I didn't have time to cook anything. We've just moved in today, babe."

Suddenly there was an almighty smash from the kitchen. Jacki flew through to see what had happened. There, on the floor, was a smashed pot and soil. The rubber plant lay broken on its side. Stuart barged past her, "Make time in future! And I fucking hate plants!" he said, storming out and leaving the mess in the kitchen.

Stuart's temper seemed to get worse and worse as the months rolled into years. Many arguments would occur with her working as a receptionist. Stuart had a terrible jealous streak in him and if Jacki so much as looked at another man, let alone spoke to one, he would fly off the handle. Eventually, he demanded that she give up her job and stay at home. The arguments continued and the relationship became volatile. But Jacki never said a word to Dot.

Stuart was becoming a slob and a drunk. Most nights he would stop by the working man's club on his way home from work and have a few too many beers. He would then go home to Jacki. Sometimes in a good mood, sometimes not – with a terrified Jacki paying the consequences.

Chapter 49

"COURT rise," the usher instructed. Lunch was over, and next to take the stand was Aaron's girlfriend, Lydia. She was very nervous as she stood and swore the oath.

The prosecution read over her statement and questioned her. Of course she had said that Tony was a violent animal that had attacked her boyfriend. She confirmed Aaron's statement and said that Tony had attacked Aaron in the queue. However, when it was Colin's turn to cross examine Lydia, she said she couldn't remember Tony hitting Aaron first. She remembered the fight but had forgotten who threw the first punch. Tony shot a look to Aaron who was sitting in the court gallery now. He looked furious with Lydia and was shaking his head. This wasn't good as this would cast doubt on his side. Colin tore her apart, going over and over her exact words from her statement which she seemed to have forgotten. Eventually, the prosecution called him off for goading the witness and she left the stand in tears. "No further questions, Your Honour," Colin beamed as he returned to his bench.

By now the time was almost 4 p.m. The judge decided to adjourn court until 10 a.m. the following morning and turned and exited. The prosecution gathered up their paperwork and hurried out.

Tony left and walked out to meet Colin and Vernon. "All going well so far, Tony," Colin said as he shook Tony's hand. Karl was beside him now, shaking his hand too. "I must dash off, but I'll see you all in court in the morning," Colin excused himself.

Tony was surprised at Aaron's behaviour today. He imagined that Aaron would have come across as a much stronger character – maybe that was his angle, his ploy to make the court feel sorry for him. *Well he had certainly achieved that,* Tony thought. He could still see the faces of the jury all glaring at him like he was an animal.

"Let's see what happens tomorrow," Karl said, giving Tony a

reassuring pat on the shoulder. "Get a good night's sleep tonight and I'll see you all in the morning. I've got a bit of business to sort out tonight with Al, so I can't hang about." Karl shook Ernie's hand and made his way out of the court.

"I don't want a late one this evening, Dad. How about we head over to the club to see all your old mates again and have a few beers there and call it an early one," Tony said, as he and Ernie made their way to the car park.

It was 7 p.m. Tony and Ernie had grabbed a bite to eat and were sitting at the bar of the British Legion Club just off the estate. It was a nice little local for Ernie when he lived here. Quite often, all the men would meet up for a game of cards and a few cheap beers. But there was hardly anyone in there this evening.

Tony had just ordered his first pint when he looked over and noticed Stuart at the end of the other bar, around the corner. He was leaning up at the bar chatting to the barmaid.

"Oh fuck, what's he doing 'ere!" Tony said. He didn't particularly like Stuart, and neither did he cherish the thought of spending an evening in the same place as him.

"Oh he ain't doing no harm, is he? Just ignore him. He's alright," Ernie said. He didn't mind Stuart.

"Yeah, if you like fucking morons," Tony said. "I don't trust him . . . something don't sit right with me and him." Tony looked over again and, at that moment, Stuart spotted Ernie and started to wander over.

"Evening all," Stuart sneered at them. He'd had a little too much to drink now and was slurring his words. "How'd it go today? Didn't get banged up today then, Tone?" he said grinning.

"Obviously not, you div!" Tony retorted. Ernie gave him a quick kick in the ankle.

"Ah don't be like, Tone. I was just asking," Stuart said. He seemed genuinely hurt at Tony's remark.

"What happened to Jacki? She said she was gonna try and pop up the court today," Tony asked.

"Oh she's not been too well today. Had a teeny tiny fit earlier she did, so she's been in bed all afternoon resting. Thought I'd better let her sleep so I'm here. I'll have pint if you're buying, Tone," he grinned at Tony with a mouth full of fillings and bad teeth. He really made Tony's skin crawl.

"I hate him, fat ponce," Tony said when Stuart had gone to the toilet.

"Don't be rude, your sister likes him. Leave it there!" Ernie's instructions were clear.

Stuart returned from the gents. Tony stood up, "Don't mean to be rude, but I'm heading off now. Got an early start in the morning. Give me love to Jacki." Tony swigged back the rest of his pint and Stuart stood up to shake his hand, but Tony ignored it.

"Hold on, I'm coming!" Ernie said, as he quickly downed his pint too. "What's the bleeding rush?"

"I just said, Dad. I got an early start ain't I?" Tony said impatiently and turned and left the pub.

"Alright, alright!" Ernie said, rushing out of the pub after him.

* * *

It was shortly after 9 p.m. that night. The phone was ringing at Dean's House. "Hello?" Dean grabbed it before it rang off.

"DEANO! It's Rob!"

"Alright, Rob? How's things, mate?" Dean suddenly realised he was supposed to keep Rob informed of Tony's trial.

"How did Tone get on today? I did try to call his phone but there was no answer. I ain't got long though, geezer. I gotta get back!" Rob said hurriedly.

"Sorry, Rob, mate. I didn't get off work today to get to the trial. Ernie said that he would call me but I've not heard from him. So I got no news I'm afraid."

"Oh shit! Are you going tomorrow?" Rob asked, he was desperate to know that Tony was ok.

"Yeah, definitely. One hundred per cent, I'm there tomorrow. Call me tomorrow evening about this time and I'll tell you what's happened," Dean said.

"Cheers, geez. Gotta bolt now. Catch ya later." The phone line clicked dead and Rob had gone.

The front door slammed, making Jacki jump. It was just after 11 p.m. She had been resting on the settee in the front room as she couldn't get to the bedroom. Her ribs were too painful to move about much and her blackened face was swollen.

A very drunk Stuart appeared in the doorway. "Feeling fucking better, are we?" he glared at her. She nodded, but said nothing. She remembered the argument now, but she didn't want to start it off again so she said nothing.

"Guess who I fucking saw this evening? Guess! *Guess!* I'll fucking tell you then! I saw your precious little brother. He's not banged up, so you don't have to worry, do ya! See, all that fucking fuss and you weren't needed there after all. And I had a drink with your old man! He's back from Geordie land for a bit."

Jacki's face lit up. "Did they ask after me?" she said.

"Nope. Why would they?" Stuart said nastily. "Where's my dinner? I'm fucking starving." He eyed about the room to see if she had eaten anything,

Jacki instantly felt the fear run through her. She hadn't made him anything to eat. She could hardly move. "I haven't made any. I came round after my fit a while ago but I can hardly move. I think I must have busted a rib."

"That was fucking ages ago! You've been lying about all fucking evening! Get out there and make me a fucking sandwich, fucking lazy bitch!"

Jacki half-crawled, half-dragged herself to the kitchen to try and make a sandwich and a coffee. The look on his face told her not to even dare to argue. She didn't need another episode like earlier.

Chapter 50

IT was 10 a.m. sharp. The court was all gathered and awaiting the judge.

Tony looked over and smiled to see that in the gallery was his dad, Karl, Al, and Dean had come today too. He felt better knowing he had all this support with him. He did notice too that Aaron hadn't appeared in court today. Neither had any of his friends or family.

Today, the prosecution said they had finished their case and had called all their witnesses. It was now time for the defence case to be heard. They called up their first witness. "Miss Suzanna Thomas," the usher called her name and she appeared at the door of the court next to the usher.

Tony just couldn't help but stare at her. The hairs on the back of his neck all stood on end – she looked amazing. He had a pain in his heart as he watched her take the stand and swear the oath. She glanced over at Tony in the dock. She smiled a very small and discreet smile at him. *God he missed her.*

Colin went through Suzie's statement. She was very adamant that Aaron had thrown the first punch. She made it very clear that Aaron had been bad mouthing Tony. She really did a good convincing job. Tony sat watching her as she answered all of Colin's questions quickly and accurately. Colin was pleased. "No further questions, Your Honour," he said, and sat down.

The prosecution walked towards Suzie. "Miss Thomas," he said, looking at her. Suzie blinked back at him and smiled. "Miss Thomas, would I be correct in saying that Mr Hayes was a fighter?"

Suzie thought carefully for a moment. "Yes, Tony has had some fights in his time. He was a boxer," she answered.

The prosecution didn't like this answer. "He has had some awful fights in pubs though, on more than one occasion, hasn't he, Miss Thomas? Would I be correct in saying that?"

"I haven't seen Tony have any fights in pubs. Not while I was with him," Suzie said.

"Wouldn't it be safe to say that, being his girlfriend, you would of course back up his story, Miss Thomas?"

Suzie looked thoughtful and said, "I'm sorry but Tony and I are no longer a couple, and haven't been for a while now."

The prosecution looked bewildered. "Why is that? if you don't mind me asking," the barrister pushed her. "Is it because he was a violent and abusive partner who regularly got into fights because he was overcome with jealousy and rage?" the barrister looked pleased with himself, as if he had uncovered a vital piece of information that might help. The courtroom seemed to hold its breath in anticipation of Suzie's answer.

"Objection!" Colin jumped up.

But Suzie continued, "no, not at all," Suzie smiled. "Tony was the kindest and gentlest man I have ever met. In fact, it was *him* who ended it with me . . . for personal reasons. I was very sad. We were engaged to get married. Do you think I would have been engaged to a monster?" she added.

The jury seemed intrigued. Everything the prosecution said, she had an answer to. He couldn't trip her up or fluster her at all. She remained calm throughout the whole questioning.

"No further questions," the prosecution had to admit defeat and give in.

After Suzie, there were a further two witnesses called onto the stand by Colin. One was a friend of both Tony and Aaron whom had given a statement to say that Tony was indeed the first in the queue. The other was a witness from the pub to say that he had heard that Aaron was bad mouthing Tony in the pub and that Aaron was threatening to beat Tony up. He went on to say that Tony had gone to Aaron's house to make amends and resolve the dispute but that Aaron had refused.

The prosecution tried every angle to make Tony look bad. They kept on about him being a boxer and referring to him as 'a lethal weapon'. The jury still had frowns painted across their faces as they heard more and more about Tony.

The judge decided to break for lunch. "Court adjourned and meet after lunch at 2 p.m. sharp." The judge left the court. Tony needed a pint.

Sitting in the pub across the road, Tony couldn't help but think about Suzie. Dean had picked up on Tony's vibes. "You ok, mate? It's hard isn't it?"

Tony looked at Dean and smiled. "Oh, mate. I felt sick looking at her standing there . . . hearing her voice. She was amazing . . . so cool and . . . just amazing. Maybe I fucked up ending it after all."

"Tony, what she did was unforgivable. You know that. Yeah, she looked good. Yeah, she's gorgeous and yeah she said some really heartfelt things . . . but . . . what can I say? A pizza always looks good, always looks gorgeous, and you really fancy it. Then you eat it and you feel sick and knew that you didn't really want it . . . you just ate it for the sake of eating. Know what I'm trying to say here?"

Tony laughed at Dean's metaphor, "Very good, mate. I feel sooo much better now!"

"Oops . . . time to regurgitate that pizza, mate," Al said, motioning towards the door of the pub. Suzie was standing there looking at them.

"Suzie!" Tony said, jumping up and heading over to her. She smiled as she watched him rush towards her. They hugged an awkward embrace and he bent to kiss her on the cheek. He could smell the familiar perfume that she wore. He really wanted to wrap her into his arms and hold her tight, but he could hear Dean's words in the back of his head. The image of a pizza suddenly came to mind, and he stifled back a grin. "Good to see you. Thank you so much for coming. Let me get you a drink," he said as he led Suzie to the bar.

"Just a quick coke, thank you," she replied.

Tony could see Dean in the background laughing with Al.

"How are you holding up?" Suzie said quietly as she sipped her drink.

Tony laughed, "Well, I'm pretty sure the jury hate me. They think I'm an animal! The judge looks like he wants to bang me up for life. The prosecution are desperate to rip me apart limb by limb . . . but all that aside . . . yeah I'm fine!"

"Yeah they're a pretty tough crowd," Suzie laughed. "But you seem to be holding it together well. If you *are* nervous, it's not showing."

"So, how have you been?" Tony asked.

"Yeah I'm ok. I'm living with Tasha now."

Tony thought back to the night at Tasha's flat. He wondered if Suzie knew – clearly not.

"Are you seeing anyone?" Tony asked her honestly.

"Yeah, I'm kinda seeing this guy. It's nothing too serious though . . . you?" she said awkwardly.

"Oh no! I'm off serious girlfriends thanks! Got too much other shit going on, as you can see."

Suzie laughed. "Listen, Tone. I've been told I can leave now. I'm not needed for any more questioning . . . so . . . I just wanted to wish you luck and I hope it all works out for you. You know what I mean. Good luck with the trial . . . let me know if you can how it goes." She lent upwards to kiss Tony on the cheek.

"Cheers, babe," he said. "Oh . . . and Suzie . . . thanks for what you said in court. I really appreciate you coming and saying all that. Thank you. I hope it all works out for you too with your new fella and stuff."

Suzie looked at Tony, "I meant what I said in there, Tony. You really were the kindest guy I've ever met." He bent down and hugged her and then watched as she turned and walked out of the pub. Dean was right. You should never go back.

"She ok?" Ernie asked, as Tony went back and sat at the table with everyone.

"Yeah, Dad. She's fine! Come one everyone, let's drink up and get back. It's almost two."

Chapter 51

IT was the afternoon that everyone had been waiting for. Tony was on the stand. The usher called him up and he was sworn in. "Mr Anthony Hayes. Please place your hand over the bible and say your oath."

"I swear by almighty God that the evidence I shall give shall be the truth, the whole truth and nothing but the truth," Tony said loudly and clearly. His leg was shaking again.

Colin approached the stand. "Mr Hayes. Would you be so kind as to read to the court nice and loudly your statement."

Tony proceeded to read his statement out. He made sure he kept looking up at the jury as he spoke so he felt he was addressing them directly. He had practised this speech and he knew it perfectly word for word. He had made himself believe every word of it too, as Karl had advised. He explained how Aaron had been bad mouthing him around the pubs and how he had tried to resolve this by meeting up with Aaron. He then explained that Aaron had instigated the fight by throwing the first punch and attacking him in the queue and how Aaron's brother had smashed his van up.

"What film were you and your ex-girlfriend, Miss Thomas, going to see?" Colin asked him.

"Sex, Lies and Videotape, sir," Tony said.

"Lovely. And what did you think of the film?" Colin asked.

"I didn't actually see the film, sir, in the end, as Suzie and I had to leave the cinema." "And for what reason was this?" Colin asked.

"Well, after Mr Harris had punched me in the side of the head, I had blurred vision and the veins in my eyes had started to bleed so we had to leave and go home, sir." Tony went on to explain that the bleeding veins were the result of a boxing injury that he had sustained when he was younger.

"So Mr Harris had punched you in the side of the temple, temporarily blurring your vision?" There were gasps from the jury as Aaron's clean-cut image suddenly had flaws in it. The judge was taking down notes too now.

Colin summed up his questioning, "Would it be fair of me, Mr Hayes, to say that perhaps Mr Harris had submitted an inaccurate statement of events, then? Seeing as he failed to mention when questioned that he had made any contact with you that had left you with any damage? Would it have been likely that Mr Harris would not have known about this boxing injury and may have unknowingly lashed out the severe punch to the temple, rendering you temporarily blinded in that eye?"

"No, sir. Mr Harris and I were friends for a fair amount of time and he was fully aware of my injuries to the eye and knew that this would be a good place to attack me."

"No further questions, Your Honour!" Colin finished his questioning.

The judge paused for a moment and read back some of his notes. He checked his watch and scribbled something down before he addressed the court room. "I do feel that this thorough line of questioning has somewhat eaten into our afternoon. So therefore, I propose that, as the cross examination is due next, and this will also be quite a lengthy process, we should adjourn for today and that Mr Hayes takes the stand first thing in the morning. If we are all agreed, then I say *court adjourned* until tomorrow morning."

The court room quickly cleared for the afternoon. Tony mentioned to Vernon that he noticed that Aaron hadn't shown up for court.

"Very observant, Tony. Yes, I had noticed that myself. It isn't necessary for him to attend court, now that he has given his evidence and taken the stand . . . though I do feel rather like he should be in attendance, whichever way the law rules."

That evening, Karl had invited everyone to the wine bar. They were all sitting at the bar discussing what had happened that day.

"I've got to be honest. I am shitting myself," Tony admitted. "I'm telling you, that jury hate me!"

"I did see them keep glaring over at you," Dean said.

"They've been doing since day one," Ernie said. "Ever since those poxy photographs came out they've hardly been on my side at all."

"Well . . . we don't know that for sure, do we?" Karl said, trying to sound reasonable. In the back of his mind though, he had a horrible sinking feeling. "And listen, we can always appeal, can't we? I've already spoken to Vern and Colin about that!"

"Ahh cheers, Karl. Thanks for the confidence!" Tony said angrily. "I ain't going down for this.I swear to God I'm not. I can't! I'll do a fucking bunk!"

"Too late for that. Where the fuck you gonna run to? You're standing in a dock!" Al said.

"I can't go down! I just *can't*! What the fuck am I gonna do?" he stood up and downed his pint. "I'm off home. I can't deal with this tonight."

"Tone, come on man. Stay a bit."

"Nah, you're alright. I'm going home. I need to be level-headed tomorrow. It's a big day for me . . . or hadn't some of you realised!" Tony turned on his toes and walked out of the wine bar. "Oh dear, I'd better get off after him. He'll be alright, don't worry. See yous tomorrow!" Ernie said, jumping up.

"And me," Dean said too. "I've gotta speak to Rob this evening. He'll be calling me to see how today went," Dean said, leaving the bar.

"Fucking hell . . . he's fucked!" Al said. "I'm telling ya now. He ain't gonna cope if he gets bird."

Karl just raised his eyebrows and shot him a look. "I know! I was thinking the same thing meself."

An hour or so later, Dean had grabbed the ringing phone off its cradle. He knew it would be Rob.

"Alright, man! How's it going, what happened today?" Rob said.

Dean explained about the day's events, how the jury had such a downer on him, and the pictures that had been passed about of Aaron showing his injuries, who the witnesses were and what they said. Rob was happy that Suzie had shown up. "It's looking a bit grim though to be honest, Rob. Vern told me it's a maximum of fifteen years if he's found guilty . . . but they reckon he could be looking at about seven years. Out in three if he's lucky."

"What? Seven years! No way! I bet Tone's freaking out. I should be with him, not here!" Rob was getting upset.

"Rob, what can you possibly do? Even if you were here, you couldn't do anything. It's in the hands of the jury, mate. He's back on the stand tomorrow being cross-examined by the prosecution. So fingers crossed that the jury go off and come back with a not-guilty verdict! Call me tomorrow and I'll let you know what happened."

"Ok, mate. Will do. Gotta go now. Cheers, Dean," Rob rang off. He was clearly upset for Tony. *What else could he have said? Lied to him maybe. He'd have found out in three weeks when he's back from training anyway*, thought Dean.

Tony was lying in his bed looking up at the ceiling. This could be the last time he saw his ceiling for a long time – the last time he saw his room and his flat. He looked around the room. *Come on, snap out of this negative thought*, he tried to tell himself. *Think positive!* He squeezed his eyes shut tight, but he just couldn't fall sleep. He sat up on his bed and lit a cigarette. He could hear his dad snoring in the other room. He'd overheard his dad talking to Margaret on the phone this evening, telling her how the trial was going. Even his dad didn't sound confident. Tony had to admit to himself that he was scared. *How was he going to cope? What if he did get sent down? All because of that stupid prick Aaron!*

It was 2:35 a.m. The number 218N night bus pulled into the bus stop at the top of the high street. The bus was empty all bar one passenger. The passenger jumped off at the stop and nodded his thanks to the driver. He dug his hands down deep into his pockets and, pulling his coat tightly around him, scurried off into the night across the estate and up the stairwell to the Hayes' flat.

Chapter 52

ERNIE was suddenly awoken by the frantic knocking on the front door. The doorbell was ringing and someone was hammering the door down. He leapt out of bed and, grabbing a wooden bat, made his way down the stairs to the front door.

Tony was on his heels, he too was wielding a bat from under his bed. "WHAT THE FUCK!"

Tony was shouting. He'd only been asleep an hour or so and now he had been woken up by this.

Ernie reached out and wrenched the front door open before it was hammered off its hinges.

His mouth fell as he opened the door. "Holy shit! What the bloody hell are you doing here?"

Ernie swung the door open fully to show Tony. There on the doorstep was a shivering Rob. He had broken out of his training and gone AWOL to come and be with Tony. Tony couldn't believe his eyes. He flung his arms around Rob's neck. "Fucking hell, Rob. What's happening?"

"Come in, come in and shut the door," Ernie said as he bundled the boy inside and slammed the door shut behind him.

Tony couldn't believe his eyes as they all sat in the kitchen. "Rob, you are gonna be in so much shit! You'll get nicked! You can't do this. You're gonna have to go back."

Ernie slid each of them a mug of steaming hot tea.

"Tony, I had to be here with you. After everything you've ever done for me, I couldn't stay there and let you go through this by yourself. I spoke to Dean earlier and he told me how the trial was going. Possible seven years! I didn't think I was gonna see you for ages if you went down . . . and it sounds that way from what Dean was saying. So I decided I'd break out just after midnight and come here so I can at least be with you tomorrow. I was going mad not knowing what was going on.

Dean said the jury are fuckers!"

Tony didn't know what to say. He just sat and smiled at his mate. His best mate!

"Best thing to do now would be to get some sleep and we'll sort this in the morning," Ernie said. "It's really late now and we've all got an early start. I can always drop you back tomorrow, Rob."

"No way! I ain't leaving here till after the trial's over. I'm staying with me mate! I'll sort it ... it'll be ok. I'll have a punishment, probably get banged up for a bit and I'm sure they'll understand when I explain it to them."

"Rob, I still can't believe you have done this for me!" Tony was still speechless.

"Come on now, let's all head off to bed. Rob, will you be ok on the sofa tonight?" Ernie said, jumping up to fetch some clean sheets for Rob.

"Yeah, of course. I'll get me nut down there, no problems. Listen, please don't either of you say anything to me mum that I'm here. She'll only worry and I won't have time to pop in. I'll have to get back straight away ... so best she doesn't know really."

Tony and Ernie understood. She'd be so upset if she found out.

Tony lay back in bed. He was never going to sleep now. He looked at the clock. It was 3:30 a.m. He had to be up in three hours or so. He squeezed his eyes tight shut. The next thing he knew, his alarm clock was going off beside him. He rolled over and slapped the snooze button; it was 6:55 a.m. It felt like he had only just closed his eyes. Suddenly, he remembered last night. He leapt out of bed and flew downstairs to see if it had been a dream ...

There lay Rob spread out, sound asleep and snoring on the sofa.

It was just over an hour later and the three of them were dressed and standing there practically ready to go. Tony had lent Rob a suit. It was slightly ill-fitting as Rob was quite a bit shorter and stockier than

Tony. Nonetheless, it was better than going in the army uniform that he had left in the dead of night in. Tony had bigger feet than Rob, but the shoes were only slightly too big. Rob stood in front of the mirror and straightened his tie. "How do I look?" he said with a lopsided grin.

"Do I look like a plank or what!"

"You'll do," Tony said proudly, shoving a plate of toast at him. "Don't get butter on the tie!"

Dean couldn't believe his eyes when he saw Rob walking into the court with Tony and Ernie. "Bloody hell! You're a sight for sore eyes! I can't believe you're here!" Dean said, throwing his arms around Rob.

Rob hugged him back. "Couldn't not be here, Deano."

Dean was pleased to see Rob, but he also knew he'd be in massive trouble when he got back. Rob took a seat in the gallery with everyone. Karl stood to greet him, "Good to see ya, mate," he said as he shook his hand.

Everyone was nervous today. None more so than Tony. He was waiting to be called to the stand and sworn in again.

"Court rise," the usher said.

Everyone stood and waited as the judge entered the court and took his seat. "Good morning, everyone," he said smiling around him. "Ok. We have a busy day and lots to get through, so we will proceed straight away with the prosecution's cross-examination," he said cheerfully and passed the floor over to the prosecution bench to begin.

Chapter 53

"GOOD morning, Mr Hayes," the prosecution greeted him.

"Good morning, sir," Tony replied.

"So, let's start by recapping on your statement from yesterday. We won't go through the whole statement . . . we don't want to bore the jury."

"OBJECTION!" Moore immediately jumped to his feet. "M' Lord, that's ambiguous to the jury."

"Sustained," the judge said to Moore. "I think we could briefly review the entire statement for the jury and the court's benefit," the judge said politely, agreeing with Moore.

The prosecution rolled his eyes as if he were performing in a pantomime. He seemed in a rush to have this cross-examination over with. "Indeed, Your Honour. Well, let's start with the night in question, shall we? Mr Hayes, there are a few details I need to ask you. You say in your statement that you were already in the queue waiting patiently with Miss Thomas, your *then* girlfriend. Although my client, Mr Harris, states that he and his girlfriend were already in the queue and that you approached him with an onslaught of punches and kicks . . . obviously causing the damage that we have seen in the photographic evidence earlier in this trial. Is that correct, Mr Hayes? Please may we see *said* pictures again. Please pass them around the jury again . . . I happen to have an extra copy here. Please have a look for yourself, Mr Hayes. You did inflict these injuries, did you not?" The prosecution handed Tony a copy of one of the photographs and smiled smugly.

"No, that's not true, sir."

"What's not true, Mr Hayes? That you did not cause this damage to my client?"

"No, sir. That's not true. I was in the queue first," Tony said, dismissing the picture in front of him.

"Well, yes, you say that you were in the queue first. However, we are here to ascertain the facts, Mr Hayes. And the facts do not ring true with your story. How would it be possible that, according to your story, you only retaliated and hit Mr Harris twice?"

"Yes, sir. That's correct. I only hit him twice and it was in retaliation."

The prosecution sniggered to the court. "Oh, Mr Hayes. Do you really expect us – intelligent and educated people – to believe and imagine that such damage could have taken place from two punches? I ask you, please to not insult our intelligence by offering such a feeble explanation of the fight. Do you realise that Mr Harris has already undergone seven constructive surgical procedures on his face to have the damage that you have caused repaired? Are you aware of this, Mr Hayes?"

"No, sir," Tony replied.

"Seven operations, Mr Hayes. That's quite a number of operations to have to endure. And you really don't expect us to believe that this damage was caused by just *two* punches? I find this utterly ridiculous!" the prosecution said to the court.

"No, sir. That *is* true. I *did* only hit him twice," Tony replied.

The prosecution continued, "Well I am sure that the members of the jury have looked at the pictures and they also would struggle to accept that this damage was caused by two punches. I put it to you, Mr Hayes, that you are lying to the court. You are lying about the queue. You were *not* in the queue first. You *did* approach Mr Harris first and you *did* attack him in a ferocious manner ... indeed showered a number of punches on my client and gave him a real hiding. Isn't that correct, Mr Hayes? So therefore, you are in my opinion, guilty as charged."

"OBJECTION!" Colin jumped up again. "Your Honour, he is misleading the bench."

"Overruled. Carry on," the judge said, holding his hand up to Colin.

The prosecution continued, "This is blatant GBH with a malicious attack on my client for no apparent reason ... other than hear'say of some idle gossip from a pub. You went out that evening intent on spoiling a pleasant evening for Mr Harris and his girlfriend. "

"No, sir. That's not true," Tony said.

"It's not true, he says," the barrister turned and mocked Tony to the court. "Ok . . . well . . . let me put it to you in perhaps another way, shall I?"

Tony looked at him. He could feel hatred rising up from his feet as the barrister went on at him, belittling him in front of everyone. His leg began to quiver again. He looked over at his dad in the gallery. Ernie was sitting there with his arms folded across his chest with a terrible frown on his face. Karl was sitting forward in his seat with his chin in his hand and he was frowning. Rob was shaking his head, muttering, and Dean was telling Rob to calm it down.

"If you had received injuries such as Mr Harris has, would you expect anybody to believe that you had only been hit twice?"

Tony could feel his cheeks starting to burn with rage. He was getting angry. He could feel Vernon's eyes boring into him, willing him to stay calm and focused. He could see Colin in his peripheral vision – he was ready to pounce any minute with an objection if he could. Tony remembered what Colin had said about this guy; h*e will try and make you flustered, try and trip you. Stay calm.*

"Well, Mr Hayes. Would you?" the prosecution pushed.

"Yes, sir. I would," Tony replied.

"Tell me, Mr Hayes. You were quite a sporty youngster, were you not?"

"I was, sir. Yes," Tony said confidently.

"And could you tell us in which sports you partook?"

Tony thought for a second. "Yes, I played rugby, basketball and I boxed."

"Oh you *boxed?* That's the one! And I believe you excelled in this boxing, did you not? In fact,

I believe that you were picked to box for your country, were you not?"

Tony shrugged, "Yes, I was very good. I was sent away on UK selection for boxing, yes."

The jury looked surprised at this piece of information. The prosecution continued, "Is that a common occurrence, or were you quite something special, Mr Hayes? Does that happen with all fifteen year-olds and under that choose this aggressive sport? Or is it only a select few? A really good few that are chosen?"

"Well, it is only a few that get selected to go," Tony said matter-of-factly.

"So would you agree that you are in the category of being perhaps one of the best boxers for your age in this country then, Mr Hayes? But ... not just a boxer, Mr Hayes ... not just a boxer. But an extremely skilled fighter. An extremely dangerous man with his fists, who would clearly know how to use them. Would you agree?"

"Boxing is a dangerous sport, sir," Tony agreed.

"You say *sport,* Mr Hayes. But you learn how to fight and defend yourself, is that not correct?"

Where was the prosecution leading with this? Tony thought. "It is indeed correct," Tony replied.

"So on this occasion, you chose to have a fight with someone who was not as skilled as yourself, and could not defend himself against a dangerous weapon such as yourself? And did Mr Harris even manage to get a single punch into you before you slaughtered him? Could you even call it a fight if he didn't hit you? Is it fair to say that a fight constitutes the involvement of two parties? I put it to you, Mr Hayes, that you attacked Mr Harris, giving him no chance to even defend himself. That is not a fair fight. That is not even a fight. That is a malicious attack on a poor, innocent victim. I therefore stand by my earlier observation that you are indeed a trained and dangerous attacker who, with all intents and purposes, deliberately rendered Mr Harris unconscious. And yet, you still expect the members of this jury to believe such a thing! I ask you again, Mr Hayes, do you really, truly expect us to believe this was *just a fight,* as you put in your statement?"

Tony was angry now. He wasn't having this. He wasn't going to stand here and let this weasel humiliate him anymore. "Yes I do, sir. As you said yourself, I am a trained fighter. Yes I do know how to defend myself. And as you quite rightly pointed out, I am dangerous with my hands. Mr Harris should have and would have known that I was a boxer and that it's actually quite easy to break somebody's nose."

"Are you a doctor now, Mr Hayes?" the prosecution interrupted.

"Pardon? No, sir. I am not a doctor. But it really isn't that hard to bust a nose. And it was a case of reacting when he hit me."

"*Oh* . . . you say he hit you now, Mr Hayes," the prosecution butted in.

"I've always stated that he hit me first. He walked up to me and swung a roundhouse punch. He hit me straight in the temple. I reacted and punched him back twice. A simple combination of boxing punches. That was it. The fight was over then. I was defending myself. I have said this in my statement. He hit me and burst blood vessels in my eye."

There was a chorus of tuts and gasps from the jury. The prosecution was revelling in his glory that he had got Tony riled. He continued his examination on Tony. "He burst blood vessels in your eye. Did you seek medical advice regarding this after he fight?" the prosecution blurted out.

"I didn't, no. It was an old boxing injury that I had sustained. If I get any knock to the head, it can burst the vessels behind my eye and my eye then fills up with blood and I'm temporarily blinded in that eye. It's ok after a few hours . . . but that night, when Mr Harris punched me, my eye filled up with blood and my *then* girlfriend and I left the cinema early."

The prosecution started flicking through his notes. "Mr Hayes, I understand that you and Mr Harris were good friends. You knew a lot about each other I take it. And Mr Harris would likely have known about this *old injury*."

"Yes, sir, we were good friends. And yes, he definitely knew about this," Tony said.

"Well, looking at your statement at another point, is it fair to say that you used to *hang out* most Fridays? You were good friends . . . you started seeing your girlfriend, Miss Thomas, and you borrowed Mr Harris's van one evening to go and see her. But you returned the van smashed up, did you not? And then, when Mr Harris asked you to pay for the van to be repaired, you replied. And I quote; '*fuck off, you cunt*'."

The court buzzed with the hum of disapproval again.

"NO, sir! That's not true . . ." Tony began again to answer but he was cut off mid-sentence by the prosecution going at him again.

"But was it when you started seeing your *then* girlfriend that you stopped hanging about with Mr Harris. You used the excuse that Mr Harris was hanging around with '*some unsavoury characters*'. You tried to paint a picture of my client being a bully and hanging around with these hooligans. He was going about '*beating people up*'. You say, and again, I quote; '*you didn't want to hang about with these characters*'. Members of the jury, I couldn't possibly believe that Mr Hayes didn't approve of beating people up . . . a trained fighter. So you became interested in women and stopped hanging about with Mr Harris. Is that true?"

"No, sir. That's not true."

"Oh, that's not true again, Mr Hayes?" the prosecution said tiresomely.

"NO, sir! I've always been interested in women," Tony shot back at him cheekily.

A chorus of stifled chuckles and sniggers came from the judge, the jury and the entire court room.

"Oh very witty, Mr Hayes," the judge said. "Very witty indeed. Do continue."

The prosecution wasn't impressed by this. He realised that he was up against someone who could fire back answers to his question. Tony wasn't as rattled as the prosecution had expected him to be. The barrister seemed distressed at the judge's comment. He began flicking through his notes again.

"I ask you again, Mr Hayes," he stuttered, "about being in the queue first. You state that you

were in the queue first."

"You've already asked me this, sir," Tony said.

"And so I'm asking you again! Please answer the question!" the prosecution almost shouted at him.

"And I'll give you the same answer again," Tony said coolly.

The prosecution seemed to have been taken completely off guard and appeared to back down after the judge had laughed at Tony. Everything he asked Tony was a repeat. He just asked him the same questions, over and over again. He got weaker and Tony seemed to draw confidence and strength from this.

"You keep asking me the same questions, sir. I have already answered this and it's the same answer I just gave you."

"Well I am asking you once more," the prosecution was getting agitated at Tony's flippancy.

"I was there first. I saw him walk across the crossing. He approached me. He struck me first," Tony said.

The prosecution kept on and on at Tony. Re-questioning him and rephrasing the same question. Tony just kept replying, "I've already answered that question," and repeated the same answer as before.

The prosecution was falling. Every time he threw a question at Tony, he answered calmly and precisely. Tony was quicker than him with his answers and stuck to every single word of his statement.

Tony looked over at the jury; they seemed to be tiring of this cross-examination. Tony caught Karl's eye and Karl winked at him.

"Mr Hayes, you are a lethal weapon!" the prosecution screeched at him finally.

"You've already accused me of that, sir. And I have already answered it three times and I'll give you the same answer if you ask me that again!" Tony said, shooting him back down.

The judge interrupted now, "I believe the cross-examination may be going round and round now in circles. Am I right in that assumption? Do you have any further questions that may be of relevance that aren't what you have already put to the accused?" the judge said directly to the prosecution bench. "I really do think we have heard all the evidence. Do you have any further lines of questioning from a different perspective?" the judge was peering over his glasses at the prosecution bench.

"No, Your Honour. No further questions." With that, the barrister threw his notes down onto his bench and retook his chair. The judge paused and stared at him momentarily with a disapproving eyebrow raised.

Tony was buzzing now. He was on fire, but as confident as he felt, he couldn't avoid the glares and stares from the jury, burning into his face with disgust. He had nailed the prosecution but there was absolutely nothing he could do now about the twelve members of the jury. His fate lay in their hands and, by the looks of it, they didn't like him one little bit.

The jury listened intently as the judge gave them his final instruction. They all looked at

Tony. He just wanted the ground to open up and swallow him.

This was it. This right here, right now. His life was being decided by a bunch of twelve people that clearly didn't like him. A group that had believed the sob story given by Aaron, who couldn't even be bothered to turn up for court.

The judge sent the jury away to deliberate and reach a unanimous decision. He also called early lunchtime. Tony looked at the big clock on the wall of the court room. It was 11:55 a.m. Court were to adjourn back after lunch at 2 p.m. to see how the jury were getting on.

He had been on the stand all morning. He desperately wanted a pint. It could be the last pint he'd have for a long time.

They all sat solemnly at the bar in the pub. "I can't believe it. I just wanted to stand up and scream at him!" Rob said, referring to the prosecution.

"Fuckin hell, he was a nightmare!" Karl said. "He was getting me wound up sitting there listening to him. What a wanker!"

Rob chipped in, "But seriously, that was funny though, Tone, when you said *I've always been interested in women.*" The friends all laughed.

"I'll remember that one for a while," Karl said.

Suddenly the mood darkened again. "Oh for fuck's sake. Come on, you lot! You're spose to be fucking cheering me up. Yes, this could well be my last drink for a long while . . . but fucking hell come on! . . . I'm not down yet!"

"I'll get another round," Ernie said glumly, "same again?"

"Tony, mate. Can I have quiet word with ya?" Dean said, pulling Tony discreetly to one side.

"Course, Deano. What's up?" Tony asked.

Dean looked knowingly at Tony straight in the eye. "I know what you and Andy did . . . " "What you talking about?" Tony shifted uncomfortably.

"That night we had the pool game and it all kicked off coz of those two stupid birds and I ended up in casualty getting me face rebuilt . . . ring any bells with ya?"

"Erm . . . oh yeah . . . vaguely," Tony lied, looking at his watch.

Dean continued, "Yeah, well I *vaguely* remember asking you not to do anything about it and to just let it go . . . remember now? The night I'm talking about?" Dean said in a more stern voice.

Tony looked up at him, "As if I was ever gonna just let that go! They could have kicked you to death! They had to be taught a lesson. Six of 'em, smashing you to shit," Tony was defiant now.

"No one does that to one of my best mates and gets away with it!"

Dean threw his arms around Tony's neck and the pair shared a very quick and manly hug.

"Thanks, buddy. I'll never forget it," Dean said quietly.

"How did you find out anyhow?" Tony asked curiously.

"Well I saw the geezer 'bout a month later. He had both his arms in plaster from his shoulders to his fingers, a neck brace on, and he was being wheeled about in a wheel chair. I thought he may have been hit by a train, judging the state of him. I saw Weaver in the pub a few days later and I eventually managed to get it out of him. He was reluctant to tell me though. You two did a proper job on him . . . he looked fucked!" Dean smiled at Tony.

"Come on, I don't want me last pint to get warm!" Tony laughed.

The hour passed too quickly. Tony desperately wanted to slow the time down and enjoy the last few minutes of freedom. Although he had needed that pint, he felt sick to his stomach. He didn't know how he was going to cope if he did go down. Karl had already said it's bad and that it can seriously screw your head up. He tried to sip his pint, but the time still ran away with itself that lunchtime.

"Time to go, mate," Ernie said sadly. Everyone looked like they wanted to burst into tears.

Suddenly, one of the solicitors from the prosecution bench walked past as they were leaving to go back to court, "Enjoy that pint. It's the last one you'll have for a while," he sniggered at Tony as the group walked past.

"Why, the fucking little prick!" Ernie said, leaping up from his stool. "I'll fucking show him."

"LEAVE IT!" Karl ordered. "That's the last fucking thing we need . . . a fucking fight in the pub with the prosecution bench. I've marked his card. I know his face . . . he'll get his comeuppance." Karl looked at Al. Al nodded and understood immediately.

Tony followed Dean and Rob out of the pub and together they headed back to the court.

"Keep your cool, Ernie, ok? I know how you must be feeling, but you gotta keep your wits about ya and keep schtum," Karl said, pulling Ernie back to one side.

"I know, son. I'm sorry. He just got under my skin with his fucking smug remark. I'll shove his words right up his . . ." Ernie stopped and saw Karl's face and apologised. Karl put an arm around Ernie's shoulders. Ernie just felt sick to his stomach; he thought the same as everyone else.

`How the fuck was Tony gonna cope inside?`

They all sat outside the court room watching the final minutes tick by. It was exactly 3 p.m. and court was ready to commence. The doors to the court room opened and the usher was calling everyone back inside. Tony's heart sank.

"Court rise," came the familiar words.

Tony was stood in the dock. The jury had been out for a total of two hours and that was all the time they needed. They had reached their decision. The judge had asked them to come back into court. Tony stood there looking at them, at each and every one of them. Not one of them made any eye contact with Tony. He quickly glanced over at his dad. Ernie looked like he was about to cry. He was holding his hands to his mouth. Tony could see Rob had tears falling down his cheeks already. He had been very quiet, unusually quiet, at the pub during lunch. Dean was rubbing Rob's back trying to calm him down. Karl looked stone-faced and offered no friendly wink or any signs of encouragement to Tony. Al wasn't even there. Tony stood looking from the judge to the jury. *This was it . . . he was fucked!*

"Members of the jury, have you reached a unanimous verdict?"

The jury spokesman stood up, "Yes we have, Your Honour."

The judge turned and faced Tony. "Mr Anthony Hayes, will you please stand."

Tony stood with his hands behind his back. His leg was shaking – it was out of control. His nostrils fared to inhale as much air as possible. He felt like he was going to faint. He was suddenly very hot and flushed. His face felt like it was burning. He couldn't breathe. He tried to take a deep breath in.

"Members of the jury, in the case of Mr Anthony Hayes. You have one count of GBH with intent and malicious wounding. Please tell the court on that one count, how do you find the defendant? Guilty or not guilty?"

TO BE CONTINUED . . .

Epilogue

May 1990

THE early morning sun rose brightly in the sky. Rob looked up and blinked in its blinding glare. He turned and gave a sad and final wave to Ernie, who was driving away from him now. He had dropped him back to the barracks at Woolwich. Half of him wanted to run back down the road after Ernie. The other half knew he had to stay and face the consequences of his actions.

It was very quiet in the campus that morning. He looked at his watch; 7 a.m. In the distance, he could hear his regiment on their morning parade.

The gates closed shut behind him as he approached the gate house, where he was immediately arrested and escorted to the colonel's office. He took one last look over his shoulder. Ernie was gone out of site.

Standing in the hallway of the main offices, he looked down at himself. All smart again in his soldier's uniform. He brushed the front of his jacket down and straightened himself. He gave his boots a quick wipe over before he raised his hand to knock loudly on the colonel's door. As he waited for the command, dread and fear crept into his stomach. He felt sick.

A loud "ENTER" resonated back at him. Taking a deep breath, he stepped forward and entered the office to hand himself in and find out what punishment awaited him.

"Well, well, well! The wanderer Sullivan returns," the colonel said immediately, standing up and walking around to the other side of his desk.

Rob was given the chance to explain himself. He wasted no time at all in telling the colonel all about Tony and the court case. How he had spoken to Dean, and how he said it was looking bad for Tony. It looked like Tony might get seven years, and it was all just a stupid fight. "Sir, I knew it was wrong what I did. But I needed to be there. I thought I'd never see him again for years."

"My heart bleeds for him, Sullivan. It really does," the colonel said unemotionally. "But it doesn't excuse what you did, and *you* have to pay the consequences."

"Yes, sir. I am aware what I did was unacceptable and wrong. But, sir . . . please . . . you have *no idea* what it meant for me to have to be there with Tony, sir. Have you ever been really low? So low that you can't physically sink any lower. And there is no way out and you feel like you are the scum of the earth and not worth the breath that God put in you? Practically suicidal. With respect, sir, I don't suppose you have. But I have. I have felt like that. And the only person that pulled me back and saved me was Tony. I would be a dead beat or even dead now if it wasn't for him. He is like a big brother to me and I couldn't have lived with myself if I hadn't been there for him. Not that I could have changed what would happen, but just being there, sir. To just be there with him and support him . . . and for him to know I was there . . ." Rob's words trailed off into a mere whisper.

The colonel sat back down at his desk and listened intently to Rob. He saw the pain in his eyes as they welled up, but Rob fought back the tears. The emotion was etched across his face. His words were heartfelt and real. It wasn't the usual rubbish that he had heard so many times before.

He could feel Rob's pain.

The colonel took pity. "Respect and loyalty, Sullivan. Do you know the meaning of those words? This is a rhetorical question."

Rob didn't dare move and was staring straight ahead, eyes fixated on the wall opposite him.

The colonel had now moved again around his desk and was standing in front of Rob. Close to him now, almost face to face. Rob could feel his breath on his face as he said, "I can see with my own eyes, Sullivan. It's quite clear that you *do* know the true meanings. I know you have always wanted to be a soldier; it's written all over you. But you must understand that the Army has rules. RULES! These are there to be adhered to. And for a reason. They apply to each and every soldier in my army. You cannot just go off and come back when it suits you! Do I make myself clear, Sullivan?" Rob nodded. "Yes, sir."

"However," the colonel continued, "on that note, I have to say that loyalty is a very admirable quality. A quality that the army needs more of in this day and age. You cannot teach somebody loyalty like that. It's inbred in them, like a dog. And you, Sullivan, are as loyal as a dog. And that is a quality that I like about you."

"Thank you, sir," Rob said gratefully.

The colonel turned back to his desk and began to write out a form. He suddenly stopped and looked at Rob. Rob's eyes shot back to the wall again and he stared straight ahead of him. "Sullivan, you could have come to me and requested compassionate leave for this."

"I didn't realise that, sir. I apologise and thank you, sir," he said, not moving his eyes from the back wall.

Rob had opened up an emotional side to himself that he never wanted to show anybody in the army. The colonel knew this and the two never spoke of it again. He was sentenced to two weeks imprisonment but not charged with desertion. He was also drug tested and deducted pay for his time AWOL, which totalled up to thirty-six hours.

Rob was immediately taken down to jail where he spent out his fortnight. He was then shipped out to Dusseldorf, where he was allowed to continue with this basic training. Later on, he was commissioned into the 16th Air Defence where he re-joined his unit.

It was only two months later that Rob was commissioned and stationed in Cyprus.

TO BE CONTINUED . . .

About the Author

Born in 1975 in East London, I was the youngest in a two point four loving family. I was just your Joe average. Going through schooling and adolescent years I was a normal teenage girl, whose mother may have threatened to throttle on numerous occasions and I never quite managed to drive my parents to drink that much!! Between now and then, I have been busy training in the art of grooming (hairdressing and beautician to be precise), worked for top London magazines in advertising, struck a pose for a camera lens, and helped run several businesses. However, writing novels had never occurred to me to be something which I would spend my time doing. I married an amazing man and we have an amazing son, who both inspire me beyond belief and make me laugh uncontrollably at times. So look at me now . . . I am a wife, a mother, a business woman, a model (although I'm not sure which one takes up most of my time) and now I can officially add novelist to my ever-growing CV list.